PRAISE FOR
THE EMPATH CHRONICLES

I started out really liking the story, but somewhere down the line that became love.

Very fast paced and exciting. Love the characters and grew attached very quickly. Made me cry more than once.

Wow, what a ride! Highs and lows, twists and turns ... A real roller coaster of a book! Loved it!

I thoroughly enjoyed every bit of this book. The characters were well developed and likable, the plot moved at a great pace and the story was fun and full of action.

Compelling, gritty and gut wrenching roller coaster of emotions. I was completely hooked.

Published by Fairies and Fantasy Pty Ltd 2020
Paperback ISBN: 978-0-6487080-3-2
Hardcover ISBN: 978-0-6487080-5-6

THE EMPATH
CHRONICLES

BOOKS 1-3

SELINA A. FENECH

EMOTIONALLY CHARGED

THE EMPATH **1** CHRONICLES

1

I stared at the crack that ran up our living room wall. The ground had stopped shaking, but tremors still zinged through my body. *Did that really just happen?*

I couldn't drag my eyes away from that lightning-shaped fracture scarring the wall. Apart from the contents of our shelves that were now on the floor — books, ornaments, a plaster "Olivia" I'd painted when I was five, now smashed to bits — it seemed to be the only visible damage. I should probably have been upset by it, but instead I felt... *excited*. The crack gave me shivers like it was carved up my spine. *That really just happened.*

1

SELINA A. FENECH

The floor rumbled under my feet and I shared a look with Mom and Dad, all three of us ready to bolt out of the home we'd just re-entered after fleeing for the first time.

The aftershock passed before we could move. Just the last little ripple after the wave.

We'd always known our town was near a major fault, but it was one of those sleepy fault lines that didn't do anything for decades, centuries even. Then just when everyone in our middle-class paradise had achieved a false sense of security, here it was, throwing a great big earthquake at us.

Dad talked on the phone to his cop buddy to get all the details and updates. He repeated the news out loud for Mom and me to hear.

"Power's out everywhere, and Terry doesn't think they'll get it back on any time soon."

Mom had already gathered up her collection of scented candles, those that hadn't broken in a fall, and lit them. Her first course of action in any blackout. The whole room smelled of struck matches and ylang ylang.

"Mom, it's not even dark yet."

"They make me feel better," she said, shrugging and lighting the last one.

Dad put his hand over the phone and looked at Mom

2

seriously. "Terry says there have been reports of people looting."

Mom paused a moment, then stomped into the kitchen and picked up a brush and dustpan. "The kind of person who would take advantage of a situation like this deserves their own personal karmic earthquake."

My imagination teased me with scenes of what could be happening out on the streets. Broken buildings where looters, police officers, and emergency response crews played their roles. I imagined a world of adventure outside. Bad guys and heroes. *Handsome* heroes.

Mom was always pushing me to follow my dreams, but truthfully, the only things I wanted were fantasies. Damseling for a gorgeous superhero, escaping to a magical world with a fairy prince, being adored by a morally vague vampire: I'd take any of the above. In real-life terms, I didn't know what I wanted. I just knew if I ever got a chance to follow my fantasy dreams I'd be there with bells on. Real life was kind of dull, and maybe an earthquake wasn't the romantic escapism I normally went for, but I could work with it. Even a sexy fireman would suffice.

I daydreamed as I kneeled down next to Mom where she worked at brushing up shattered ornaments that had fallen from our shelves. Her collection of ceramic owls would never be the same. I helped pick up the few which had broken into larger pieces and put them aside. Mom loved her owls. Maybe some could be glued back together.

Dad's news report continued. "We were lucky. A lot of people have lost homes. And the old post office is flattened, but we've been expecting it to fall down for years. How many times did I try to tell the council to get it renovated?"

Mom counted on her fingers and Dad added his own fingers into the count too while he listened to the phone again. "There's a shelter being set up in Livvy's high school for anyone whose house is unsafe."

I bet they needed volunteers. The shaken world felt full of possibility and I wanted to be part of it. Even handing out blankets had my mind brewing up dreams of romance. Mopping at the brow of a dust covered EMT who'd just saved a puppy from a crumbled home...

I have to get out there. "Mom, can I go and help at the school?"

Mom looked up at me. A glow of pride and the darkness of worry showed all over her face.

I could read the emotions clear as subtitles. For as long as I could remember, I'd been able to see energy shining from a person with their emotions. Not like an aura or anything; that sounded so New Age woo-woo. I was just good at knowing

4

how people felt. Always had been. It was my one and only superpower. When I was a kid, I used to dress up and play at being a caped crime fighter, Awesome Olivia. Then I'd realized reading someone's feelings wasn't the kind of power that was useful in a fist fight. But it did come in handy sometimes.

I pre-empted the inevitable worried mom speech with soothing words. "I'll just be helping out in a shelter, under the watchful eye of aid workers, responsible adults and doctors. Probably the safest place at the moment, right?"

"You know I like to let you make your own choices but things sound pretty rough out there. I don't want you to get hurt." She looked at the dustpan and brush in her hands as though making a point about the damage the earthquake had done. Her startling blue eyes turned back toward me. Why couldn't I have inherited those? My eyes were brown instead, to match my hair which she guilted me out of dyeing. Harsh chemicals didn't fit her idea of green living.

I could win *this* debate though. "Just think how appealing some volunteer work will look on my college application as an extracurricular activity. And I can swing past your shop and make sure it's okay."

"I hope there's not too much damage. I just had a porcelain shipment come in. Great timing, right? I'd go check myself but there's so much to do here." She paused, chewed at her bottom lip. "All right, off you go then, but be careful."

Dad finished his phone call and kissed the top of my head when I stood up, his moustache tickling my forehead. "I think it's a beautiful idea, Lollipop. Good on you for wanting to help out."

Mom walked over to empty her dustpan, sighing as shattered owls tumbled into the trash. Shards of pink rolled in and I knew it was the remains of her favorite one. Dad gave her a hug as though they were standing by the grave of a beloved relative.

I saw how sad Mom was and gave her a peck on the cheek. "Thanks, Mom. I'll be careful. And I'll keep an eye out for any owls needing adoption on my way." I threw on my red trench coat, chucked my phone, keys and wallet in the pockets, and headed for the door.

"Buses are still running, Livvy," Dad called out. "There's a clear route to your high school. Just a couple of hours, okay? Be safe."

"Of course," I replied. "See you soon."

The air outside had a hint of dust and sense of silent awe. People filled the street, gossiping in relieved whispers. A hairline crack across a nearby pavement had drawn the attention five or so local kids, who stared at it the way I had stared at the one in my home—as though it could snap open like a monster's maw at any second and engulf me.

Sirens sounded in the distance.

The possibilities of what could happen tonight, and an intense desire for adventure ... or *something* ... made my body hum. I pulled my trench coat tight around me and set off.

2

This. This was what I was made for. I felt like I was actually glowing or vibrating, or something.

"Bless. You're just an angel." A woman with a cloud of white hair patted my hand as she took a blanket from me. She smiled, but I felt the tremble in her palm and sensed her fear.

It made me tingle.

I felt like some kind of weirdo. These people were here because their homes were too unsafe to stay in, or gone entirely. I saw fear and sadness on every face, *felt it* in my bones, and there I was, bubbling over on some kind of weird high.

What is wrong with me?

EMOTIONALLY CHARGED

I'd felt it before I'd even reached the shelter. On the bus ride, a buzz had built in me the closer I'd got to the school and it'd been non-stop since. I wasn't sure how many blankets I'd handed out or how many people I'd escorted into the gym, finding them a patch of ground to rest on. Any injured went straight to the hospital, but I still felt like a warrior helping out in the aftermath of a battle. Handsome heroes so far had been non-existent, sadly. I remained hopeful and kept busy. I'd listened to people's stories of the earthquake, dragged restless children back to their parents, and helped unload the cartons of bottled water the local U-Mart trucked in. The cartons felt feather-light—I was on such a high. *I'll probably be aching tomorrow.* I'd tripped over twice, my feet wanting to move faster than I could keep up with, and my hands twitched and jittered. It was probably adrenaline. Maybe I needed to take a break.

I found my way to the volunteer's area and cracked open a bottle of water. I squeezed it too hard as I was drinking and splashed water all over my chest. *Well at least it's a perfect set up for a meet-cute.* I held my breath, wishing this was the moment my hero would appear and be enamored by my clumsiness. But the only man approaching was my history teacher. I sighed and patted myself dry with paper towels.

9

Trevor was also the coordinator for the shelter. Any other day he was Mr. Jones, but today he insisted on being Trevor. He leaned on a bench next to me and pushed the sweat up off his forehead and back over his head, slicking graying hair away from his face.

"Thanks for all your help tonight, Olivia." His voice came out as a long sigh. "I wish I still had a teenager's stamina. Is this your first break? You've been at it for hours."

Hours? It felt like twenty minutes, tops. My eyes popped wide. "What's the time?"

I pulled my phone from my pocket for the first time and saw it was half past eleven. I also saw three missed calls and two texts from my mom, and a couple from my BFF Nati. *I should have checked in with her. Where is my head tonight?* Maybe it wasn't me buzzing, just my phone doing its vibro-dance in my pocket.

Trevor watched me with concern as I grimaced. "Sure you're okay?"

"I'll be fine, as long as my parents don't kill me." I tapped the screen to call them back and got nothing but failed calls. No bars meant no signal. The messages left by my parents were all from back before seven o'clock. The last bus ran at ten-thirty, and thanks to my parents' hippy car-free household policy, last bus translated to curfew and I knew it. *Especially* on the evening of a mid-level natural disaster. I was going to find myself on the wrong end of a serious lecture, assuming I could find a way home.

Trevor watched my hopeless phone poking. "Phone towers have battery backups which work for a couple of hours, but in a long blackout like this they will have cut out by now."

Even if I could get through, I had no way to get home that wasn't going to put out the neighbors, or worse, Terry. I cringed. A ride with him in his cop car was not the way I wanted to arrive home.

Maybe I could stay in the shelter for the night. I just had to let my parents know I was here and safe.

"Sorry Mr. um… Trevor. I sort of maybe kind of missed my ride home."

Trevor looked around the gym. Everyone was settled in, many asleep already. Even half the volunteers had curled up in a corner somewhere as the influx of new people had slowed down. "I could ask around for a lift for you, or—"

"I'm happy to stay."

He sighed. "Yes, fine, you can stay, if you can find a spare blanket and bit of floor. Landlines are still working if you want to use the phone in the office to let your parents know. Briefly. Have to keep the line clear for official calls."

"Do you think you could call them for me?" I hated talking on the phone. I couldn't see people's reactions, couldn't tell how they were feeling and always ended up saying the wrong thing, even at the best of times. And now was far from the best of times. "It would just be better if a teacher told them, instead of me. You know, someone of authority."

And yes, I was also dodging the lecture.

Trevor rubbed his forehead, the pen still in his hand marking it blue. He added my name to his clipboard. "Go on. I'll call them. School's off for the week and people are going to be here a while, so if you want to help out again tomorrow everyone would appreciate it."

Sounded like an offer I couldn't refuse. I nodded gratefully and he took down my number and left for the office to make the call.

I still had my phone in my hand, and voice mail was down so I checked the texts my mom had sent. The earliest must have been while I was still on the way in—Mom reminding me of the bus schedule. The next, five minutes after the first, asked me to check the boxes of new stock that had just arrived at her shop.

I'd missed the bus home *and* I had completely forgotten to go past her shop on the way in like I'd told her I would. *I can't believe I spaced so bad. The winner of daughter of the year? Not me.*

I *could* still go now. Real quick, just zip out and back before anyone noticed I was gone.

Heading out onto the streets seemed a bit crazy but I really wanted to do this for Mom. Knowing her "Duck Egg Blue" home-wares boutique was okay would mean a lot to her, especially after she'd lost her owls. Her little shop wasn't far from school. Normally a ten-minute walk, but tonight I felt like I could fly.

Another family trudged into the hall armed with pillows and suitcases, prepared to camp out with everyone else, looking sad and lost. I felt bad for them, but there were other volunteers who would help them out. I needed to check on the shop before it got any later and this adrenaline kick I was on ended and I crashed.

I waited until no-one seemed to be watching me and slipped out the gym entrance and through the school gates, and jogged down the street. The chunky heart pendant I wore thudded on my chest like a second heartbeat.

Just checking on Mom's shop, I repeated to myself, while a deeper, quieter voice whispered of heroes and adventure and what-if.

If only I'd remembered that with adventure, comes danger.

3

O nce away from the school, where generators were running and floodlights lit up every corner of the grounds, it
was quiet.

I hadn't ever seen the town so deserted. The police weren't
even out driving around. They must have had a lot more on
their plate than patrol. It was quieter than any other time I
could remember.

Mom always called the town 'sleepy'. On this night, though,
I would call it beyond sleepy. It had an almost post-apocalyptic
feel.

In reality, there were still plenty of buildings standing and no enormous cavern in the middle of the street like there might have been in some end-of-the-world movie. Which probably also meant no grisly-but-good-hearted savior riding in on his motorbike to sweep me to safety. It would have been a lot more interesting if there had been, but for now, I needed to get to Mom's shop and back to school before they noticed I was gone.

For some reason, the details of the older terrace housing which backed the main street appeared clearer than I'd ever seen before, even in the dark. It was like I could see better than normal. I looked around for a full moon or some other light source to explain it, but found nothing. Shame. I felt like I wanted to howl at the moon. I almost giggled at how good I felt and then thought again how strange it was, that I could feel *good* in the midst of such chaos.

No matter how many times Dad had said the post office was going to come crashing down someday, the sight of it as I passed by was eerie. Water flowed from a burst pipe and piles of mail were strewn throughout the wreckage, snow drifts of letters white on the ground.

Slowing my pace, I enjoyed the excitement of the solitary darkness. So I got a bit over-excited tonight and missed my bus, but I helped people tonight and it had felt *amazing*. Mom would understand. She was always understanding and encouraging.

Checking her shop out was the least I could do.

She loved her shop like she loved her owl collection. When I was younger, she'd talked about getting a real owl. I'd looked at her like she was crazy. "Ew no, so messy! You have to feed them real meat. So difficult."

"Life should be like that. Difficult, messy, and real," she'd replied. "You have to do what you have to do to make your dreams come true."

Now, I understood what she meant. So maybe it was crazy I wanted a rich, handsome prince to sweep me away to far-off lands of adventure, intrigue and decadence. But I didn't want my life in half measures. I wanted real affluence, real excitement, real romance. Mom's dreams had come true, and I wanted to be as happy and in love as her and Dad one day.

On the main street the shops were all still standing. Some had cracks running up pastel-painted fronts, splitting quirky logos with jagged smiles. The arty mosaic archway leading into the boutique district had crumbled, blocking the road so cars were unable to pass. I felt a pang of grief for it, knowing it was a humpty that couldn't be put back together.

A lot of windows were broken, spilling glass onto the street and making the shop displays sparkle as though the shabby chic furniture or gourmet cupcakes had been sprinkled with diamonds.

Then I noticed it wasn't just a lot of windows. It was every window. It made sense the earthquake had broken glass, but just around the corner I hadn't noticed any windows broken on the rows of townhouses.

A beam of light shone out of a building up ahead. I froze. *Someone's in there, but someone good or bad?* I didn't need to see the exact pastel shade of the shop to know it was Duck Egg Blue. The light jiggled, then vanished. The sound of shattering porcelain echoed in the street followed by a boy-like chuckle.

I'm guessing not good.

"Hey!" The word came out before I stopped to think. "Hey, get out of there!"

The humming inside me had grown louder, anger pulsing through my veins. *That's my mom's shop.* The hell I was going to let someone trash or loot it. Getting called out should make them run away.

The possibility it wouldn't only struck me when four figures in hoodies jumped out through the cleared window, bringing with them an avalanche of retro dinner sets from the display. I cringed as plates smashed on the pavement.

The gang turned my way and I saw they were just boys, younger than me. I didn't recognize them from school, and they didn't dress like teens from this area either. More like

17

kids from the housing estate a couple of 'burbs over who sometimes crashed parties around here. The kind of kid Mom always told me to be understanding of. They had tougher situations than we did, but it was hard to be understanding when they were smashing up my mom's livelihood.

Two shone flashlights my way. I squinted into the harsh glare.

I stood taller than a couple of the thugs, but it was still four against one. Why did I feel like I could deal with this? The fizzy high I was on had my confidence up and blocking the part of my mind that knew this could be dangerous, and that feeling of invincibility could just make it worse. A point proved when the boys headed for me instead of making a guilty dash.

"Stay back. I have pepper spray." I bluffed, reaching my hand into a pocket of my trench coat. I grabbed for my phone instead, swiped it on, but couldn't dial on the touch screen without looking, and I wasn't sure the emergency number would even redirect and work with most of the network down. What would they do if they saw me dialing? Back off, or advance faster? It didn't seem worth the risk when it could take ages for the cops to arrive.

"Pepper spray? I eat that stuff on my breakfast," one of them joked.

I took steady steps away as the boys came closer. Every one

was dressed in black, like they were in uniform. They had no distinguishing features visible apart from slightly varying heights. I started imagining being a victim who couldn't identify her attackers and I didn't like it.

I tried to warn them off again. "I'll call the police."

"Relax, we're just out for some fun." He chuckled, the same chuckle I'd heard when he was smashing things in Mom's shop. His idea of fun worried me.

Glass crunched on the concrete footpath behind me. I spun around. Another boy, all in black loomed over me.

He grabbed for my arm. I gasped, stepping quickly out of his reach.

Anger shone from him and my body flared with adrenaline. The five thugs penned me in and took turns pushing at me or grasping for me. I reacted on instinct, my body taking control. I dodged, avoiding a lunge from one side then a snatch from the other. They jeered and taunted, trying to get their hands on me. Fingers wrapped around my arm, but I easily twisted out of them.

But the more I avoided them, the more I saw the anger in them build.

No one had ever been this mad at me before. It scared me. It set my whole body on fire.

19

SELINA A. FENECH

"Someone help!" I cried out, but my voice was lost in the wide street. I doubted anyone would hear. No hero would come and save me. This wasn't one of my daydreams. This was a nightmare.

I ducked under a wide swing from the closest guy. He snarled violently. They weren't playing anymore. Remembering my self-defense class, I pulled my keys out of my pocket. I grabbed my phone with the other hand. I made a wild jab at the thug's chest with my longest key while I looked at my phone screen, thumbing in an emergency call.

The key sank into flesh, startling me. I didn't expect it to break skin at all, let alone slide right into him like a dagger. My hand warmed with the guy's blood. *What the heck?*

I paused too long and was shoved in the back.

I fell flat on my face. My phone dropped from my hand and skittered out of reach. On the ground, my mind helpfully recalled the second part of the self-defense lesson emphasizing the importance of disabling your attackers, not just pissing them off even more.

I barely felt the fall, but when I tried to call for help again there was no air in my lungs. Numbly, I registered broken glass jutting out of my palms.

One of the guys grabbed my shoulder and rolled me over.

20

I snatched his hand in both of mine and twisted. I swear I heard bones break. He screamed.

I also thought I heard footsteps approaching, fast. I might have just been hearing things. Just wishful thinking as the guy cradled his wrist, called me something I wouldn't repeat and kicked me in the side of the head.

4

My world swam in darkness. Sounds of scuffling faded in and out, and energy surged through my body.

Snapping my eyes open, I watched a man in a white button-down shirt throw one of the hoodies against a power pole. Actually picked him up and *threw* him. The others were already running, or stumbling, away.

Someone had come to save me. It was a miracle.

The kid thrown against the pole slumped there, unmoving. My eyes widened, hoping he was just unconscious.

Dusting his hands, my savior turned around to reveal the face of a male model. I blinked, and in that instant he went from all the way over there to over beside me. I blinked again, confused and unsure of reality. Because now I really had gone into daydream world.

The new guy's shirt accentuated his V-shaped chest like it had been tailored for a perfect fit and his blond hair sat flawlessly as though he hadn't just dealt with a bunch of looting delinquents. His sleeves were rolled neatly below his elbows, and although he only looked about twenty, the watch on his wrist was expensive. I'd seen it in classy magazine ads.

"Are you all right?"

Even his voice was dreamy.

I tried to sit up so I wasn't so awkward and prone, wanting to be more presentable for this god-like figure. "Hngh. Ow. Crap."

Damn it.

The guy chuckled, and his smile made my heart shiver like a nervous bunny. When he grabbed my hands and helped me up with perfect care, I thought I would lose it entirely.

"You were amazing," he said, bending to collect my phone and keys from nearby. "When I heard someone calling for help, I came as quick as I could. Saw most of the fight while I ran down the street. I thought you had them dealt with on your own for a minute. Very impressive."

I groaned, reliving my misguided foray into heroism.

"Impressive like a high-jumping lemming."

He half-smiled. "Cutest lemming I've seen in a while."

Gulp.

He handed my phone and keys back to me, giving me a scrutinizing look. "But really, how do you feel?"

How did I feel? I'd just been thrown on the ground and kicked in the head, but actually I felt... "Good? Does that mean I'm in shock?"

"Maybe. Maybe something better. My name is Jake." He took my hand, gently cleaning blood off it with a tissue, and I forgot to ask what was better or whether I needed a blanket and hot chocolate in case it was shock after all.

"I'm Livvy," I replied, without stuttering, which was the second miracle of the night.

"Let's find you somewhere to recover then, my lovely Livvy."

Guys had tried calling me that before and it had always sounded corny until now. This guy's voice was so tasty I could lick it.

He looped my arm in one of his like a Victorian gentleman and I trotted obediently alongside him. I pretended to need the support more than I did, just to squeeze a little closer. I was going to make the most of this, in case I woke up and discovered it was a concussion-induced dream.

24

We walked to the end of the street and sat at a bus stop on the corner. It was beautiful, a real work of art. Designed to bookend the archway that used to stand at the other end of the strip, the heavy concrete bench was covered in colorful mosaic tiles.

My mind refused to help me out with anything to say. *Thank you for saving me* was the obvious thing, but it seemed so inadequately lame I couldn't make it come out my mouth. Jake kept looking at me, and I read amusement and satisfaction all over him. *Oh God, he smells so good.* I couldn't say that out loud either.

He broke the silence after what felt like forever, but was more likely only seconds long. "I bet you feel better than good, don't you?"

I shrugged. I did still feel pretty tingly. I looked at my palms, where glass had poked from my skin, and found them clear and clean. What?

Maybe I'd imagined it. My brain had been MIA. "I think I've been on an adrenaline kick most of the night."

He chuckled. "Getting kicked like you did, aren't you surprised you're already feeling okay? You don't realize how fast you were moving back then, do you? And did you know you almost ripped that guy's hand off?"

"I did *what?*"

"It's fine. It was self-defense." Jake paused for a moment. He assessed me with piercing eyes. "What if I said you were more than normal? Something different, better, possibly even supernatural? Would you freak on me or—"

"Would I think it was a dream come true? The latter." I nodded with wide eyes, waiting to see what he'd reveal. I half-expected he was setting me up for some epic punch line, but there was an energy in the air I couldn't deny. A magic I wanted to embrace. And if this guy had the key to that? Dream. Come. True.

Jake pointed his finger at my chest and then his. "You, me—we have superpowers."

Tingles. I eyed him up and down, looking for outward signs of mental illness. But I felt his sincerity and wondered if this was what I'd been waiting for my whole life. If by some miracle my dreams were about to become true. *Things come in threes, right?*

And the things I'd seen him do, the things I had done tonight, were they more than normal? I wasn't one hundred percent sure. It had all been such a blur. "Okay. That sounds great and all, but this is a bit outside the realm of real life. I'm going to need some kind of proof to be onboard here." *Please have proof. Please have proof. Please have proof.*

He raised a perfect eyebrow. "How about a visual demo?"

Jake took my hand and pulled me off the bench. Turning back to it, he gave it a swift kick in the center. The bench cracked down the middle and fell inward in a kaleidoscope of tiles and crumbled concrete. It was as completely destroyed as the archway down the road. The bookends matched even more now.

I stared, mouth open, and he waited for my response with a smile.

"Where are we supposed to sit now?" I giggled, edging on hysteria at the scope of what was happening. "And also, what the how?"

Down the road, headlights broke through the darkness and a car swung around the corner, heading down the street. Jake waved at it and turned back to me.

"You're like me, like us." He gestured to the car, speaking fast as it approached. "You've always been able to read people's feelings, right? You feel stronger when people are angry, or full of energy when others are scared. When emotions surround you, you think faster, move faster, heal faster."

I found myself nodding to his words, realizing what he said was the truth. This wasn't just a dream. I'd always been like that. My one unique feature, hidden on the inside, was more special than I had ever realized. His words repeated in me. *You're like me, like us.*

"It's real. I can tell you feel it. We're empaths. That's why I'm here. We're always on the look-out for other people like us, and the easiest time to find them is during a natural disaster when emotions are heightened across the whole population. It's often the first time empaths really experience their power, like you have tonight."

The black SUV skidded to a stop beside us and the front-side window opened. I couldn't quite see inside but I heard a man talk. "We've been driving 'round looking for you for ages. What's the deal, Jake?"

Jake tilted his head to me and simply said, "Got one."

A girl not much older than me burst out the back door. "You really found one? Zomigosh, it's a girl!" She squealed and came toward me, her shimmering red hair flying around her from her leap out of the vehicle. The front doors opened and two guys stepped out. They were stunning, every one of them. I made an effort to keep my mouth from hanging open.

Everything was happening so fast. I had superpowers. Jake had superpowers. Now I was meeting so many hot people with superpowers.

I reached out a hand to the girl to introduce myself and she wrapped her arms 'round my shoulders, hugging me as she jiggled a little dance. "I thought I might have been the only one. Don't get me wrong, I love my boys, but I've been dying to find another girl 'path."

Jake cleared his throat. "Everyone, this is Livvy. Livvy, that's Emma, over there's Donny." He nodded to the tallest guy, whose velvety black skin rippled with muscles which barely seemed to fit under his clothes. "And this jerk is Jamie." Jake grinned at the last guy, a few years younger than all of them. He and Jake looked like they could be brothers. Jamie gave Jake the finger, smirking all the while, then shook my hand. Donny just nodded silently.

"So, you guys come to natural disaster areas to help out, and hope you find more people like you—like us?" I couldn't believe I was talking to a team of real-life superheroes. I needed to sit down but the bench option had been removed.

"That's pretty much what we do," Jamie said.

"How did Jake find you? How long have you known what you are? Did you already know? Are you from around here?" Emma overflowed with questions and I couldn't find a gap to answer any.

Jake cleared his throat. He leant on Jamie's shoulder and

gave me a bashful smile, threatening to liquidize my legs. "I know you just met us all, and I know it's late, but we'd really like for you to come with us."

I exhaled a little too loudly. "With you? With you where?"

"Just to hang out for a bit, chat some more. I know I unloaded a lot on you all at once. I'd love to talk it over more and explain things properly because there aren't many of us. Empaths need to stick with our kind. We're stronger together. That's why we have our team."

Hang out and chat. I could do that. I had to.

This was really happening. My impossible dreams were coming true, and I had to find out more. I couldn't let these empaths just leave me in my normal life again. My parents weren't expecting me home now and with so much going on at the shelter, I doubted my absence would be noted. I could spend all night with Jake and his team if I wanted. And I *wanted*.

I knew I should be thinking about this more seriously, but I had trouble focusing on anything other than Jake's smile, and the warm feeling it gave me inside. I couldn't sense any dangerous emotions coming from any of the empaths, just warm, happy fuzziness. The desire to jump in the car with them proved overwhelming. "Sure. Let's go."

Jake and Emma beamed. Jamie's smirk remained in place.

Donny didn't show much expression. His face remained still, like the carving of a god. He checked his watch, also expensive. "We're meant to be flying back tonight."

"Oh. In that case..." I hesitated.

"We can chat in a café at the airport until we fly out." Jake looked down at me, his eyelids half closed and a small, pouting smile on his lips. "Come with us."

A rush of warmth flooded me. I felt so secure, so sure. I nodded.

Looking past their attractive forms was difficult, but in their emotions all I read was excitement and pleasure at finding me. They wanted me. I was special. Like them? Maybe not quite, but they wanted me anyway. Jake and his friends didn't feel like strangers at all. They already felt like family, as if I knew them. I trusted them and going with this group, this team, was the only thing in the world I knew I wanted. It could be my only chance to live my dreams. Mom would tell me to go for it.

Somehow we went from chatting in the rental car, to chatting in the airport, to chatting on the plane.

It wasn't the first time I told my parents I'd be in one place but went somewhere else.

But it was the first time that going somewhere else involved a first-class flight.

5

First class was *wow*. Everyone treated our group like royalty. Jake sorted out everything and the airline squeezed me onto the flight at late notice. Even with strict airport security we breezed through with the team's excess baggage, no questions asked. Jake reassured me we weren't going far, and they would fly or drive me back home any time I wanted. They only flew up to get to the quake site fast, and were only a few hours' drive away from my Bellscroft.

Why were they leaving my home town so soon? Wasn't there any more they could do for people after the earthquake? Maybe they'd done their sweep and were happy no one was trapped under rubble somewhere. We didn't talk about that at all. Mostly they had questions for me about who I was, and what I knew so far about my abilities. Which I had to admit wasn't much, with that night being my first experience. But I explained how it seemed like I was moving crazy fast and the firey strength I felt, and they all nodded like they knew exactly what I meant. Because they have felt it too. Then they relaxed into the flight as though they had been working hard, and I relaxed alongside them, basking vicariously in their post-heroism glow.

Once off the plane at the airport, I spotted a payphone while Emma was spending fifteen minutes freshening up in the ladies room and Jake was arranging the valet for his car. *I really should call my parents.* My phone battery was way too low, but I had some change in my wallet and had one of my parent's numbers memorized. My mom's cell. When I rang, it went straight to voicemail. Network mustn't be back up at home yet. After the beep, I had no idea what to say either. How could I sum up the events that brought me there?

"Umm, hey, it's me, I'm fine. Don't worry, everything is fine and I'll call you again soon to explain." I hung up, hoping they'd get the message soon. I worried about them being worried, but then Emma was back and Jake was there again too and my whole world turned sunny again.

If the flight was decadent, their house was something from a fairy tale. Not a house. An abso-frikkin'-amaze-balls mansion. Not too old-fashioned, not too modern. Perfectly classy. It was mid-morning by the time we got there and the sun sparkled off the building like a dream. *I wonder which one of them has the trust fund. Probably all of them.*

At first sight of the mansion, all I could do was splutter like I'd spontaneously learned another language. "Ung, thas, wha?"

This was luxury on a level I'd never imagined. No, that wasn't true. It was luxury on the level I daydreamed about every day but never dared think I'd experience. I'd fallen in with a group of super-powered superstars and felt more than a little afraid at how I was meant to fit in. *If* I was meant to fit in. Who knew how long they'd want me around?

"Does anyone else live here?" I asked, when the English language had returned to me.

"Just us. Service staff come and go. A cleaner and a gardener. Oh, and a cook, of course." Jake pulled his car up at the front steps and we all unloaded. His gorgeous sporty wheels looked right at home parked out the front of this place.

"Of course," I whispered.

Jake threw a duffle bag over his shoulder from the trunk of

the car and made an "after you" gesture with his other hand.

I took a tentative step toward the wide front doors. Emma grabbed my hand and dragged me at a run. "You're going to have the room next to mine. Come on, I'll show you around."

I get a room? For how long? Something felt twisted and defiant, deep down inside me, but this was obviously what I wanted. I *wanted* to be here, with other empaths, with Jake, with all of this magnificence. I was probably just hesitant because everything was happening so fast.

Emma's tour was informal at best. She dragged me fast-paced down wide halls that mostly looked the same to me, with walls painted stark white and floor-to-ceiling windows showing a view of the sea.

"Garage is downstairs that way. Living rooms and all the general stuff through there, but there's a second lounge area back that-away. Kitchen is 'round there; it's near my room, so that means it will be near your room! The boys' rooms are all off down that hall in the other wing." She pointed in vague directions. Even if she'd stopped and showed me each one, I was sure I'd get lost in there anyway.

"Whose place is this?" I asked.

"It's a serviced rental. We kind of move around a lot. I think Jake's planning another move soon."

"Oh?" I asked nonchalantly as my heart sank.

"Or he was before we picked you up." She grinned at me. "I hope we get to stay here a bit longer now. This is our best place yet."

"It must be so nice, travelling around, going on adventures, helping people." I cringed and smiled bashfully at Emma. "So, that sounded lame. But I won't lie — you guys are my new idols. How did you all get together?"

Emma twirled and started walking backward to look at me while she talked. "Jake and Jamie are brothers. You probably noticed."

I nodded and followed along after her. They had that brotherly vibe, as well as being like different-sized versions of each other.

"They've been doing this gig most of their lives. I guess the whole 'path thing runs in families sometimes, or whatever causes it can hit siblings or people growing up closely together. We don't really know what it's all about. We just know we have it and it's cool." Emma flicked her hair as if to emphasize the coolness.

I had to agree, but had hoped they'd have more info to share on this 'whole 'path thing.'

Emma kept talking. "So anyway, Jake and Jamie found

36

Donny first. None of us know much about Donny. He's the quiet type. But a good guy. That's when they realized there really were other people like them out there, outside their family, and made more of an effort to look. Wasn't long after that they found me. At a funeral, would you believe it?"

I wasn't sure what to say. Who had died? Were the deceased and Emma... close?

Emma kept smiling, despite the flash of grief and guilt coming from her. "Then it's been, like, forever, with just us. I've been wishing for another girl on the team. And here we are. Ta-da!" Emma swung a door open and gave me a nudge into the room with her hip. "Nice?"

I shook my head. Not nice. *Incredible.* There was a king-sized modern four-poster bed with billowy sheer white drapes. Wide-screen wall-mounted television. Doors to what I imagined were a walk-in-robe and en suite. Wide bay windows. Ocean view. A *balcony.* I panted a little.

"I know, right?" She grabbed my hand and gave it a squeeze, sharing in the excitement. "I told you you'd love it here. I called ahead and got Ms. Penny to set the room up for you while she was cleaning. You probably want a shower after being up all night. I know I do. There'll be towels in the bathroom, and you can borrow shampoo and stuff from my bathroom next door. Help yourself to whatever you like."

Emma opened the door and showed me the en suite. The other door was a walk-in closet, empty except for a bathrobe and slippers. I was suddenly conscious that I only had one set of clothes with me—the ones I was wearing.

I compared my average, straight-up-and-down figure to Emma, who was tall and impossibly curvy for her slim frame. She was dressed like a celebrity's supermodel girlfriend, in a tight leather skirt and deep-necked dress-shirt and high heels. I doubted she'd have much that would fit me, let alone suit me.

"I didn't pack," I muttered, dazed. I didn't do anything other than get on a plane without planning. I sat down hard on the bed, opposite the doorframe where a small white box was mounted. What was that? Where were the phones? I hadn't even told my parents where I was going. *What was I doing? I didn't think things through very well.* My skin turned clammy.

"Honey, we'll buy you whatever you need. You're special, like us; you can have whatever you want. And now I have a girl to go shopping with! We are going to buy you so much stuff." Emma came and sat next to me. She put her arm over my shoulder and squeezed. "You okay? Oh, you're probably coming down from the buzz. That would have been your first major use of the powers, right?"

"Is this what happens? I feel like I don't know anything yet. Do I need training or something?" I flopped back onto the bed, my feet still dangling over the edge.

"We don't really do the training thing. More like learn on the job. It mostly comes naturally anyway."

"So it just happens? Or do I need to make it happen?"

"A bit of both. Some of the power kicks in naturally, but you can focus to absorb even more." Emma lay back on the bed as well, propped up on one elbow. Her hair fell around her like a curtain and smelled of raspberries. "It's like when someone is feeling a strong emotion, it sort of floods out of them. Like the human mind—or heart, I don't know—can't hold so much feeling inside." She made her hand into a fist and placed it on her chest. "Ever felt like that? Like your emotions are more than you can stand? It's that excess we can tap into. I mean, emotions are powerful, right?"

I put a hand on my own chest, mirroring her. "When those looters came at me, I managed to protect myself, sort of. They were so angry and it was like their energy rushed into me, and I moved faster than I'd thought I could. And I should have bruises and cuts, but I don't."

Emma shifted down onto her back as well and punched her hands at the air above her. "It's bad ass, right? Hate sets up our bodies to fight, gives us strength and healing. Excitement gives us energy. Fear speeds us up. There's obviously a lot of overlap with emotions so it all gets a bit fuzzy."

"What about other emotions? Sadness?"

"Ick. Avoid sad people. Despair is just useless." Emma stuck her tongue out like she'd tasted expired milk.

"Love?"

"Aw, you're cute! I wouldn't go holding out to experience tapping into true love if I were you. Lust is where the power's at." She winked at me and I blushed.

Emma's pocket started pinging and she tugged out her phone from the skin-tight skirt. "It's Jake. Ooh, another job already?"

Wow. This place was so big, they texted each other inside.

"Come on. Let's go get the info." She grabbed me by the hand and we were off again. I was caught up in a red-headed whirlwind and her enthusiasm was contagious. I found myself giggling at how lost I was when we reached a lounge room lined with bookshelves where the guys waited.

The boys had showered, and somehow, they looked even more handsome than they had before. It made me self-conscious of the scent of overnight flight I wore. Jake had changed into a tight black tee under a leather motorbike jacket. I barely noticed the other two guys who stood either side of him. It was as though their hotness just enhanced Jake's. Side-kicks beside the most powerful superhero.

He smiled at me and I felt like I was in the right place again.

"What is it?" Emma bent at the knees and sprang up like an excited child.

"I'll tell you on the way. We have to leave right now if we're going to get anything done. Livvy, I'm sorry to do this to you, but we really can't miss this one. I'd bring you along, but it's too dangerous for someone so fresh."

My inner voice whined like a little puppy being left home alone. I didn't understand why they couldn't even tell me where they were going or what they were doing. Paranoia scratched at the corner of my brain. Jake patted me on the shoulder and all my worries floated away. *Don't be selfish, Livvy. They've just got important hero stuff to do.* "Yeah, I understand. Umm... what should I do?"

"Get settled in, cleaned up, relax. Ms. Penny left after her morning rounds but Sophie, our cook, is in, so feel free to call the kitchen on the intercom for whatever you need and she'll help you out." Jake pointed at an intercom near the door. I had seen one like it in my room too, but I hadn't known what it was at the time.

"Take a car into town if you like, or just hang here. We've

got all the channels," Jamie added, and they headed to the door and down the hall.

Emma popped her head back in. "I'll take you shopping tomorrow, I promise!"

I nodded and remained planted in the room as their footsteps faded.

My first move was to inspect the intercom, and press the button labelled 'Kitchen'.

A husky woman's voice buzzed out of the box. "This is Sophie."

"Hi, um, I'm Livvy." I paused, embarrassed.

"Hi, love. What can I do for you?"

"I think I'm lost."

6

Sophie managed to find me from my description of the room in which I had been left, and gave me a slightly more formal tour than Emma's. The house layout was actually well structured and not nearly as daunting as I'd first believed. She made me a range of cute brunch-style snacks that looked like they were from a fancy restaurant and left me to explore.

It had been so good spending last night with them all. A bond had formed between us, and it was as if I really belonged. A secure contentedness had made me glow and want to stay with them forever.

Now I was on my own, hours from home. I felt like an

intruder here without the team. I kept feeling confused, concerned about how I'd ended up here and what I'd left behind. Like a pair of uninformed parents, and my phone charger. My phone lay lifeless on the bed.

The day was getting on. Even if Trevor had assumed I went home, or my parents had assumed I'd stayed longer at the shelter, sooner or later one would contact the other and there would be trouble. *What was I thinking? My parents must be freaking out.*

I attempted to turn on my phone, hoping for a last scrap of power, but it didn't respond, and there were no cables of the right kind in the house. Even Sophie had left her phone at home, and this palace seemed to be designed for room-to-room communication only with no visible landline. And with Jake off who knew where for who knew how long, getting home again was off the cards as well, for now. I felt stuck. Almost trapped.

I filled my stomach, took a shower, and put my dirty clothes back on, feeling apprehensive and, well... flat-out grouchy. Angry at myself for getting into this situation. Upset at being left alone.

To fill the time until the team returned, I decided to find the garage.

I never found it.

Instead, I stumbled across what had to be a prestige car showroom. When Jamie said to take a car, I didn't realize what sort of selection he meant. They had six cars between them, each of which probably cost as much as six ordinary cars, or, you know, a *house*. I barely recognized the badges, except ones like Maserati, and I only knew that one from TV shows about rich people.

I buzzed Sophie in the kitchen again and told her I'd be going for a walk. I didn't have a driver's license yet—thanks again to my parents' no-car policy—and even if I did, the stress of scratching up one of those cars could turn me prematurely gray.

But I did want to get out of that place. The big building left me at a loss without the others around, and I was never very keen on watching TV alone. On screen, I saw changes in the faces of the actors, but they lacked energy or the connection I felt in real life.

I figured I'd head into town and kill time at a cinema. While TV left me cold, I always loved going to the movies. I guess I understood why now. My empath abilities couldn't pick up emotions across a small screen, but they could pick up the vibe of a room of people sitting in the dark, all feeling the same thing.

Sophie asked if I'd be needing dinner. I still had twenty bucks cash on me, so I said I'd find something while I was out.

I hoped I'd also find a pay phone. She gave me the visitor's security code for the keypad entry to get back in and I headed off. I felt almost surprised, and relieved, that I was allowed to leave. Was I being paranoid or what?

The mansion was at the top of a hill, and a long, winding road led down into town, past a few other mansion-like estates perched on the rocky cliff-side, overlooking the sea. A salty breeze from the ocean pushed at my back.

Sophie had given me directions to the cinema and it proved easy to find. I bought my ticket but was disappointed when I went in and was the only person there. It proved more depressing than watching TV.

By the time the movie was over, it had grown dark, and so had my mood. I found myself wandering aimlessly through the unfamiliar town, trying to get my thoughts in order. I questioned how long I'd been wandering but had no way to check the time. I'd made my way into an area where every second storefront was boarded up and layered in crude graffiti.

Despite the lofty elite on the hillside, the town looked like it had seen better days. It made my hometown look downright posh with its little boutique shops like Mom's.

Mom.

I swallowed hard. Mom and Dad must have been frantic.

46

I hadn't found a pay phone that hadn't been vandalized and was no longer functioning. I dreaded making the call to my parents even if I did have a way. I had no idea what I'd tell them, or how much trouble I'd be in.

I tried not to beat myself up too much. I'd just had some life-changing events take place. I was fine, and I'd let them know as soon as I could.

It was fine. They'd be fine. Everything was fine.

Who am I kidding? I went missing during a natural disaster. There was probably an amber alert out on me.

I've stuffed up big time when I really need my parents to be okay with this.

I needed to be able to tell them that my dreams were coming true and I had to follow them. Could they be okay with that? With me staying with the team? I would have been off to college in a year anyway… now I didn't even know if I was going back to school. I had no idea what was ahead of me, but it wasn't as though college had an Empath 101 course I could take. But still, how did working with these guys equate to money? Earning a living? Or would their trust fund look after me?

Shaking my head, I decided I needed to stick with Jake and the team. Regardless of anything else, I trusted Jake. One way or another, I felt that he'd look after me. It was why I was here, despite it seeming completely crazy.

While my mind did loop-de-loops trying to justify my actions, a sound caught my attention. A range of noises reminding me all too clearly of my confrontation with the looters—taunting, laughing, the sounds of anger and hard objects thudding against flesh.

It came from a side street up ahead.

My pace slowed. If someone was in trouble, maybe I could do something. It wouldn't be like last night. Surely I could use my powers properly, now I knew what they were.

I wasn't the old me anymore. Now, I was superhero princess me. Awesome Olivia was there to help.

I approached the side street carefully, going over the pros and cons in my head. No chance to call the cops this time. My flat phone had been left back in my room. If I did this, I'd have to do it with caution. I'd have to be clever. Jake hadn't mentioned secret identities yet and I didn't see the other guys wearing costumes, but I assumed it was best not to flaunt my powers.

I peeked around the corner.

Under a flickering street light, two guys were beating on a third. They had him pressed to a wall between them, taking turns slugging him in the stomach. They called him names—homo, trailer trash—disgusting, offensive names. The guy they beat didn't struggle and I worried they'd already done serious damage.

I tried to tap into their emotions, get some strength, speed, something I could use.

A cold emptiness crept over me instead.

Maybe I wasn't close enough? *Damn it, how did this work?* Their victim looked in a bad state and they showed no signs of slowing down. I had to do something fast.

Stepping into the alley, I took a position hidden in the shadows and yelled, "Police. Stop what you're doing."

All three jumped at my voice, and the emptiness cleared. A wave of anger, excitement and fear flowed off the attackers, and power built inside me. *Oh yes, I can do this.*

The two holding the third guy down blocked most of my view of him, but they all seemed about my age. The pair of bullies wore beanies, one blue, one red, probably from sports teams, but what would I know. My family was more likely to attend an art gallery opening than watch a football match. They muttered between themselves, then one of them called out, "You're no cop. Just get gone. You seen nothing here."

I flexed an arm, feeling the strength in it. I reveled in that power. Part of me wanted to use it, fly in like a superhero and show those bullies how it felt to get a beating. But I tried to stay smart. The power was my safety net only. Also, I really didn't want to nearly rip someone's hand off like I had last time. "Come on, guys, just leave him alone. I'm not going anywhere, and I don't think you want a witness here."

The beanie twins did that chin-lift thing guys do when communicating without words. One kept a hold of their prey and the other stalked toward me.

I took a step back out onto the main street to see if there was anyone else around, but it was empty. *Up to me then.*

I stepped forward and squared off against blue-beanie-boy. He twitched and swayed slightly. He had a badly grown goatee and up close, he stunk of alcohol.

"She's just some skinny chick!" he called back to his mate. He laughed and turned away. "Get lost!"

He spat out a swear word and headed back to his friend.

I followed at his heels. "I'm not going to let you keep beating that guy."

"Don't." The grunt of opposition came from the guy against the wall. He slouched, as though he'd fall if red-beanie-boy's hand on his shoulder didn't pin him in place. Stringy hair fell over his face. His effort to talk earned him another fist in the stomach.

"See? No one wants you around." Blue-beanie-boy spun back at me and thrust out an arm to push me away.

EMOTIONALLY CHARGED

I sidestepped easily and he lost balance. His whole body fell forward after his arm and he landed hard on the pavement near the overflowing trash cans.

As he hit the ground I felt the force of his anger burst around him, accompanied by his loud swearing. I made an effort to absorb it all, like soaking in sunshine through my skin. My body responded, every cell working at perfect efficiency. I pulsed with strength.

He pushed himself back off the ground and dusted off his knees. "You're going to get it!"

He came at me swinging.

I maneuvered around a street sign and his fist cracked on the metal instead. More swearing. I had no problem keeping away from him, drunk and uncoordinated as he was, but I was only making him angrier. I wanted them to back off and leave without having to hurt anyone. Brilliantly, all I'd done was prove for a second time that me on my own wasn't intimidating enough to scare off angry guys.

After another bout of swearing, his friend let his victim go and came to join in. He didn't stumble around like drunken blue-beanie. The two of them advanced together. I stepped away, not wanting an all-in brawl. They backed me into a urine-scented corner of the alley. Their expressions were vicious.

I lifted my fists, ready to fight back.

Down the street, a siren wailed. *Perfect timing.*

I shrugged innocently. "Did I forget to mention I *already* called the cops? Time to run, kiddies."

Their anger shed from them, replaced instantly with fear. After a quick glance at each other, and more swearing, they finally took my advice and bolted off into the night.

I took a few deep breaths and the siren passed by the other end of the alley, revealing the red of a fire truck. *Close one.* The bullies were well on their way though, and didn't notice my trick. It was over.

I just saved someone. All on my own. I let out a whoop and punched the air, grinning like a fool.

The guy they'd beaten had slumped down against the wall, his knees against his chest. He seemed to be catching his breath as well.

I held out my hand to help the guy up. "Are you okay?"

He ignored me and pushed himself to his feet with one shoulder against the wall. A breath hissed out through his clenched teeth. "What were you thinking? You shouldn't have gotten involved. You could have been hurt."

I froze with my hand still outstretched but my smile slipped right off my face. Not exactly the response I'd expected. "I...

I just wanted to help."

He turned and faced me fully. Average build, baggy clothing, dusty brown hair, pasty skin—nothing special at all. But his eyes transfixed me. Gray like wet concrete, they held me like a trap and the coldness I felt earlier crept back in.

"I didn't need your help. This happens all the time."

"A playful rumble, huh? What if they went too far?"

He just shrugged like he didn't even care. He winced as if each small movement hurt him, even talking. He was in pain but his face was blank, and I couldn't read a single emotion from him. It irritated me more than his criticisms of my rescue effort.

He glanced at me again with those eyes, looking me over as though checking for damage. "You were lucky they didn't mess you up."

"I wasn't lucky, I was..." I couldn't tell him what I really was, that I had superpowers. But even if I didn't. "I was clever, and capable, and I saved you!"

I found myself yelling. I couldn't read him at all and it threw me. *Why wasn't he happy I helped him? Happy to be saved?*

Blood dripped from his nose onto his light gray T-shirt. He zipped his jacket up over it and pulled the hood over his head. "Whatever."

He walked away.

All energy was drained from me. I spent my last cash to get a taxi back up to the mansion. I found it empty. Confused, frustrated, and alone, I crawled into bed.

I couldn't sleep. Gray eyes kept haunting me. Stupid, unappreciative eyes.

7

Jake and the team returned mid-morning. Seeing him again knocked my dull mood away. It also felt better having clean clothes. Ms. Penny had washed and dried what I'd been wearing while I had breakfast in bed in a robe and slippers. Pretty people and decadence took the edge off real quick.

We all sat in a lounge room. I wasn't sure which one or what its exact designation was, but a different one to yesterday. The white leather couches were immaculate and the rug so dense and fluffy, I almost wanted to sit on it more than the couch.

The guys relaxed from whatever their secret overnight mission had been, yawning and checking their phones amid a pile of empty energy drink cans and coffee mugs.

I didn't want to disturb them, but I had to deal with contacting my parents. I felt lame bringing it up, but none of that could match how upset my parents probably were.

I mustered up the will to speak. Jake smiled at me, and I almost lost it. Concentrating on something other than his perfect features proved difficult.

"Is there a way I can get my phone charged? I need to call my parents."

Jake sat next to me with his feet up on the glass coffee table and his head back. He straightened up to look at the powerless phone I exhibited in my hand. "Don't worry about it. We'll get you a new phone."

"Oh, I just need a charger, really. I don't need—"

"Ems, you taking our new girl out shopping today?" Jake spoke over me.

Emma had draped herself full-length down the opposite couch, leaving Donny and Jamie in designer egg-shaped armchairs, which looked more fancy than comfortable, at least for guys of their size.

Emma moaned and pouted, lifting her head with exaggerated effort. "Yeah, sure. I could probably stay awake for shopping. Let me chill out for a bit first though, K?"

The longer this waited, the more the knot in my stomach tightened. What would my parents be thinking? They probably thought I was buried under a collapsed building somewhere. "It's just, I really need to call my parents, like, yesterday. Maybe could I borrow someone's phone to let them know where I am?"

Jake shuffled across the lounge and put his arm around my shoulders.

The knot vanished. A warm glow replaced it and I tried not to purr.

"You're worried about your folks, about them worrying about you? I forget sometimes what that's like. Me and Jamie have been on our own for so long. Do you want me to take you home?"

He sounded so disappointed, like I was a child who'd had enough of a birthday party. Yesterday I might have said yes to leaving, but not now the team were all back here with me. I didn't want to be anywhere else. "Oh, no, I can just call them. I'm sure they'll be angry, but I need—"

Jake gave my shoulders a squeeze. "Do you want me to sort it out for you? Look, I'm great with parents, and it's always better to deal with things face-to-face, right? I've got to head back to your town tomorrow anyway, so I'll stop by and smooth things over. Save you from bearing the parental brunt."

I tilted my head and winced, working up to say no, which was hard. But seriously, my parents could have called me in as a missing person by now. I had to fix this.

Jake took my chin in his hand, leaning so close I almost thought he was going to kiss me. "Let me do this for you."

Warmth washed over me. I exhaled over wobbly lips. I smiled and gave my okay. My parents could wait another day if it meant getting an in-person explanation instead of dodgy phone call, and I just knew Jake could make them understand. He made everything better just by being there. He would explain everything, and everything would be okay. I could feel it.

"I could go with you, if you'd like. See my parents too and—"

"Livvy, we want you right here this week so at first sign of an event nearby we can take you with us. It's time to get to know you better and see how your powers manage," Donny said.

Emma sat up with far more energy than she'd shown before. She clapped her hands together. "Then you can be part of the team for real!"

I glowed, and wondered if it was visible to them all.

"What do you want me to tell your folks?" Jake asked.

I thought for a moment. "Tell them I'm following my dreams."

Emma did take me shopping that afternoon, but we didn't get a new phone. We mostly bought new clothes for Emma.

She held nothing back, snapping up every designer item taking her fancy, paying cash for everything. And everything wasn't cheap. She tried to encourage me to do the same, but I only managed to humbly request a new pair of jeans, two tops, some PJs and some underwear. At least I had some clothes to change into now. I was sure that soon I'd feel more comfortable taking what I wanted like Emma did.

Soon, I'd be part of the team for real.

During the week each of the team members ducked out individually for this or that. They weren't much for explaining what they were doing or where they were going, and I didn't want to seem naggy with my questions. Maybe they had day jobs? I somehow doubted it, unless it was just as cover for their secret identities. No way did they need the money.

No one did any empath power training, which disappointed me. There was so much I wanted to know, but they didn't even seem as interested in it as I did. The only training done was daily body-sculpting workouts. I joined in and they encouraged me, even though I was pathetic.

Jake returned from Bellscroft with a new phone for me, already programmed with the team's numbers, and a report on my parents.

"They were worried, of course, but my top-notch empath

skills had them feeling better in no time. Here, check this out."
Jake opened the photo gallery of the new phone and showed
me a ten-second video of him sitting on my couch with my
parents, all three smiling and waving.

"What did you tell them?" I had run through that discussion
so often in my own head. Of course I wanted to be a good
daughter and be honest, but the truth in this case was kind of
wild, and not just my secret to keep.

"I told them we were friends from school, that we picked
you up and let you stay at ours instead of the shelter. Made a
few other excuses about flat phones, extra volunteer work
together, following your dreams, yadda yadda, and they're
happy to let you stay with us as long as you like."

I wondered if *forever* was included.

It felt sort of wrong to have not told them the whole truth,
and there was something weird about seeing them so cheerful
in that video. Was I upset that they weren't more worried?
Maybe, but I was happy too. I needed to go back home myself
for a visit sometime soon, and I reminded myself to give my
parents super-hugs for letting me do this.

I knew Mom would understand. Mom ran away from a
backwater slum when she was fourteen and lived on her own
for years, waitressing in cafes during the days and working

nights and weekends building her own business. She met the man of her dreams and now ran her own shop. My mom was amazing and always encouraged me to follow my dreams too. Not that I could compare my little adventure with what she'd done.

I thanked Jake for the new phone, and tried it out by taking a photo of us together. I spent most of my free hours for the rest of the week staring at that photo.

On Sunday night, Donny and Jamie called in from the industrial district across the city. A warehouse had gone up in flames. They said it looked like a good first event for me.

It was time for me to prove myself, although the idea of a whole burning building intimidated me. I'd never witnessed a real fire before. What would I be expected to do?

I felt too embarrassed to ask and appear dumb to the others. I just agreed to go.

This was my chance to use my powers as a part of the team. Maybe I could save someone's life.

8

Jake drove the Maserati there faster than I thought was safe. Emma took the front seat and I squeezed into the pocket-sized back with Emma's reasoning that I had the shortest legs.

Maybe Jake sensed my anxiety, because he explained the situation more as we stopped down the road from the pillar of black smoke marking the fire.

"Don't stress. There's no one in the buildings. The whole industrial park has been evacuated. Nothing but stock and structures at risk." Ever the gentleman, he popped his front seat forward and helped extract me from the back of the two-door sports car.

I noticed Donny's black Jeep parked a little farther down the street. He and Jamie loaded something into the back. We wandered down to meet them.

"So, what will I be doing?" I tried to sound brave and eager.

Jake nodded to the other guys before coming back to my question. "Just watching. The firefighters are working hard to get the fire under control before it spreads. There's some serious adrenaline and emotion involved in that, so just feel out the situation and see what you can use. Then show us what you've got."

We were still a building or two away and I already felt the heat. I wondered if it was from the fire or the emotions of those fighting it. Or maybe just the warmth I always felt from being near Jake.

We ducked through a hole in a chain-link fence, sneaking closer between the warehouses. We found a viewpoint nearby and hid behind a stack of wooden pallets so the officials wouldn't send us away.

"What would you guys normally be doing, if I weren't learning?"

"For a fire? Not really a lot. Empath powers don't really make us more effective at putting out flames. We don't suddenly get super flame-retardant breath or anything. But If someone was inside, I'd rush in for the save, of course." Jake smiled and winked.

Could I rush into a burning building to save someone? Mouthing off at punks seemed altogether different to that level of heroism.

But I wanted to be someone who would do that. And I wanted to be *with* someone who would do that.

I stared happily at Jake for a moment too long before the fire drew my attention.

The two-story warehouse glowed like a jack-o'-lantern. I gaped in awe at such destructive, beautiful power. Flames painted the walls and the heat dried my unprotected skin even from this distance. The smell was off, like bad eggs and car burn-outs. Fortunately, most of the smoke blew the other way.

We watched the fire fighters doing their thing, calling orders back and forth, dragging hoses, working pumps on the truck. All knew their roles. They worked as a team. I'd be part of a team like that soon, but even better. I looked sidelong at Jake, his hair and skin glowing golden in the firelight. *Part of his team.*

Excess emotions flowed off the firefighters and I made myself a magnet, letting the power soak in through my pores.

Jake bumped my shoulder with his. "How are you feeling?

Got the mojo yet?"

"Yeah, feeling good. Awesome even."

Jake held up his palm flat in front of me. "Give me your best shot."

"Really?"

Jake rolled his eyes. "And don't be holding back. We don't take wimps."

I raised my eyebrows and lifted my fist to the challenge. I could feel my muscles tense and coil. The sensation and awareness, the pure power, made me feel giddy.

I smacked my fist into his palm. The sound echoed like a log smashing the ground.

Jake whistled, shaking off the hurt dramatically. "Nice, some real potential there. Let's see how fast you are. How about a race?"

My imagination went on its own race into the future, Jake and me running through deserted warehouses, giggling, speeding after each other, tumbling into a heap, our lips so close and then...

Something caught my eye over at the fire.

My sight had improved as well, the way it had the night after I volunteered at the shelter. A sheet of corrugated iron peeled itself off the roof, lifting under the hot gusts from the fire like a strange kite. It lingered in the air then fell in a deadly dive bomb straight at one of the firefighters.

I ran.

I bolted toward the man. I'd never moved so fast. *Was I still visible or just a blur?*

I collided with the firefighter in a tackle and we rolled six feet, tumbling together. The corrugated iron scraped and tore on the concrete right where he had been.

The firefighter looked from me to the jagged, red-hot iron and back again with his jaw unhinged. His face softened and I held my breath, waiting for the praise I'd missed with the last save I made.

Instead I found myself wrenched to my feet and dragged away.

"Idiot! What were you thinking?" Jake hissed as he pulled me along, jostling me roughly as I stumbled to keep up. We moved fast and were back at the car before I knew it. "We can't be seen here. You can't do things like that! People will start asking questions."

I stuttered, screwing my face up to stop myself crying. He might as well have slapped me. "I... I didn't do good?"

"It's important we all keep a low profile." Jake's eyes had turned stony. "You're not going to be trouble for us? Trying to be a big hero?"

"No, I..." I had been trying to be a hero. Was that wrong? I felt like a dumb, naïve child to have thought saving a life in the real world would be like it was on TV. Everything had repercussions and I had acted without considering any consequences for myself or Jake's team. I hung my head. "I just wanted to help him. I'm sorry. I get we have to do things carefully."

Emma, Jamie and Donny caught up. I looked around them for support but could tell they were all irritated, or downright angry. I felt broken inside, and tried to wipe away a tear before the others saw it on my cheek.

Jake softened and my world turned right again. "It's okay. It's easy to get caught up in the power sometimes. You did a good thing. Just remember, if you're going to be part of the team, you have to learn to take orders. No running off and being a hero on your own."

I nodded, relieved as the team's anger at me lessened. "Of course. I can do that. I'll follow orders. I want to be part of the team more than anything."

No one talked on the drive home. I kept busy berating myself internally. I had to be smarter or they wouldn't accept me. I should have known I wasn't special enough as is to get an easy A on their empath tests. I never was good at exams.

Those thoughts mixed with the thrill I'd felt when saving

the fireman's life. Even if it was wrong to expose myself or my powers, deep inside I felt like I'd done the right thing. Jake was probably just angry I got there first and beat him at his own hero game. Maybe he was secretly impressed.

Would the fireman have thanked me if he'd had the chance?

Of course he would have. Only emotionless gray-eyed robot types didn't thank people.

Once those eyes came into my head, I couldn't wipe them away again for the rest of the night.

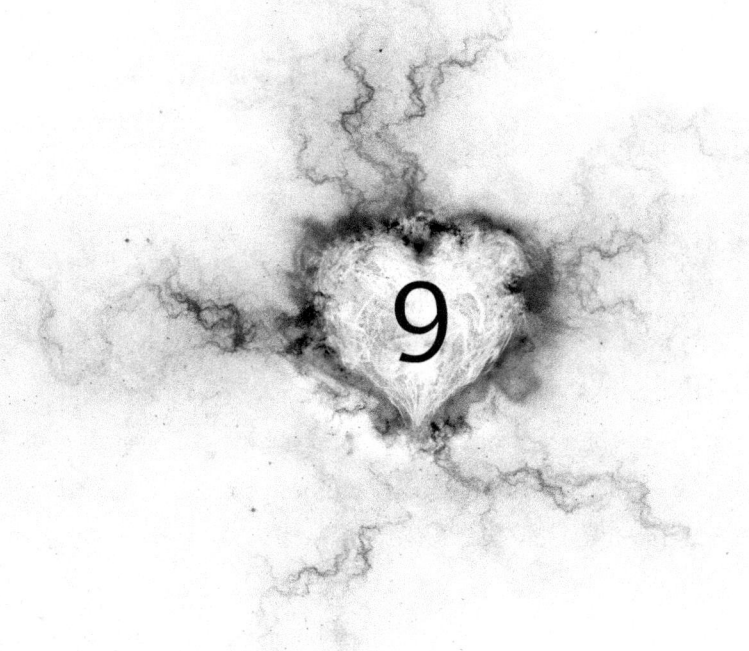

9

woke up the next morning to Emma jumping on the side of
my bed. I gasped, shocked out of sleepiness by her sudden
appearance in my room.

She giggled and headed back out the door, calling over her
shoulder. "Come on, get up. Make yourself pretty and meet us
in the formal lounge. We'll be waaaaaiting."

Could it be? Formal lounge, formal initiation into the team?

I rushed through a shower and put on my best choice of limited
clothing. I tried three options for my hair then left it out long,
running Emma's straightener over just the front to tidy it up.

I tried two lounge rooms before I found the formal one

where everyone waited. I wasn't sure I'd been in this one before. A massive gilt-framed mirror dominated one wall, and everyone sat in armchairs around a stool in front of it.

Emma stood up, squealing. "It's makeover time!"

She ushered me onto the stool and I sat awkwardly, feeling like the star of a very terrible one-woman show. "Makeover?" I didn't see any wardrobe or makeup or hairdressing stuff.

Jake leant forward in his armchair and smirked, his wide shoulders on display in a fitted shirt. "We want you on the team, Livvy."

He wants me on the team. I didn't screw up. I beamed.

Jake continued, "So we need you to be the best you can be."

"Be. Yourself. But. Better!" Emma shouted, punctuating each word with a clap.

Okay, and that meant makeover? Could be fun. Just like on reality shows. I could go a fancy new hairstyle for sure. The prospect of dying it something other than brown had me smiling. I was getting the princess treatment again, and I liked it.

I had worried I'd blown it last night with my hero stunt. Jake didn't seem angry anymore, but eyed me critically, running a hand through his golden hair and rubbing his chiseled chin.

I tried to sit tall and not be overwhelmed with self-consciousness as everyone visibly judged my appearance. It was the hardest thing I'd done since *ever*.

Emma circled me and played with my hair. "You're already so pretty; there won't be too much work to do. Just need a few things to really make you pop."

I burned with a blush. People had told me I was pretty before, but I'd figured I was average-pretty at best. And *pretty* wasn't *amazing. It would be nice to be amazing like everyone else in this room.*

"If you have suggestions for my hair, I'm up for anything." I poked my loose hair to highlight my fashion cluelessness.

"We'll do the hair for sure, and much more. Don't worry. Any work you have done is on us." Emma grinned.

Hang on, what? "Work done?" I asked.

Jamie spoke up. "She should get her lips and tits filled."

I laughed out loud but no one else did.

My laughter shut off fast. "Oh. I thought you were joking."

Jake cut in with a soft tone. "Sorry, Jamie can be a bit crass. Don't worry; it wouldn't be that extreme. Not as much as Emma's had done. It wouldn't suit your frame."

Emma folded her arms under her abundant bust as though to demonstrate.

"She could also have the bridge of her nose taken down a little, and narrowed at the base," Donny said in his quiet, authoritative voice.

Jake nodded. "You're right, Donny. Always with the eye for detail."

I wanted to hide. Were they seriously talking about cosmetic surgery? Sitting there deciding on how to rebuild my body? They were pranking; they must have been. Just pushing it to see how long they could keep me going.

At least Jake wasn't joining in being as critical as the others.

"She needs to get some dental work done too. The crooked front teeth have to go," Jake said.

Something shattered inside me.

There was no joke here.

My mouth fell open as the concept settled in. *They expect me to get cosmetic surgery to be part of the team. And dental work.* I closed my mouth. Did I really think someone like Jake could be attracted to me as I was? Maybe not, but I'd hoped. I'd hoped he'd seen beyond the brown-haired, brown-eyed, average-pretty to something special inside. That had been my dream. Not him wanting to change me into something else.

"Honey, don't feel bad! It's not like it's just you. We've all had work done." Emma hugged me around the shoulders then pounced back into an empty armchair. "We're talking about way less for you than I had. But then, I wanted a lot of it myself."

All of them? Even the guys? I looked around at them, all like fresh-out-of-the-box action figures, and they suddenly seemed too perfect. All of them had been carefully designed and crafted. "Why?"

"To be this fab-u-lous," Emma drawled, posing like a model in her chair.

Jake tilted his head and gave me a kind smile. It helped settle my nerves better than hot chocolate. His smile made everything better and I started wondering if I could get plastic surgery, for him, if it would keep him near me, so I could always feel this warm and safe. "We all do it because it helps with our powers. Same with keeping ourselves in good shape. It pays off to be attractive."

"I told you. Lust is where the power is at," Emma said.

I frowned. "I don't understand."

Donny's voice was dryer than usual. He spoke slowly, like he was trying to wake a sleepwalker, or talking to someone really dumb. "When people are physically attracted to us, we receive power from that emotion. It means we can get them to do what we want. Anything we suggest is accepted easily, a bit like hypnotism. The more attracted they are, the better it works. So we make ourselves physically desirable. Did you really think we were all born this perfect?"

Emma chimed in. "Haven't you ever had it easy picking up guys and getting them to do whatever you want? Buy you drinks, give you their number, give you their whole damn wallet?"

Not really. There had never been anyone I was interested enough in to try picking up. I was waiting for my prince, my Jake. Sure, there had been a couple of guys who had hit on me before but I'd never thought that I could use that to my advantage, and why would I ask for their wallet?

Just how open to suggestion did this attraction power make people?

The air rushed out of me so quickly I felt faint. Would that power make someone open to the suggestion of leaving home with a group of strangers in the middle of the night?

Everything spiraled. *It can't be...* I stared at the floor, trying to take steady breaths.

I should have asked more questions. I should have gone home and thought about what I was doing. I should have asked my parents. Any sane person would have done those things. I liked to think I was, but I also didn't like the idea that Jake had used his powers on me. The two concepts couldn't co-exist.

I looked up to ask something, anything to get the reassurance that he hadn't done what I thought.

Jake smiled. His perfect smile. My concerns fell away like

sand under a wave. In the past, that wave buoyed me and left me floating blissfully, but now the water was cold, leaving me feeling numb and confused. Was it happening again? I could hardly tell my own desires and emotions over what I was being told I should do. *I do want this. I'm following my dream.* Maybe body alteration didn't fit into my dream but I hadn't ever been really clear on what my dreams were anyway.

"So, my lovely Livvy, the question is—what are you willing to do to be part of the team? If you can't even handle some cosmetic surgery..."

The thought that my chance to be part of the team was slipping away made me panicky. I didn't think I could cope with going home, being normal again after seeing how Jake and the others lived. The way I felt after saving the guy in the alley, after saving the fireman—maybe that was the dream I should be chasing. If I wanted to be a hero, to be exceptional, my best chance to do that was with these people who were unlike anyone I'd ever met before.

"Anything." I took a moment, my smile wide. This was the right decision. "I'll do anything."

10

I moped up and down the shopping mall, arms loaded with fancy bags from deluxe boutiques.

I should have felt like a celebrity, out on a spending spree with a fat wad of someone else's cash, but I was stressing about buying the right things to make myself look better. Like if I bought the right dress, the team would decide I looked fine just the way I was. Even if that could work, how was I supposed to know which dress that was? I was no style expert. I wished Emma was here to guide me, but she had gone off on some important lunch date. She had great fashion sense and everything she wore looked perfect on her, like it had been custom fitted.

Or was it her that had been custom fitted to the clothes? Just how much work had she had done to look so magazine-cover perfect? How did she look before?

After the 'makeover' meeting, Jake said he wouldn't rush me into anything major. It was all just something to think about for now. They wanted me on the team and seemed happy I was willing to do what I needed to be with them.

Jake told me there were so few people like us. Maybe he felt they couldn't leave me out, that they needed every empath they could find. But I had to step up and be valuable to the group. I had to be the best version of me, to fit in with them. *I just hope I can do it without going under the knife.*

Whether it was my thoughts or the swag weighing me down, I felt exhausted. I needed fuel, and stepped out of the glittery mall onto the street to find a coffee shop.

That was when I saw him again.

He sat across the street in a park. His eyes were down, reading a book, but I didn't need to see them to know their exact shade of gray.

I felt bad that I'd yelled at him. Sure, I'd saved him from further beating, and that was a point to me, but yelling at the victim wasn't very heroic behavior.

I decided to apologize and see how he was recovering. Now

we were in a less stressed environment, maybe he'd also say thank you, which I had to admit I really wanted. It wasn't just a validation thing. I needed reassurance to know I'd done the right thing, since "the right thing" was starting to get very fuzzy in my mind.

I took a deep breath to build up some courage and marched across the road.

Very few people were in the park, and if they were, they rushed through it like a shortcut rather than lingering in the neglected space. The swing set was rusted and both swings had been tangled up around the top beam. A wooden play fort dominated the central area. It was the kind which wouldn't get built these days for being too dangerous for kids, but the kind kids loved. A maze of timber rooms and too-high balance beams and splintery surfaces—it looked like adventure. One boy pointed longingly in its direction before being dragged the other way by his dad. The lawn throughout was uneven, spotted with dandelions and longer than it should be.

I shuffled through it to the bench where the guy I'd saved sat.

I stood still in front of him, and he didn't move.

Whether he was ignoring me, or absorbed in the dog-eared paperback, I couldn't tell. The same weird, cold, emptiness I'd felt when I first saw him crept into my bones. I cleared my throat and he looked up.

He looked better in the daylight, less pasty and more ivory skinned. I spaced out for a moment, wondering how my olive skin would look pressed against it. *Where did that thought come from?*

"Hi?" He sounded confused. Did he recognize me? I was wearing the same red trench coat I'd been wearing since leaving home, which I figured was pretty memorable.

There was a slight rosiness to his cheeks and under his eyes, almost like he'd been crying, but I couldn't get an emotional read on him.

"Do you remember the other night? I was, uh, in the alley, and those guys, and, um, I'm Livvy." My inability to sense any hint of emotion from this guy threw me. It was just like watching TV. I saw the movement and angles of his face and body but couldn't sense anything real. Almost as though he wasn't even really there.

"I remember." He nodded slowly. I wanted to face palm. Of course he remembered. It wasn't the sort of thing you'd just forget, like what you had for lunch last week. I shuffled on the spot, ready to leave in embarrassment.

"I'm Dean," he said, and a tiny smile emerged. Or maybe it was a nervous tic. I couldn't tell either way with this blank slate.

Even Donny showed mountains of emotion in comparison. But that tiny smile gave me courage.

"I was just about to get a coffee. Want to join me?" I thumb-pointed over my shoulder at the café in front of the mall.

Dean stared at it for a moment, then back up at me, his eyebrows twitching. He closed his book. It was so worn, it had no real cover anymore. I wondered what he was reading.

"Sure."

He stood up and I juggled my bags back into carrying order as we crossed the road.

I paid at the counter for a cappuccino with extra froth and Dean waved off getting anything, just helped himself to some table water. We took a booth and my bags piled around me on the bench.

"So..." I struggled to be casual. "Are you feeling okay? Since, you know, I saved you from those guys?"

Dean shrugged and nodded but didn't say anything.

The red around Dean's eyes made them look less gray, more the color of worn denim. They had a depth I kept falling into, like a deep, icy lake. I couldn't help staring, trying to get some hint of what this guy felt. But all I got from him was that same chilling, hollow feeling.

He leaned back in the booth and unzipped his jacket. The

baggy shirt underneath was gray and it struck me that he seemed to be wearing the same clothes I'd seen him in before. Not that they were unique in any way to tell for sure. They were clean, and I smelled plain soap and a smoky musk as he took off his jacket. The stitching had come undone around the collar of the T-shirt and the fabric looked thin.

His hair fell in front of his face, feathery and also clean. Maybe it just looked stringy the other night from sweat.

His lips moved.

Shoot. I had completely missed what he'd said. "Uh, sorry, what?"

"I asked if there was something specific you wanted to talk to me about." When I hesitated, feeling foolish for the whole situation, he continued. "Are you okay? You seem upset. At least, you aren't smiling like a fool like you were after chasing off those guys."

Great. I had no idea what he was feeling and here he was making guesses about me.

I pulled my lips closed tight. "It's just my teeth. They're all crooked. I didn't mind so much before, but now I kind of hate them."

"You're prettier when you aren't doubting yourself."

He said it so plainly, like it was nothing. Not praise, not

flattery or a shot at getting something from me. He said it just like a fact, like *the sky is blue*.

Nothing Dean said felt like it had any emotion so I clung to his words for meaning. Like how he said *prettier* and that maybe the "er" meant he thought I was pretty even now when I was doubting myself. My heart was doing silly maneuvers and I shook my head, looked into my foamy coffee and added another sugar.

"Your teeth give you character. It's cute, the way one crosses over the other a bit at the front—"

I put my hand over my mouth.

"Sorry, I'm saying dumb things. But you shouldn't feel bad about them. I suppose you're going to get them fixed though, aren't you?"

I shrugged, not entirely sure if it was up to me.

"I guess you've got the money to get whatever smile you want." Dean eyed the bags surrounding me.

"Oh, the shopping. I kind of came to stay with friends for a while without packing and needed some things. The money isn't mine. It's sort of complicated." I shuffled around on the seat as though it would hide some of the mountain of purchases behind me, suddenly embarrassed by it all.

"What about that necklace? You were wearing it the other

night too. Silver, or...?"

"White gold." I wrapped my hand around the heart-shaped pendant I had been wearing since the earthquake, covering it from sight. "My parents bought it for me when I got a B on my last tests."

"Shouldn't that have been an A?"

"Probably, but B was the best I could do. It's not like I don't try; I just suck at tests." *And my parents are big softies.* My vision glazed with tears. I missed them so much. I blinked the wetness away.

Dean rolled his eyes. I didn't have to sense emotions to know the blatantly sarcastic 'poor you' look.

Did he think I was spoiled? Was that what he was getting at? This whole conversation had been weird. He was all questions and no answers. I wanted desperately to know why his eyes were red, whether he had been crying or not. Whether he had any feelings at all. I wanted to know how he felt about being attacked and how he felt about me saving him, and I couldn't read a thing.

Embarrassment unfurled inside me without warning, coloring my face. I gulped my coffee to hide it. Dean stared.

A beeping noise distracted me, and it took a moment to recognize the message tone of my new phone. I apologized and pulled it out of my pocket.

83

A message from Jake. I smiled at seeing his name, then pulled my lips back over my teeth again.

Coming to pick U up. Meet west mall exit. C U in 15. Team stuff.

I typed quickly. *Cya soon.*

I slipped the phone away and told Dean I had to be somewhere.

He helped me load my bags up again and thanked me for the coffee, even though he didn't have anything.

We stood for a moment, facing each other silently.

I wasn't sure if I'd see Dean again after this and I kind of wanted to. In the whirlwind my life had become, the last twenty minutes had felt like the only time recently when my feet were safely on the ground. There was something cooling, calming, and down to earth about Dean. Also something frustrating and confusing, but that just made me want to work him out even more.

I could ask for his number, but then what? He didn't seem that interested in me. He probably only came over for coffee to be polite. I should have just said goodbye, but instead I blurted out more crazy words. "You really think my teeth are okay?"

Dean half-smiled and walked away.

11

Donny's jeep screeched to a stop in front of me where I waited on the curb, doing a balancing act with my purchases. I threw them all in the back and climbed in next to Emma who shuffled into the middle seat. It was a full house, with Donny driving, Jamie shotgun, and Jake and I in the back with Emma as an unfortunate barrier between us. I handed the remaining unspent cash to Jake, and he pocketed it.

"So, team stuff?" I asked, hoping it was fun, heroic team stuff and not 'let's all point out Livvy's flaws' team stuff.

"Last night at the fire we were getting to know the strength of your powers. This afternoon, it's time to prove you're one of us, part of the team." Jake gave me a serious look, with just enough flirty smile to make me swoon. "We're doing a fundraising activity."

"Oh, like, charity work?"

Emma barked a high-pitched laugh that faded into a giggle. I frowned. *Since when is charity work funny?*

"Fundraising for us, for the team," Jake continued. "We're headed to a bank to make a withdrawal. We need to stock up on the spending cash."

Donny drove us downtown. The glitzy mall area made way for the industrial and housing estate district.

I shook my head. *They're just going to the bank? Why did this need to be done as a team?* Unease gurgled in my stomach. My paranoia grew sharp claws but I still refused to let it scratch down my perfect painted world.

Emma fished around in a massive designer handbag on her lap and threw what looked like a dead animal to Jamie. She grabbed more hair from the bag—wigs —and passed a black one to Jake. She took a blond wig in each hand and dangled them in front of me. "We're both going to be blond, like sisters! You're going to look so cute."

I took the wig with numb fingers. A buzz of excitement came from everyone else in the car. "We're not really withdrawing money, are we?" I wasn't sure I wanted to hear the answer.

"Sure we are," said Jamie. "Just not ours."

"Um..." That was the answer I hadn't wanted to hear.

Jake sighed, shaking his head. "My little brother and his abundant tact. Don't freak out. It's not a big deal. This is an easy job. Breeze in, breeze out. You're with us on this, aren't you, Livvy?"

"Um..." I hesitated again.

"We have to do this to stay a team. Do you think we should have normal jobs with our powers? We're better than that."

Donny glanced at me in the rear-vision mirror. "Taking on a new member is expensive too. Got to earn that back. Where did you think the money you spent today came from?"

Trust funds? Inheritance? Lottery winnings? That was all a bit naïve to assume. This was the real world, not one of my fantasies, even if it had felt like a dream come true. Did I really expect to just take and spend their cash with no strings attached? I'd gone out and spent their money, like I'd had every right. I'd put myself into debt with them. I shivered cold sweats.

"Are you really talking about robbing a bank here? That's all kinds of dangerous, and, well, illegal." My heart pumped hard and I wasn't sure what to think. It was all just too surreal. This was only-happens-in-movies stuff, not just-left-the-mall stuff.

"Honey, it won't be dangerous at all. We have superpowers, remember? We're just going to walk in, bat our eyelashes, ask for the money, and walk out with it. We already scoped this bank, and it's old school. No security screens or anything." Emma tugged her wig into place and reached between the front seats to adjust the rear-view mirror to preen. She then turned her preening onto Jamie and Jake's wigs, also now in place. They looked so different, their hair now jet black with mature cuts. It made them seem darker, more dangerous, somehow. "My lunch date was with a worker from there who told me all about the place. We would have left it a bit longer, but now's the best time to hit them. It's welfare check day, and the bank tops up its tellers for everyone coming in to cash their checks. Easy pickings."

Jake brushed Emma away and put on dark sunglasses. "Livvy, you're just going to be lookout for us this time. Until you get some work done, we won't have you taking on a teller, just in case."

I breathed out very slowly, letting the air puff out my lips. "I don't know if I can do this. Isn't it wrong?"

"No one will get hurt and the bank won't miss a few cash drawers. We're not taking the vault or anything insane. And we'll use the money to help us do more heroic stuff later on.

Promise." Jake winked, and I swore I heard Jamie chuckle.

Jake looked me in the eyes and I felt him forcing the sense of trust, warmth and contentedness on me. I pushed it away. It was easier now. With Jake's recent words and actions, I wasn't as attracted to him as I had been before. I saw clearly, felt clearly, and the horror of it almost overwhelmed me.

A physical pain crept into my chest. I was scared of Jake. Scared of what I was doing. Terrified of all of them and what they would do if I didn't cooperate. I had visions of jumping out of the moving car and trying to run away, but these guys had had use of their powers for longer than me. I was going to guess they'd be much faster than I was.

Jake watched me, waiting for my response. I felt trapped, but I couldn't let him see that.

I put the wig on and smiled. I read once just the act of moving your muscles into a smile made you happy and hoped it would be enough to cover my fear. I tried to shut off the part of my brain saying *no, no, no, no, no,* and focused on Jake's smile. It didn't help. *That fake smile.* How much of him was real at all? Everything felt wrong.

Emma tilted her head at me and giggled. "Donny, drive around the block a couple of times while I sort out this girl's hair."

12

Donny waited with the car down the street and Emma and I walked into the bank first.

It was a reasonably large place, old-fashioned, like she'd said, standing in a row of mostly closed shopfronts in a dying business district. Only a pawn shop, second-hand clothing store and tobacco shop were still open nearby.

Inside the bank, a musty smell rose from the threadbare carpet, and the wooden counters looked more like something out of an old western movie than a modern bank. Plexiglas dividers had been bolted on top of them, and a ticket machine stood at the entrance like a welcoming robot, but they were the only parts of the place that felt like they weren't from the 1950s. Even the customers were old, mixed in with a few younger tradesmen and laborers.

I was in a bank. About to rob a bank.

We were seriously going to rob a bank.

I played through my memories of how I'd ended up here, as though this were a pick-your-own-adventure book and I could just flip back to the right point and avoid this outcome.

So much of the time since the earthquake was a blur; I'd been hypnotized by these perfect people. *Perfect criminals*, I realized. But I couldn't only blame them. I'd made my decisions. I had wanted this.

Well, not *this*, exactly.

I made sure my oversized sunglasses were still in place and tugged down my wig as though I could cover all of my face with it. *If I just get through this, there has to be a way I can back out gracefully from this whole team thing, right? Will Jake just let me go?*

Emma scoped a security guard and went to do her job, flirting with him and keeping him entirely occupied. I just had to take a seat and keep watch. Only the bank was busy, and there were no seats left. Small detail, but I had to breathe through an anxiety attack as I tried to stand casually in the corner.

91

Jake and Jamie came in not long after us and took numbers from the machine. I practically counted the seconds waiting for them to be called to a teller, sure we were all about to be arrested at any second. I felt so thoroughly guilty, I was sure it could be seen oozing from my pores. I considered just flat-out bolting, but Donny was watching the street.

Jake was called, and Jamie a split second after as two tellers cleared. They were middle-aged ladies who I could tell were already swooning at the boys' approach. Maybe this would be easy after all.

I watched with fascination as Jake leaned forward, his lips almost up against the Plexiglas barrier. I saw the attraction radiating from the lady. She probably would have played with her hair if it weren't back in a very tight business-like bun. She kept on talking and giggling with Jake as she pulled a cash bag from the desk and opened the cash drawer, stuffing bills into the bag one wad at a time. No alarms went off. No one seemed to think anything suspicious was happening. It was business as usual and a bag of free cash for the team. I didn't like it. It felt so wrong. But I just wanted it to be over so I could breathe again.

Coldness crept across my skin.

I hoped it just meant the air-con had kicked in, but this felt familiar.

I'd felt this sort of chill before.

The teller with Jake froze, and her flirty grin dropped into a frown. She looked at the bag in her hand like she'd discovered she held a dead fish. I couldn't hear what she said, but her jaw wobbled up and down. I couldn't tell how she was feeling either; my empath senses had turned off. Jake kept working his act but she wouldn't calm down for him.

Jamie called over to Jake. He was having trouble too.

Jake called back, loud enough for me and Emma to hear, "Change of plans."

The teller stood and made to move away, and suddenly Jake had a shiny silver handgun pointed at her.

No, no, no, no, *no.*

Jamie pulled a gun from his jacket too, waving it at the waiting customers. "Everyone get back against that wall. You know the deal. If nothing stupid happens, then nothing stupid happens."

A large man in grease-covered clothing didn't budge. He drawled in a husky voice, "Come now, boys. Don't do anything rash."

"Stupid." Jamie dropped his aim and shot the man in the leg. He crumpled, gasping, clutching at the wound, trying to hold in his blood.

I yelped, my heart hammering. Jake shook his head at me, warning me with his expression. Others in the crowd screamed as well, cowering back.

I turned to Emma, just a few steps away from me with the guard. She couldn't be in on this. Not *this*.

She held a petite pistol in one hand and she relieved the security guard of his weapons with the other.

"Ems?" I hissed.

"Chill, sister," she hissed back. "A little firearm action will get the sheep scared and our powers kicking in again. Then we can get our goods and clear out fast."

But my powers weren't kicking in.

I didn't feel anything, not the slightest tingle, only the cold inside. People shuffled toward the wall, mumbling outrage and prayers. I looked over their faces, all of them terrified.

Except one.

His face was blank and his gray eyes stared at me, at my heart pendant, at the same clothing he'd seen me in just half an hour before and my disguise, the blond wig.

Dean.

I looked away, ashamed.

"I'm still not getting the vibe!" Jamie yelled at Jake, who was busy getting the teller to keep clearing drawers.

94

"Swap," Jake called back, and Jamie swung his gun to the teller, taking over.

Jake scanned the room, coming to stand beside me. "You feeling anything?"

"Just... cold." My eyes turned toward Dean automatically, just for a second too long. Jake's gaze followed mine and he grunted.

"A blocker. We've got a blocker!" Jake yelled to the others.

"Oh shit," Emma spat.

The hostages against the wall cowered. Dean stood motionless and continued to stare right at me.

Jake patted me on the shoulder. "Good pick, lookout. We'd be in trouble if you hadn't spotted him. You're making yourself valuable."

I didn't want to be valuable like this. I didn't understand much of what was happening and liked even less. "Why? What's a blocker?"

"People who shut away their feelings so hard it breaks something inside them. They mess with our powers," Jake ranted. "Best to deal with them when they show up. I've seen one block off an empath's powers for good."

Jake aimed his gun at Dean and smiled his comforting smile at me. That smile chilled me more than the blocking coldness coming from Dean. "Don't worry. Once we get rid of him, our powers will work again and we can get all this under control."

"Get rid of? What? No!"

I stepped in front of Jake to try and talk him out of it.

Jake swore and jerked the gun to the side.

Sound exploded through my skull. Everything went numb. My ears rang.

It took a moment to hear the screams behind me, to feel the burn in my cheek. My over-sized sunglasses hit the floor.

I turned in slow motion and saw an elderly woman falling to the ground. The pool of blood around her made acid rise in my throat. I knew she was dead, just knew it.

Other customers cried and ran.

Jake had lost control of the situation. People stumbled right over the old woman's body, stampeding toward the door. Emma and Jamie headed for the door as well. Sirens wailed in the distance.

Dean dodged between the crowd but didn't make for the exit.

"Run, get out of here!" I screamed at him.

He kept coming my way.

I felt hard, hot metal press against my temple.

"Jake?" I whimpered. I wanted to be strong, but it turned out a gun at your head could cause whimpering.

"I should have known you wouldn't work out, but I didn't think you'd screw things up this much!" he yelled at me, so close spittle hit my face.

His finger on the trigger tensed.

The gun fired. A body slammed against my side, pushing me away.

Dean cried out as he fell past me and hit the floor. Blood flooded through the fabric of his hoodie sleeve.

The coldness faded. I felt some power come back to me, like it had when I'd surprised Dean and his attackers that night. I guessed when he was shocked, he wasn't keeping his feelings under such tight rein and his emotional block didn't extend out. Or something. I didn't know. I just knew I had to act fast before Jake felt his powers kick in again too.

I had stumbled when Dean pushed me clear of the gunshot but I regained my balance fast. I spun with the momentum and knocked the gun from Jake's hand. I continued the spin and cracked my elbow against Jake's jaw, making him fall backwards.

I grabbed Dean by the arm, pulling him to his feet, practically threw him over my shoulder, and made a run for it.

13

I raced down empty alleys and side streets. Sirens blared around me, and I changed direction to avoid them. I was sure Jake was right on my heels, sure I would hear a gunshot go off again and that would be the end.

Dean bounced where I had him slung in a fireman's carry over my shoulder. Blood from his arm ran slick and warm down over my coat and onto the crisp white of my peasant blouse, the cutest of three tops I had chosen from to wear this morning to be judged by those... *bad guys*. How had we gone from makeover planning session to gunfight in just one day?

I hoped the jostling didn't hurt Dean too much, but I couldn't slow down. He was still out of it, which I guessed was the only reason I could keep moving at superspeed, could support his weight so easily. I couldn't risk being caught, but I had no idea where I was going or what I should do. I needed to help the guy who'd just been shot saving me. I only remembered one thing from first-aid class that seemed relevant: the DR ABCs. I had to get Dean and myself out of Danger then check his Responsiveness. That meant I had to get us as far away from Jake as I could. Airway, Breathing and CPR... *it better not come to that.*

Dean moaned and coughed and for a split second I felt relieved.

Then the coldness sank into me, leaching all my strength.

My legs buckled and we both hit the cracked concrete footpath. My knees grazed through denim as Dean's weight on my back crushed me forward.

I tried to roll him to the side without hurting either of us more. He moved off me, and leaned up against one of the graffiti-covered high metal fences enclosing the backyards around us.

His upper arm still oozed blood.

He opened those gray eyes and stared at me.

I blushed red all over. I had no idea what he thought of me right now. This was all my fault.

"We should get you to a doctor, or a hospital. We have to do something about your arm."

He turned his head to the gunshot wound, staring at it for a moment, expressionless. He brought his other hand up to suppress the bleeding. "No. Hate hospitals." He flinched at his own touch and stared at me again. "I don't understand you."

I coughed a hysterical laugh but only a breathy noise came out.

"Were you with *them*? Or are you just wearing a wig for fun?"

Reaching up, I patted the side of my head, feeling the curling blond waves of the wig. I tugged it off and dropped it on the weed-covered pathway.

"It's complicated." I didn't know how to explain without sounding bad, because there wasn't a way. I'd done the wrong thing.

"Complicated. Like your shopping money not really being your money. But you tried to stop them. Why? You have a death wish, taking on people like that?"

"I'm not a criminal. I mean, I didn't mean to be. I just got caught up with the wrong crowd. I thought they were the right ones. I don't know." I glared at the pile of synthetic blond hair on the ground, angry at my own excuses. "I just wanted to be a hero."

"A dead hero by the sounds of it." Dean pushed himself to his feet and walked away, cradling his arm.

I almost took out my phone but didn't know who to call or where to go next. I sat on the concrete and tugged at the weeds, tearing them out in showers of dirt, taking my pain out on them. Jake had tried to shoot me, kill me. He'd definitely kill Dean if he saw him again. Everything told me if I wasn't with Jake, I was against him. He'd come after me. I couldn't go home; Jake knew where I lived. I'd given him the address. He'd been there, seen my parents, manipulated them.

I had no money left for travel or accommodation and didn't know the area well enough to get myself moving in any direction. Tears built up along my bottom eyelashes and the first broke free, splashing on the ground and turning the concrete the color of Dean's eyes.

"Do you have somewhere to go?" he asked.

I looked up, and Dean stood next to me again. I shook my head and another tear spilt.

"Come on then."

14

Dean and I both moved slowly. I jumped at every sound, expecting a gunshot or an empath to burst out from behind a corner and attack us.

Dean kept a steady pace but wobbled as he walked. He'd lost a fair bit of blood and must have felt woozy. I'd be woozy just from the pain with a hole in my arm like that. I offered my shoulder for support, and the second time I did, he accepted.

We only walked two blocks, to where a trailer park spread from the end of a cul-de-sac. Dean pulled out his keys and let us into a mid-sized trailer, permanently fixed in place like most others around it. The screen door rattled and inside, a man lay sprawled across the couch.

I stiffened and looked to Dean. He just shook his head, put a finger to his lips, and led me past a kitchenette piled in beer cans and a tiny bathroom to a room at the end. The man let out a gurgling snore as Dean closed the door behind us.

His room barely passed eight-by-eight feet in size, with a small bed, beanbag, and set of drawers taking up most of the space.

Dean scooped up an old towel from the floor and held it against his bleeding arm.

Boys. I frowned and snatched it off him. "Do you have any kind of first-aid kit? Bandages or something? Alcohol? At least something *sanitary*? If you won't go to a doctor, we better clean that up properly ourselves."

Dean left the room. He returned with a box of Band-Aids, scissors, a clean cotton dishcloth and a bottle of vodka with just a finger or two left in the bottom.

He handed them to me and shrugged, then sat on the side of the bed, looking extremely pale.

"Okay, we can work with this. Can you take your jacket and shirt off?"

Dean looked away, almost as though he was shy.

"I just mean, I might need to cut them off around your arm

if you can't."

"No, I think I can manage." He let out a slow hiss of air as he unzipped his hoodie and peeled it away from the wound. I helped him pull the sleeves free of his wrists, since he worked one-handed to undress. He inched his T-shirt off. It took him a while so I cut the dishcloth lengthways down the middle, and started working around in a zigzag line to turn one half into a long strip. I dropped the makeshift bandage on the bed and soaked the other half of the cloth in vodka.

Clenching my teeth against nausea, I bent forward to inspect Dean's arm. A mixture of running, dried and coagulated blood created a gory horror-show. I dabbed around the mess on his bicep until I could see the bullet hole clearly. I leaned so close to Dean I felt his body heat radiating off him and his breath against my face, contrasting with the cool chill he gave me inside. The smell of blood mixed with the smoky-musk scent I noticed on him before. He didn't smell like a smoker. Maybe just someone who lived with one.

With the blood cleared, I saw a clean hole passing straight through the edge of his muscle. *Thank all things sweet and fluffy I don't have to pull a bullet out.* Just half an inch to the side, and the bullet would have missed him completely. A couple of inches the other way and I didn't want to think about it.

I'd just finished cleaning it off when it started bleeding again.

Dean spoke, his voice low. "You okay? You're turning all kinds of green."

I nodded but didn't open my mouth to reply, worried I might throw up.

I stood back up, away from the blood, and took a deep breath. I held up the bloody wash cloth. "You have another clean one?"

Dean started to get up but I put my hand on his shoulder. He took the hint and told me where to look in the kitchen. I walked back into the room and cut a second cloth in half as well to make some padding for the entry and exit wounds. Then I started wrapping his arm.

I felt Dean's eyes on me. I tried to focus on the bandaging.

"How about your cheek?" His breath tickled the fine hairs on my neck.

"What about my cheek?"

Dean lifted his uninjured arm to the left side of my face, but didn't touch me. I placed a hand there myself and felt a sting. The first shot Jake had fired. I remembered a pain on my cheek at the time, but then I saw the dead woman and people started screaming, and Jake kept pointing his gun and the world was upside down... I'd completely forgotten about it. My hands shook as I looped the bandage around Dean's arm.

"Is it bad? How's it look?"

"A thin line, just a graze I guess. Doesn't look like it bled much. You were lucky."

Maybe my empath powers had helped it heal fast. Maybe it would have been healed completely if it weren't for Dean's blocking. I wished I understood it all more.

I sighed and tried to wipe blood from my hands with the already soiled cloth. "Yeah, well, we both must be lucky since we're not dead. You should have just run. You wouldn't have been shot at all. Why didn't you run?"

Another shrug. No emotion I could read in his face or body language.

My first-aid results looked pretty dismal when I was done. I stuck the bandage closed with half a dozen adhesive band-aids. At least it didn't seem to be bleeding through yet.

Dean stood up and pulled a clean T-shirt from the drawers near the bed. He faced the other way as he put his shirt on in slow, careful movements. Muscles on his back shifted under the skin and I couldn't help but notice how nice his body was. With the baggy clothes he wore, I'd had no idea. I blushed, a mixture of embarrassment for looking and anger at my thoughts. How I'd stared so lustfully at the empaths' attractive bodies.

Them and their workout routines, creating those pretty shells.

"You work out?" I asked, sounding cattier than I meant to.

Dean finally had the shirt over his shoulders and let it drop loosely to cover his chest. He turned back toward me. "I *work*. I do some cash-in-hand jobs for a construction company. Manual labor stuff. Keeps me fit."

He reached into the drawer again and seemed to dig down through to the back to extract a packed of painkillers. He popped a couple out and swallowed them without water.

My thoughts became ragged. I was so angry at myself it overflowed onto Dean. I had no one to blame for my part in that messed up situation but myself, but if Dean hadn't been at the bank, maybe guns would never have come out. It would have been in and out. Easy pickings, like Emma had said. No one would have gotten shot.

No one would have died.

"Why were you even at the bank? Were you following me?" I snapped.

Even without being able to read his emotions, I could tell from Dean's frown just how dumb I'd been. The bank wasn't far from the mall and park, but we drove and went around in circles for ages while I got my wig right and panic buckled down. Dean could have walked to the bank in that time, but it was unlikely he'd followed us in Donny's jeep.

"The world doesn't revolve around you," he said. "I don't know where you're from, but this is my town; that was my bank. I was in to cash my dad's welfare check. I try and do it myself if I can so it doesn't all go on... my dad."

The shake in my hands had spread up my back, up my throat, and my head shook. "I'm sorry, I—"

"Who were those guys? What was the trigger-happy fashion model talking about, about blockers and powers? Why was he set on shooting me? And don't tell me it's complicated."

"They're empaths, like superheroes, but they weren't super-heroes. I just thought they were superheroes and that I was like them and I went with them but they weren't. They were the bad guys, and you're something else as well that does stuff to our superpowers..." I kept babbling. I shook and tears streamed down my face, stinging the graze on my cheek.

Dean put his hands on my shoulders and I rattled under his touch. "Okay, you're really freaking out."

He steered me to the unmade bed and sat me down. I scooted across to sit with my back against the wall and pulled the covers up around my shoulders, trying to fight the chill racing through me.

"You're in shock. Maybe something hot will help. I'll go see what we've got. Put the TV on and just try and relax a bit."

I squinted at the small, blocky television sitting on the cluttered top of the drawers. "Where's the remote?"

"Doesn't have one."

"Really? Retro much? You can't even give this kind of box away anymore. I know. My mom has tried." I tried to smile a bit and lighten the mood, but my teeth chattered and I must have looked a little insane. I imagined how my hair must look after its release from under the wig and the mental image rounded out nicely.

"It's a whole two feet away. I'm sure you can manage."

I tried to follow his instructions and not be completely useless as the guy with the bullet wound looked after me. Dean had made me a hot chocolate by the time I worked out how to get the television on. I set the volume extra low, worried I'd wake his dad.

Dean went to take a shower, to shake off his own shock and clean up some more blood. I told him to keep his bandages dry if he could, but didn't know if that would help.

I settled into the blankets with the mug of hot goodness balanced on my knees, and my shaking became less intense. I still felt teary, confused, and sick to my stomach. The news report on the TV didn't help.

The bank robbery was the top story.

They showed some security-camera footage, but it was too distant and grainy to make out any details. I had been right, though. The old woman Jake shot was dead.

Was that my fault? If I hadn't stepped in front of Jake and he hadn't swung the gun away... no, then Dean would be dead. If Dean wasn't there, they might never have brought out the guns. But if I hadn't drawn attention to him, they might not have spotted him in the crowd. If I'd refused to go at all, the whole thing might not have escalated. Or Dean would have been dead. I was like a hamster on a wheel, going round and round. *I could go crazy thinking like this.*

I thought the news report was over, but it continued. Footage from another scene I recognized, the warehouse fire. Warehouse fire and theft, apparently. While one building burned, valuable goods had been taken from others nearby. There was evidence of arson. The news reporter said police felt confident linking this event with the bank robbery and other crimes in the area over the last month. The pattern also matched crimes from a number of cities previously. They used the term 'terrorist cell' and I pulled the blankets up closer around my face.

I hadn't even questioned Donny and Jamie loading the car at the fire, or the extra luggage when we flew back from my earthquake-stricken hometown.

They were looters, but worse, even setting up disasters to take advantage of the emotions, making bad stuff happen on purpose. Not once had I seen them do anything heroic. I'd just assumed they did and they'd let me believe.

Even Jake. Would he have even saved me if I wasn't one of *them*? He said he saw some of the fight before he helped. How long did he wait and watch until he decided to step in, to make sure I was one of them, just because he wanted another 'path on his team? What if I'd just been a regular girl in trouble?

I heard the shower still running through the thin wall between Dean's room and the bathroom. Dean was shot. *I* was shot. Someone had *died*. It was a nightmare and it didn't even faze Jake.

Just what else had he done in the past? What was he capable of?

I had to stop them. The only way Dean and any other victims of these villains could be safe was to shut the team down. Permanently. Block off their powers for good.

Jake said Dean could do that.

How? I had no idea. Dean probably didn't know either. He didn't seem to know what was going on at all. He might not even want to help.

I finished the hot chocolate and put the mug on the drawers next to the TV. My eyelids felt leaden and sound of the running water calmed me.

But maybe Dean could learn how to shut down empaths. He could practice on me. I would give up my powers.

I'd give up the whole superhero fantasy if it meant everyone was safe again.

15

I stared at the screen of my phone. I'd been staring at it since I woke up. Half an hour, according to the clock. I'd tapped in my home number but couldn't hit Call.

Dean slept across from me on the beanbag. I'd fallen asleep in his bed before he got out of the shower and the idiot hadn't kicked me out like he should have.

He curled on one side, holding the bandage on his arm with the other hand. It didn't look comfortable. I noticed no coldness from him while he slept, but couldn't read any emotion from him either. That could have just been because he was asleep. What did I know? It wasn't like I'd had training with this stuff.

I sighed and looked at my phone again. I should call my parents, but at this point what could I say? *Sorry for leaving, I'll be back as soon as I take down a bunch of superpowered criminals.* Yeah, that wouldn't freak them out at all.

The beans in the beanbag rustled and hissed like a snake. Dean shifted and opened his eyes. I gave him a shy smile in return. He probably felt more awkward with me here in his bed than I felt. If he felt anything at all. His expression was blank. The coldness crept into me again.

I turned the phone off to save battery and put it down on top of the drawers.

"Morning. You calling someone?" he asked.

"I was going to call my parents." I took a deep breath. Time to sell Dean on my plan. "But I want to finish all of this first."

As calmly and as rationally as I could, I started from the top, trying again to explain the empath powers, who Jake and the team were, and what Jake had said about Dean being a blocker.

Dean looked skeptical.

"I know you think I was babbling like a crazy thing last night, but it's real, the powers, the whole thing. I need you to believe me."

Dean seemed to think for a moment. "Then show me."

"I *can't.* You're a blocker, remember? When you're around,

you stop my powers from working."

"I'm not doing anything on purpose."

"I know. But that's how it is. At least, unless you're surprised by something, or unconscious."

"Well this is all pretty surprising stuff, but you still don't have superpowers."

I folded my arms. "I don't know exactly how this stuff all works, okay?"

"Okay. Let's work it out then. What sort of range does my... *blocking* have?"

"Oh! Right, maybe I can demonstrate the superpowers from a distance. Good idea. Let's go outside and I'll see what happens. I'll still need some strong emotion to tap, though. Anger or fear emotions are easiest."

"Sure, okay." He still looked unconvinced, but I was grateful he was at least humoring me. "But you probably shouldn't go out looking like that."

Dean dropped his gaze to my chest and I blushed. Then I looked down too and saw the crusty bloodstains across the front of my trench coat and shirt that I'd slept in.

Dean dug out what he assured me was his smallest T-shirt and I went into the bathroom to change and clean up.

I peeled off the old clothes, and after giving myself a quick wash down, tried to clean them off too. The blood rinsed easily off the plasticky material of my trench coat, which I was happy about since it was almost the only thing I had of my own now. The white peasant blouse was unsalvageable.

I put on the shirt Dean had given me. The fabric was old and worn to super softness and there was a picture of a cartoon super-critter on the front. *Is he having a laugh at me?* I tried to tuck the shirt in, tie it to the side, do anything to make it not look like I wore a tent. Nothing worked, so I just left it untucked.

Dean paused and looked me over before we left the trailer. "Looks good on you."

He said it in the same matter-of-fact tone he'd used when he complimented my smile the day before. I just shook my head and tried to cool my face. I never understood why guys liked girls wearing their shirts. Wearing a guy's T-shirt felt like the most unflattering fashion ever.

It wasn't too early, but no one else seemed to be out and about in the trailer park. Still, it turned out finding some anger to tap proved easy. Just a few trailers down the sounds of a domestic came clearly though thin walls. I stood outside, and Dean backed away until I felt the cold leave me. I gave him a thumbs up.

I let the heat of emotion radiate into me, trying my best to absorb it efficiently, and my muscles burned with strength. A stop sign across the laneway seemed like a decent target for a superpower demonstration.

I checked Dean was still watching, grabbed the pole with both hands and put my foot against the middle. I pulled with my hands and pushed with my foot, and the solid metal pole bent easily in half.

It felt good to be so effective with my powers, and I couldn't resist a smile when I saw Dean's jaw drop. I had probably looked the same when Jake had demonstrated his powers by smashing that bench. *Ugh. Way to break a mood.*

I didn't even care then how much work someone must have put into the careful mosaic artwork on the bench Jake had destroyed. Neither had Jake. He'd just demolished it to make a point without a second thought. *I should have realized then what I was getting into. Destruction of property isn't exactly good-guy behavior.* But I'd been blinded by surface things, not to mention dazzled by an empath much better at this stuff than I was.

I felt bad for having busted an important street sign. I strained to straighten the pole, which proved harder than bending it in the first place. Once bent, it just wanted to remain crooked.

A red flash caught the corner of my eye. I turned to look

down the long laneway through the trailer park toward the road that passed the other end. Jake's Maserati cruised by at a speed designed for scoping.

In a blur, I dashed back to Dean as fast as I could until my powers waned in his presence. I still had just enough momentum left when I reached him to push him out of the middle of the lane and into the cover of the nearest trailer.

"Okay, I believe you!" Dean said, looking down at where I had my hands still on his chest from pushing him. I dropped them away and gave him some space.

"No, it's them. The car down there."

"The ones from the bank?"

I nodded. "I don't think they saw us. But that was them, looking for us. It's why I need your help."

"My help?"

"Yeah. I have a plan."

We waited until the Maserati had continued on, then we snuck back to the sanctuary of Dean's room.

The minor effort of our excursion had left Dean looking paler than normal. Some blood showed through his bandage, and I worried it wasn't healing right. He took the last couple of painkillers from his drawer.

He took a seat on his bed and I paced in the small space in

front of him while I presented my plan. A plan to block Jake and his team's powers for good.

As I thought, Dean had no idea how to even begin blocking an empath's powers permanently.

"That's why I want you to practice on me." I looked into his gray eyes, and spoke as earnestly as possible. "You can learn how to do it by locking away my powers."

He didn't respond. He just stared with his usual blank expression.

"Look, I know it's a lot to ask, making you learn how to do this and take on those guys, but you saw how dead set Jake was to get rid of you. It's the only thing I can think of to keep you and others safe, so you can protect yourself properly. Without, you know, turning to assassination or something. We can't even call the cops on them—not while they still have their powers."

Dean nodded. "I understand. I can try, but it still feels kind of crazy. I don't even know where to start."

"Me neither," I admitted. "I only really found out about my own powers last week. I know less about yours. It's not like there's an Empaths Help hotline. We just have to experiment, I guess." I slumped down onto the beanbag. "When I use my powers, it feels like sun warming my skin, filling me with energy, spreading heat through me. When you're around, I just feel cold."

Dean made a face. Normally, I would know exactly what that meant, but without my powers, as far as I knew, the emotion could be anything from anger to just passed gas.

"I just mean, if energy is warm, it's like a cold lack of energy. Can you, I don't know, try and visualize projecting more coldness?"

It felt stupid even as the words came out of my mouth, but Dean tried anyway. I could see him concentrating, but nothing seemed to change.

We gave up and had toast for lunch.

Dean's dad wasn't around so we sat in the living room. It smelled of stale beer and weed. I pretended not to notice.

"Why are we even like this?" Dean said with his mouth full. "I mean, how do we even have these powers? If I understand them more we might get further."

I tried to piece together the few bits of information I had. None of it sounded particularly scientific in hindsight. "Well, for empaths, we just sort of absorb excess emotion from people and it makes us stronger."

"So you're like emotional vampires, feeding on other people's life force."

"That's silly."

"Fine, leeches then, or some kind of parasite."

"Harsh."

"Okay maybe, but really, excess emotion? You think people don't need every bit of the emotions they are feeling? That anything you can tap into is just fair game? That it's yours to take?"

"I..." I hadn't thought of it like that. "I just thought the powers were part of being a hero."

Dean had inhaled his toast and pushed crumbs around the empty plate with his finger. "Pretty people, hot cars, wads of spending money... was that your idea of being a hero, too?"

"Just the perks?" I fake smiled, toothy and pleading and not even caring about my crooked teeth. I was being lectured, but I deserved it. Dean had a way of seeing things I'd been blind to. I needed to hear what he thought. "What is your idea of a hero?"

"Someone who doesn't think about themselves, who puts others first always, even before their own life. Someone like..."

Dean stood up without warning and dumped his empty plate into the sink. He paused there for a moment then came back to sit next to me on the couch. I chewed my toast slowly and stared at the floor, wishing I could understand Dean more. Without my emotion-sensing powers, all I had were questions.

Really hard-to-ask questions.

"I wish I knew how you were feeling." I blushed and rambled on. "I just mean, something has made you block all your feelings away, so much it extends out and blocks empath powers too. There must be a reason. If I knew more about how, or why, it might help."

Dean made eye contact for a moment before returning his focus to the stained carpet. I didn't want to push too hard, so I took a different tack.

"Maybe if you could work out how to let emotions out a little, it might be easier to also pull them in more, create a more powerful block than your normal one. Something that could lock down an empath permanently, like Jake said blockers can do. Do you think you could try letting some emotion through?"

Dean shook his head. "I don't think I can just... do that."

My suggestions weren't working, and Dean seemed less and less interested in trying them. And very uncomfortable talking about emotions at all. But he had let emotions through in the past, or at least had been surprised out of holding them back so much they blocked my powers. In the alley, and when he was shot, he was too shocked to keep a tight rein on his feelings. I hadn't actually read his emotions those times, but I hadn't exactly tried. Other things on my mind and all. If I could just surprise him again now, I could see what happened, see what he was really feeling.

But how could I surprise him? I didn't know why I thought the first idea that popped into my head seemed like a good one, but I acted on the impulse before common sense or embarrassment could stop me.

I leaned over and pressed my lips against Dean's.

They were soft and cool and spread slightly under mine. My eyes fluttered closed and a shiver crept over my scalp. Then I felt the coldness leave me and I opened my eyes, surprised my impulsive action worked.

Dean's gray eyes looked into mine, inches away, just as surprised.

I focused on reading any emotion I could in them, drawing them into me. What I felt was heavy with depression, a sadness as deep and hard as a glacier. Hiding within it was something small, tentative and warm. Something guarded so closely I couldn't identify it. I moved my lips back away from Dean's. His breath was fast and hot on my face.

The sadness I'd tapped overwhelmed me, like a heavy weight around my chest dragging me into black water. I backed away to the other end of the couch, shaking my head like I'd just been boxed in the ears. "Too much… bad feelings…"

I could tell Dean felt confused, hurt, and then the icy chill spread through me again and I couldn't read him anymore.

He finally found his words. "You did that just to get my guard down?"

"And it worked, yay?" Clearly not yay. "I'm sorry; it was just an idea that came to me. Your emotions were just a bit much for me to handle. But I'm sorry, anyway. I shouldn't have done that, or I should have asked first. But I couldn't have asked first or then it wouldn't have surprised you."

"It's okay. It doesn't matter." Dean had closed off completely. He didn't look sad, or upset. He didn't even look angry. He had gone back to complete emotional shutdown. But now I knew on the inside he kept hidden a deep well of grief, pushed down, out of sight. Emotions I couldn't even handle for a few moments. No wonder he blocked them away.

I could tell his life wasn't easy. Everything around us screamed poverty. His dad didn't seem to work, and was possibly an alcoholic.

Dean came across as smart, and able, and so... kind. Even when he'd pressed me on acting spoiled, which he'd been right about, he could easily have been much crueler. With the pain he held inside, I was surprised he wasn't.

I tried to smooth things over with Dean. He didn't talk

much for the rest of the day, but remained cooperative, nodding and trying a few more suggestions to practice his powers. We tried some visualizing techniques but honestly, they just felt wanky. It was still early when Dean started looking gray and tired, and I could tell his bullet wound troubled him.

We ended the day frustrated and without any headway on locking down my powers.

I insisted Dean kept his own bed and I curled up on the beanbag. He fell asleep before me, and for a while, before I found my own rest, I stared at him, remembering the sensation of the deep, black despair he kept hidden inside.

16

Thursday morning, I woke up to Dean trying to tiptoe around me.

"What time is it?" I asked, squinting at the window. The mostly bent blinds didn't block much out but barely any light showed through them.

"Six thirty. I need to get to work." Dean put on a dark-blue hoody with holes at the elbows. "I'll be back about three."

"What? No." I bolted upright in the beanbag. It shifted under me and I almost fell on my side. "You can't. If you're out working all day, Jake might find you."

Dean sighed and didn't look at me. "I have to work, Livvy.

I didn't even get to cash Dad's welfare check this week, and I'm out of money."

"No, I won't take any arguments. You can't work anyway, not with your arm like that. I bet it's hurting." I said the words, but my stomach cramped with guilt. *Out of money?* Not only had I been taking up all his time, eating his food, and getting him in trouble in the first place, it was also my fault he couldn't get to work or a bank. I had just come from Jake's mansion where the staff handled everything and cash was handed to you in rolls. Even before that, at home with my parents, I'd never had to worry about running out of money. I had an allowance and my parents bought me whatever I needed. I knew, sort of, that some people lived day-by-day, only just earning enough to get them by, or sometimes not enough. But this was the first time I'd ever *felt* how privileged I had been. Part of me wished I hadn't handed the change from my shopping trip back to Jake. That would have made things a bit easier right now—although it was stolen money. *Why did everything have to be so complicated?*

I'd work something out. I had to stop being the spoiled brat and start working harder for Dean.

Dean sat down on the bed again with a slight wince.

"Yeah, I thought as much. Can I have a look at how it's healing?"

SELINA A. FENECH

Dean nodded, and took his hoodie back off.

I lifted the sleeve of his T-shirt. The shoddy bandaging was twisted and had a bled through. "We should put a clean dressing on it. Or at least that's what people seem to do in movies. Then you can walk me into town and I'll see about some cash."

"And that will be safer than me going to work?"

"I'm not going to rob a bank, if that's what you're thinking. If you show up at a construction site with a bullet hole through your arm, people are going to talk and Jake will find out who you are and where to find you. I don't plan for us to be out long, and at least if I'm with you, I could knock you out or something and use my powers to get us out of there if things go wrong."

"Well, you have worked out one way to shock me out of my blocking ability," Dean mumbled.

I blushed and went to get more makeshift first-aid supplies. There weren't many left, and they felt so inadequate. Once I got some cash in town, I'd purchase some real bandages and dressings. I made a mental note to also buy him some more washcloths to replace all the ones we'd used up.

I unwrapped and gently cleaned Dean's arm. It didn't seem to have gotten any better. The skin around the wound looked red and yellow and inflamed. I bandaged the area with the last clean washcloth available in the trailer, and Dean walked me into town.

It proved hard trying to walk casually while still keeping an eye out in all directions for Jake and the rest of his team. I felt like an exaggerated cartoon character, sneaking up to corners and ducking when cars came past. But no one seemed to pay us any attention, and we made it to the main street without any sign of the other empaths.

The bank was closed up, police tape webbed across the front and flapping in the slight breeze. My stomach seemed to flap the same way. Dean had lent me one of his hoodies since it was cold but I couldn't wear my too-obvious red trench coat. I hugged the worn, soft fabric to myself and smelt him on it.

I went into the pawn shop I saw last time I was here and sold my white-gold heart pendant necklace. I got less than half what my parents had originally paid for it, but it was something. Enough to get by a couple more days. I only hoped this would all be over by then.

I asked Dean about somewhere good to eat, and he took me around the corner to a tucked away diner with a drug store conveniently next door. I bought a first-aid kit which had bandages, dressings, and everything we should need, then went into the diner, insisting on buying lunch for us both.

The diner had a mix of cracking plastic table sets and a line of tall booths along the wall. It was still early for lunch so the place was practically empty, and we took a booth in the far back corner that looked nice and secluded.

I bullied Dean into ordering something substantial, sure his body needed it, and after I set aside what I needed to pay for lunch, I slid the remainder of the cash across the table.

"What's that?" He was already shaking his head.

"It's for you."

"I can't take that."

"Sure you can. It's your pay. I'm paying you to work for me, to keep trying to do this blocking thing. If you can't get to your job because of me, then I'm your job."

We locked gazes, both unwilling to budge, the money sitting untouched on the table between us.

The waitress arrived and put a massive hamburger down in front of Dean, and two milkshakes that came in tall retro glasses in the middle of the table. My fish and fries were in an actual basket, the paper lining it spotted with grease. The waitress raised an eyebrow at our strange stand-off.

I smiled at her, then pouted. "I'm trying to pay him back and he won't take it."

She wiped her hands on her apron and flicked her curly

hair. "Just take the cash, kid, before I consider it a tip."

Dean pocketed the money begrudgingly and the waitress left us to our food.

"As long as you don't make me call you Boss," Dean muttered.

"You're no fun," I teased back, but couldn't crack his façade.

Dean took a big bite from his burger and chewed it for a while. "You didn't have to sell your pendant. Didn't it mean something to you?"

"Other things mean more."

I picked through the fries and battered fish bits. They were good, but I didn't have a big appetite.

Dean seemed to barely be putting up with my presence. I wasn't surprised, considering the trouble I'd brought him, not to mention crashing his space and sleeping in his room. Each day, he seemed more and more irritated sharing close quarters with me. Or maybe it was my crazy plan and nagging to get this to work. But we had to succeed. At every moment I worried Jake would find Dean, or go to my parents to find me.

He had to be stopped before he hurt anyone else.

Back in the trailer after lunch, Dean and I sat in the living room and tried again to practice his blocking abilities. We attempted turning them off and on, making them stronger or weaker, but nothing worked.

Dean's wound bled through a second time so I rewrapped it with the new proper dressings and the result looked a lot more professional. I hoped that meant it would also heal better. I didn't like the way it was looking one bit.

Dean was just putting his shirt back on when his dad stumbled in the front door.

"Just finishing up with your little whore?" His words sounded slurred.

I winced. I had no idea how to deal with an angry drunk. I liked him better when he was passed out and snoring.

"Dad, don't." Dean stood up as a buffer between the two of us.

His dad's gray hair was greasy and while his eyes were the same shade as Dean's, they bulged, bloodshot, and gave him the look of a crazy man. They fixed on me over Dean's shoulder.

"I know you been sniffing around last few days. I see it's going on. Don't think you can go shacking up here. No money to be sniffing for anyway, and you can't be having more of my drink."

I opened my mouth to try and defend myself but just shook my head. I looked to Dean for a cue on what I should do, worried how embarrassed he might be. I got nothing. I might as well have been a figment of his dad's drunken imagination.

Dean put a hand on his dad's shoulder, leading him like a

sleepwalker to the room at the opposite end of the trailer to Dean's. "Why don't you go lie down for a while?"

His dad swatted the gesture away. "You two stole my vodka! Don't try and hide it. I know what's what and what's gone. You get rid of that whore, Dean. Get her out before she goes leaves anyway! Just like your mom."

He turned the other way and left out the front door again, cursing and stumbling.

I sat speechless on the couch.

"Sorry." Dean stared at the closed front door and didn't look like he would turn around anytime soon.

"Is that it? Is that why your dad's like that? Because your mom left?" I blurted. I clenched my shaking fists. Dean hadn't stood up for me. He'd just let his dad call me a whore and rant like that to my face.

Dean remained still. "She didn't leave. She died."

"Oh, crap. No, I mean, I'm—" Sorry didn't cut it. I was such an idiot. I should have realized, from the amount of pain Dean carried inside him, that it was something more. All that pain, and I was angry at being yelled at.

"I'm so sorry." I said the words anyway, even though they weren't enough.

"He wasn't always like that. He just couldn't handle the

way she left." Dean leaned on the back of the door and still didn't face me. My heart warmed and ached for how he was defending his dad. I had no way of understanding what they'd been through. I'd never lost someone close. I wanted to poke, to pry, to encourage him to keep talking, but decided keeping my mouth shut was the best option right now, in case another foot tried to squeeze in.

The silence extended and I thought he might not have anything else to say. He stayed leaning on the door. I stayed watching anxiously from the couch.

Finally, he spoke.

"My mom got sick. Like, never-getting-better sick. We weren't badly off and Dad gave everything, every saving, every dollar he'd earned on any kind of treatment he could find. Everything, and more. Dad refused to let her go, refused to give in or stop doing whatever it took." He spoke softly, slowly, as though he were calming himself before each word. "The medical costs bankrupted us. We lost our house just to keep Mom in hospital in palliative care."

He shook his head, as though he could deny the past. "She didn't want to be there. She faded, slowly, painfully, and steadily. She was ready to go and knew what the drawn-out illness was doing to our family."

Dean didn't move. His words held just the smallest edge of pain.

I mopped up flooding tears with the neckline of Dean's T-shirt I was wearing. I kept quiet, didn't sob, but the tears just ran.

The sadness I'd felt in Dean when I kissed him all came back to me. How long had his mother's illness gone on? What had their family been like before? What had Dean been like before? I'd never seen him really smile. I bet he was gorgeous if he really smiled. It would reach those gray eyes and they would sparkle in a way they never did now. The neck of my shirt was sodden.

Dean's next words came a long moment after the others.

His voice broke so slightly I wondered if it was my own imagination.

"Mom took her own life."

I'm sorry. They were such useless words, so flimsy. What everyone says when they don't know what to say.

I thought back to my parents and the strength of their love. If what happened to Dean's family happened to ours, under those circumstances, would they break? If I lost one of them, and then lost the other to alcohol, I doubted I'd manage half as well as Dean. I'd up and left them behind for this adventure gone wrong, but only because they were so permanent. Like no matter what I did, I could always go back to home, to comfort, and there they would be. Even when distant, my parents were a safe place in my heart. The idea of losing them seared my insides.

If that happened to me, I would probably lock all my emotions away too. Stop myself ever having to risk loving and losing anyone again. Do anything to hide from that pain.

Dean shifted and I wiped frantically at my face to dry it in case he turned around.

I stuttered, hoping my words weren't completely useless. "I'm sure that she didn't want to leave you behind. If she thought she had any other choice, I can't imagine—"

"I know. I know she left so her illness, and Dad's obsession with saving her, wouldn't destroy us completely."

Our conversation from the day before came back to me.

"What is your idea of a hero?"

"Someone who doesn't think about themselves, who puts others first always, even before their own life. Someone like…"

When he clammed up, was he going to say someone like his mother?

I couldn't emotionally grasp what it must have been like for her, to feel like the burden of her illness did more damage than her choice to leave. It must have been an impossible decision. It seemed like Dean's dad wasn't going to accept her death either way. And despite Dean saying he understood, it had clearly broken him as well.

And yet he was still so strong. Opening up to me, telling me all of this, couldn't have been easy. My voice broke as I said, "Thank you, for sharing that with me."

He faced me and I shivered.

I grew colder inside than his presence had ever made me. Anything Dean had opened up, he'd now closed again tighter than ever before.

He sat back next to me on the lounge and asked about what we were going to try next.

I casually caught another tear with the flick of a finger and suggested we take a break and spend the rest of the day watching TV.

We sat close, our shoulders just touching enough to share warmth between us, but inside, the sensation of cold only grew.

That night, I wriggled myself into a semi-comfortable position on the beanbag again before Dean could say anything about sleeping arrangements. He came back in from his shower and stood still in the middle of the room for a moment before getting into his bed.

"I'm sorry," he said. "For being angry that night we first

met. For not saying thank you for what you did."

I didn't know what to say. I had obsessed over it at the time, but when everything went crazy, I'd forgotten about it again until he brought it up. It just didn't seem to mean so much anymore. "That was you angry? I was the one yelling like a lunatic."

"I was angry, and I'm sorry."

"It's okay, really."

Dean paused, his jaw clenching briefly. "It's just, I saw this mousy girl—"

"Hey!"

"—willing to take on two big guys, willing to risk her life to save a stranger. To do something like that, you have to be someone special. It made me so angry, the thought that someone so special could have been hurt, for someone like me."

"I guess I was just trying to be a hero." I shrugged, trying to make it seem like nothing. I hadn't done it for him, not really. I'd done it for myself, to be praised. I'd had no idea what it meant to be a hero, not then.

"My mom taught me what a hero is. And she taught me that heroes die."

My gaze drifted down to the bandages on Dean's arm. How he pushed me clear of Jake's gun, how he preferred to be beaten to a pulp by those bullies than have me risk myself to help—he seemed determined to save me from what he thought was a hero's fate. And at the same time, he was taking that path for himself.

No. I wouldn't let him. My breathing grew fast and my eyes burned hot, and tears fell before I could hide them. "Your mom did what she could with nothing to work with but tragedy. We've got superpowers. I'm going to make sure we both survive this."

Dean reached across and wiped my tears from my cheeks, then turned away.

Neither of us said anything else.

The next morning, I woke and saw Dean sitting on the side of his bed, watching me. His expression was intense, yet calm. Longing, yet withdrawn. Something inside felt different, a turmoil of hot and cold, and then it happened.

Ice grew in me, crystallizing and encasing every sensation of empath power I knew. And then I felt nothing at all. Not the warmth of absorbing emotions, not the cold of Dean's blocking. *Nothing.*

I ran through the trailer park, trying to connect to any emotion outside of my own but nothing came.

It was done. Dean had learned how to shut down an empath permanently.

I was normal.

17

At night, the overgrown park across from the mall felt like a scene from a horror movie. The wooden play fortress loomed in the shadows and a slight breeze made tree branches creak against each other. Streetlights at either end of the space provided lighting, and both flickered. It was cold and my red trench coat swirled in the wind like a cape. I pulled it closed over the T-shirt I wore—*Dean's* T-shirt. It smelled of him and my heart beat a little faster.

This plan had better work.

I kept imagining every possible way things could go wrong. The idea of Dean getting hurt following my plan made anxiety dance like a jittery sickness inside me.

I hoped the cold would give us an advantage, so Jake and his posse wouldn't sense Dean's presence until too late.

I'd called Jake earlier that day. He wasn't happy to hear from me, and I'd begged, I'd begged shamelessly to be given another chance to be part of their team again. He hadn't been as interested in me as he had in finding the blocker. He'd sounded obsessed.

"Where is he? You know, don't you?" he'd snarled over the phone.

"I don't know where he is. We went separate ways after the bank. I'm sure you don't have to worry about him anyway."

"Every blocker is worth worrying about. Every one needs to be put down. We are *better*, better than any normal human, and those blocker scum drag us down to nothing. They are the enemy."

"I know, and I should have listened to you before. Please, give me another chance."

"So you think you can manage it now, doing what we do? You want it bad enough? You got us into all kinds of trouble with your stunt at the bank."

"I'm sorry." The words tasted disgusting in my mouth. I was glad he couldn't sense my emotions over the phone. "I screwed up big time."

"Why would we even want you back on the team? What do you have to offer? Maybe if you could tell us where the blocker was, we'd consider it. But if you really don't know—"

"Fine, okay, fine." I'd let him think he'd called my bluff, but this was just the bait I needed. "I helped him get home, so I know where he lives. I'll tell you where you can find him. But only in person."

Jake had been more than eager to arrange the meet-up then.

I shivered, and wondered what time it was, whether the team was late. I felt like I'd been here for hours. But Dean and I did get to the park much earlier than we needed, to give Dean a chance to get hidden.

The kid-sized hiding spot looked uncomfortable, particularly with his arm still hurting him so much. He'd suggested the park while I'd tried to think of somewhere with a place Dean could hide, public but without other people around. Somewhere that wouldn't seem more suspicious to the team than I thought this already must.

A car pulled up beside the park. Not one of the team's usual favorites, but it was them. My blond prince charming who had turned from beauty to beast strolled up followed by his pack. They seemed confident and I sighed in relief. It meant we'd cleared the first part of the plan that could have gone wrong. They could have sensed Dean the moment they got here, but either the cold night was masking his presence, or Dean was able to hold in his blocking power.

He said he thought he could do that now. He seemed sure of it. I'd only realized that Jake's team sensing his effect could be a problem after Dean had already locked me down, so we had no way to test what he could do. But Dean said he'd worked something out. He had something inside now he could use to control his abilities. Now I just had to hope he could keep holding in his general block and still individually shut each of the team down for good.

Jake wore a dark leather jacket over a stark white designer shirt. He stared at me with disdain. I marveled at the face I'd once thought so dreamy that now spoke of nightmares. His attraction-based hypnosis powers had no chance on me anymore. Unfortunately, his general intimidation levels still worked.

"So, uh, hi. Um." *Wow, lame start.* I had to get my brain working, keep them engaged, talking, so Dean had time to do his part. But Jake and the team were so daunting, they flicked the off switch in my head.

"Oh honey, living rough?" Emma almost sounded sympathetic as she smirked at me and my slept-in clothes. She, of course, looked ready to hit a red-carpet afterparty—minidress, stilettos, perfect blow-out and all.

"Yeah, things have sucked on my own." That was a direction I could take, playing to their egos. "I should never have left you guys."

Donny was frowning. "Jake—?"

Jake waved him silent, his eyes remaining on me. "I'm surprised you didn't try and go home," Jake said coldly, and my heart whumped. Had he checked? Had he done anything to my parents?

I tempered my emotions, trying to stay calm. I had to keep them here, keep them talking as long as possible. "Who could go back to normal life after this?" I gestured to them, as though they summed up everything normal life couldn't give me.

Jake nodded like I'd spoken gospel. "So you understand we have to find and stop the blocker?"

"Totally. Who would ever want to lose these powers?" I had to turn the conversation back away from finding the blocker again, because the moment they pressed me for his location, they'd know something was up.

Donny looked more and more uncomfortable as we spoke. He tried to get Jake's attention again but Jake kept shushing him, too busy enjoying a good gloat at my expense. *Come on, Dean.*

I scrambled for more words. "At the bank, I didn't know what I really wanted, and it messed everything up. I thought I was doing 'the right thing'." I emphasized those words as sarcastically as I could. Jamie scoffed at the very idea. "But who says what's right anyway? If we're stronger, better, if we can easily take the things we need—why not? Isn't that evolution? We deserve to be happy."

"Wow, sounds like she finally gets it." Emma laughed.

"Yeah, but she doesn't deserve it. Not until she tells us where to find the blocker." Jake strode around me in a circle, a panther waiting to snap. He must have been able to tell how uncomfortable this whole situation made me. I hoped he thought it was just nerves in his oh-so-glorious presence, the bastard.

"Yeah, of course. I'll tell you. But how do I know you won't leave—"

"No buts. Tell me!" Jake came to a stop behind my back. He groaned softly. "What is that? I feel…"

Donny looked off-color, drained. "I've been trying to tell you, something's happening. I think the blocker is *here*."

Jake grabbed me and turned me to face him, shaking me. "Is he here? Did you bring him here?"

Last-ditch effort. I shrugged, but my shoulders shook with fear. "It's probably just the cold you're feeling."

Donny stared at his hands, his expression distraught. "I think he's locked me down. I've lost it all."

Jake shoved me away in disgust and yelled at the others. "Find him! He's got to be close by."

Jamie moved in a flash. Dean mustn't have gotten to him yet. He sprinted around the park, checking the perimeter, behind trees and fences, in high grass. My teeth bared in disgust knowing it was my fear he was using, stealing from me, to get that speed.

Donny moved slower. He went to the play equipment and wooden fort. I tensed, and tried not to watch and make it obvious where Dean hid. As he climbed through it, Donny's adult footsteps clunked heavily on the timber. I hoped for a plank to snap under his weight but no such luck. Still, they weren't finding Dean.

Emma watched Donny's slow, normal movements for a moment with her mouth agape. Her voice held pure terror. "I can't. I can't lose my powers. I can't go back."

"Snap out of it, Ems. Help us find the damned blocker!" Jake hissed.

She looked at him only briefly. She met my eyes for a second too and I saw a strange moment of hesitation. Without my empath powers, I didn't know what it meant. Then she fled.

146

She moved so fast she was just a blur till she reached their car and took off in it on her own. So much for team loyalty.

Jake growled and pulled a gun from the behind his back. He pointed it at me, and his hand shook. "I'm not losing this power, Livvy. You're dying first."

I'd known Jake wouldn't be shy about turning to guns once powers failed them. The bank job had taught me that much. Dean had figured as much too, and didn't like my plan with him hiding and me in the firing line. So I'd come up with a back-up plan that comforted Dean's concerns for me, but I wasn't so sold on it actually working. I just had to do anything I could to keep Dean safe until Jake and his crew were all locked down.

I threw the back-up plan out there and hoped it would fly. "If you shoot me, you're done. I've given that phone you gave me to someone, and if I don't show up safe by midnight, they have instructions to turn it in to the cops, along with all your numbers, that lovely happy snap of us, and notes on all of you and your activities."

Jake's face became a feral mix of snarl and smile. "You think I care about that? I've still got plenty of cash to get away clear and can change my face if I have to. But I won't have to. I will still have my powers, and with my powers *I* am the law. You hear that out there, blocker?" Jake called into the park where Donny and Jamie still hadn't found Dean. He kept the gun held in front of my face. "The second you shut me down, this girl is dead. Crawl out of wherever you're hiding and we can all just sort this out."

I flicked a glance at the wooden fortress, at the join between two sections of the construction that had been badly patched up when the original builder's plans didn't line up quite right. The planks shifted.

"Dean, don't!"

The wall hinged open, revealing a standing-room-only space, and Dean stepped out and walked toward us, holding his hands up in a gesture of surrender.

Jake whipped his gun away from me and fired.

No hesitation. No time to stop him. No time to talk him out of it. No time for anything.

He shot Dean, just like that.

18

The blast of the gun echoed like thunder around me. I ran to Dean, but it felt like a dream where everything was too slow.

A look of shock hung on Dean's face and he stopped still. He stared at his chest like he couldn't believe the way the blood pooled and spread across the fabric of his shirt. Like he'd spilled ketchup on himself, and might just laugh with embarrassment and brush it off.

Then his legs buckled.

I ran. I was too slow.

I skidded under Dean just before his head hit the ground,

catching it in my lap. But I had been too slow to have stopped the bullet, to have pushed him out of the way, to have saved him.

Dean's skin was more blue than pale. He kept his teeth clenched, panting between them.

"Help!" I screamed into the night uselessly. If the gunshot hadn't brought anyone, my scream wouldn't either.

His chest bled so much.

I tried to hold it in, pressing down. The blood oozed out between my fingers.

I let out a wheezing cry.

"Liv?" Dean grasped for one of my hands. "Listen. I'm sorry."

"Sorry?" Nothing made sense. He'd done nothing wrong. His apologizing lips were spotted with blood. *This can't be happening.*

"Sorry. For pushing you away. Being scared of you. Of feeling for you."

Jake yelled at me, a muffled hum, unimportant. Only Dean mattered. But Jake kept yelling. "Stand back up, Livvy. I want you facing me."

I didn't want to hear him. I only wanted to hear Dean, to keep hearing him talk so I knew he was still okay.

"Didn't want to feel like that. To risk losing someone again.

The feeling—" He coughed, winced. "Too intense. Shutting that down, that gave me control of these powers."

He held me trapped in the gaze of his gray eyes. "But I don't want to anymore, don't want to shut it away. Not if... I'm dying. I want you to know..."

"You're not going to die. Heroes don't have to die," I sobbed.

My chest burned. The fierceness of what I felt for Dean, the pain and pure need, blazed through me. And not just my feelings. Emotions came from Dean as well, intense and raw, warming me throughout like a nearby fire.

"Livvy, I—" Dean breathed.

Arms, hard like steel, yanked me away from Dean and I screamed like I'd been torn apart. Jamie pinned me up against him, pulling me back. I kicked and wrenched my body around but his grip was charged by emotion. Emotion he stole from me. My pain. *How dare he?*

"Let me go! Let me go back! Dean!"

Jamie dragged me toward Jake. I struggled against him, useless—at first. But he felt weaker and weaker.

No. I was stronger.

Any ice inside me that had shut my powers away had melted. Power unfurled within me, wild and mighty. That warmth of emotion, shared between Dean and I, that *feeling* ... he'd used it to unlock my powers again.

Along with my powers came hope. Now I could fight back, get help for Dean, save him. There was still time. *Please, please let there be enough time.*

I tore one arm free of Jamie's grip and turned so I could see Dean again.

I had to let him know it had worked. That everything was going to be okay.

His eyes were closed. His body gave a startling shudder then went still.

I let out a sound between a scream and a roar.

That *feeling*. That warmth. It was love.

I'd fallen in love with him. Had he been trying to tell me he felt the same?

I screamed again. I ripped into Jamie. I clawed his arms off me. Donny came to help him, unpowered, but still strong and twice my size. I sparred back, ducking their blows and kicking, scratching, jabbing between them with more strength than they could ever know. I drew the power from myself, from the fury of my own emotions, not stealing the scraps from others.

Jake kept his gun aimed our way, but didn't seem to want to take the risk of hitting one of his own. I was surprised he had even that much moral fiber. He stashed the gun and came

EMOTIONALLY CHARGED

to join in by hand.

I knocked back Donny just in time to be grabbed by Jake. I pulled free from him just in time to take a hit to the ribs from Jamie. I held my ground between the three of them, outmatched but determined.

I fought for my life and for Dean's, if it was still there. Dean had taught me what it meant to be a hero, a real hero. He'd taught me kindness, and selflessness. He'd been right; heroes weren't the fake fairytale dream I'd thought they were. But he had to be wrong about heroes dying.

I couldn't accept that.

I loved him. I couldn't lose him.

I chanced a look at him again, hoping, wishing to see him pick himself up, to be okay.

Dean still didn't move. He looked dead.

Jake caught me with a blow to my jaw that slid me back along the ground. I didn't even feel it. I launched myself at the men again, feral with grief. I didn't hold back, unleashing all the overwhelming emotion surging through me. I broke ribs, snapped knees, pulled arms from their sockets.

I set loose all of that emotionally charged energy against them but still the pain inside me grew.

I knew despair like I never had, like I couldn't begin to

153

handle. A black, bottomless pool drew me in like quicksand, drowning me.

Darkness overwhelmed me. The despair fed on everything I had inside, consuming any feelings of morality or mercy.

And it remained ravenous.

I turned it on Jake, Jamie and Donny, and I let it feed. I used that black energy to tear into their very beings, absorbing everything I could from them. All their power, all their energy—I stole every emotion from their bodies.

They fell to the ground like human husks. Just pretty shells.

My mind reeled, burned, darkened, then lit up like an exploding fireworks factory. My muscles were a flash fire of pain. My only thoughts were for Dean.

I stumbled a few steps towards his body.

Then I fell too.

19

Everything was too bright. Too loud. Machines beeped and whirred. Colors bled through my closed eyelids.

Why was there so much pain?

I remembered the night in the park. I remembered Dean being shot. I didn't remember what had happened next.

I stirred, and when I opened my eyes I found myself in a hospital bed, strung up with tubes attached to the back of my hand and wires stuck to my chest.

I was alone in the room except for a petite, dark-skinned nurse who leaned over me to press the call button.

She smiled at me as I blinked myself awake. Golden energy

glowed off her. My head pounded and I winced.

"There you are. Came back to us. Shh-ssh, don't move. You've been out for a while. We'll get a doctor in to look you over."

Her smile hit me like a solid wall of energy, the sheer strength of her happiness making me nauseous. Who was ever *that* cheery? All around me, emotions seeped through the walls from people celebrating, people grieving, people fighting enemies in their own bodies to stay alive. Every emotion invaded me, crawled into me like tiny spiders digging under my skin.

I rolled over to the side of the bed.

The nurse must have seen me turn green because she was ready with a pan to catch my vomit.

She had helped me clean up and was taking my blood pressure when a doctor came in, bringing a billow of orange, blue, and purple emotions with him.

Am I going crazy?

I leaned back in the bed and took deep breaths, trying to slow the spinning inside. The doctor started checking me and my attached machines.

"Good to see you're awake. You have some nausea?"

I nodded only slightly but my head hummed with pain. "What happened? Is Dean...?"

The doctor took a seat next to my bed and pulled out a

156

notepad. "We were hoping you could tell us what happened. No one else has been able to after how you were all found, with one boy shot and you and three others injured and unconscious."

I looked down at my hands, remembering the fight, the blows I'd taken. There wasn't a mark on me.

I remembered the blood spreading across Dean's chest.

One boy shot. "Is he...?" I couldn't say the word aloud.

"The cops are flustered too. They've identified the shooter from the bank robbery, and the two other men carrying guns are his associates. But they are very curious to know how you and the boy who was shot come into it." The doctor glanced across to the door, where out in the hallway, a uniformed officer was pacing, looking back to the doctor for his cue to come in. "But you don't have to talk to them yet if you don't want to."

My mind raced over all the evidence of my involvement with Jake's team. Photos, phone calls, texts, leaving home, my stuff at their place, the video from the bank. I had to tell the truth, as much as would be believed. That I didn't realize who Jake and his companions were until it was too late. It was going to be a long story, and a long investigation, and I couldn't handle it now. I could barely think.

"Can't now. Later." I turned my head away.

The doctor nodded and gave the side of my bed a sympathetic

157

pat. "Of course. Whenever you're ready." He paused, tapping his pen on his notebook. "But, if you can give me some idea of what happened, I'd appreciate it. Anything to help understand what is causing the symptoms in the others. They aren't unconscious anymore, not really. But they are completely catatonic, all three of them. We can't get any response. Their brain activity is almost completely non-existent."

Just pretty shells.

I could tell him what happened, now I realized what I'd done. *I killed them.*

Or I might as well have. I ripped all their emotions right from their bodies, leaving them as vegetables.

I bent over the side of the bed a second time, my eyes watering and my chest convulsing. The nurse held a pan out for me again and I retched, but nothing came up. My body rolled inside with pain and guilt and I wished I could vomit it all out, clear all these feelings from me.

I had taken lives.

And at the same time, I had somehow absorbed, stolen their powers. That was why everything was amplified. Why I felt everything so much more vividly.

I deserved this torment, the screaming of every emotion around me drilling into my skull. It could send me insane, and

EMOTIONALLY CHARGED

I almost hoped it did.

I only had to know one thing first.

My voice was a harsh scratch, and I spoke to the floor, still bent over the side of the bed. "Did he die? Is Dean dead?"

My heart grew small and painfully tight, waiting for the answer.

The nurse replied, "He's been in and out of consciousness since surgery. He almost—"

I was already moving, throwing back the sheets, tearing drips and wires off me.

The nurse tried to talk me down. The doctor stepped in front of me to urge me back to bed. I shoved him weakly, and he flew back against a wall, bringing a beeping machine down with him. I was much stronger than I realized.

"Sorry!" I clenched my teeth as my body ran riot with overloaded emotional power.

I bolted out and down the corridors, not giving a thought to the state of my hospital robe. I followed my nose, or rather, my heart.

I felt him, felt his presence, before I saw him.

I stumbled into the room Dean lay in, grabbed his hand, and dropped my head onto his shoulder.

I found quiet there.

Next to Dean, the pains and pleasures of others were muffled. I wept with relief.

"Hey." Dean's voice was dry and husky.

"You're alive. You're awake," I whispered into his shoulder.

"Yeah, you too."

I didn't feel any coldness—just soothing warmth. He wasn't holding back. He wasn't keeping any of his emotions from me, but he still calmed me with the abilities he'd learned.

The love I sensed from him made me weep more, but happily. I wished he could experience how I felt for him in return.

I lifted my head from his shoulder and kissed his lips.

The kiss was gentle, lingering, and I put everything into it that I couldn't give justice to in words. It tasted of salt tears and summer days, heating us both with glowing joy and desire.

He put a hand around my waist and pulled me onto the bed next to him. He let out a small grunt of pain when I pressed against him but still kissed me harder.

I pulled my lips away just far enough to talk. "I'm sorry. You okay?"

"Worth it." He smiled like I'd never seen before, and his gray eyes sparkled as they stared into mine.

I heard shuffling from the doorway but couldn't turn my eyes away from Dean's.

"Livvy?" It was my mom.

Her voice, and the jolt of worry it contained was enough to pull me back from Dean to see her and Dad.

"Mom!" Tears filled my eyes. They came in and hugged me. I tried not to break them when I squeezed them back.

My nurse cleared her throat and stepped into the room as well.

"We just arrived but you weren't in your bed." Dad frowned, and nodded to the nurse. "Tara said you'd just run off, and probably come here."

Tara looked from me to Dean to my parents, crossed her arms, and said, "Five minutes, then he needs to rest again."

She took a quick glance at Dean's heart monitor then left us in peace, tapping her watch on the way out.

I still clung to Dean's hand, but my parents only had eyes for me, looking deep into my face as though they'd find written there what they needed to understand everything that had happened. A soft cyan halo surrounded them.

"We came as quick as we could." Dad smoothed my hair back with his hand. He explained how they'd been so worried when I'd disappeared, but then my 'friend' had shown up and explained I was fine and I'd be away with him for a while.

"It seemed to make sense at first, but the longer you were

gone, we couldn't understand why we'd accepted some stranger's explanation." My mom's voice was choked, as though she were the one apologizing to me, as though they had failed me. "When we found out you'd been brought into hospital—"

"It's not your fault." There was so much I had to explain, to fix. I wanted to tell them everything, but I had no idea how. I tried to keep it simple. "I made mistakes and fell in with the wrong crowd. I'm sorry. But I'm still here. I'm okay."

My mom nodded, then looked past me, down at Dean, and our tightly joined hands.

"And this boy, was he part of the wrong crowd?" Her tone wasn't accusing. It was soft, tentative with care.

"No. He's the one who saved me. And I saved him."

20

I hadn't slept very well since the whole final confrontation-with-evil-super-powered-villains thing happened.

I had to keep using those words. *Evil. Villains.* I had to use them to stop myself feeling awful for what I'd done to them. It didn't really work.

I'd spent almost every minute by Dean's side since we were admitted to hospital. Our little romance and bizarre brush with death was the gossip of the staff and came with a mix of sweet sympathy, coos of cuteness, and tuts of "just a silly teenage thing."

They didn't understand that I really might die without Dean

by my side. After whatever I did to Jake, Donny, and Jamie, everything I sensed, every emotion of the people around me, hammered into my brain like the drummer of a death-metal band thrashing his skins.

There had been other changes as well. Everything was strange and different and painful. It was only near Dean that I found solace. The hospital staff didn't know; they just saw my puppy-dog eyes for him and, as long as I didn't interrupt his care, let me camp out in the armchair in his room.

My parents were great about it all. I knew there would be a big talk with them down the road, but for now, they were just being here for me, and letting me be here with Dean. Mom and Dad took shifts so at least one of them was with us during daylight hours, but often they had to duck away to get back to the contractors repairing the house and Mom's shop after the quake. We were still in Dean's hometown, and since we didn't own a car they'd had to hire one, and had been driving two hours each way to be with me.

I felt guilty as all get-out about it. But it made me love them even more.

On top of that, I wasn't sure what was happening with health insurance, or what the extended stay in hospital and all the tests were costing, or whether Dad's leave from work was paid or unpaid, but they were being good adults and organizing everything so I was oblivious to the details.

I even had a visit from Terry, my parents' cop friend. I was sure he was more curious about the case than my wellbeing because he asked a bunch of questions about Jake's team and what had happened in the park. Apparently, he'd recently been promoted, so maybe he was practicing his detective skills. Maybe he thought he was helping my parents out with answers. I don't know, but it was beyond awkward so I was glad when he left.

The doctors didn't know what was wrong with me, which made them hesitant to discharge me. To them, five kids came in bloodied and unconscious and only two had woken up, and I'd woken up as a gibbering mess. I tried to act as normal as possible and not let on anything to do with the whole super-powers thing, but it was hard with my mind so messy. Not sleeping wasn't helping the issue.

I'd like to say I was getting used to the lumpy vinyl armchair in the corner of Dean's hospital room, but it was just as much of a torture device as it had been three days ago. Still, I slept—or tried to—in there beside him rather than go back to my room down in a different ward.

I needed to be by his side.

I *wanted* to be by his side.

Daylight streamed in through the blinds despite them being drawn, but I was exhausted from another night of broken sleep and stubbornly kept trying to snooze. Dean's cocktail of heavy-duty medication meant he slept easily and often, his body working hard to mend the damage from Jake's bullet.

"Mumble, mumble, tests, mumble, mumble." A voice reached my sleeping mind.

"Huh?" I tried to swallow, my mouth dry and tasting like hospital. My eyes didn't want to open. Maybe I'd dreamed it. I tried to let sleep take me again.

"Wake, mumble, mumble, time, mumble, mumble."

I groaned, exhausted.

I thought it was a nurse. I remembered something mentioned yesterday about tests. Right. I had to have some scans done. The doctors were still trying to work out what had happened to me and the others, what with the weird comas and all. *Sure*, I tried to say, but just flopped my head forward in a vague nod and tried to stand up.

"Poor girl, mumble, happened, mumble, recover, mumble."

A soft squeaking sound approached me. I was barely conscious, yawning and trying to get my stuck eyelids to open as Tara, the petite nurse who'd been looking after me, put an arm around my shoulder and helped me into a wheelchair. The one that had been sitting nearby for Dean's use since he was under strict no-walking orders.

I wanted to argue I didn't need the wheelchair, and something else, there was something else I needed to argue. But I was already being wheeled down the hall.

I couldn't turn my brain on. There was too much noise in my head. I tried to wave back at the nurse but she kept pushing me along. I shook my head, trying to clear it, but the pressure was building too quickly.

"You okay, love?" Tara slowed down to check on me, but it was too late. I wasn't sure how far we'd walked, but I knew it was too far.

I was awake now. And I was too far from Dean. Too far from his blocking powers, and my head felt like it was going to explode.

Because of this place, this hospital, full of people who were sick and dying, and the loved ones of people who were sick and dying. People who were angry at the world for their prognoses. Women in the pain of labor and experiencing the elation of meeting their babies for the first time. People about to go into surgery, or even simply preparing to receive an injection. And without Dean to block my powers, every one of those scared, sad, angry, or elated emotions came flooding into me at four times the strength it should have.

I wasn't just an empath anymore; I was four empaths.

And it was too much.

Not only did the power from the emotions rampage through me, but now I could *see* them. Flowing streams of shimmering and juddering colors. Auras that haloed bodies and reached out to me like iron filings to a magnet when I passed by.

Wincing in pain, I reached back and clutched at Tara's hand. "Go back." I pleaded the words out, and they were followed by a rough cry.

My vision blurred and my head lolled back. The nurse crouched beside me, flashing a light in my eyes. She spoke, but I couldn't hear past the pounding sound in my ears. With a concerned look, she started pushing the wheelchair again. Faster. In the wrong direction. *No. No, wrong way.*

The world spun around me and my veins and muscles felt like they were about to burst. I grabbed onto the arms of the wheelchair and felt the plastic split and crumble, the metal bending like butter in my fingers.

In the swirling faces around me, I saw a familiar one. *Dad.* The expression on his face said everything about how I must have looked. He ran down the corridor towards me.

"Take me to... Dean!" I tried to hold eye contact with him but kept wincing from the waves of emotion. I needed him to understand. I used every last bit of my focus to get the words out. "Must. Be. With. Dean."

Dad turned away from me, looking to the nurse for answers as she continued to push me along. She didn't have the answers. *Dad, listen to me!*

I pushed myself out of the chair as it was still moving. The force of my action knocked Tara and the wheelchair across the corridor. The momentum was too much for me too, and I landed facedown on the ground. I could feel myself losing control of my body, my muscles jerking and seizing from the uncontainable influx of energy.

Dad knelt on the floor with me, cradling my head as my body shook and I slipped into unconsciousness.

I didn't know how long I was out for, but I slowly came to. The first thing I saw was Dean, his body bent with pain, supporting himself on his IV stand. He was so far away, but I saw him like a beacon, the lighthouse to the storm of emotion raging through me.

I blinked, the rest of the world coming into focus. There were nurses all around, checking on me, on him, and on Tara where I'd sent her flying.

"So sorry," I whispered to her through clenched teeth. She looked embarrassed more than anything, as though she'd somehow caused this with a self-destructing wheelchair. Everyone seemed at a loss to explain what had happened. I guessed 'that girl's got superpowers' was pretty low down on what most people would believe.

Dad looked down at me, frowning, but he sighed with relief when I looked back. He glanced across at Dean, then back to me, then to Dean again. Dean was pushing through the chaos to get closer to me. His nurse was following behind, scolding him for being out of bed, but he didn't listen.

He knelt on the ground next to me, those blue-gray eyes calm yet intense. "I woke up and you weren't there. Came to find you. Figured I should just follow the signs of chaos."

"Thanks," I replied. "I hope you didn't bust your stitches."

"I'll survive. Looks like you needed, well…" His sentence faded out.

Him. I needed him.

I smiled my thanks. I swallowed my guilt at being so dependent on him.

Dad was halfway through a discussion with the nurse about my seizure.

"This is exactly why we need to do the tests," she said.

"She needs to recover first," Dad argued.

"I'm fine. I'll be okay, really. I can do the tests. But …" I looked to Dad, hoping he'd understand, "… can you and Dean both stay with me?"

21

Dad could have said no to letting Dean tag along to my tests. But he didn't.

I wasn't sure how much he saw, or believed, or understood from when I collapsed, but I saw him talking to Mom when she came in, and I saw them talking to the nurses, and I saw forms being signed and arrangements being made, and suddenly I was moved to a private room right beside Dean's. Well, my belongings and medical charts were moved. I'd remained right by Dean's side. I didn't want to suffer through an experience like that again. And I liked being near him. He made my heart do a soft, gentle *flutter-flutter.*

EMOTIONALLY CHARGED

Having my own room, my own bed, with only a thin wall between myself and Dean made a huge difference. I got to sleep and wow, I'd really needed that.

It was hard at first. My mind still wouldn't turn off and I found myself reliving the moment Jake shot Dean and what happened after, and my half-asleep self would turn the moment into a nightmarish vision of vampire me sucking the souls out of the people who'd wronged me.

But soon I did sleep, and it was long, and deep, and much-needed.

The next day I shuffled around into Dean's room. I felt sheepish, knowing he could have his privacy now. And maybe he wanted it after having me by his side every moment recently. But he greeted me with a small smile. The kind of small smile that from him, I knew, was huge.

Dean was poking at a tray of hospital food.

"I never used to understand why people complained about hospital food. When I was a kid, I loved sharing my mom's food when I visited her."

I moved closer and sat on the bed beside him. I wanted to be even closer, I wanted to hold him through what must have been a sad memory, but it was always hard to tell with Dean. He'd changed a lot, and was so much more open. But he was still Dean.

"Now I'm a bit older... yeah, I can see what people mean about this food being awful."

"You're still eating it anyway," I pointed out.

He looked at me with his mouth full of fruit jelly. "Well, yeah."

My heart swelled happily at his display of typical teenage boyishness. He seemed to be healing well.

"Want some?" He pushed the tray closer to me.

I'd just had my own breakfast but grabbed a piece of chewy cold toast to nibble on anyway.

"Okay, so," I said, trying to get focused, "I've got Detective Phillips coming in this afternoon. And I have no idea what to tell him. And I don't think he'll be satisfied with the *I'm not ready to talk yet* response again."

Dean put his plastic cup of fruit jelly down. "How much are you planning to tell him?"

"I don't know. I mean, I want to tell the truth. I don't want to lie. But that's only going to make me seem crazy. I can't really prove it, and what I can prove about my powers, well, I'm not sure I *should* be proving that. Feels like revealing that could come with way too many consequences, you know?"

Dean nodded.

"But the police are still wanting some kind of answer though, for how we all ended up out there, passed out in the park like that, and why the others still haven't woken up."

"What else could cause something like that? Drug overdose?"

"Been screened for that already. It's one of the tests they ran straight away."

"Gas leak?"

"Out in the open? And how do the broken bones get explained?" I cringed, having flashbacks of our fight. I never thought I could be so violent.

This would be the third time the police had come to talk to me. The first I'd just said "later," and considering the state I was in, they'd accepted that. The second time I'd tried to explain that all I did with Jake was hang out, and I hadn't known they were criminals. Or at least not until it was too late. I'd already embellished the story beyond the truth. I'd blushed when I lied and said Jake was obsessed with me, which was why he'd come after us and why he'd shot Dean.

After he'd shot Dean... that was when my story fell apart. And those were the answers the authorities were still waiting on from me, that I knew the detective would be pushing for the next time I met him.

"Hypnosis," I suggested with a sly shrug. "I'll tell them Jake was a master hypnotist or mentalist type, and he'd manipulated us all into a death cult and made us attempt to commit suicide by not breathing until we fell into self-induced comas."

"Wow." Dean raised his eyebrows, impressed. "Yep, that's the winner."

I half whimpered, half sighed. "I am so screwed."

22

Detective Phillips sat across from me in my new hospital room, adding a strange elegance to the place with his neat suit and well-groomed appearance. I was tucked into bed, messy hair on display, giving my best impression of 'poor girl still recovering.' Dad stood beside me. Or 'loomed protectively' would be more accurate.

Dean had offered to be here as well, but I didn't want any added stress for him. I'd bet anything he was probably sleeping right now, and I knew he needed it. He'd done his time with the detective already. All the police really wanted from him was a finger pointing at who pulled the trigger.

They seemed to want a bit more from me.

I looked Detective Phillips in the eye and knew I could manipulate him, make him think and do what I wanted the way Jake had done to me. The detective may not have been physically attracted to me, but power rushed through me and emotions blazed from him that I could use to smooth through all his defenses. But I didn't want to. I couldn't manipulate someone like that. Not unless I really had to.

"The moment this goes beyond what my daughter is comfortable with, I'm calling in legal counsel," Dad said to the detective.

"Of course, Mr. Mirawi." Detective Phillips flashed a 'just think of me as a friend here to chat' smile. "Now, Olivia, has anything more come back to you from the night in Stanford Park?"

"No. Sorry." It was the best option we could come up with, after going over ideas. Saying I simply couldn't remember anything seemed safest.

I waited anxiously for the questions to continue.

Detective Phillips just nodded. "I've been talking to your doctors, and while they don't know what caused your collapse, they say it's likely that brain function would have been impaired at the time, so amnesia is completely understandable. I won't press the issue, but if anything does come back to you, it's important to share any detail, even if it seems small."

I tried not to look too relieved, but then I realized he wasn't leaving. He had a tablet device in one hand and swiped to scroll through whatever he was looking at. "We've been reviewing evidence surrounding the bank robbery and the surveillance video corroborates your testimony that you weren't aware of what was going to happen. It's a little blurry at times, but we could still clearly see you trying to protect the people in the bank."

I gulped, knowing it had all been caught on video. The reminder of that awful event sent my stomach plummeting. "It was so horrible. I couldn't believe they were like that, that they would do those things. After the bank, I didn't want to see them again, and we only met them at the park because I was trying to talk them into turning themselves in, to stop what they were doing." It was a small lie, but still a lie. I blushed and I wondered if the detective had worked out my tell yet. "I guess that wasn't the right decision, but I didn't know what else to do."

Dad put his hand on my shoulder. "You could have come to me and your mom, Lollipop. You know you can tell us anything. We could have helped you."

I nodded, but knew I couldn't have gone to them. Not that time. They didn't understand the danger it would have put them in. They didn't know the whole truth.

"I have another video here to show you, if you think you're up to it," Detective Phillips said. His expression was calculated and my shoulders tensed.

Another video? Of what? It was clear I was only going to find out by agreeing to watch it here with my Dad. But then what would he discover about me or empaths?

I was still gaping, unsure, when Detective Phillips turned his device around, the video already running on the screen.

It showed a hospital room with three bodies laid out on life support. Two gorgeous and blonde, the third statuesque and dark-skinned. Jake, Jamie, and Donny. I frowned, looking from the screen to the detective, confused as to what I was looking at, when movement on the screen caught my eye and there was Emma, standing over the beds. She watched them for a short time, then the image changed to the view of a corridor at night. The video quality was good enough that I could see the room number. Dean's room number. And Emma stood there, staring through the small window in the door. The expression on her face was not a nice one.

"She was watching us? When was this?" I gasped.

"Can you confirm that this is the same girl from the bank? That she was part of this group?" the detective said.

"Yeah, that's Emma. Sorry, I don't know her last name."

"That's all right. We already have her details—just wanted to confirm it with you."

"Has she been caught?" Dad asked.

"No, we're still looking for—"

"Is she a risk to my daughter? Shouldn't there be an officer on protection here?"

The detective didn't seem guilty at all as he said, "There's been a plain clothes officer outside the whole time."

To protect us or to keep watch? I wondered, worried about what they might have seen or heard, and why they had kept their presence secret.

"We're doing what we can to apprehend the other girl," the detective continued. He put his tablet away and stood. "Thank you for your time, Olivia. I will be in touch, but feel free to contact me first if you do remember anything that could help us bring Emma in and help keep you safe."

23

The hospital courtyard was small and enclosed on all four sides with glass and brick, and filled mostly with people sitting and drinking coffee. But the grass was soft, and the trees created a soft, dappled-green light around us that lifted my spirits.

Dean sat on a bench about twenty feet away from me. He was off his drip and had been told to get some gentle exercise, so we walked slowly down from our rooms to get some fresh air, and do some testing. I needed to see how far his influence on me extended.

I took another step backwards and winced.

"There it is." I wandered back to Dean and sat next to him. "That's about it. I mean, I might be able to push a bit farther, but that's the point when things start hurting."

I rubbed my temples. "Hospital is probably one of the worst places to have enhanced emotion-based powers. *So many* intense feelings here. Maybe out in general public I could get farther away before things became too much for me. And at some point, I'm guessing I'm going to have to go back to high school."

"Do you think it will be as bad as in hospital?"

I gave Dean a look that showed what I thought about the emotional levels of people in a high school. I made a little whooshing sound and mimed my head blowing up. "I need to get this under control though. I need to be able to be away from you. Not that I don't like being with you—I mean, I do—but I'm sure you don't want to be forced to follow me around all the time, and really, we only just met each other, and now we're like, squish, together, with the close-proximity thing all the time and..." And I was rambling.

"I really don't mind," he told me softly. "Really."

My heart fluttered and I fidgeted with my fingers. "It's not ideal though. I don't want you having to feel responsible for my sanity like that. It's too much."

Dean nodded, his expression vacant.

"Maybe you could block me again. Permanently. Then I wouldn't have to deal with any of this. I'd be normal."

I glanced over at Dean as he thought through my proposal. He was still so pale, and a small shine of sweat on his skin told me everything his lack of expression didn't about the pain he was still in.

"But what about Emma? What if she comes back, decides she wants revenge or something? I'm safe; I can block her if she comes after me, but if you're normal again, you won't be able to protect yourself."

"Then I'd need you to stay close by anyway. So no solution there. But to be honest, if she comes after me again, I kind of want to have my powers to fight back with."

I hung my head, kicking at the dirt under the seat. My hand rested on the bench right beside Dean's and he lifted his little finger and placed it over mine. We hadn't really touched much, or kissed, or done anything romantic since I'd first woken up. And we hadn't really talked about that night. What he wanted to tell me. What I felt for him.

Things were kind of awkward.

But that small action, that small touch between our fingers, meant everything to me. It gave me the strength to ask more from Dean than I wanted to.

EMOTIONALLY CHARGED

"We're going to have to work something out." I looked him in the eyes. "And to do that, I think we're going to have to tell my parents. Everything."

24

Mom popped her head around the corner of my door. She had a huge smile on her face. "Guess who's getting discharged today!"

Dad walked in beside her. "Is it me? Gosh, I sure hope it's me."

"Daaaad," I groaned. I sat cross-legged on my bed, and Dean was in the armchair by the window, as we'd both been waiting anxiously for my parents to arrive.

"Well, it does feel a bit like we've all had a long hospital stay. Aren't you ready to go home?"

I paused and bit my lip. "Not really. I don't think I can come home yet."

"Do you think she's scared about re-integrating into society?" Mom asked Dad, cheekily.

Dad looked at me, offended. "It can't be that you like the food here more than you like my cooking."

"I'm serious, guys. I... kind of can't leave until Dean leaves."

I didn't need empath powers to understand the looks they were giving me.

"It's not what you think. This isn't just about some teenage crush. There's more to it than that, and I know it's going to sound crazy, but just hear me out. This is truth time, okay?"

At the word truth, I had their full attention. Mom sat on the bed beside me, dead serious. "Okay, Livvy. We're listening."

"There's so much to tell you..." I took a deep breath and started at the beginning. I explained what I'd experienced the night of the quake, and leaving with Jake and his team. I explained my powers and how they worked. I explained how Jake was able to manipulate me, and them, with those same powers. I explained what had happened the night in the park, what had really happened, and what I'd really done. That I remembered it all, and the effect it was having on me now. I explained that was why I had to stay close to Dean.

My parents listened. They didn't say anything. But what could they say when presented with it all?

187

"I know this is a lot to take in, and I know you are having trouble believing any of it is real, which is why I asked you to bring something in for me."

Mom reached into her tote bag, looking dazed. "The phone directory? I had to ask around our neighbors to find one. What is it going to do?"

I half-smiled at my mom. "Hopefully, it will prove to you what I can do. It's my disposable demonstration tool."

I took the brick-sized book off my mum, and let the emotion I could feel nearby channel through me. Even with Dean in the room, I was still 'on.' With his blocker ability, he basically brought me back down to normal empath level. I had plenty enough strength for my demonstration, and without even flexing, I easily tore the phone book in half across its spine.

Mom gasped.

Dad picked up one of the halves and had a couple of unsuccessful goes himself, inspecting it for clues as to how I'd done it.

"It's not a trick. And you know I've been screened for drugs—this isn't some steroid- or meth-induced rage strength," I reminded them.

The room was silent for a while.

188

EMOTIONALLY CHARGED

"Okay," said Mom.

"Okay?" I replied.

"Okay."

"Okay," added Dad.

"Okay," Mom said again for emphasis.

She looked back at Dad and at me and at Dean.

"Well, this is huge. Okay." She took a deep breath. "I don't know what to say."

"Congratulations on having superpowers?" Dad half-smiled, and I laughed out loud.

"This is really real?" Mom asked, and Dean and I both nodded. "Okay. I believe you. I do."

Dad became serious again. "Who else knows?"

"Just the girl, Emma. And the other guys that got brought into hospital, but... you know. I don't think the detective knows. I've tried not to give anything away."

"Good. That's smart, Lollipop. We're going to have to think about this some more, work out what it all means. But thank you for telling us. You really can tell us anything. Even when you develop superpowers, since that seems to be what you teenagers are doing these days."

"Oh, my girl," Mom sobbed and stepped across to wrap me up in a huge hug.

"Are you the same, with super-strength?" Dad asked Dean.

"It's a bit different for me. Not as exciting."

From within Mom's embrace, I said, "His power is what's keeping me stable now. He has sort of a dampening effect. That's why I need to stay near him now my powers are overloaded. Dad, you saw it in the corridor that day."

He puffed out a breath and rubbed the back of his head. "I did see something. I could see it was real, but I thought it was psychological trauma real, not *paranormal superpowers* real."

I reluctantly withdrew from Mom so I could get to the next big issue. "That's why I can't get discharged until Dean does. I figure it will be easy to make them keep me in longer again. I just have to have another seizure."

"On purpose?" Mom looked shocked. "We can probably just ask to hold off on discharging you. I know they are short on beds, but still."

"Trust me, I'm not looking forward to doing it. But Dean could easily be in here another week or two, and they won't let me stay that long without a reason. I mean, if they try and wheel me out of here, it's going to happen again anyway."

"Let us at least talk to the doctors first. We'll say we saw some odd behavior from you just now. That should be enough to get some more time," Dad said.

Mom took a chair by the bed, shaking her head slightly. "This is all so... Dean, how did your parents handle this when you told them?"

My whole body froze and I tried to somehow suck Mom's words back out of existence, but there was no way of dispelling the tension they'd just dropped into the room.

Dean didn't look phased, but he rarely did. He spoke calmly, and I gritted my teeth and tried not to cry as though every bit of emotion he was blocking ended up channeled into me instead. "My mom died a while ago, and my dad won't visit hospitals. We haven't told him anything. He's not very... reliable."

"He hasn't visited you?" Mom looked enraged. "At all?"

Dean actually looked worried. He shrugged and mouthed 'no'.

Mom stood back up and went straight to him, giving him a hug that was even longer and more smothering than the one she'd given me. I could feel Dean's shock hit me like a wall as his blocking abilities disappeared for a moment and a huge swell of emotions washed over me.

Luckily, he recovered quickly, and he even brought his arms up and returned the hug. No one could deny a mom hug.

"What happens once you are both discharged from hospital?" Dad asked me, looking like he had already thought through what was going to happen next and wasn't sure he liked it.

I put on my 'please forgive me' face. "Can Dean live with us for a little while?"

25

I t had taken another seizure to convince the doctors I needed to stay, but we'd made sure Dean was close enough that it didn't last too long. It still left me feeling like I was a sack full of vomiting cats.

I'd become the hospital's favorite lab rat, with various specialists going over my case and seeming way too excited about the completely abnormal and inexplainable brain activity my scans were showing. I wished it all wasn't on file, but I just had to hope there wasn't some neural marker that screamed 'this person has superpowers!'

The doctors decided to try a range of different medications, which I disposed of secretly instead of taking. I played it weak for a while after the seizure, then showed sudden improvement when the doctors started talking about releasing Dean.

It was another week and a half before Dean and I were both discharged at the same time.

I packed all the clothes and belongings my parents had brought in for me into the bag I'd been living out of. Dean didn't have anything with him to take. No one had brought in belongings for him—no clothes or necessities for his stay. He'd mostly been living in hospital gowns at first, and more recently, his nurse had found a couple of changes of clothes from lost-and-found and charity boxes for him. The clothes he'd come into hospital wearing had been cut off him during surgery and were so covered in blood they were disposed of with the biological waste.

In the wait between being told we were being discharged, and actually officially being discharged, I thought I would go mad with impatience. I paced anxiously, but knew it wasn't all just the waiting. There was something else. Something I didn't want to do, but felt I had to all the same.

I had to stand on tiptoe to peek through the small window in the door of the dorm-style ward they were in. I wasn't brave enough to go inside, but even from here, I could see them straight away. That Hollywood-crush-style blonde hair.

It was growing out now. I could see dark roots showing at both Jake and Jamie's scalps. Of course. Everything about them had been fake. The casts on their arms were real though.

Dean had come with me, but I didn't think he cared to see the person who'd shot him.

But I felt the need to see them again. To say sorry maybe, or goodbye, or I don't know. After what I'd taken from them, I didn't know what I could do or say to make up for it.

Even if they were able to hear me.

I almost pushed the door open to step in when I noticed other people in the room. Between Jake, Jamie, and Donny's bed, a doctor was standing with an older couple, going over paperwork. One of them turned, as though sensing I was watching, and I ducked down out of sight.

I figured they were probably more detectives, based on how they were dressed. Detective Phillips had told me there were others working on Jake's case, with the team gathering enough evidence to tie them to a number of crimes in the area and elsewhere. Regardless of what was going on, I didn't want to disturb people in an intensive care ward.

As Dean and I walked back to our room, I said a silent goodbye to the hospital that had started to feel like home. Now we really were going home, I didn't know what life would be like anymore. With Dean moving in, and dealing with our powers, and whatever our relationship was now, and my parents being involved in the lot of it—it was going to be complicated. I was going back home, but nothing could take me back to how things were before.

Everything had changed. *I* had changed.

I'd started out with such romantic, selfish notions of heroism. Now I had a new understanding of what being a hero really meant. The power, the risk, and the reality of danger and sacrifice.

Dean and I had survived our brush with heroism, but only just.

Doing whatever I could to go back to being normal was the best plan now. But I could couldn't deny the fire of pure power, the desire to be more, have more, simmering inside me, fueled by emotions.

My experiences with Jake's team, with Dean, had shown me there was injustice all around. I didn't want to be a hero just for heroism's sake anymore—but if I had the power to make a difference, didn't the world deserve that? And how did that fit into my everyday existence, going to school, dating Dean and being a daughter to two amazing parents?

EMOTIONALLY CHARGED

I didn't know. I only knew that now I had changed, the world had changed for me too.

How could I ever be normal again?

EMOTIONALLY
SCARRED

EMPATH CHRONICLES EXTRA
EMMA'S STORY

I wish I could use magic to stop people staring at me, or enchant myself to be beautiful, but the magic powers I have are different. I'm not really a witch, no matter what the other kids call me. I'm not a superhero either, even if I do have special powers. Heroes aren't ugly.

The lime-green shade of my new school's corridors set my teeth on edge. Everyone watched me, and why wouldn't they? I was the new girl with a target right on her face. My sneakers squeaked as I walked and I felt so completely conspicuous. Cruel laminate flooring. My own body betrayed me as well. I was taller than most girls, which just made me easier to spot.

I wanted to love my bright red hair but I hated that it attracted attention to my face.

The other students stared openly at me and gossiped as they pretended to poke through their lockers. A tide of emotion followed their stares, the usual mix of sympathy and disgust that I was used to. That was my superpower — to sense how people were feeling, so strongly that I felt their emotions burrowing into my pores. I hated it. I hugged my new textbooks close to my chest and tried to ignore it.

Chin up, Emma. Don't let them get to you. You're beautiful on the inside. You're special and important, no matter how you look.

I tried to believe that my outer appearance didn't matter and that *real* friends would like the *real* me despite how I looked. But I was smart, smarter than most kids my age, and it made them think I was even weirder. My intelligence made me as much of a target as my face. I tried to act like everyone else, dress right, talk right, do all the right things. I had gone from being a child prodigy down to a C average. I stuffed tests on purpose, half-hearted my assignments, and worked harder on giggling mindlessly, and pretending I actually like music where dudes sing about their sexy bitches. Anything to just fit in.

It didn't work.

EMOTIONALLY SCARRED

This year was supposed to be better. Operation: New Me. I finally convinced my parents to let me change schools. Well... by convinced, I mean I was expelled from my last school when I got into a fight with this girl who kept calling me names. I had a weird adrenaline rush and broke her arm. Oops.

A little extra begging on top and my parents finally let me have the mole, the bane of my existence, removed. The mole that had made me the brunt of bullying my whole life. This was no cute beauty mark, oh no, but a brown blob of ugly flesh that covered half my chin. That's why I was called a witch at my last school. Marked by the devil, dribbling sewage, fecal face; I heard it all from the other kids.

My life was a living hell. If they also knew I could read their emotions like some kind of freak...

But all that changed. I was going off to a new school, and in between, I'd have the mole removed. Then it was meant to be like in the books, where a group of great friends would adopt me and the hottest guy in the school would fall for me. I wouldn't be teased. I would be happy.

The whole plan plunged into epic fail. My plebian parents didn't realize I needed a proper cosmetic surgeon for the work, to actually make my face look like the mole was never there. Sure the doctor removed the mole, but in its place he left a jumbo pink scar like a deformed fetus.

Determined to be positive anyway, I came to this new school with a plan. I dressed up, smiled, and waited for people to ask, wow, where did you get that scar? And I would tell them crazy cool tales of my heroism, saving a baby girl from a pit bull attack, only to have a chunk of flesh bitten off my face. I'd say it was nothing, I did what I had to do to save a child. Beloved school heroine, here I come!

Except I didn't have a chance.

Someone knew someone from my previous school and gossip of my mole, and the botched removal attempt, became the new school joke. It took no time for mortifying "before and after" photos to make the rounds, and the fact that I'd lied about how I got the scar turned everyone against me. Not one student would even talk to me. Their hateful emotions seeped into me like poison, chilling my veins, making me ill.

I hadn't escaped.

I wish I could turn my powers off, to just ignore all those emotions for just a second. Or turn them back the other way and make everyone else know how I was feeling. Because right now, walking down this school corridor with my chin up pretending to smile was the hardest thing in the world.

My eyes stung. No way, if I cried in the middle of everyone, it was all over.

I turned to face the wall and got lucky. There was a notice board right there, covered in fluoro fliers for me to pretend to read while I got myself under control. There were fliers for cheerleading try-outs, chess clubs and the whole spectrum of other cliques that wouldn't take me.

Just breathe.

The corridor stank of bleach from a recent cleaning. If anyone saw my eyes damp and asked if I was OK, I'd say my eyes were sensitive to the chemicals. I always had an answer for everything. I just needed someone to ask.

I closed my eyes, and when I opened them again, Rafael, who I'd already identified as the most handsome guy *ever*, was leaning next to me. He had one elbow against the wall and his hand played with his sun-bleached hair. I don't blame him; my hands would love to do that, too.

Rafael had the looks of a 1950's movie star and he knew it. He played it up, wearing a leather jacket with turned-up collar like he was James Dean and said things like doll, daddy-o, and swell. Yeah, I've been eaves-stalking. Just a bit.

And here he was next to me, looking at me. What was going on? I scanned my surroundings for hidden cameras.

"Since you're new, I'll give you some advice." He spoke in

my ear, closer than I'm used to anyone getting. I shivered.

"Advice?"

"Don't join the chess club," he said.

I let what must be a dumbfounded expression stay on my face and spoke slowly. "But... the checkered boards are so pretty, and I like the little horsies."

Rafael looked at me like I was a poor dumb girl and I worried I'd missed my shot. I raised an eyebrow dramatically, hoping he got the point.

A moment passed, then he chuckled at my joke and I let out a massive sigh. Internally. Externally, I kept my cool and gave a flirty-yet-coy grin. I was stupidly proud of myself. Maybe I could do this. I could be funny and charming and fab-u-lous. I was beautiful on the inside, and he would be the first person to see. And really, I'd kick ass in chess club, but I'd never let him know that.

"I'm Raf. That's the other important thing you need to know, new girl."

"Emma," I said. I extended a hand to shake his, leaving just one to hold up my books. They shifted, almost fell, and I rebalanced them in a way that squished my boobs up into prominence.

"Oops!" I giggled as though I hadn't done the whole thing

on purpose. His smile in return was hungry, almost predatory. I could sense the lusty excitement in him, but also something chilling, a darker emotion hidden under his grin.

"Careful, you'll need those, for, you know, learning."

"No problem. I can shake hands *and* balance books. Get me a job in the circus, I have the skills."

The bell rang. Too soon... I didn't want my time with Rafael to end. This was the nicest anyone had ever been to me and my heart raced with hope and confusion and the close proximity to hottest guy in the world.

Rafael sighed as the bell finished clanging. "Better move. I don't want to get you in trouble on your first day."

Right. I'd been here two weeks. Well, he's noticed me now at least. I had to give him a reason to remember me. Dare I?

"I don't mind getting into trouble sometimes, if it's for a good enough reason."

Raf bumped his shoulder into mine. "You're a firecracker, aren't you? Say, you want to meet up after class? Hang out?"

My lips trembled. "Sure."

"Come to Siren's Haven. You know it?"

I nodded, casually, like I went there all the time. Siren's Haven was an abandoned set of a failed pirate movie, still standing down by the river. I knew all about it because Dad was big into collecting movie props. Tacky replicas mostly, but real stuff too when he could.

"See you there at six, at the main pirate ship. It'll be a gas." Rafael winked at me then headed off down the corridor.

This was too good to be true. I hated that I doubted this, doubted that there could be anything about me he'd find attractive. I was about to split apart, torn between hope and suspicion.

Too jittery for class, I skipped out, went to the girl's bathroom, and did the Snoopy Dance.

Between when I talked to Rafael and the time for our meet up, everything changed. I almost didn't go. I almost curled into a ball of sobbing tears never to face the world again. Then I came up with my plan.

I took so long trying to decide what to wear that I risked being late. I ended up staying in what I wore to school that day: sneakers, black stockings with enough carefully manufactured runs to look every-day, short shorts, and an oversized dusty-red sweater. I'd spent long enough picking it out in the morning anyway and I didn't want to look like I was trying too hard by having an all new outfit on. All I did was change my bra. I also had other preparing to do, and the loose-fitting sweater worked well with my plan.

Twilight lit the fake pirate town, turning grayed wood and dusty weeds varying shades of lilac. I squeezed through the hole in the chain link fence and when my top snagged on one of the cut wires I had a mini panic attack while getting my outfit in order again, covering up what the sweater hid.

I couldn't lose the shakes that had been with me since my conversation with Rafael. They only grew as I made my way to the half-built pirate ship, propped up on blocks down the path. Used spray-cans littered the road like a rainbow and I kicked them along to try and distract my nerves.

Siren's Haven had been abandoned a year ago when issues with actor contracts tanked production. They closed up shop and left it all standing while they tried to get back on track, but in the meantime it had become a playground. I climbed up the weathered wooden ladder onto the ship's deck. Empty beer cans lay scattered around the remains of fires. A couple of old lounges had been dragged in. All the signs of a regular party destination for parties I never got invited to.

Rafael waited for me, reclining on top of a cluster of barrels like a real swashbuckler.

"Hey, sweet cheeks." He rolled onto his side, shifted over, and patted the spot next to him.

"Hey." I strolled across the deck and paused at the barrels. A foam mattress had been thrown on top of them. It made squishy noises when he moved. Ew.

"Come on, don't be shy." Raf patted the mattress again and its moldering stench reached me. "No pressure, I'm not going to try anything. I'm a gentleman."

I already knew how untrue that statement was. But even still, I wanted to give him the benefit of the doubt. Some dumb part of me still hoped that what I'd overheard wasn't true. For the part of me that despite everything hadn't yet turned bitter, I had to let this play out.

"Can I admit something?" My voice quavered, but that was ok, I was aiming for cute and vulnerable. But really I was super nervous about what was going to happen. "I haven't been here before. I want to have a look around. Can you show me?"

"A tour? Sure, doll, sure." He hopped down onto the deck with a smooth jump.

The wood squeaked in warning under us, fragile and not meant to have lasted this long. Rafael put an arm around my shoulder and led me to the prow. I hadn't expected him to touch me. My heart thudded. If he had put his arm around my waist the game would have been over.

From the prow of the ship you could see the whole film set.

EMOTIONALLY SCARRED

There were mermaids carved into the front wall of the pirate bar (which, like most of the buildings, only had a front wall). Tall grass sprouted everywhere, even from the façades themselves. There was a fake rock pool to our left, and the place might have been pretty if it weren't crumbling and trashed.

"Beautiful, isn't it?" Rafael breathed heavily into my ear. "But not as beautiful as you."

Where did this guy get his lines? I hated that they still made my heart race, even though I had no reason to believe him. Before I could mutter the obvious denial, he kissed me.

It was a small kiss on my temple, soft and a little cheeky. I lost my breath.

"Hey," he said, and turned me toward him. I let him move me as he wished. He smiled down at me and it was a beautiful smile. His emotions told me how excited he was. Excited, and smug.

He whispered in my ear. "Take your top off for me."

The last fine cobweb of hope I'd clung to snapped. I knew this was coming, but I clung anyway, and now I felt myself fall. I could stop this and leave now, or I could follow through with the plan I had stupidly dreamed that I wouldn't have to use. Rafael saw my pause and misread my internal conflict.

"It's OK, you're beautiful. I just want to see you."

I nodded slowly and grabbed the bottom hem of my sweater,

lifting it up over my head.

I heard the cla-click sound effect of his camera app as I dropped my sweater to the ground.

The hidden camera finally revealed.

He held up his phone, admiring the photo he had taken. "Grade-school underwear, much?"

I had changed out my nice bra that afternoon for a plain black sports tank that covered as much of me as possible. I came prepared. I reached around to the back waistband of my shorts while he examined his photography.

He stood there, still pointing the phone at me, playing his cruel trick.

And I stood, pointing a gun right back.

Checkmate.

"What are you doing? Are you crazy?" He took a clumsy step back and looked around as though there'd be someone to save him.

"I knew. I knew what you had planned!"

After he first talked to me and I danced like a happy fool, thinking he actually wanted me, the fear that it couldn't be true took over. So I went to find Rafael, to follow him and find out more. I knew there had to be something going on with him, and I daydreamed that he just had some cool, dark secret that only I could know, like he had freaky powers too, or he really was from the 1950's. Instead it turned out that he was simply a jerk.

"I heard you talking to Gavin. Saying you had me eating out of your hands, and you were going to get a photo to blackmail me with to make me do whatever you wanted." I jabbed the gun at him as I talked, my voice growing louder.

"I knew about it all, and even then, I still hoped maybe you were just saying that to your guy as a cover but you really did want..."

I shook my head. I had to stop saying stupid stuff in front of him, as though I were still waiting for him to reveal he cared for me.

No. I had my plan. I knew this was coming, despite any crazy hopes I held. I came here knowing what I would do so that I'd come out of this on top either way.

"Throw your phone over," I said.

He did, and I deleted the photo of me.

Rafael trembled visibly. His expression was frozen but with my powers, his fear was tangible to me. He had his hands raised in front of him. I pulled out *my* phone and flicked on the camera. Set it to video and kept the gun aimed at him with the other hand.

"I want you to tell the world, Raf, what a jerk you are. A horrible bully. Come on, I'm easy pickings, right? Go for the girl with the mangled face, why don't you."

His jaw moved, but he said nothing.

"Say it!"

"I... I'm a jerk, and a bully."

"You are. You take advantage of girls. Say it."

"I take advantage of girls."

The fear flowing off him made me giddy. I hadn't felt such an intense emotion before and it filled me with energy. A grin spread on my face.

"You're nothing but a small-dicked, derivative, misogynistic coward..."

He repeated me on cue.

"Who is about to *die*."

I squeezed the trigger and Rafael twisted like he could dodge a bullet. He couldn't even dodge the spray of water shooting from the gun. Working replica water pistols formed a large part of my Dad's prop collection.

Not all the wet on Rafael was from the gun. His pants were soaked. I giggled as I turned the video off on the phone and slipped it into my shorts pocket.

"Wow, a better performance than I could have hoped for.

Now listen carefully, Mr. Popular. You're going to be my new bestest friend at school. You'll help show everyone how fab-u-lous I can be. Because if you don't, I will show everyone who you *really* are."

My plan complete, I turned to strut away, the proud victor.

I felt the change before I saw anything. The fear gushing from Rafael shifted to blinding fury. The heavy sound of footfalls charged at me.

He shoved me hard from behind and I landed on my face. The aged wood deck grazed my hands, turning them into splinter pincushions. I rolled onto my back, looking up at him. The anger on his face was terrifying, the strongest anger I'd ever sensed.

"No one is going to see that video, ugly bitch!"

He reached down, grabbing at the pocket of my shorts.

I wrestled against his hands, swatting him away.

"No way are you blackmailing me. You're going to suffer."

He slapped me in the face.

Something strange was happening with my powers. I felt Rafael's anger flow down onto me, bathing me, seeping into my muscles and warming them. I felt strong, the same strength I felt when I broke that girl's arm. The splinters didn't bother me. My cheek felt hot where Rafael had slapped me, but didn't sting. I felt powerful.

Rafael swung at me again and I knocked his arm away easily. He pulled back, shocked, and nursed his arm where I hit it.

I knew then I was stronger than him. My powers had always felt like a curse before, but now I realized they were something more. I was something superhuman.

I leapt onto my feet, grinning and staring Rafael down. He shied away from me.

That's where I should have left it. I should have made some witty comment, and walked away. But my hands balled into fists, wanting more fight. With this strength running through me I felt out of control. I wanted revenge for every painful word or look I'd ever suffered.

I kicked high and hard, hitting Rafael right in the centre of his chest.

He *flew* backward, like he was wired up for a movie stunt.

I was a witch after all.

Rafael hit the figurehead at the prow of the boat with a sound that made me feel sick. I instantly regretted lashing out, and went to help him up, to make sure nothing was broken. Even if he was a jerk, I hated myself for being so violent.

I took one step and a squealing groan came from the ship, followed by popping and cracking noises of wood splitting. I felt the deck shudder, and knew the ship would fall.

I looked at Rafael, groaning as he tried to get back on his feet. My body screamed with energy. I felt strong, fast, and confident, like I could reach him, throw him over my shoulder, and leap to safety in time. But he was so far away, all the way at the other end of the ship, where I had kicked him to.

The ship lurched to the side as the hull split open and I ran for him. I leaped over holes that tore open in the deck. Something huge fell into my field of vision and I saw the main mast collapse down into my path, right in front of me. Unable to handle my new speed, I slammed into it and rolled to the side. My momentum spun me too fast and I fell from the side of the ship, tumbling to the ground.

Coughing dirt, all I could do was watch as the pirate ship collapsed in on top of Rafael.

I bolted away from Siren's Haven before the dust settled. I had to sneak back inside so my parents wouldn't see that I'd lost my sweater and come home half-dressed.

It wasn't my fault. It was my fault. It wasn't my fault. It was my fault. My brain was stuck in a loop of guilt and denial. There were too many variables, but I knew one thing—if I had held back, if I hadn't let my anger loose, Rafael might still be alive.

I deleted my video of Rafael for fear it could be used as evidence against me. I fretted about the sweater I'd left behind and hoped it would be considered just another piece of trash, not a clue to a crime. I plotted various excuses and alibis for if I was questioned. I had answers for everything.

But no one came for me.

A week later, I went to the funeral.

The grief I felt from Rafael's family ached, pounding into my skull, and I told myself it was the punishment I deserved. But not everyone grieved. Two rows in front of me, gleeful relief came from a small huddle of girls from school. I wondered what Rafael had done to them, whether they were on a long list of blackmail victims. I tried to cheer myself up by pretending I was a hero who saved those girls from Rafael's conniving schemes. But it didn't work. No matter what he did, I knew he didn't deserve to die. Heroes bring people to justice, not beat them up and fail to save them.

After the ceremony, I wandered through the crowded church, exploring the mix of emotions held by the funeral-goers. Some kids from school just thought it was cool to be there, since Rafael was so popular. His death made big news, and parents were already lobbying to have the "death trap" film set demolished.

EMOTIONALLY SCARRED

They all believed it was an accident, and nothing could have been done. I was the only person who knew that wasn't true. My brain played through hundreds of alternate endings for the night if I'd made different choices. I wish it would stop. I couldn't take back the choices I'd made.

There were a couple of guys I didn't know drifting through the funeral crowd, taking donations for some vague anti-teen-death charity. They looked like brothers. Both had the same cute, roguish charm. Their faces showed commiseration, but my powers told me they felt smug, the same kind of smug Rafael had felt as he pulled his trick. I wondered just what trick these two were up to. Every single person gave them money. A LOT of money. I watched with interest from a quiet corner.

Gavin, Rafael's best friend and blackmail confidant, found me there.

"You were with him, weren't you?" His voice was a growl.

I acted shocked. "Me and Rafael? Why would *he* have been somewhere with *me*?"

"I know he was going to meet you. You had something to do with him dying, I know it. You've been acting weird all week. Why were your hands all scratched up? What happened?"

He loomed over me. I saw anger in him, bubbling under his skin like the glow of lava. But now I knew what I could do with someone else's anger. I couldn't let him reveal to anyone I was with Rafael that night. I had to scare him off and I had the power to do it.

"I don't know what you're talking about," I drawled. I rested a hand on the crossbar of a stone crucifix next to me. "But whatever happened to him could happen to you too if you don't keep quiet and leave me alone."

I squeezed my grip and the stone crumbled like chalk. The patter of the pieces falling to the floor was covered by the talking crowd. Gavin looked at me like the freak I was. My demonstration clearly had the desired effect.

Gavin ran away, leaving me with my regrets. Was I really a witch, or a monster? Was that the path I was fated for, using my powers for evil? I started to wonder how much I could achieve with my newfound abilities. Maybe, one way or another, I could still turn my life around.

The older boy with the donation bucket stared at me. I stared back, waiting for him to glance to my scar, be disgusted and turn away. My glare was a challenge.

But instead he smiled.

He came over and introduced himself. His name was Jake, and he was there with his little brother Jamie. They'd read about the funeral in the newspaper and came to see what donations they could get for their own "charitable cause".

"I saw what you just did," Jake whispered, dramatically low considering no one was interested in our conversation anyway. He kicked at the broken stone on the floor and raised his eyebrows.

"I didn't do anything. It was dodgy craftsmanship, broke on its own."

"You're a fast thinker, too. Perfect," he said. "Don't worry, I know what you can do, because I can do it, too. I'm so glad I spotted you. It's rare to find someone special, like us. How about we get out of here and talk more. Doesn't all this sadness give you a headache?"

I couldn't stop my eyes widening. "You really feel it too?"

Jake grinned. "The emotion reading, the super strength, the whole deal."

The idea of other people with powers like mine made a strong need for belonging bloom in my chest. My voice sounded way too vulnerable when I asked, "Can you help me understand what I am?"

"Sure. Come with me. I want to tell you how sticking by me will give you everything you ever wanted. Everything that people like us deserve."

Every nerve inside me ached to go with Jake, my body

rebelling against my better judgment. Jake was charming and so handsome it made my palms sweaty. There was something downright supernatural about how tempting he was, but also something wrong and disturbing. I wouldn't fall for sweet talk again, and could already tell he wasn't one of the good guys.

I shook my head. "No. Go away. You're not my type."

Jake looked stunned. I doubt he got turned down... ever. He stared, assessing me again, his gaze lingering on my face.

He handed me a business card.

"What's this?" I asked.

"A gift, something I'm guessing is high on your wish list. I'll let Dr Rachenko know you're coming and to put any work on my tab. I've written my number on the back so you can get in touch again when you've seen what I can do for you."

I stared at the card. *Dr Rachenko- Discreet cosmetic surgery and enhancements.*

Jake tapped the card as I held it in my hands. "Everything you ever wanted starts here."

Jake called his brother over and the two of them left the building, counting the money they had been collecting from the grieving crowd. Definitely not on the good guy side.

I stared at what Jake had given me, my fingers clenched and shaking around the thin cardboard. Jake had offered me a new life, a new skin, and all I could wonder was what trick he would play on me, what catch this promise held. I couldn't stand the idea that his offer wasn't true.

And if the only catch was that I wouldn't be one of the good guys either, could I do that?

Deep inside I had always wanted to be something good and special, but it seems that I was born to be something other than a hero. I never had that sort of strength in me, the strength to stay beautiful on the inside. Ugliness had crawled inside me, driven in by the cruel words and games of my peers. It sat there, next to the dull ache I felt in my chest whenever my mind replayed the night at Siren's Haven. A montage it chose to replay often.

I shook the guilt and regret away, denying it. It didn't matter anymore. I would become beautiful on the outside. Everything I wanted, I would take. I had great plans. Operation: New Me, Mark II would not fail.

EMOTIONALLY
UNSTABLE

THE EMPATH 2 CHRONICLES

I t was funny how little I knew about Dean.

In the chaos of what had happened to us—discovering empaths and our powers and almost getting killed—I had grown to feel so much for him, but I didn't even know his last name until I saw it on his hospital chart. Dean Lasslow. And he was apparently eighteen, a year older than me. When Mom and Dad agreed to let him stay out our place for a while, they started making arrangements and it turned out he'd dropped out of school halfway through his final year to work. As soon as Mom learned that, she got straight to action and enrolled Dean at my school so he could graduate with me. Apparently, there was no way I was using any of the recent events as an excuse to skip my normal education.

Dean left hospital with strict orders not to lift anything heavy or perform strenuous exercise. He was given a huge list of post-hospital-care instructions about how to change the dressings on his wounds, plus a large paper bag full of medication, and that was pretty much it. He had almost none of his own belongings with him.

Mom and Dad had offered to pick up some of Dean's things for him, but he didn't want them having to deal with his dad on their own, so it was agreed we would all go by his place together to pack before heading back to my home.

Mom pulled up the hire car in front of Dean's trailer. Down the laneway, surrounded by trash and weeds, some unsupervised kids were smashing bottles for fun, and a cloud of anger and depression drifted to me from the untended homes around us. Dad reached over and held Mom's hand. I knew her childhood hadn't been great, but she kept most of the details from me. She always preferred to focus on the positive. But from the way Dad moved so quickly to reassure her now, and the dark blue chill of sadness that surrounded her, I wondered how many of her childhood memories were being relived. I wanted to hug her for any pain she was feeling, and for who she turned out to be despite it all.

"Wait here. I'll be right back," Dean said. He stepped gingerly out of the car, the still-healing bullet wound making such movement difficult. I wanted to hug him too.

Dean didn't even make it to the front door before it flew open, metal screen clattering against the side of the trailer home. His dad burst out, like he'd been standing there waiting the entire time Dean had been in hospital. Standing there waiting, and drinking.

Dean had left his car door open, and we could hear every slurry word.

"Gone f'weeks, and look at you—nothing wrong with you. Think you're just waltzing back in after the trouble you caused? Sending cops banging down my door?" His shirt was stained, and he had an almost empty bottle of bourbon in one hand.

"I'm just here to collect my things," Dean said coolly. He took another step and his dad blocked his path, thrusting out a palm against Dean's shoulder.

I was out of my seat so fast the car was left rocking in my wake. My parents were right behind me. After they got over the impact of the shuddering car.

"Leaving me again? Good. Sick of you stealing my paycheck."

"Mr. Lasslow!" Mom yelled.

229

"He's not stealing anything; he's just picking up some clothes," Dad said in the calm voice of someone trying to defuse a situation. Then he seemed to rethink the whole plan and addressed Dean. "Maybe we can pick you up some basics at a store for now, come back another time for the rest."

Dean's dad stepped right up in front of Dean. Dean flinched away from his breath. "Weaseled yourself a real sugar-mama family to look after you, huh? Too good for this place now?"

Dean breathed out slowly, and in the calmest voice, said, "I'll just get some things and be right back."

He tried to sidestep into the trailer, but his dad grabbed the shoulder of his too-large charity T-shirt and wrenched him backwards.

I was there in a flash. I rebalanced Dean as gently as I could to stop him from stumbling over. I didn't want to know what a rough fall would do to his healing internal organs. I stood between him and his Dad, ready for anything.

Or I thought I was, until Dean's dad spat in my face.

My jaw dropped and I wanted to vomit. I wiped frantically at the slippery ooze on my chin.

"Little whore, stealing my only family from me," he growled.

Anger fired through me. Mom and Dad rushed to my side, and it took their strength combined to drag me back to the car, even with Dean blocking my full powers.

"We're leaving. Now," Mom said, and Dean followed us.

I was shaking with fury, and heartbroken for Dean, that all the family he had left in the world was that disaster of a parent. Dean deserved so much more. "We can't just go. What about your stuff?" I said to him.

Dean looked back at the rusty, gray trailer surrounded by monstrous weeds, and his drunk dad, waving his arms and yelling obscenities at us. "There's nothing there I need."

We all took our seats again and Mom started the engine. The gravel road crunched as the car started rolling away.

"Well," he added, "except my motorbike."

"Your *what?*" I turned back, surprised, and caught the glimpse of a wheel of what could have been a motorbike around one corner of the trailer.

"It's just an old dirt bike. My mate was borrowing it when you visited before. But if I leave it there any longer, Dad will probably sell it."

My mom turned halfway around from watching the road. "Would your friend be willing to bring it to Bellscroft to our place for you?"

Dean watched out the window quietly as we drove away from the trailer park. "Yeah, yeah he might."

Dean called his friend and made arrangements in a series of short monosyllable sounds. His phone and wallet, all he'd had in his pockets when we ended up in hospital, were all he had of his own now.

The drive was silent for a long time after that. The emotions flowing off my parents ranged from angry to sad to worried then back to angry. Dean remained his unreadable, cold self.

The trip took an uncomfortable two hours. On the way, we stopped at a strip mall that had a budget department store draped in 'clearance sale' signs. My mom mumbled about the ridiculously cheap clothing prices and unfair work conditions in Bangladesh, but begrudgingly agreed it would do for now. Dean picked out some basics, plain T-shirts and jeans, a hoodie and underwear, deodorant and a toothbrush, socks and a pair of sneakers. He checked every price tag and mouthed a running total to keep track. He picked the cheapest every time and didn't seem fussy about what he bought, unlike the kind of dramas I'd pulled in the past about what my wardrobe should include.

At the checkout, Dean pulled out some of the cash remaining from the sale of my necklace, my 'wages' to him when he couldn't work because of me. He checked and counted out how much he had left before he tried to pay.

But my parents weren't having it and Dean wouldn't accept them paying, and it quickly turned into a scene. I couldn't call it an argument, Dean was being too polite for that, but a large queue of impatient customers was building up behind us.

Mom took Dean by the wrist and led him away from the checkout. From the look on her face and the fountain of red and orange emotional energy flowing from her, I wasn't going with them, and neither did Dad. We just helped push our purchases to the side so other customers could move through around our drama.

Over beside a rack of magazines and gum, Mom had crouched down in front of Dean, looking up at him as she talked with the most intense expression on her face. There was some conversation back and forth. I tried to imagine what she was saying to break through his pride and let them help him. Had she ever been in a similar situation?

Dean seemed to be standing firm on something, and soon, I saw Mom yield to him. But he must have also yielded to her, because when they came back, Mom paid for his clothes and other items.

On the way out Mom pulled through a drive-through liquor store and picked up a six-pack of beer, which Dean paid for.

"What ... what?" I stuttered.

"*These*," Mom said, emphasizing the word, "will be staying in our possession until the necessary time."

I looked across at Dean for an explanation, but he was staring the other way, out the window.

When we finally pulled up out the front of our house, I couldn't believe how happy I was to see it. I was almost ready to jump out of the car and start kissing the garden path.

Home. It felt like so long since I'd been there. All my stuff. My room. My parents. All where we were meant to be.

Inside, everything had been cleaned up after the quake, and the section of living room which had the crack running down it had been repaired but not yet repainted, the white plaster stark against the smoky lavender walls.

My parents showed Dean to his room, which was really Dad's office with a sofa bed in it.

"Showers are three minutes or less, and hang your towel in your room to re-use a couple of times before washing it." Dad was rattling off his list of green-living house rules. Water conservation, recycling, low power habits. I was used to it all, but Dean listened carefully like it was life or death. If I didn't know better, I'd say he looked nervous.

"Yes, Mr. Mirawi," he said for about the fifth time in a row.

"Once the hire car is returned, there's no car, so Livvy can help you get used to the bus-and-train routine around here. Curfew for getting home is ten p.m. unless otherwise discussed."

"Yes, Mr. Mirawi."

"And we also have one new rule," he said, looking at me now. "A new curfew. Neither of you are to be in the other's room after dinnertime, and no closed doors at any time you're alone together in a room."

Dean didn't reply. He shot me a look.

"Daaad." I blushed. "We're not ..."

Mom gave me a no-nonsense look and I knew her no-nonsense attitude was about to embarrass me. "We've talked about relationships and sex before love, and we do trust you to look after your own body. But you've both just been through a very traumatic time, and brains don't always work their best after trauma. The new curfew is temporary, but it will be strictly enforced until our lives start coming back into the realm of reality."

"Okay, Mom, okay." My blush grew hotter all the way to my ears.

We gave Dean some time to settle in on his own and unpack the couple of shopping bags worth of new belongings into the side cupboard Dad had cleared out for him. I went and lay down on my own bed and cuddled my own pillow and cried in relief.

It wasn't long before the doorbell rang. I answered, and a guy was standing there with two helmets, rechecking his phone and our house number. Behind him on the street was a banged up dirt bike.

Dean stepped up behind me, and introduced his friend Mako. I stood back and let them have a chat. Mako seemed highly amused by the whole situation, and especially pleased with getting to 'heist' the bike out from under Dean's dad's nose. Mom and Dad appeared with the six-pack and it all made sense. It was payment for bike delivery. Payment Dean wanted to make himself. On top of that, Dean used what I figured was the last of his cash to pay for his mate's public transport home.

Dad wheeled the bike into the garage which was otherwise used as a second storeroom for Duck Egg Blue stock. Then we all stood at the door and waved goodbye to Mako, something he found very funny.

Once he'd walked off to the bus stop, I exhaled a few weeks' worth of stress. That was it. All sorted. Time to just settle back into my life and get back to normal, if that were even remotely possible.

"It's nice to be home," I said softly.

Mom made a sucking noise through her teeth. "Just one more new house rule, though."

236

EMOTIONALLY CHARGED

I sighed, knowing I was in no position to debate parental authority right now. "Sure, what is it?"

"You're not to go on that bike."

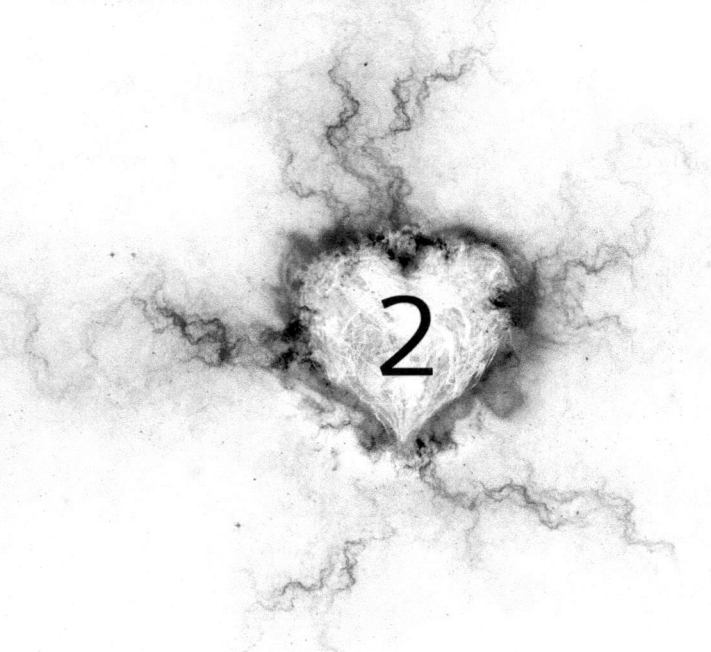

2

Dean put his hand on my shoulder to steady me.

We edged closer.

"I was wrong. I'm not ready," I mumbled. Energy flooded me, like overactive bees humming through my veins. It already felt like it could drive me crazy.

"You can do it. You're strong."

We took another step closer to the school gates.

"Oof. Do you think you can ramp up your blocking amount at all?"

Dean shook his head. "Not really. I think if I try and do much more it will be getting into the territory of shutting down your powers for good."

I looked at the crowd of teenagers moving around the school yard. Their emotions felt like a thick cloud, surrounding me. I couldn't even clearly define them, just this rainbow-swirl mass of intense *feeling*. I felt like I could either punch a hole through a brick wall or suddenly take off flying—*if* my brain didn't spontaneously combust first.

"Okay." I took a deep breath. "Here we go."

We made it in through the gates and were heading up the gum-spotted concrete path to the main building to take Dean to the office when I heard a long, high-pitched sound.

"Liiiivyyyy!"

Even the pressure in my head couldn't stop me from being excited.

"Natiiiiiiiiiiii!" I squealed back.

She appeared like magic from behind a group of kids exchanging class notes, and ran towards me in pretend slow motion. A huge toothy smile shone on her dark skin and her ringlets bounced in perfect rhythm along with her.

I opened my arms for a hug, laughing at her dramatics, but she stopped short a couple of steps from me and changed to a pouting, hands-on-hips stance.

"Where *were* you?" she accused. "You disappear for weeks

and not a single call or message or So-Snap?"

We had a plan for this situation. Me and my parents had decided that if I shared anything about what had happened, it would be exactly the same story I'd told the police. Consistency was everything, since we figured some news might have spread already. Nati seemed completely clueless though, and I wondered, maybe vainly, whether anything about what had happened to Dean and I had made the news at all. It didn't seem that way, which was odd.

I was only just opening my mouth when Nati started up again.

"You've been sick, haven't you? Wow, look at you—you look like the walking dead, babe. It's not contagious, right?"

I half smiled. I did feel pretty awful. Dealing with the relentless level of heightened emotions was taking a lot out of me. I felt clammy and jittery, and hoped Nati didn't jump from sickness to just-out-of-rehab with her assumptions. "It's not catching; don't worry. I'll give you the whole story soon."

"Oh. My. Smosh." Nati's eyes widened as she *noticed* Dean. "And who are you?"

"D-"

"You little con-artist!" Nati interrupted, turning back to me with the slyest expression. Man, I didn't realize how much I'd missed her, and this display of pure Nati was making me giggle.

"Pretending like you've been off sick and coming back to school with a honey at your side? You've got some insane-level spillage to do!"

"I know. I'll catch you all up soon. Cross my heart. Last period, chemistry?"

"It's a date." She grinned. "Are you around for good, new guy?"

Nati, you've no idea how complicated that question is. "Dean's enrolled. He'll probably be here for a bit."

"That's bonkers!" she shouted. Dean and I looked at each other, confused. "Two new guys in one week! The other guy, Ash? I have to say, he's easy on the libido as well. Oh, oh!"

She ducked in close to me and lifted her chin like a pointer to the corner of the red-brick building. "There he is, and he's totally looking at you!"

I peeked over my shoulder, and saw him. An Asian boy with bleached white hair really was looking straight at me. He caught me looking and I averted my eyes, then looked at Dean, who had his eyebrows very slightly raised. I shrugged. Not like I had control over who was looking at me.

"What is this? Livvy love week? Is it this new waif look you're rocking that's got the boys flocking?" Nati said with a little shimmy of her hips.

I was saved from any further embarrassment by the bell. I

hugged Nati quickly and promised again to chat in chemistry.

"Your face is chemistry!" she yelled gleefully as we headed off in different directions.

Dean and I made our way to the office and dealt with both his introduction to the school and my recent absence from it. My parents had sorted most of it out; there were just forms and timetables, homework and textbooks to pick up before getting to our classes, all of which had been arranged for Dean and I to be together, which couldn't have been easy. But Dad did a large share of volunteering for the school so he had favors he could call on. Dean got a photo taken for his student card and would have to pick it up in the afternoon.

He was looking unsure about the whole being-back-at-school thing. And I knew he was here mostly for my benefit, but I hoped he would get something out of it too. I mean, it was high school, but it was a good high school with some good kids and teachers I even liked, like Mr. Jones, who we had first up that morning for history.

As we walked into the class, Mr. Jones tapped me on the shoulder and said, "Glad you're back. Was worried when you disappeared on us that night."

"Sorry about that. I hope my parents explained everything." I ducked past before he could reply, and took a seat near the middle of the room next to an empty desk for Dean. He paused to introduce himself to the teacher and hand over some paperwork.

Ash slipped right into what should have been Dean's chair. *Ugh. I should have put something on it to claim it.* I wasn't thinking straight with the rainbow of emotional auras creating a haze in the room, including the bright sunshine yellow beaming from Ash as he grinned at me.

I shot Dean a look of apology as he moved to another available desk behind me.

It was still close enough to get a decent blocking effect, but I silently cursed Ash for meaning I couldn't have Dean at my side.

He didn't seem to notice and, still smiling, started talking in a strong Australian accent. "Hey, you new to this place too? I'm Ash."

"Livvy," I said, busy getting my textbooks in order. "And I'm not new. Just been away for a while."

"Yeah? Where to? On holiday?" His grin stayed large. He was as cheery as a kid's TV host. He glowed almost too bright to look at.

I rubbed my forehead and turned to the front of the classroom, trying to make a point of paying attention to Mr. Jones who had begun the lesson on the smart board. Something about an assassination causing World War I. I was behind on the details there. I glanced to the side and Ash was still staring at me, waiting for an answer.

"In hospital," I hissed.

"Whoa. What happened?" He sat sideways on his chair to face me better and looked me up and down, as if seeking clues as to my illness or injury. "Was it serious?"

I shot him a glare. Was he trying to get us both in trouble? Why so many questions? Maybe I could have avoided an interrogation if I'd lied and said I had been on vacation, but that wasn't the plan. Stick to the script. Stay consistent. Or just avoid giving busy-bodies any unnecessary information entirely.

"I'm fine now. Shh." I tilted my head to Mr. Jones who seemed to have noticed our conversation. I had my pen in hand, trying to take notes, but between Ash's prying and the distracting buzz of emotions swarming through my body like angry ants, I was having trouble concentrating.

"You look knackered. Sure you're not still feeling a bit off? Or is it because it's so cold in here?" Ash continued looking straight at me. Like he was oblivious to the rest of the room. Or to me being annoyed. Or the increasingly bewildered teacher who stared right at him, tapping his foot.

"Ash Len," Mr. Jones snapped. "Private conversations are for outside the classroom. If you feel the need to talk so much, maybe you can go have a chat to the principal."

"Sorry, Mr. Jones," he said, his cheery grin still in place. "I'm just so excited to be in this new school, with so many interesting new people to meet."

Confused laughter swept across the room, as though the class was unsure if this guy was trying to be a clown or not.

Mr. Jones also looked bewildered at Ash's behavior. It seemed almost arrogant or cheeky, like he was the kind of person used to getting away with anything. His comment about it being cold popped back up in my memory's ear. *Huh.* I narrowed my eyes, my suspicions twitching.

Mr. Jones cleared his throat. "Well, some more interest in the lesson would be appreciated."

"Sure thing, mate," Ash said, turning himself to the front of the room again, pen in hand, head down.

He didn't talk to me again for the rest of the lesson, but every time I glanced across at him, he was also glancing right back at me from under his straight white hair. Grinning. Not taking any notes.

The school bus stop was a swell of jostling teenage bodies, wired from a day in school and ready to be free. A couple of supervising teachers near the gates kept trying to remind us to stay calmly in our bus lines but it was futile. Between the hot tin roof and the concrete floor, students dueled in games of handball or huddled together, streaming funny videos on their phones or taking selfies. In the corners farthest from the teachers, couples pressed their bodies together, making out or just staring dreamily into each other's eyes.

My gaze drifted up to Dean beside me. He stood close, with his shoulder pressed against mine, but there wasn't that intimacy or rush of lust between us that the other teenage couples seemed to have. At least not in the Dean-to-Livvy direction. In the Livvy-to-Dean direction, just a glimpse of those intense gray eyes made my whole body whimper. But I held back, uncertainty a wall of ice between us. Were we even a couple? Was it always going to be this hard to know how Dean was feeling? Would I always doubt us?

Dean caught me staring, and without saying a word, he wrapped his hand around mine. *There he goes being a mind reader again.* But Mom always did say I had a face like an open book.

His hand felt good in mine, and the flutters in my heart grew fierce as a tornado.

"You two are so cute together. Like Romeo and Juliet, except

246

ones who kicked death in the ass!" Nati had proclaimed during chemistry class. She had gasped all the way through my explanation of my absence, how I'd gotten caught up with a gang, the bank robbery, and the fact Dean had been shot. Gasps were punctuated with a lot of 'No way!' and 'Shut up!' She ate up every detail, her eyes sparkling with a fierce, protective awe.

After class, it was like she didn't want to let me out of her sight, offering to drive us both home even though it was out of her way. I declined, happy to catch the bus and return to normal routines.

Our bus pulled up out the front of the gates, and kids started filing into line, pushing through the rest of the swirling crowd of students to get on. Just before reaching the gate, Dean's hand slipped out of mine and another student pushed in between us. Then my wrist was grabbed again from behind. A sharp tug pulled me out of line.

"Hey, Livvy! It's Livvy, isn't it? I've met so many people today, it's a bit of a blur." Ash grinned at me. He let go of my wrist and I just nodded to him, trying to head back to the bus as the last student in line got on.

He grabbed my shoulder and stopped me from walking away. I knew I was stronger than him, but didn't want him to also know that, so I let him get away with it. "Ash, I have to go."

"I wanted to ask you something," he persisted.

"Dude, that's my bus," I snapped at him.

I heard the *whoosh* of the bus doors closing. I turned to find Dean, and spotted him on the bus as it pulled away. Without me.

3

Dean stood in the aisle of the bus. He'd noticed I wasn't behind him anymore, and looked out the window. Our eyes met, both wide with fear.

Down around the back of the covered bus shelter, I heard raised voices, as a couple of girls started pushing each other around. The buzz of emotions from my fellow classmates was building up in me. *Fast.* I had to get to Dean. I really didn't want to be seizuring out in front of everyone on my first day back at school. Or at all.

Ash still held my shoulder, saying something I wasn't paying any attention to.

I stepped out of Ash's grip, pushing him back at the same time, and left him stumbling with a look of sheer astonishment on his face.

I ducked quickly between the other students, sidestepping behind some larger bodies until I was out of sight of Ash and any watching teachers, then slipped away behind the covered shelter walls.

The street was visible through the thick bars of the school fence, and a row of busses had stopped just outside, waiting for the green light. My bus was one of them.

I had to get to it. And I had to do it without totally revealing my powers.

I dashed to a section of fence where bushes grew on either side, hoping they'd be enough to obscure the view if anyone was watching me run around the schoolyard like a weirdo.

Giving the fence a calculating glare, I ran straight at it. I moved fast—there was obviously enough fear around for me to use. I hoped there was also enough anger, so I'd have the strength to make the jump. I judged my moment and leaped. The tops of the metal bars skimmed the soles of my shoes. Dirt swirled as I landed behind the leafy bush, feet firm and heart pounding.

But the bus was already pulling away again, down the street.

EMOTIONALLY UNSTABLE

I ran along not far behind, trying to keep out of direct view of people on the street and the vehicle's windows. Thank goodness school was in a quiet part of town. I ducked behind parked cars then sprinted ahead in a blur of speed when the coast was clear. It wasn't hard keeping up with the bus at first, but I knew just around the corner they'd be moving into a faster speed zone and I wasn't sure if I'd make that pace while staying covert. I needed to get in the bus.

Or maybe *on* the bus ...

Just around the corner was a billboard truck that had been there for months, advertising a new dental surgery. I just hoped they hadn't moved it.

I rounded the corner, anxiously scanning for it and—*there.* Yes! It was still there. The slope of the double-sided A-frame billboard was steeper than I'd remembered, almost straight up and down. My shoes had basic rubber soles that I hoped would give me enough traction, because this was my last chance to get on the bus, and not get a seizure in the gutter.

I gunned it, using every bit of speed and strength I could muster. It felt like I was running at a wall, but when I reached it, I scrambled up the face of the white-toothed grinning woman on the ad, toes and hands moving together to pull me up to the top. And there was the bus in front of me, just in front of me and starting to accelerate.

I didn't slow down. I pushed off with both feet and sprang from the top of the billboard, my hair flying about as the world disappeared from under me. My chest tightened. *I'm up in the air.* It was amazing. And terrifying. *Please let me come down in the right place.*

I landed neatly on top of the bus in a crouched action pose, and couldn't help but smile.

I did it. Now *that* was superhero stuff. I felt like I had flown through the sky, and my heart raced faster than I had.

I dropped down onto my stomach. It wouldn't pay to have anyone see a teenage girl riding a bus around like a skateboard. After catching my breath, I slid over to the edge, ducking down to look through a window. Dean stood up the front. He seemed to be arguing with the bus driver who waved him back, probably telling him to take a seat. With the bus on its way, it wouldn't come back for students who'd missed it, or let anyone off outside of a designated stop.

The other students seemed too involved in their own conversations or phones to be looking my way, so I took a chance and waved to get Dean's attention.

Halfway through a sentence, his eyes turned my way and he stopped, mouth open. I grinned, giving him a thumbs up.

He said something else to the driver then took a seat, eyebrows raised at my upside-down face.

Another kid turned my way, and I moved out of sight. I took off my backpack and flipped over onto my back to watch the blue sky for the rest of the ride home, pretending I was still flying.

When the bus pulled up on our street, I waited for Dean to get off, and then jumped down off the back of the bus as it left, landing out of sight behind a gray van.

"What happened?" Dean came over to me. "I thought you were right behind me, getting on the bus. Then you weren't. I tried to get them to stop but the driver wouldn't listen."

"I know. It's okay, I was held up by someone, but did you see me? I was so fast, like *so* fast, and I jumped onto a fleeping bus. Right onto it!" My empath powers had calmed again now I was beside Dean, but my heart and mind were still in crazy-excited mode. "I went full superhero."

We started the walk up the street to my house, and I skipped around Dean as he half-smiled at my enthusiasm.

"I don't know if I've ever run like that before. Or jumped! Or landed! Do you know how I landed? Not on my face! It was like POW." I demonstrated by jumping a little on the spot and landing in an action pose.

"You are such a huge dork." But Dean smiled, as though he really liked it.

Mom met us at the front door. I bet she'd been hovering. She knew I'd been worried about my first day back at school. "How was it?" she asked.

I tried to contain my grin. Pure nonchalance. "It was fine. No dramas at all."

I rapped my knuckles lightly against Dean's door. Mom and Dad were watching a movie in the living room downstairs. Dean and I were meant to be catching up on homework before bed. Separately, in our own rooms, because it was after dinner.

I'd had a soothing bath and changed into pajamas and tried to relax and just focus on studying.

But the excitement of today still zipped through my veins. I couldn't stop thinking about the race I'd run, the sensation of flying, and the way Dean had held my hand in the bus shelter. So I had fearlessly snuck down the hallway, desperate to see Dean to have someone to share those feelings with.

I heard some shuffling but the door didn't open. I didn't dare knock louder, so I pushed the sliding door open a crack and peeked in. Dean was sitting cross-legged on the sofa bed, wearing only gray sweat-pants, reading a paperback.

My breath caught and my cheeks heated. I almost backed away, but Dean looked up and rested the book on the bed, like a sign it was okay for me to interrupt. I stepped in and closed the door behind me, careful not to make a sound.

"Isn't this against the rules?" he whispered.

I answered by grinning mischievously and wriggling my eyebrows.

Dean didn't share my delinquent delight. He reached across and grabbed a shirt, pulling it on quickly. "I don't want to get in trouble off your parents."

"I just wanted to chat." My enthusiasm dropped quickly. For all I could tell, Dean didn't want me there. But I could never really tell what he wanted, or if he wanted. *What would this situation be like with a normal boy?*

I almost bit my tongue. *Normal?* I'd never been the type to want normal.

I sat next to Dean and studied his face, his skin smooth and pale like no laugh lines had ever marred it. Those gray eyes looked like they could be thunderstorms but held none of that wild energy.

I could never sense his emotions. What he was feeling. If he felt at all. But I knew his heart. I'd once felt the pain he held so deep in there. I knew his kindness. I knew he felt *something* for me. It was just hard to tell exactly what and how much when he didn't show it.

I found myself lost for words after having just said I wanted to chat. *Ugh, so awkward.* I picked up the book he was reading. It was a space opera classic, probably off one of the shelves in the room. One of Dad's favorites. "You like reading?"

"Yeah. It helps me shut out the things around me, to escape." He coughed softly. "And it was easy to find cheap second-hand paperbacks back at home."

"Paperbacks? Haven't you discovered e-books yet? You can borrow my e-reader if you want since I mostly read on my phone. I have so many books in my collection," I said as my mind served up the image of Dean's tiny trailer room. Even his phone looked pre-smart-phone era. He had been working to support himself and his alcoholic dad, and there I was, boasting about my e-book collection and how many devices I had. Including the brand-new phone my parents had given me while I was in hospital since my own phone had been left behind and the one Jake got me had become evidence. Me, who had been so excited by the idea of affluence and opulence that I got involved with criminals.

Thankfully, Dean didn't seem as mortified by me at that

moment as I was. He just said, "Sure, sounds good," as I tried to get my brain functioning in an acceptable way.

My life had changed so much. My eyes had been opened so wide, I felt like I didn't know how to exist anymore. Like I couldn't be the person I used to be. But my identity hadn't quite caught up with that memo yet, hadn't grown into it. I was a toddler wearing her dad's Superman costume.

And then there was Dean, who made me want to be worthy of a love he might never be able to express. How was I supposed to act around him?

My mind was muddled. What had originally been planned as a fun secret meet-up was turning into a confusing mess. What had I wanted, really, when I snuck down here?

"Are you," I started, hesitantly, "having trouble feeling normal again?"

Dean's eyes were on mine, and I wondered if he'd been studying my face the way I had his. "Yeah. I'm not sure how normal I ever felt, but yeah, I know I've changed, from who I was before all this. You?"

I bit my lip and nodded. "And it's not just the powers. I mean, it's hard to feel normal when you have super strength and speed, and who knows what else. But other things too. I feel ... different. In a good way, but also a way I just don't know how to make work yet."

Dean nodded.

We sat in silence and I considered reaching out and taking his hand, or leaning my head on his shoulder. Instead, I reached over and placed my palm on his shirt, so gently it was barely a touch at all. Through the thin material, I felt the plasticky square of post-op dressing covering his bullet wound. The action moved us closer. Dean's breath ghosted over my cheek.

I whispered, "Are you feeling a bit better?"

"Yeah." Dean looked down at my hand. "I was worried about you on the bus today. When you didn't get on, I just kept imagining you on the ground, hurting."

The pain I'd felt when I saw Dean on the ground, shot and bleeding, was far greater than a seizure had ever caused me. But maybe that was how he felt now, knowing what happened to me when he wasn't close by my side. "I'm sorry that you have to be here for me all the time now."

"I really don't mind. Honestly, I'm not sure my life was really going anywhere before. Or, I mean, I don't think I had it in me to want my life to go anywhere." He turned back to look at me and the edges of his eyes were just slightly red, the only hint of emotion on his face. "I think all I was doing was … existing. You, and being here for you, has given me something to care about again."

I exhaled softly as though trying to release the butterflies from my stomach. "And is that okay? Caring about something again?"

Dean shook his head just the smallest bit. "It hurts. But in a good way. It means I'm feeling *something* again, when I haven't felt anything in so long."

A single small tear spilled over my eyelid, surprising me, then I surprised myself again when my lips met Dean's. The kiss was soft at first, until I pushed harder, seeking, and his mouth opened under mine. He wrapped his arms around me, pulling me up into his lap, holding me tight, and pressing my chest against his.

The *flutter-flutter* in my heart was no longer gentle. It raged with a burning intensity and all I could sense was Dean and the kiss and his hands and his tongue, and that was all I wanted.

But the intensity kept growing. Too fast. Too strong. A pounding in my head and electricity in my veins. Fire in my muscles. The world grew blurry and dark. I clung to Dean's T-shirt and heard it rip as he backed away from me, pushing me off him onto the bed where I fell, close to convulsing.

"Livvy? Liv? Are you okay?" He was leaning over me, a hand on my forehead. I blinked my vision clear to see his expression blank and calm again, and my body started coming back under control.

"How did that go so wrong?" I grunted.

"I'm sorry." Dean helped me sit up on the edge of the bed, and crouched in front of me. He held my hands and looked at them instead of my face. His words were measured and his voice monotone, as though he were doing everything he could to remain emotionless. "I couldn't keep my blocking power going. When I was kissing you. The way I feel about you … I couldn't control it. And I hurt you."

"You didn't hurt me. It isn't your fault I'm like this." I could have cried. I'd wanted proof that Dean felt something for me, and I got it, right along with a clear message of *no, you can't eat the cake too.* The rollercoaster of the last five minutes had left me teary and frustrated. "What does this mean? Can we never kiss or …?"

"I don't know."

"But do you want to? Kiss me, I mean?" It seemed like the wrong question to be asking. But I wanted to. Despite what had happened, I still wanted to be kissing Dean right then, to have my arms around him and be with him, in a way that felt like I was *with* him. I wanted to know what our relationship was and have all the good things that came with connection. Like kissing.

"I don't think we can. Not until we find a way to fix your

powers. I don't want to hurt you again," he said eventually, perhaps reluctantly.

I just nodded. He was right. I had to do something to fix myself. I couldn't live like this forever. Even with him right there, I could still sense emotions around me so clearly, like I could almost tell how everyone on the street was feeling. Including two angry bodies just outside the door.

Oh, butts. We were busted.

4

slipped back out of Dean's room and closed the door behind me so that whatever happened next didn't have to involve him.

"Olivia Poppy Mirawi," Dad said, sternly.

Ouch. I knew it was serious when my parents full-named me.

They both stood there, arms crossed. Mom glanced at Dean's closed door, and beckoned me to follow her with a flick of her chin.

I obediently shuffled along behind them, glad they didn't give me an earful right there where Dean could hear everything through his door. In horror, I wondered how much my parents had heard through that same door.

EMOTIONALLY UNSTABLE

On the way down the stairs, I looked out the window onto the dark street below, and noticed an unmarked gray van out the front. It looked like the same one I had landed behind when getting off the bus. *A surveillance van?* In the past, I'd write that off as my imagination being its wild self, but these days, I wasn't so sure. I thought about mentioning it to my parents, but they'd think I was just trying to deflect. I filed it away with my suspicions about Ash to review at a later time, under the heading 'When did I become so paranoid?' My imagination used to feed me budding romance plots at every turn, and now I was seeing enemies in every corner.

Once in the kitchen, Dad pulled out a stool at the counter for me and Mom started making herself a cup of tea. I could sense the anger in both of them, but they were clearly restraining it.

"I'm sorry. I know it was past bedroom curfew. It was entirely my fault; I went to him. I just wanted to talk to him." At first, at least, until the kissing started.

"You're only sorry because you got caught," Mom pointed out. She slowly dunked her teabag as she placed her cup on the counter, then sat down across from me. "And I understand. You wanted to spend some time with him and didn't think that our rules were important to follow. But you know we put rules in place for a reason."

Dad stayed standing up, behind Mom. "Look, we remember what it's like to be a teenager, and the feelings that come with it. We also remember that teenagers don't always think straight, and make mistakes like sneaking into a boy's room when they've been told not to. So you're getting a free pass on this one. This. One. Time."

Phew?

Dad opened his mouth as if to speak again. No, they weren't finished yet. Not phew.

"It's not that we don't want you following your heart or having sex," Mom said in a matter-of-fact way that left my jaw on the counter. "We'd prefer you to be having sex under our roof where we know you're safe and making the right choices, rather than sneaking off somewhere less safe."

"Mooom," I gasped.

"Normally," Dad added. "But these aren't normal times. You know that, right?"

I nodded. I really, really knew that. But now wasn't the time to let them know I wouldn't be kissing Dean again anytime soon because of what it did to me.

Dad tilted his head, his anger shifting to sympathy. "Lollipop, you kids have been through some serious trauma. You can't trust what your bodies or minds are telling you right now. That's why we have to set these boundaries. And stick to them."

"That's also why," Mom said, looking down at her darkening tea, but still not drinking it, "we've made an appointment for you and Dean to go and see a therapist."

"You think we're crazy?" I squeaked.

"No, of course not," Dad said. He came over to stand beside me, and put his arm around my shoulders. "We believe you. We know what you've experienced is real. That's the whole point. You need help dealing with what has happened. Gaining superpowers, challenging your entire view of reality—it's kind of a big deal, dear."

"Having someone professional to talk to about things can be really helpful for anyone. Counselling will help you understand how you're really feeling when all your feelings seem to blend into a confusing mess."

I didn't like the idea. It felt like a betrayal, despite them saying they believed me. It felt like they were saying I was broken, or wrong, and that I needed fixing. Defensively, I muttered, "What I need is to find a way to control my powers. Will they be able to help with that? Can I even tell them about my powers or will they lock me up?"

Mom and Dad looked at each other. "You'll have to skirt around the superpowers detail. We still think it's best that stays between us, professional confidentiality or otherwise. But they still might be able to help you. You said your powers are based on emotions, and who better to help you understand emotions than a therapist?"

I nodded begrudgingly. Maybe there was something to it. I had no other plans yet on how to even start getting my powers under control. It wasn't like my parents could find an empath specialist to send me to. They had to find the next best thing. They were trying their hardest. I was just too riled up to appreciate it.

"Okay. Fine. I'll go. I guess it might be good for Dean, too. In other ways."

I wondered if he'd ever had counseling when his mother got sick and died. I doubted it. All their family's money had gone to her medical care; there probably wasn't anything left for Dean.

And maybe a counselor could help me get my powers under control. Maybe there was a cure there. Was that what my parents wanted after all? Maybe they thought I could be cured entirely, and go back to being their normal girl again.

But there was no going back for me. I had changed.

Forever.

5

The next day at school brought with it another history class, and another lesson with Ash. He was hovering near the door when Dean and I arrived, and I made sure Dean got a seat right beside me this time. I was still sour at Ash for making me miss the bus. Whether he'd meant it or not, he'd caused a risky situation. So far, no one had come up to me at school to ask why I could run at super-speed though, so fingers crossed on that front.

Ash followed us over, and I smiled when another girl, Roxy, took the remaining seat on my other side. But then Ash outright asked if he could swap with her.

I tried to signal her with a shake of my head but she'd already grabbed her books, grinning at Ash, happy to do as the cute new guy asked. She hung around to flirt with him a bit more, but he'd already turned to talk to me. Roxy flopped down in a seat diagonally behind us.

"You disappeared on me yesterday," Ash said, sounding disappointed.

Groan. I tried to tell myself Ash was just a normal guy. Any weirdness was probably coming from him being eager to make friends in a new place. But I didn't need any more complication in my life right now. I wanted things to be as simple as possible.

I brushed some dust off my table and pretended I didn't hear him. Where was Mr. Jones? What was taking him so long?

The classroom was a noisy mix of a dozen different conversations. Half the kids in the class were away from their seats, talking to their friends, sitting on desks, or playing catch with balled up paper.

"You're really strong, you know that?" Ash said.

I spun towards him. What did he know? Had he seen?

He watched me, and there was something more calculating now in that cheery grin of his. His eyes searched mine and I frowned. *Damnit, boy, stop being so suspect!*

"Ash, this is Dean," I deflected. I almost added *'my boyfriend,'* but I didn't know if we were label-ready. "Have you met each other yet?"

Dean waved politely and reached out a hand. Ash met it and they shook hands behind my chair. My heart sank. Making new friends was something Dean really did need. I just wasn't sure if Ash was the best option. I didn't miss the way Ash shivered when he came into contact with Dean. It didn't help me lay to rest my questions and suspicions. Still, I tried to get the two of them talking, mostly so I could avoid Ash, as I flicked more dust off my desk.

What was with the dust?

I looked up to see a small crack in the ceiling above me. A thin stream of dust trickled continuously down to my desk like a gossamer waterfall.

I pushed my chair back slowly, staring at the crumbs of ceiling hitting my desk. My heart thumped.

A letter-sized piece of plasterboard crashed down onto my desk loud enough to shut the whole room up.

Then the whole roof came down.

Fear crashed into me like a tsunami. Dean had either stopped blocking out of shock, or the sheer quantity of terror was enough to turn on my powers in a big way even with him nearby.

Pain shot through me, and I winced, fighting against it. I had to act, but had maybe only seconds before the level of emotions I was absorbing would be too much.

Time seemed to slow to a crawl, but it was really me, moving faster, thinking faster, seeing faster. *I could make these seconds count.*

The roof was collapsing right into the center of the room. Dean, Ash, Roxy, four other kids and me were directly underneath it.

I shoved the chair out from under me, jumping to my feet. I kicked out, hard, at the desk in line with the students in danger. One, two, three were caught up in a tangle as desk-hit-student-hit-chair-hit-desk, skidding them across the room. Probably bruising and winding them too. *Better than the alternative.*

Movement flickered in the corner of my eye and I saw Roxy, Ash, and one other boy were safe under the teacher's sturdier desk.

The rest of the class had made it to the edges of the room, shielding their heads with their arms from the smaller debris.

There were just Dean and I left. I gritted my teeth, trying to stay focused. *Dean.* My heart pounded his name as my eyes searched for him through the growing cloud of dust and greenness of fear overwhelming my system.

Dean moved in slow motion, reaching out to me. I reached out to him in return and sped the two of us into a corner. Our bodies pressed together, as though we were each trying to be a human-shield for the other. His blocking power returned. I gasped in relief as the empathic intensity lessened and time returned to normal speed.

The ceiling that had seemed to hover for those few split seconds crashed down like thunder. Plasterboard, concrete, and roof tiles hurtled down all around us.

I hope no one was left under there. Clouds of dust rose as the sound of falling debris softened into a rain-like patter.

Mr. Jones appeared in the doorway. "What on earth? Is everyone okay?"

I could see him do a headcount around the room and I followed his gaze, counting as well. Chalky dust hung in the air, making it hard to see, but everyone was clear. A few students cradled sore spots on heads and waists where either the debris or the sliding desks had hit them. A couple of kids were crying.

The largest slab of roof that came down heavy lay flat on the floor with nothing under it, no human pancakes in sight. *I did that*, I thought proudly. *I saved us.*

"Out," Mr. Jones yelled. "Calm and quick. Leave your bags." He split his attention between ushering the class out of the room and yelling down the hall for another teacher to call in emergency services.

Our class had just made it outside when we heard sirens.

Ambulance, police, and an emergency rescue vehicle showed up within moments of each other. We were all giddy. The shock and adrenaline of the event—and the lack of serious casualties— turned into teenage excitement, and everyone was gossiping and recounting their version of events.

EMTs began triaging kids, dealing with those who'd taken something to the head first. Some were given oxygen to help with their breathing.

Dean had a small gash on his forearm, and was taken into an ambulance to get it cleaned and dressed. I hoped he'd get them to have a quick look at his wound site too, in case he'd strained it. I tried to go with him, but had already been checked over and given the all clear, and had to remain away from the medical workers.

I recognized Terry, mingling around and checking up on everything. It didn't make much sense for him to be there now he was a detective, but he always was very 'community minded,' as Dad would say. He saw me too and waved. I wiggled my fingers and smiled awkwardly in return, not really wanting everyone here to see I was friends with a cop. I turned my attention to my phone so it seemed I was busy, and there was a text there from Nati.

Nati: OMGGGGGGGGEE gurl! You OK? They won't let

us in that part of the school. Kids saying the whole building is flat *Crying*

I typed out a quick reply, reassuring her everyone was all right. When I looked up, Terry was there anyway.

"Hi, Detective Pence," I said, as politely as I could.

He smiled and brushed at some dust on his uniform where a kid must have bumped against him. "Olivia. So glad you're okay. Especially after how upset your parents were due to your last little adventure." He grinned perfect teeth at me as though we were co-conspirators and he wasn't just rubbing salt into my guilt. He always put on the buddy-cop performance though, and with his sparkling eyes, blond hair and million-dollar smile, sometimes he sold it.

"It seems as though the earthquake damaged parts of the school's roof—more than anyone realized," he started explaining to me as I fidgeted on the spot, hoping he'd move on. "Really lucky there were no serious injuries. Really lucky."

"Yeah. Lucky." My mind raced. I hoped what I did back in the room hadn't been too obvious, too visible to everyone in the class. Did they see me kick out and push the desks? Was I moving fast enough to be unnoticeable, or just fast enough to look like I was moving weirdly fast? One kid who had been right beside me was walking with a limp. It must have been from where the desk hit him. He didn't seem to be paying me any attention, and just seemed happy and no doubt shocked that he wasn't under a pile of rubble right now.

And then there was Ash.

I looked around the covered learning area where we'd evacuated to and spotted Roxy talking to another police officer. She was gesturing wildly about what had happened, and saw her point at Ash. I frowned. I'd seen something move fast in the room. At a time when everything normal seemed to be going in slow motion.

Ash was making a phone call and then turned to leave. I wasn't sure if any of us were supposed to be going yet. But part of me was glad he wasn't sticking around for questioning as I wondered again what his deal was.

"Yeah. I don't know what happened," I said, covering for myself and maybe Ash as well. "We were all just really lucky."

Terry nodded, flashed his grin again, and moved on to talk to some teachers.

"Hey," Dean said from behind me. I turned and almost threw myself into his arms, until I saw the bandage wrapping one of them.

"You okay?" I asked instead, putting my hands in my pockets and hoping I hadn't leaned too awkwardly close to Dean.

"Fine. Was just worried about you. But you saved all of us." Dean's voice was low, just for me. He held my gaze intensely, and gave me a single nod.

"I, ah, I don't think it was me only."

Dean looked across to the school gates, dropping his voice even more. "Maybe, yeah. You think Ash is an empath?"

"*For sure* an empath!" I whispered back, relieved to be on the same page.

"What does that mean? Trouble?"

I opened my mouth, but didn't have an answer. Ash wasn't just displaying a reaction to Dean's presence. He'd *used* his powers. Maybe it was just on instinct, the very first time they had kicked in for him. It didn't seem that way to me, though. And while he seemed nice and friendly, I'd been tricked by people masking their true selves before.

"I don't know," I said. "We'll just have to wait and see, and be ready."

6

Dean took off his motorbike helmet. "You keep on making me break your parents' rules."

I could hardly hear him through the helmet I wore. My hands were still on his hips from the ride and we'd just pulled up into the parking lot outside of The Bellscroft Mental Healthcare Facility. Or as I called it, *The Asylum*.

The psychologist we were meant to be seeing did counselling out of an office here and the whole thing just made me feel even more like my parents really did think I was insane. Even though they kept referring to her as a counsellor, and our visits as counselling, I had visions of electro-shock therapy in my future.

EMOTIONALLY UNSTABLE

"Don't worry, they won't find out," I bluffed, worrying that my parents always seemed to have ways of knowing, like they could read my mind. Or maybe I was just never as covert as I thought I was.

I pushed at my helmet, the snug fit making it feel like my head was going to pop off along with it. Dean hopped off the bike and helped me. I shook out my hair and smiled. It had been a fun ride, and a good excuse to lean into Dean and feel his warmth as we rode down through town. My parents had wanted to take us to our first meeting, but it was straight after school and they were working, so I said we'd catch the bus directly to the appointment. Then we conveniently forgot until we were back at home, and with no busses scheduled for another half hour, Dean's bike seemed like a better option than being late to our first appointment. I didn't want it to seem like we were avoiding going. I was sure that would be a psychologically red flag.

The grounds of the facility were nice, and not at all creepy or foreboding like I'd imagined. Set on a large block downtown, there were high fences, but inside neat gardens surrounded an art-deco era mansion that, despite being old, was more welcoming than spooky.

"Ready?" Dean asked.

"As I'll ever be. You?"

He nodded, eyes on the building.

Both of us had been shaken up by the roof collapse at school. On its own, it didn't seem like a huge event compared to what else we'd been through, but it was a bit like the straw on the camel's massive pile of trauma.

I spent most of the night afterwards in my comfiest clothes, eating crisps dipped in ice cream, and alternating between hugs with my teary, relieved parents and snuggles on the couch with Dean. I had nuzzled up next to him and he'd, somewhat stiffly, put his arm around me. In some ways, he seemed more distant, colder than he had been when we'd first met, but I was starting to understand that that was how he dealt with things like this. Things like *yet another near miss of losing someone he loved.*

That thought alone warmed me—maybe I was someone he loved. I had planted one kiss on his shoulder, then let him be as we'd watched cartoons together.

That was a week ago, and I knew in some ways we were both looking forward to having a chat with a counsellor. The trauma was real. But I also had no idea what to expect. Would it be like on TV shows? Would she ask me, 'How does that make you feel?' a lot? I guessed I was about to find out.

A pleasant woman with wiry black hair directed us from

the front desk, down a corridor to where we'd find the waiting room. On the way, I couldn't help but snoop, arching my neck and peering down side corridors or into rooms, curious about what really happened in places like this. It all seemed very normal, a bit like a regular hospital, but there were less outward signs of illness—less IV stands and bandages, and more comfy chairs and social areas. The people were mostly calm, and seemed content, if quiet. We passed an elderly man with hollow, glazed eyes being helped down the corridor by a nurse, and a shiver ran down my spine.

"Is it cold in here?" I asked Dean.

"Not really."

I glanced back at the old man and frowned. He had an identification tag with what looked like medical care notes clipped to his chest, but all I could read was *Holbrook*.

We reached the waiting room and I was called in right away. Dean gave me a searching look and a small nod, which I returned, adding a half-smile.

The counsellor said, "Call me Debbie," and welcomed me into her office.

She was a tiny woman with a sweet face made quirky by eyes that were slightly too close together. She gestured to one of the two simple office chairs in the room and took a seat.

Beside me was a glass of water and a box of tissues. Certificates hung on the walls, books on psychology filled shelves around the room, and a few baskets of toys sat in the corner, probably for her younger patients.

The session was ... interesting. Debbie got me talking, just prompting me to chat through everything that had happened. I stuck to the mundane details and left out anything beyond normal. I did tell her that there were things that had happened that seemed ... *strange*, that I couldn't explain, as backup for the likely case my story didn't add up. I thought that would be when she started scribbling secret notes about my sanity, but she said it was to be expected. Trauma could often leave people confused about what was real and what they experienced, make them seek fantasy excuses for terrible events.

Even with Dean just out in the waiting room, I was still picking up a lot of emotions in the building. It made me twitchy and I rambled. Debbie just listened, sometimes asking me to explain a bit more or giving me a moment to think about *how it made me feel*. I wasn't sure how that was going to help me, but I thought it did. I even used the tissues, twice. The session was a lot like on TV and also not. And it was over before I knew it.

I tag-teamed Dean, and as he walked in and closed the door,

part of me wished I could hear what he would say. How much would he open up? Would he reveal more to Debbie than he did to me? Would he simply state the facts or would he let some emotion break free?

My strange counsellor-related jealousy was banished by a commotion down the hallway. It was the first sign of trouble I'd seen since we arrived, the sort of cliché I was expecting from a horror-style institution. Three very flustered nurses were struggling to subdue a small boy—or was it a girl? Someone petite and blond and from this distance, very non-binary.

Red emotion swirled around all of them. The heat of the nurse's anger reached me and my muscles tensed and grew strong. I felt like I could punch a hole in the wall, and part of me wanted to, just to release the tension of all this power.

The kid was given an injection of some kind, calmed quickly, then was ushered away. How did one small person need three big men to hold them down? I was worried that I knew exactly how.

By feeling the way anger just made me feel.

I was on my feet, but they were already gone. I couldn't risk following or I'd get too far away from Dean.

I sat down again, my heart racing. Was that kid an empath? And the old man before who gave me chills … was he a blocker?

Or was I looking for paranormal answers to regular events? Was I seeing empaths everywhere, in Ash, in the people here? Maybe the kid was an addict in a drug-fueled rage. Maybe I just felt cold. It could all be nothing.

But I couldn't get past the worries. If no one had explained my empath powers to me, how sane would I feel right now?

My thoughts were still spinning when Dean's session finished and he came out. His eyes seemed red around the edges and I wanted to hug him, but instead just stood close enough that our hands touched.

We both thanked Debbie and made our way to the exit. I bumped my snooping up a notch, but didn't see anything else suspicious.

"I think I saw an empath in there," I told Dean almost bashfully when we reached his bike.

He looked thoughtful for a moment. "You think they don't know what they are?"

He understood right away, which made me even more certain I was on the right track. "If we didn't know what we were, what was happening with our bodies and emotions, I think I might be a permanent resident in there too."

"What can we do?" Dean asked.

EMOTIONALLY UNSTABLE

I groaned. "I don't know. I'm not even sure it is what I think it is. I guess we wait and watch again. Maybe next time we can try and talk to them, if that's allowed. I get the feeling the rules might be strict about that sort of thing." I felt hopeless. I wanted to help, but didn't even know where to start. This seemed so much bigger than pushing some kids out from under a falling ceiling.

We'd taken the wait-and-see approach with Ash, but hadn't even seen him again since naming our suspicions. Which was odd in itself, unless he also hadn't known what he was, and was gone because he wasn't coping with the experience of finding out about his powers. I pouted like a very sad clown.

"You'll work something out." Dean handed me my helmet. "Since we're breaking rules anyway, I think I know what might cheer you up. Something I know you enjoy."

"What?" I asked, my fingers lingering on his as I took the helmet from him.

"Flying." Dean put his helmet on and swung his leg over the bike. He slid to the back of the seat, and patted the spot in front of him. "I'll show you how."

My grin in return was massive and mischievous.

7

School took a while to return to normal after the ceiling collapse.

Everyone wanted the full story from those of us in the room, and rumors had spread about Ash, who hadn't returned to school since. Mostly from Roxy, who was obviously pining for him. She believed he was the one who saved everyone's lives through some kind of martial arts prowess, which I thought seemed like stereotyping.

But maybe I was stereotyping by thinking he could also be an empath. Him and the people at the institute. I felt like I was seeing empaths everywhere and I doubted they'd be that common. Maybe it was like Debbie said—I was seeing the paranormal in the normal because of the trauma I'd been through.

Nati, Dean, and I had a free period at the end of the day and even though we spent most of it in study room, we still ended up down at the bus stop before any supervising teachers or most of the other students. Nati normally drove home since she owned her own car, but that car was a beat-up relic which frequently found itself at the mechanics to stay roadworthy. I was quietly grateful for more time with her.

Dean had been holding my hand since we left class. A detail neither I nor Nati found small. I wondered if the counselling had anything to do with this huge-for-Dean public display of affection. Nati found it squee-worthy and practically skipped around us as we waited at the school gates, like she was about to break into the K-I-S-S-I-N-G song any moment.

"I can cover for you guys if you want some alone time. I am an awesome lookout for make-out-stopping interruptions."

Dean's hand tensed, and I remembered our last attempt at making out. "Thanks, Nati. We're okay for now."

Nati gave me a look up and down, then gave Dean a look up and down. "Oh hi, hot teenage girl. Oh hi, hot teenage boy. How are you two not smushed together twenty-four-seven? This sexual tension is driving me insane and I'm just a bystander."

Yeah, I knew how she felt. Where Dean's hand sat in mine, the gentle pressure of his fingers around mine, it seemed to set my whole body on fire. I wanted more, and I knew I couldn't have it.

"Nati, I love you, but seriously, just drop it, okay? There's other stuff going on than just ... just drop it."

As if I'd been talking to him, Dean let go of my hand.

Nati frowned, realizing she'd gone too far. She pouted, widened her arms into a hug position, and baby-stepped toward me.

I accepted her silent apology and hugged her back.

She let go then turned to Dean, her pout now cheeky. "You get one too!"

Dean had no chance of escape as Nati wrapped around him. Dean begrudgingly accepted her hug, and even patted her awkwardly on the back.

I was chuckling quietly at them when I heard a vehicle pull up behind me and the sliding sound of a van door.

Hands grabbed at me, locking around my arms.

I was dragged off my feet. Nati and Dean broke their hug, shock all over their faces. Two figures in black SWAT-team-style outfits dragged me toward a gray van. *I told you so!* My brain announced with ironic triumph, over my fear.

The surprise dropped Dean's blocking away, and I was hit with a wall of energy as he no longer subdued my rampant powers.

"Livvy!" Dean and Nati yelled in unison.

Dean tried to get to me and one of my assailants knocked him flat onto the concrete. "Dean!" I screamed, furious they'd hurt him. I tried to fight back, but the attackers were strong. *Super* strong. I was hefted and thrown into the back of the van. I landed with a thud. The door closed.

I screamed, lashing out at the door, trying to pull it open. I cracked the interior panel with my fist and felt the metal bend underneath my pressure. The engine rumbled, and I was thrown to the side as we sped away. Away from Dean, way too fast.

My vision blurred with streams of colorful energy, emotional auras and power rushing into me unchecked. I turned to the closest threat and threw a punch. They blocked with their forearm and I felt it crack. The van spun around a corner and my next hit missed. My mind buzzed, swirled, faded.

I cried out as the waves of emotion became too much. I flailed, fighting the air. The attackers grabbed at me again, two, maybe three of them working together, and I was pinned facedown, just in time for the seizure to hit.

Darkness took me.

I gasped back into consciousness. My head ached, but was clear. My mouth tasted of blood.

I was … lying on a mattress? In a weird, sterile space. It was an odd room, like an office or meeting room, but set up with a simple metal-framed bed, basic kitchenette, and a table and chairs. My hands weren't bound in any way, and I reached straight for my pocket, where my phone should have been, and found it gone.

Ash sat on the table, his feet on one of the chairs, hands clasped over his knees, watching me.

I sat up slowly. A low level of energy hummed inside me, but I could sense almost no anger or fear or any strong emotion nearby. It was as though Ash was the only person for hundreds of feet around, and he was eerily calm.

I wasn't.

"Ash? WHAT THE ACTUAL FLEEP?" I rubbed my forehead where a small bump had risen. "Did you get kidnapped too? Who were those guys?"

"Hey Livvy," he said, like we were best friends. He smiled his cheery grin, but the calculation in his eyes remained. "Time we had a proper talk."

"A *talk*? You … did you do this? Did you seriously just have me kidnapped to have a talk?" I couldn't make sense of why I was here, and why Ash was here, or where *here* was. There were no windows or clues as to our location. *What in blue-blaze-balls is going on?*

"Since you found out I'm a proesthian too, there's no point trying to hide it. Not for either one of us."

My confusion made me squint. "A pro-what?"

Ash frowned very slightly. "A proesthian."

I stared blankly.

"A primal?" he tried again.

I blinked, continued staring, frowned.

"An empath?"

"Oh," I said, before realizing maybe I shouldn't give him confirmation I understood even that much.

"There we go." Ash hopped down off the table and walked up in front of me. "You don't seem to know much about empaths. But you like them, don't you?"

My hands became fists. Did he mean Dean? Did they, whoever *they* were, kidnap Dean too? He must be here somewhere, otherwise I'd still be a twitching drooling mess. Was he in another room nearby?

I swung my legs off the bed and stood face-to-face with Ash. He suddenly seemed older, smarter, than he ever did at school. He squared his shoulders to mine.

SELINA A. FENECH

"Where is Dean? Did you and your mercs kidnap him, too?"

"Why would we—?" Ash frowned, and rubbed his temples. "Look, I'm sorry about how we had to get you here. But I needed to be alone with you, and you were never alone. But now we are, just you and me. You know I'm like you. Isn't there … anything you want from me?"

SERIOUSLY? The word flashed in my mind in giant neon letters. "Even not counting the abduction, I'm really not interested in you in that way."

Ash half sighed, half chuckled. "I didn't mean …"

What else could he mean? "Oh, like information or training or something? Is this some kind of weird superpower hazing thing? You need to quit with the cryptic because I'm just not getting onboard here."

Ash's shoulders dropped. He must have been tense. His whole body had been on guard. From me?

He turned and looked up into the corner of the room. I followed his gaze and noticed a camera. He talked directly to it. "My assessment stands. I don't think we've got the right one. She seems completely clueless."

"Insult me like I'm not standing right here. Why not?" I muttered.

A loud, mechanical unlocking sound came from the door and

290

it opened. A man and woman wearing suits came in, both pale-skinned and grim-faced. Weirdly, they were followed by an Asian girl who looked about twelve years old and far too colorful for the situation. Before they closed the door, I saw a glimpse of half a dozen adults in the SWAT-style uniforms in the hall outside. They looked as if they were ready to make a move, and yet also somehow really calm. So much for it being just Ash and me. And so weird that I couldn't sense their emotions.

The woman held a tablet device which showed the camera-angle view of the room we were in. She swiped it closed only after I'd seen it, as though she wanted me to know they'd been watching.

I looked carefully at her and the man.

I knew them. I'd seen them before. I raced through my memory, trying to work out where I knew their faces, and it pinged. They were the couple from the hospital who I saw looking over Jake, Donny, and Jamie.

My confusion levels were epic, and fear also started to shake me up. What had I gotten myself into? Myself and Dean? This was some serious shady organization stuff.

I giggled nervously. "Is this the part where you give me some answers, or the part where you make me disappear?"

The woman gave me a chilling look. "Take a seat."

I dropped into a chair like an obedient puppy. The older

couple sat down across from me and Ash and the girl stood behind them. The girl seemed super calm. Not calm in the nearly robotic way Dean seemed sometimes, but in a really chilled and contented way that made me feel good inside too. Her My Little Pony multi-colored pastel hair and lemon-yellow cardigan also made me happy.

But If I knew only one thing, I knew I was dealing with empaths here. Ash definitely—the guys in the van, probably. The girl, maybe. What kind of empaths, I wasn't sure, now there were empaths and blockers and pro-whatsies on the table apparently too.

I couldn't trust my feelings. I had to stay alert. I hadn't been restrained or bound in any way, but the door had made a locking sound again when it closed. I didn't know if I was some kind of prisoner, or if I'd be free to get up and leave. The SWAT guys could still be outside, and I wasn't sure I could take them all on. My powers felt weird. Different to when Dean was keeping them subdued. More low-level, like there was nothing around to draw from rather than actually being turned off.

So for now I would sit and see what these people had to say.

"You can call me Dr. Crossman," the woman said. With her pin-up hair style and lazily beautiful face, she looked like she'd just walked out of a detective noir movie. What kind of doctor was she? "And this is Mr. Crossman," she said, gesturing to the man.

I confirmed wedding rings on both of them. I thought they gave off a couple sort of vibe, a bit like Bonny and Clyde might.

Mr. Crossman had a clean-cut boy-scout type appearance, thick black hair, and a sparkle in his eye that didn't seem wholesome and boy-scout like at all. "You've probably worked out by now that Ash was placed in your classes to observe you. His empath powers were revealed during the roof-collapse incident so we had to pull him from the mission, but we weren't finished assessing your risk. That's why we decided to bring you in."

Beyond Ash being an empath, I hadn't worked anything out. But I liked that they thought so highly of my deductive abilities. "And have you finished assessing my *risk* now?"

Dr. Crossman held my gaze in a way that unnerved me. "We're hunting for an empath who has been stealing power from others."

My chest grew tight. They must know what I did to Jake, Jamie, and Donny. *That's why I'm here. For … punishment?*

I rambled. "I'm not, I mean, I didn't mean to. I didn't want to steal anything." Panic made my vision swim. I jerked to my feet; my chair fell back. But the door was locked, I was surrounded, there was no window, no escape.

The girl moved quickly to me and put a hand on my arm and one on my face, turning it toward her. "Shh, it's okay."

"Careful, Rayni," Ash said, following her to my side. They had matching accents.

"We're okay, aren't we?" Rayni smiled up at me. Golden-yellow contentment and calm swirled around her and washed over me. It pushed into me so forcefully that it seemed to force out all other emotions, like a rainbow cloud leaving me.

The panic faded. I could feel my emotions dulling, my adrenaline wearing off. I tried to fight it, to stay in charge of how I felt, but the calm pushed back harder. Ash righted my chair, and I drifted back down into it.

"She's a strong one." Rayni seemed out of breath, and stayed at my side, one hand on my arm. This was nice. She was nice. Everything was okay. *Golden.* My eyelids drooped half-closed.

"Thanks, Rayni," Dr. Crossman said. "As I was saying, we are trying to track down an empath who is hurting other empaths, taking their powers. We wanted to test you by giving you a situation that, if you were our target, you couldn't resist."

In my calm came a sort of clarity. "You used Ash for bait? Was he trying to get me to drain him?"

"He was perfectly safe; we were monitoring the whole thing."

EMOTIONALLY UNSTABLE

I remembered the camera and the men outside, and nodded as though it made perfect sense. I could feel the small pressure in the pit of my gut from my emotions silently screaming. "But Ash said I'm not the one?"

"You clearly didn't have any idea what was going on," Ash confirmed.

"But you have drained empaths before," Dr. Crossman said coldly.

I nodded, and my eyelids started to slip closed. My breathing was short and shallow, like my body had decided it wasn't necessary anymore. Everything was okay.

Ash grabbed my shoulder before I faceplanted on the desk. "Rayni, ease up a bit."

"Omigod, I'm so sorry! She's just so strong. I haven't pushed that hard before."

My emotions eased back under my own control. The fear and panic and worry, the confusion and disgust that these adults had used Ash as bait, all became my own again. Followed by the anger that they were holding me here, that they'd kidnapped me, and that I didn't know what they would do to me next.

"What are you doing to me?" I wanted to cry.

Rayni looked genuinely upset, flushing a sickly aqua-blue aura, her lips quivering. She looked entirely like the child she was. She quickly got her emotions under control again and returned to a calm state. But whatever she'd done a moment ago she wasn't doing anymore, not to the same levels. I wasn't being smothered.

"Rayni is here because of your reaction to us acquiring you." Mr. Crossman said.

"Kidnapping me," I muttered.

"We know absorbing additional powers can result in heightened emotions and unstable behavior. Rayni's emogen ability is helping to keep you level, and keeping those around us level so you aren't drawing in too much. Frankly, we're amazed you've done so well on your own so far."

Every answer they gave raised a dozen new questions and I wasn't keeping up. So Dean wasn't here somewhere? Did they not know about him? Rayni was the one keeping me from frothing on the floor? What in empath-land was an emogen?

I didn't have time to ask anything before Mr. Crossman picked up the tablet device and opened a screen showing footage from the bank shooting. He swiped across and there was a police report from the fireman I saved. He swiped again, and kept swiping, and there were photos of the park marked out with crime-scene tape and evidence flags, and a video of Jamie, Jake, and Donny in hospital beds. And then, a surveillance camera view of the park. That night, with me fighting the others, tearing their emotions from their bodies. I could see Dean lying still in the foreground of the video. I watched with my mouth open and tears started running down my cheeks. There was no visual sign on the video of the emotions leaving them, no glow or aura the camera could see, but the moment was clear. One by one, they dropped to the ground.

"How did you get that? Why don't the police—why don't they know?" My voice was hushed with guilt and sadness.

"We made sure this video disappeared before the police could get it."

They covered it up. These people, this organization, whatever it was—they hid evidence. And what else? Detective Phillips seemed to give up on me so easily, and after the bank, none of what happened had made the news. *That was just the sort of manipulation organized empaths could perform.*

Dr. Crossman softened a little. "The video always seemed to tell the story of a girl fighting for self-defense. And then things went too far. We've known of the criminal actions of this group for some time, and it's clear you got caught up in it and were only with them briefly. But still, we wanted to be sure that what we saw was true. Sometimes images lie. Maybe you were the one infiltrating their group, manipulating their actions in order to steal their powers."

I shook my head and a tear splattered on the table. The Crossmans clearly knew everything. There was no point denying what I'd done. But they didn't seem to know anything about Dean, so I made sure to keep him out of it. "I didn't mean to do it. I didn't even know what I was doing. I'd only known about empaths for barely a week, and I know nothing about emogens or proessie-thingies or any of this. I don't even know how I took from them what I did. I'd give it all back if I could. I'd do anything to give it back."

Dr. Crossman gave me a piercing look. "I hope you really mean that. Come with me. I need to show you something." She stood up from the table, and that seemed to signal everyone else in the room to move as well.

The Crossmans left the room first and I followed after them, with Ash and Rayni behind me. As we headed out into the corridor, the people on guard there separated to let us through, and then followed along behind as well. *Guess I'm still not entirely trusted yet.*

Wherever they were taking me, they were taking me there silently. The halls we walked down were plain, like they belonged to an office building or budget motel, and all doors were closed, so I couldn't sticky beak. We reached an elevator and, based on the internal buttons, this building was a decent size, taller than any in Bellscroft. We were on the sixth floor of ten.

Mr. Crossman pressed the button for the first floor, and addressed the SWAT team. "We should be fine from here."

I eyed him and wondered what type of empath he was, now I knew that empaths had types. With Rayni keeping my emotional levels subdued, I wasn't sure I'd be able to beat even her and Ash if it came to a violent getaway, let alone two expert adult empaths of whatever type the Crossmans were.

The elevator opened up to another plain hallway and we headed off to the right. Mr. Crossman stopped at a double door and swung one open, letting Dr. Crossman then myself through first. I held my breath, waiting to see where they had led me. I half expected it would be my prison cell.

Instead, I saw what looked like an intensive care ward.

A dozen hospital beds were laid out next to each other. On seven of the beds lay lifeless bodies.

Machines hummed along near each patient, reading vital signs and providing nutrients through feeding tubes. Half hidden behind a partition curtain, a nurse worked on massaging and exercising one of the patient's legs. He saw us come in, nodded to Dr. Crossman, then left us in privacy.

"What is this place?" I whispered. "Who are these—?"

299

People, I was about to ask, then I saw the beautiful face of the body closest to me. *Jake.* His re-growth-streaked blond hair lay greasy and flat against his head.

My eyes darted around, confirming my suspicions. *Jamie. Donny.* They were all there. My heart pounded, flighty, like a scared rabbit.

Something rubbed past my leg and I jumped nearly three feet into the air.

"Mew." A black and white cat circled us, as though greeting me, Ash, Rayni and the Crossmans.

No one else seemed confused or surprised by the cat. *Oookay.*

Dr. Crossman, who until now had been so composed I hadn't seen a hint of color on her, started to show wisps of blue sadness. "These are the three empaths you drained. And four more, drained by someone else."

That was why the Crossmans were at the hospital. They must have gone there to collect the three of them, to bring them here.

"Each of the other four were found one at a time. When you drained these three all at once, it didn't fit the pattern, but we had to be sure. Finding the leech is our biggest priority."

"There's someone out there with four other empath's powers?"

My voice cracked. How were they even functioning? I couldn't say too much about my own case without letting on about Dean, but I had so many questions.

"At least four. There have been a couple of other empath disappearances where we couldn't locate and confirm the cause. But we are sure the leech is actively hunting and absorbing other empaths' powers."

I glanced at Ash, no longer cheery, and Rayni, so young beside me, and shivered. "What can I do?"

"We want you to try and restore the empaths you have drained. If it can be proven possible, there is hope for the other four as well. If we can discover the identity of the leech and capture them."

"Do you think it's possible?" If it was, then all the intensity would stop. I could be myself again. I could be with Dean. I was hopeful, but I was also still ticked off at the whole kidnapping thing. These people had hurt me, and there was no telling what they would do in the future. What would they do if I simply wasn't able to do what they asked? "I really know nothing about what happened. I didn't even know what type of empath I was before today, or that there were other types."

"There's a lot you don't know," Mr. Crossman said. "If you agree to help, we can train you, teach you everything. Maybe we can find a solution."

"What about you? I mean, you're obviously the expert empaths here. Why can't you try and do something?"

Dr. Crossman and Mr. Crossman both stiffened. I knew I'd said the wrong thing, but I had no idea what it was. She stood beside Jamie's bed, and her hand rested on the mattress near his shoulder. The blue aura of sadness around her intensified and flowed towards me. It almost buckled my knees and I bit back a sob. Rayni also winced, noticing my reaction, and Dr. Crossman's aura dulled.

"We're doing all we can." Mr. Crossman reached into his pocket and pulled my phone out, then handed it back to me. A quick glance at the screen showed it had only been about two hours since I was kidnapped, but there were dozens of missed calls and texts from my parents, Dean, and Nati.

"Will you help us?" Dr. Crossman asked.

Rebellion roiled in me. *Why should I help these people who kidnapped me?* A tear rolled down my cheek, thinking of the worry my parents, Dean, and Nati must be feeling for me right now, but also something else. Even with Rayni using her powers to dull the emotions, I could tell Dr. Crossman was intensely sad. The same kind of sadness only caused by losing someone you love. Regardless of what she'd done, I wanted to help her.

"I'll try. But I'm not the only one you need to win over," I said, and met Dr. Crossman's gaze. "If you want me on your team, kidnapping me wasn't the way to go about it. My parents are going to be pissed."

8

I stood at my front door, flanked by the Crossmans. The sun was just starting to set and the flowering lavender in the herb garden swayed in a slight breeze. It was nice to be home. Kidnapped and back before dinner—Limbus were efficient.

Rayni had to come along as well when it had become clear I wasn't coping without her emotion-controlling presence. Ash had apologized for the whole ordeal, and remained behind. I didn't blame him.

It only took one knock on the door for it to burst open, and Mom, who opened it, to burst into tears.

Dad was right behind her, and on the phone. "Terry, she's

home. No. No. Look, I'll call you back," he said.

Dean and Nati spilled out of the house after my parents.

Mom held me. She shook, and swaths of blue sadness flowed off her, replaced with orange and green tones. Relieved, but still worried, almost angry. The colors surrounded us like a blanket.

Nati soon joined in the hug, squeezing past Dad to get in first. "Omigod, that was like something from a movie but it really happened. Did it really happen? Omigod, I don't know how to process this," she said, all in one breath.

Dean stood to the back, still and calm, but something intense filled his eyes. I sighed, happy to be within his blocking aura again. I was worried one of the other empaths would react to his presence, but the Crossmans didn't seem to notice anything. Only Rayni looked a little confused.

A flurry of questions and emotions hit me next. Was I okay? Did they hurt me? Did we need to call the police?

"Yes. No. *No*," I answered as quickly as I could in the short pauses between conversation.

Mom looked warily from me to the Crossmans. "Who are these people? Police? Did they rescue you?"

"Um. No. They're actually the kidnappers." I held my hands up in a pleading 'just hear me out' gesture. "But it's okay. It was sort of a mix-up. They're okay, but we need to have a talk."

"A mix-up? They abducted a child! Broad daylight abduction!" Dad roared.

I held up my pleading hands a bit higher. "They'll explain everything. And you can always call Terry on them if you decide you aren't happy with their explanation." Not that it would do much good, considering how they'd swept evidence of my last adventure away so efficiently.

I reached over and took Nati's hand, squeezing it. "I'll have to tell you all about it later, okay? You should get home; your parents are probably worried too."

She looked teary and overwhelmed. "Only if you think, if you really ..."

"Yeah, it's all good. I'm fine." I smiled my best smile.

"Our driver could give you a ride if you like," Mr. Crossman offered.

"Hells no am I getting a lift with kidnappers! I'll catch the bus, thanks." And after one more tight hug, she was gone.

"Rayni, I'm okay now that I'm home. Feeling much more relaxed. You can take a break. Maybe you can wait in the car?" I suggested, getting concerned she was going to pick Dean as a blocker. She shook her head slightly, as though trying to clear it. Poor thing. She was so young to be involved in this.

She looked to the Crossmans for confirmation. They nodded

and she trotted back down the front yard path between my mom's overgrown herb garden.

"What about the boy?" Dr. Crossman asked, realizing all too easily that I was clearing out people I didn't want to hear this conversation.

"It's okay. He already knows all about me. You've seen the videos; you know who he is. You can trust him."

She didn't look convinced, but nodded and stepped closer to my still frowning parents.

"Dr. Crossman. You can call me Lola." She extended her hand to shake, but my parents looked at her as though she was riddled with leprosy.

"Vincent Crossman." At least he was aware enough to not try and shake their hands. "We apologize sincerely for what you've just endured, but we assure you it was necessary. We had to assess your daughter's risk due to a larger threat we're facing. May we come inside and discuss?"

Dad looked to me. "We can make them leave if you want. Just say."

I sighed. "No, it's okay, really. This is important. Let's go in and talk."

We all took seats around the dining table, and the Crossmans caught my parents up on why I was kidnapped. They spoke a lot more officially with them than they had with me. They were from an *organization* called Limbus, and were seeking a *rogue threat* within the *empath community,* and given my recent activities, they had me marked as a *potential suspect,* and circumstances required I be *forcibly acquired for interrogation.* Same stuff. Bigger words.

"Limbus is dedicated to studying, policing, and training empaths." Dr. Crossman leaned toward my parents across the table. "On record, we work as a freelance spy agency for the government, and as far as the government knows, that's all we do. But Limbus has been a secret empath organization for decades."

"*Secret* being the key word here," Mr. Crossman emphasized. "We expect you understand the importance of keeping the existence of empaths hidden, as it directly affects your daughter."

"We do understand. I also understand you wouldn't be telling us all this if you didn't want something from us or Olivia," Mom said, tapping the table with two fingers.

"Besides our silence on the whole kidnapping affair," Dad muttered.

Dr. Crossman's lips grew thin. She hesitated, then continued her spiel as though she hadn't been interrupted. "Limbus has a science and development division, special agent division, and monitoring division. We offer training in all these areas, which will give your daughter a greater understanding of her talents, and also job opportunities in the long run."

"You mean you want her to sign up with you lot? After you kidnapped her?" Dad's tone was incredulous.

Mr. Crossman replied, "We already have a small group of youths in training at our Bellston Main facility. Olivia is familiar with two of them already. Joining them would be of great advantage to her, and it's better for all empaths to be under the Limbus umbrella, especially with current circumstances."

"Which are?" Mom asked tersely. She tapped her fingertips around her cup of tea, which she hadn't taken a sip of yet.

I answered quickly, hoping hearing it from me would get my parents onboard. "Someone's attacking empaths. Another empath, seeking out and stealing their powers."

My parents leaned back in their chairs, as though pushed away by the words. Dad rubbed the bridge of his nose. "Sounds like a good reason to me to *not* be around other empaths right now."

"Dad, they know so much more than me, like about proesthians, and that there are different kinds of empaths." My eyes strayed over to Dean briefly and then back to my parents before my look could betray him. I was still curious why the Crossmans didn't seem to notice him at all. They hadn't mentioned blockers at all yet. Maybe they didn't know. Maybe Dean was focusing all his blocking on me and making sure not to block them? It was something he'd been able to do in the past, but so far, our levelling up of skills had been hit and miss. Maybe training with Limbus would be good for him, too. Still, I didn't want to reveal him just yet. Just in case it didn't go well. And it should be his choice, either way.

I looked down at my fidgeting fingers, unsure even of what choice I wanted to make myself. "There's just ... so much I don't know."

"Do you even understand the core theory of empath powers?" Dr. Crossman asked. Her tone was curious more than mocking, but I still felt embarrassed when I shook my head.

"As our scientists currently understand it, empaths are a subset of human evolution, with far more advanced adrenal and social-neural receptors. We believe empaths evolved to be protectors within human social groups." Dr. Crossman held my gaze. I could tell this was an area she was passionate about, the science side of things. I couldn't help compare her to Jake, and how little he seemed to know about empaths, and how little he cared to know, beyond what the powers could gain him.

Dr. Crossman continued. "Even from the time we lived in simple tribes, proesthians, like yourself—"

"Primals is the more common term," Mr. Crossman slipped in, like he thought we needed layman's terms.

"*Primals* were always the strongest, fastest warriors in the tribe. Because humans are a community animal, if one member of that community feels scared, it could mean there is danger to be scared of. In that case, being able to move the fastest is a great benefit and could save your life and the lives of others. If there is anger in the community, it's a warlike emotion, and the need to be able to fight might be important, so strength is increased. It's like a super-heightened fight-or-flight response. Primals have the ability to turn the very emotions of the community around them into what they need to protect that group."

"What about happiness? Love?" I asked, reminded of my conversation with Emma when she scoffed at the idea. How would Dr. Crossman respond?

"Happy emotions don't have as much direct physical effect, since a happy tribe doesn't generally signify the presence of a fight-or-flight situation," she said.

I wanted to argue that love had been the emotion that gave me my greatest strength. That beyond fight-or-flight, love was the emotion needed to give you the desire to protect your tribe, and the power.

But I said nothing. They clearly knew a lot more than me

about the science side of it all. I knew I wasn't wrong, but I knew there was so much I still needed to learn. The idea of learning with them gave me mixed feelings.

"You seem to know your stuff," Dad said.

"I've worked hard to do so," Dr. Crossman replied.

Mom finally sipped her tea, then placed the mug down heavily on the table. "I think that's enough for now." Everyone turned to her. "We'll talk about this with Livvy, but right now, I'd like you to leave my house. If Livvy does become involved in Limbus, expect her to come along with a formal complaint about your actions today."

Dad stood up to see them out, the threat in his tone clear. "And that's a really big *if*."

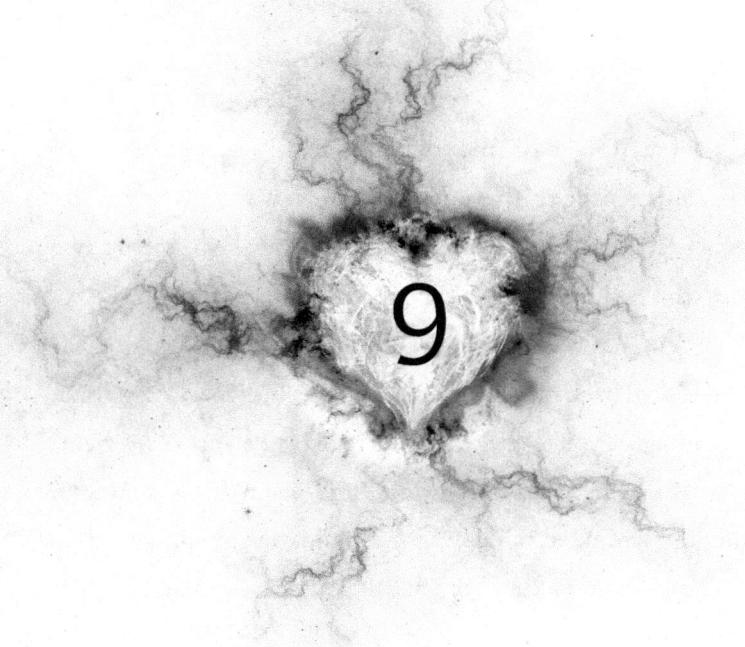

9

Awkward wasn't even close to explaining the thick silence that surrounded us as we sat at the table, waiting for Dad to return. He had walked the Crossmans to the door and was probably letting it hit them on the way out.

I had no idea how I felt, other than bombarded. We'd all been hit with so much information in so little time. I hadn't even mentioned that the Crossmans had also put me in a room with the guy who shot Dean, who was still in the coma I'd put him in, who they wanted me to revive.

The clinking of the teaspoon in Mom's cup reverberated through my skull. Rayni's powers had somehow managed to control my intake of emotion while Dean wasn't around, but it was different to the effect his presence had, and it had exhausted me. Or maybe the exhaustion was the result of having that whole kidnapping thing happen.

"Well, that was an all-new and unnerving experience." My dad walked back into the room with a business card in his hand. "I'm just glad you're back, and you're okay. You are okay, right?"

I looked between him, Mom, and Dean, all watching me intently. I nodded, clutching my hands in my lap so no one could see them shaking. "I'm fine. It scared me at first, obviously, but I get why they did it."

Mom scoffed. "I don't. How hard was it to come to us and talk first?"

I shrugged. "If I was the one they were looking for, they couldn't take the risk of me knowing they knew about me, you know? I mean ..." I rubbed my forehead, trying to soothe my swirling mind and make sense come out of my mouth. "They were just taking precautions until they knew it wasn't me who'd been hunting empaths. This other empath *leech* sounds pretty dangerous."

I remembered all of the bodies lying motionless in the hospital ward—some put there by me, some by the leech—and a chill ran from my neck to my fingertips. I reached out for Mom's hot tea and drank some without even asking. She didn't say a word.

The silence returned as everyone seemed to ponder what *pretty dangerous* really meant in our changed lives.

Mom let out a deep sigh. "I think we need a break." She stood up and clapped her hands. "Come on. We need to get the shop fixed up, and I think we could use a distraction from all things supernatural. A bit of mundane work might give us time to think. If you don't mind helping out, Dean."

"Of course. Whatever you need done."

Dad nodded in approval. "I like that attitude. Lollipop?"

I pouted. Work was the last thing I wanted, with shower and sleep being much higher on my list. But I couldn't let Dean show me up to my own parents. "Sure. Fine."

Mom's emotional color-space had been a sickly green–orange since I'd gotten home, but a fragile stream of yellow happiness shimmered within it now. She waved us off to get ready. "Change into something you don't mind seeing ruined. I want to be on the next bus."

The whole ride to Mom's shop, Dean remained silent. The few times I caught his gaze it was intense, as though I could see right into his soul, see the war between his emotions and his denial of them. No outward sign of those emotions escaped. No wisp of color was visible.

The bus was full, cramped with the grumpy, the irritable, the overworked and the underpaid, smelling of body odor and dirty socks. Dean reached over and laid his hand on mine, pushing his blocking power a little harder, knowing exactly what I needed. Just his touch made me feel better, calmer than before. I mouthed the words, *"Thank you."*

Half the shops along the street were still boarded up after the quake and the damage those kids had done, smashing everything the shaking earth hadn't. Duck Egg Blue's front window had been temporarily replaced with a sheet of plywood, but I could still vividly remember the sounds of shattering porcelain coming from inside the last time I'd been there.

I could still hear Jake's charismatic voice ringing in my ears. *You're like me, like* us.

Inside, the shop had been cleared out. I didn't know how much had been broken and had to be thrown away, and what had been salvaged. I'd missed that potentially heartbreaking stage of the clean-up. There had been some structural damage too, and a couple of tins of paint sat in front of a freshly patched-up wall, along with brushes and rollers.

"Pick your weapon," Mom said, as she cracked open the tin

of blue-green pastel paint.

Dean picked up an edging brush, and I took a roller, my hands too shaky still for anything requiring precision.

For a while, we all painted in silence. Dean seemed to know what he was doing, and his steady hand brushed perfect lines of paint along the edges, his face a picture of meditative calm. He wore one of his usual gray T-shirts, and as he tensed to apply the paint, the muscles on his arms distracted me from my work more than once. While I began as tired and overwrought, soon the repetitive crackle of the roller moving over the wall soothed me. It felt good to put the strength and anger filling my muscles towards something that created a satisfying result.

Mom and Dad worked together on the opposite wall.

I broke the silence, words spilling from my mouth about how being pulled into an unmarked van made me feel, how I still felt bad that I might have hospitalized some of the agents who'd grabbed me, and what Limbus had shared with me about their leech problem.

"They have the people the leech has drained there, on life support. Along with guys from the gang, the ones who—the ones I—" I kept rolling one spot on the wall over and over with a roller long since exhausted of paint. "They want me to try and revive them, because if I can do that, they might have a chance of making the leech revive the others if he or she can be caught."

Dean put his brush down in the roller tray and took a paint rag to wipe where his line had just gone crooked.

Mom came over to tip some more paint into the tray for us. "So they want to train you, teach you, so you can learn how to do that. And it sounds like if you can, it would benefit everyone, maybe save some lives. But that's assuming everything goes the way everyone wants it to—that you learn how to do it, that doing it doesn't hurt you in any way, that those boys can be appropriately dealt with once revived, and that learning to revive them doesn't make you a target for this leech person."

"Wow." I stopped rolling. Mom had already projected consequences into the future much further than I had. "I hadn't really thought about the risks, as usual."

Dad dropped his brush into a bucket of water and wiped his hands clean. "You're a positive thinker, Lollipop, and a helper. And we love that about you. We understand you want to help these people, but we also want you to understand that you don't have to."

I nodded. "I don't know what I want. I'm just a little over-whelmed with things."

"Of course you are. It's been a whirlwind ever since you left the house to help out at the shelter." Mom took the unmoving

318

roller from my hand, then gave me a tight hug. "We're all trying to figure out what our new normal will be. Just take it one day at a time."

One day at a time. I barely make it one minute to the next these days. But it was nice I had time to think about this decision. That I had people to take advice from. I had already raced into one negative experience, between my own yearning impatience and the empathic manipulation Jake had used on me. The very fact I was here, doubting and planning my decision with my parents, softened me to the Crossmans and Limbus some more. From what I felt and guessed, they hadn't even tried to use any compulsion powers on me to affect my choice. I'd felt none of that same warm befuddlement in the Crossmans' presence as I had with Jake.

Mom let me go. We had all stopped painting. Dean's lips were pressed thin and he looked away from me. Dad looked at the two of us, then patted Mom on the back. "Let's go check the inventory in the back room, just you and me."

"Subtle," I mocked, but I was grateful as he led her away.

I sat on the spotted drop sheet and picked paint from my hands. Dean sat beside me.

"You're worried," I guessed. "About the whole Limbus thing."

Dean shrugged. "I don't think that you working with Limbus

would be necessarily a bad thing. But I do worry about you."

And I worried about what him worrying about me did to him. I wanted to show him that loving someone could be a beautiful and happy experience, and not just one filled with pain and the fear of loss. That was hard when I kept getting into dangerous situations. Usually, people said that knowledge was power, but for some reason, with so many decisions in front of me, I felt like knowledge left me vulnerable and scared. How did I know which decisions would keep us from danger? And would they also be the *right* decisions?

"I could learn *so much* from Limbus. I could fix my mistakes."

Dean nodded, his gray eyes shifting back and forth between the floor and me. "Yeah. And if it all works, maybe we could have a ... better relationship."

My eyes immediately darted to him. As confusing as our relationship could be, I knew my heart belonged to him. But I had to admit things between us could be better, and to hear him admit it too was a big deal. "You're right. If I can give these excess powers back, you won't have to be on-duty all the time."

"And maybe I won't have the kiss of death." Dean *blushed*. He actually blushed. What world even was this? I didn't know, because the mention of kissing had wiped my brain clean.

Dean leaned closer to me, reaching out and running his

hand down my arm. "But the question is, what do you want? It's your life."

I desperately wanted the kissing to start again right now, please and thanks.

I gave myself a mental cold shower and closed my eyes, bringing the question into focus. *What do I want?*

It was my life, but it had all felt out of my control until now. Before everything happened, my head had been in the clouds, dreaming of being a superhero.

Now I could really think about my future, and I really wanted to learn how to use my powers to the fullest extent. I wanted to be around people like me, people who weren't going to judge me or think I was crazy or turn out to be criminals. I wanted to make a difference, to help people.

"I'm sitting here weighing it out in my mind, but to be honest, I already know what I want to do. The moment the Crossmans asked me to help, I told them I'd try, and I meant it. I want to go for it. I want to figure out just how far this rabbit hole goes."

Dean half-smiled, but I couldn't feel his happiness. "I thought so."

"Honestly, the hardest part is going to be working out how to explain any of this to Nati." I chuckled.

"I suppose you can't really tell her you're joining a secret superhero organization."

I frowned. I wasn't quite sure I was ready to call them superheroes yet. Not after my mistake assuming that last time with Jake. So far, Limbus had only described their work as dealing with empaths and freelance spy stuff for the government. Even at my tender age, I knew enough to be jaded over what that work could entail. But it still seemed like a good opportunity to learn. "What about you? I don't think Limbus knows about you yet, but I'm sure they'd be interested to get you on their team too."

He shrugged. "I'm not really a team kind of guy."

"You could be."

Dean hesitated, swallowing something down before shaking his head. "What if we hedge our bets? If they turn out to be a society of super-villains I'll be our secret weapon."

"I love a good plan B." The excitement of the afternoon, the thrill of having made a decision, and the surprising development that Dean could *blush* had left me feisty. I leaned forward on my hands and knees, bringing my lips close to Deans. "But let's hope plan A is a success this time. So the kissing can happen again soon."

Dean blushed again, and even the threat of a seizure wouldn't have been enough to keep me from him if my parents hadn't come back into the room right then to announce the working bee was over and pizza on its way.

I groaned at their perfect timing, sure they'd probably been listening in. But pizza sounded amazing, and I felt good knowing what I wanted. "Dad, you still have that business card? I've made my decision."

The Crossmans were openly pleased with my choice, and wanted me to come in again the next day to talk some more and show me around. I was doing mental gymnastics trying to work out how to get there. The Limbus building was an hour's train ride away from Bellscroft, down in the city of Bellston Main. I couldn't ask Dean to chaperone me all the way there and wait around to take me home again, and I couldn't risk him going into the empath beehive in case his powers were recognized.

Thankfully, Mr. Crossman offered to send their driver, and I made a quick decision. "Sure, but could you also send Rayni, if she's available? Just a bit on edge still after last time and might need her to do that calming thing for me again."

"We can probably arrange that." Some muffled noises on the other end of the line could be heard. Something about *class time, child safety,* and *building trust.* "We'll send her, along with her brother, to pick you up."

Dean and I waited outside the school gates the next afternoon. I paced, my backpack full of textbooks swaying on my back, and Dean leaned on the fence and watched.

"I can go with you if you like," he offered.

"And lose our plan B? No, I think you're right about keeping you secret for a bit longer. And remember to hold back, if you can, when they get here too."

A black SUV pulling up in front of us halted my pacing. The back door opened, and Ash and Rayni climbed out.

I raised my eyebrows, looking up and down the street. "What? No super-creepy grab-and-nab this time?"

"Again, super sorry about that," Ash said, with his usual one-thousand-watt grin. My lips twitched, wanting to return that smile. Now I understood him better, I found I missed his cheeriness since he'd stopped coming to school. Since his mission cover was blown.

He couldn't be much older than me, could he? Where was

the line drawn between training empath kids and creating secret agents? And was it weird that I kind of liked the idea of both?

"You were just doing your job," I replied, eventually.

"I'm glad my job wasn't being in that van. Man, the stuff the ops guys have been saying about you! Kind of wish I'd seen the action."

I raised my eyebrows at him.

"But yeah, ahem, super sorry."

Rayni pushed Ash to the side and dipped into a small bow that made her rainbow hair bounce. "Hi Olivia. I will try to do better for you this time."

She sounded so mature, and again wore a prim cardigan, but in pink. Maybe they were both older than I'd thought. "No problem. And you can call me Livvy."

As though we'd just become best friends, her grin shone in a way that completely defeated Ash's. Maybe she wasn't older after all.

"Ready to go?" Ash thumb-pointed to the car and the waiting driver.

"Almost, just waiting—" I spotted my dad walking around the corner from the street with the bus stop, and I waved to him. "Here he is."

I turned back to Ash's confused expression. "What?" I

grinned, enjoying myself. "You didn't think I was coming alone, did you?"

The Limbus building was tall, gray, and boring. It was a military-like structure with straight lines and few windows. There was a sign by the wide foyer entrance that said *Limbus,* small enough that it wasn't visible until you pulled into the parking area.

Although I'd seen some of it the day before, the stress of the situation meant I hadn't really absorbed what I was seeing. The parking area was open and surrounded two sides of the building. On one other side of the building was the deep channel of a stormwater drain, and on the remaining side, a vacant block, leaving the building appearing isolated despite being near the middle of the city.

Dad had chatted amiably to Ash and Rayni on the drive in, and they had done a good job of talking up the training and Limbus in general. They were technically boarding with Limbus, while both of their empath parents were 'out in the field.' I could only imagine what it would have been like to have grown up knowing you were an empath, with parents who were as well. Dad joked about coming into his own powers late, and hoping he'd get laser vision.

Only Ash laughed.

"Actually, empaths can't get laser vision," Rayni piped up like a grade-A student.

When we walked into the shining glass and polished timber lobby area, the Crossmans were there to greet us.

Hands were shaken all around and they began their tour of the facilities. Ash took his leave but Rayni remained beside me, taking her duty seriously. She didn't so much turn off my powers like Dean did. Instead she seemed to be controlling the emotions around me, making sure there was nothing too extreme reaching me in the first place. She made everything calm just by being there. Could she control emotions in other ways too?

The Crossmans led us to the ward where the drained were cared for, but we didn't go in. Standing outside the doorway, Dr. Crossman cleared her throat. "There's something we need to be open about."

Dad and I simply nodded, as we'd done to most of the information they'd given us so far.

"Jake and Jamie are our sons," she said, her voice calm and matter-of-fact.

"W-what?" I stuttered. Jake and Jamie who I'd run off with, never even knowing their *full names,* were the sons of the

Crossmans? I wondered if I should be doing a runner, but I wouldn't get far without Rayni beside me, nor could I leave my dad. *I wonder if I can carry them both?*

"I wanted to tell you before you found out some other way. And I want you to feel assured that we don't blame you or seek retribution for what you did. If anything, we are at fault for their behavior." She began walking again, as though she expected us to follow. She didn't go into the ward but continued down the corridor. "We knew what they were doing, and that it was going to end badly one way or another. We had been trying to bring them in for a while, but they were just too good at avoiding authorities. Which is also our fault."

Dad and I side-eyed each other, then trotted to catch up.

Mr. Crossman took over the story. "We used to be con artists. A family business, using our empath powers for greed—it's how we raised the boys. Then we came across a blocker."

My spine straightened. They did know about blockers. I gulped, remembering Jake's attitude towards blockers and hoping again they hadn't pegged Dean as one.

Rayni explained, "Blockers are a rare form of empath, and they have the ability to negate a proesthian's abilities or turn them off permanently."

I silently sighed with relief. If she felt the need to give me the textbook definition, it was doubtful they knew about Dean.

"The blocker shut us both down, Lola and I, permanently. We got away, but our sons outright abandoned us after that. Without our powers, they considered us lesser. Worthless. That was a real wake-up call for us."

No wonder they seemed awkward when I suggested they used their powers in our previous meeting. They didn't have any.

After a short elevator ride, we arrived at the door of a large corner office. A black leather desk had files spread out over it, and abstract paintings dominated each windowless wall.

Dr. Crossman stopped in the doorway, which had a brass label with her name beside it. "We ended up turning ourselves in. Mr. Kairu, the blocker, was a good man, and took pity on us. He was the head of Limbus at the time and gave us honest jobs. Taught us more about empaths than we'd ever imagined. He's also one of the victims of the leech.

"The point of telling you all of this is to hopefully convey that we believe strongly in second chances, and our great hope that the drained can be revived." Dr. Crossman swept her arm to invite us into her office.

"Thank you for your honesty," Dad said.

"I'll do what I can to help bring your sons back," I added. Because *no pressure, right*?

Before we stepped inside, Mr. Crossman made a sharp inhaling sound. "Ah, I left some of the information sheets and intake forms we need down at reception. Rayni, would you—"

I was already shaking my head when Mr. Crossman realized as well. "I'll go get them. Actually, Mr. Mirawi, if you would like to come with me, we can go over some of them on the way back up. I'm sure it's the kind of thing that would bore a teenager."

Dad gave me a checking glance, but I nodded, and the two men headed back to the elevator.

Dr. Crossman still stood with her arm out, and Rayni and I went inside. Rayni took a seat on a lounge away from the main desk, and I could see she was looking tired. Was it from this extended use of her powers? Dr. Crossman ushered me to the cluttered desk and we sat across from each other.

I couldn't help looking at the files. A sheet right in front of me had a photo of a red-headed girl who looked familiar, and yet entirely unfamiliar.

I turned my head to the side and furrowed my brow. "Who is that?"

"That's Emma," she said, nodding to the picture as though she didn't mind me looking. "Although she looked quite different when you met her."

331

My mouth dropped open. Now I'd been told, I recognized her, but it was definitely pre-cosmetic surgery. It looked like a school yearbook photo from around middle-grade, and the face I knew was there, just less magazine perfect. But the most obvious of the spot-the-difference between then and now was, well, the spot. She had a huge mole, or birthmark, or *something* right across half her chin. I could only imagine how badly she got picked on for that.

"She had a pretty rough childhood, and it didn't help that her dad was more interested in collecting replica weapons than he was in saving his daughter from bullying." Dr. Crossman began gathering up the files, then gave me a thoughtful look. "How close were you with her?"

She'd offered to share her clothes. She'd been so excited to have another girl on the team. She'd called me 'sis.' But what had all of that amounted to?

I shook my head. "Not very. She was nice, but kind of flakey. I'm sure she was probably trying to figure out some sort of revenge when she was peeking into Dean's room at the hospital."

Dr. Crossman shook her head, then smoothed back one of her pin-up rolls of brown hair with a hand. "No, I don't think so. Actually, we just tracked her down."

"Where?"

"Not close enough to worry about. She popped up again a town over, in San Corale. We found her when she raised several red flags with the company she's taken a job with—this Three Minute Miracles service that hires masseuses to corporate events, parties, conventions, and so on. Sounds like she's using her empathic gifts to get a whole lot of extra money out of her clients."

"Yeah, that sounds like her all right," I muttered. "Are you going to arrest her?"

Dr. Crossman tapped elegantly manicured fingernails across the closed file. "We were actually hoping we wouldn't have to. We'd like to bring her in peacefully, if possible. She's young and has been misguided by ... con artists. We feel as though she deserves a second chance. I was wondering ..." She looked at the doorway, then back to me, lowering her voice very slightly. "Would you be able to talk to her for us? Ask Emma to come in peacefully? Explain the threat of the leech out there, and how we can help her, teach her the right way to use her powers? We are really hoping all it will take is a face-to-face talk with Emma, especially since you were, at least briefly, her friend."

Biting the inside of my lip, I saw the photo of the younger Emma again in my mind. My stomach gurgled. "Where exactly would I find her?"

Dr. Crossman slid a piece of paper across the table to me.

"The Three Minute Miracles will be at this comic convention tomorrow. There is a cosplay party starting at three in the ballroom. Emma will be working there."

I looked at the sheet, taking in a deep breath. Carefully, I folded the paper and stuck it in my pocket with a nod. Doctor Crossman smiled and returned the gesture.

She put the files away and we were chatting more casually about the mix of empaths to non-empaths working at Limbus when Dad and Mr. Crossman returned, but my stomach still churned at the idea of seeing Emma again. If I did see Emma again. If my parents allowed it. If I told my parents.

I felt like I'd been given my first secret mission and I hadn't even received my superhero costume yet. Because while in the Crossmans' minds Emma might just be a misled young woman, in my mind, she was a villain.

11

" I feel as though I'm giving my child permission to join a fight club." Dad looked more than a little uncomfortable as Ash and I stood across from each other on a sparring mat.

We were on the ground floor of the agency in a large training room, with exercise machines, gym mats, and even a running track. Motivational posters had been tacked up onto the walls. Dr. Crossman had brought us there after suggesting we should end our visit to Limbus with 'a bit of fun.'

"There will be no attacks against Olivia today. She won't be harmed, and we'll all get an idea of just where she is in terms of controlling her powers." Dr. Crossman pulled out a tablet and stylus, ready to take notes.

"I'm the volunteer punching bag." Ash grinned, tossing a few juggling balls in one hand. He'd changed from the jeans and jacket he wore when picking us up to sweatpants and a tight tank top. He had the kind of tiny waist only a growing teen boy could manage to achieve.

They had offered me some gym clothes too, but I was more comfortable staying in my own outfit. The yoga pants and tunic shirt I wore were comfortable enough for a bit of action. I clenched and unclenched my fists, embarrassed under the spotlight. "I haven't, you know, had any kind of martial arts training or anything. This isn't going to be some cool montage of me being a kung-fu prodigy. I've only ever been in maybe four fights"—Dad frowned. *Aw, man. I should not have revealed that number*—"and I just reacted on instinct and scraped through."

Ash grinned, juggling the balls behind his back. "Instinct can go a long way, especially with superpowers backing it up. But regular training will mean having muscle memory to back up your super-speed, and knowing how to punch properly to capitalize on your strength. Then maybe you can be as awesome as me."

I chuckled. "Fine. What do you want to see me do?"

"Speed test?" Dr. Crossman suggested.

I nodded, but with Rayni keeping things cool and calm, I

couldn't sense enough fear to use. "Um, there's no green energy around."

Dr. Crossman's eyes widened. "You get visual emotional feedback? You see emotions as colors?"

"Yeah." Everyone was staring at me now. "I mean, only since, you know, I ended up with the extra powers."

"Oh, I see. That makes sense. Some gifted empaths have that ability naturally, but it's rare." Dr. Crossman took down some notes. "Rayni, can you bring a bit of fear up in the room? Not much. We don't want to overwhelm Olivia."

Rayni looked pale and yawned, but she also nodded. "Sure. To who? Livvy's dad? Do you mind if I send you some emotions?"

Dad blinked a few times. "You can do that?"

"I'm an emogen. I don't get any of the cool superpowers like the primals. I kind of send emotions out to people. Just remember what I'm sending isn't really real, so just feel it but don't act on it, okay? Especially if I make you angry." She grinned a super-cute kidsy grin, like she could never make anyone angry.

"I'll try," agreed Dad. "I do pride myself on my emotional awareness."

Rayni nodded, and I could see a faint stream of green flowing from her through to Dad.

"Okay, this isn't a great experience." Dad looked like he

wanted to vomit or bolt.

I focused on him, on the new fear flowing through him, and brought that energy over into me. Not too overwhelming, just enough. Only a hint of wooziness.

"Ready," I said.

Ash nodded, and without warning, he tossed all three juggling balls across the hall at once. "Catch."

One, two, three. I caught them with my eyes first, deciding my path. Then I sped after them. The first and second weren't far apart and I caught them easily, one in each hand. The third I pushed as fast as I could, blurring across the distance in a blink, and managed to fumble the catch because my hands were already full. I knew I'd been faster in the past, but between balancing my powers and hitting complete emotional overwhelm, I thought I did okay.

"Decent access to speed powers." Dr. Crossman made notes as I came back to the middle of the room.

Dad looked impressed and terrified. "Amazing, Livvy. I'd cheer but I'm worried I'm going to wet myself."

Rayni stopped sending him fear.

Next they had me do a strength check with a simple weights machine, recording how much I could lift while Rayni sent Dad anger. He paced, fuming and muttering about second-guessing working with *these people*. Afterwards, Dr. Crossman had Rayni send Dad a range of subtle emotions, and asked me to pick them based on their color and my empath senses.

"Good, good. How about some fun now? Let's see if you can land a hit on Ash. Ash will act in defense only, and Olivia, feel free to use your full powers. He can take it."

Between using Ash as bait the day before, and letting him be a punching bag now, I wondered just how highly she thought of his skills. I guessed I was about to find out.

Rayni amped things up with a range of emotions going out to both Dad and Dr. Crossman.

Ash bounced a little on the spot and gave me a *come on, then* gesture.

My first swing was sloppy, timid. He leaned slightly to the side, crossed his arms and shook his head, his straight white hair shimmering. I tried again, faster, but without my full strength behind it. I wasn't close to touching him.

"Aw, *Lollipop*," Ash teased, like I was a child, grinning all the while. *Where had he heard that?* Right. It had been his mission to observe me.

Oh, it was *on*. My arms moved swiftly, chasing his dodges with my swings. The problem was, he was just as fast, if not faster. I couldn't lay a finger on him, let alone a hit. He'd had potentially a lifetime of training, and what did I have? Instinct?

But that instinct had saved my life in the past.

I let it take over again.

Our movements were so fast they would have been barely visible to a normal eye. I kicked out and he jumped. I jabbed left and he spun right. But then it happened. I caught sight of his eyeline—he kept his gaze on my fists and shoulders. I was projecting my every move.

So I projected again. When he reacted to my fake-out I ducked down and grabbed him by the ankles, heaved him skyward and slammed him down on the mat with a primal roar of triumph.

Followed by a hasty apology. "Omigod, are you okay?"

He laughed and waved my apology off. "Mate, pretty glad right now that you don't know how to punch properly. Ouch." He got back on his feet, gave me the thumbs up and walked off the mat, amused and, it seemed, sore.

Rayni clapped loudly, glowing golden approval showing at my defeat of her big brother. "Yay! Livvy is amazing!"

She had stopped sending fueling emotions out, but had also stopped calming the space, and her cheerfulness smacked me. "Oof, sitting down now." I swooned and landed cross-legged on the mat.

EMOTIONALLY UNSTABLE

"Sorry!" Rayni squeaked, and quickly got things under control again.

I gave her a limp, long-distance high-five and gulped in air, winded from the fight. Dad and Dr. Crossman seemed to be taking a moment to recover too.

Rayni looked at me with glittery eyes. "That was so cool. I wish I was a primal too. Being an emogen is lame." She whispered the last word like it was a curse.

I scoffed dramatically. "Uh, no way. What you can do is amazing. You can control emotions! Of more than one person at a time. Like, wow. And you are so young; you have no idea where you could take it."

Rayni tilted her head. "What do you mean?"

"Girl, you reached inside me the other day strong enough to make my body think it was cool with just shutting down and sleeping forever. Which is terrifying, might I add, but also one super powerful superpower. If you can do that, imagine what else you could do."

Rayni looked thoughtful. "Still, your strength is awesome. Like you could lift a house and toss it on somebody."

"That would be epic," I replied, rubbing my chin. "Definitely putting that on my list of goals."

Dad walked over and put his arm gently over my shoulder.

"You're giving my daughter bad ideas. Next thing you know, she'll be on the news because she started throwing houses at people. Try to explain that one to the police."

Dr. Crossman muttered distractedly while looking at her screen. "Try explaining anything about empaths to the mundane authorities. They either think we are completely insane and try to lock us up in a mental ward, or they laugh us away. Hence the secrecy." She waved a finger in the air as though to demonstrate the entirety of Limbus around us. After a few more taps, she looked up from her screen and smiled, but it showed little pleasure. "You're quite strong, Olivia, with the additional powers in you, but also, it seems, highly reliant on calm surroundings or an emogen to support your unstable state."

"Yeah. Without help to keep this stuff under control, I'm basically a drooling mess." I winced, worried I'd said too much and given Dean away, but Dr. Crossman seemed to be focusing on her own tangent.

"I'm positive we can help you harness your abilities and keep them under control, until you can return your excess powers." Her eyelashes fluttered as she tactfully skipped over that those excess powers came from her sons. "From the drained we know of, Mr. Kairu was the third victim of the leech; his other victims all proesthians. Based on seeing your symptoms, I think the leech must have sought out a blocker to drain as a way to self-medicate, as it were." She seemed to be thinking out loud, but the implications sprouted scary thoughts in my head too. That there could be someone with all the strength of at least four proesthians like I had, but the inbuilt stability of a blocker as well. And that was the person out hunting for more empaths?

"I think I want to go home now," I said.

"I'm with you." Dad offered me a hand up. "That was one wild rollercoaster."

Ash and Rayni came with us again on the trip back, but we didn't talk much. From finding out the Crossmans' relationship to Jake and Jamie, being asked to talk to Emma again, and the thrill of test-driving my powers with other empaths—my head was spinning.

I could never imagine being so cruel to my own parents as to disown them. I loved my mom and dad, and superpowered or not, they were amazing. It was just another sign of the kind of people Jake and Jamie were. And Emma too.

The same Emma I'd been asked to find and attempt to deliver back to the agency.

I wasn't so sure about second chances. She deserved to pay the consequences for what she had done.

343

12

Dean met Dad and me on the garden path before we reached the front door. He had his hands deep in his pockets and his shoulders high around his neck. "How was it?"

Relief filled me at being back in his presence. Rayni did a good job, but she had been getting really tired by the end and the final part of the car ride had been rough. I wanted to hug Dean and soak all of him into me. "It was good. Exhausting. Lots to share."

I waved back at the black SUV as Ash and Rayni were driven away, then we all went into the house.

Mom had the same question for Dad and I as Dean did, and

EMOTIONALLY UNSTABLE

I replied the same way.

"Sounds like your normal reply for every time I ask how your day was. *Good*. Not like you were just getting a tour of a clandestine society for superhumans or anything." She crossed her arms and pouted.

Dad chuckled. "Your mom's just jealous I got to go with you and she didn't. I'll tell you all about it, hon."

The two of them headed off into the kitchen with Dad giving Mom a full recap, leaving Dean and I alone. We sat in the living room, and I pulled a fluffy mohair throw blanket over myself, needing the comfort. I put the TV on a random cartoon channel for some cover sound, then gave Dean my own recap.

"They want you to go and see Emma?" Dean's pitch was a few tones too high.

"Shh! They asked me while Dad was out of the room. My parents don't know about that bit at all."

"And that's not a red flag to you? Don't you think you should tell them?"

"I won't have to, because I'm not going to do it anyway." I shook my head, the silky fibers of the blanket tickling my chin. "I've been thinking it through, and why should Emma get a chance join the Limbus team too, like we're all best buds? She had plenty of chances to do the right thing—at the bank, at the

345

park, and probably a million times before that. She's a selfish fake and doesn't care about anyone, so I figure she can just keep on fending for herself."

Dean nodded slowly. "Could also be dangerous, seeing her again. Sounds like the best idea to not. But what are you going to tell Limbus?"

"I'm going to lie to them," I stated matter-of-factly. "I'm going to tell them that I *did* talk to Emma but that she refused to come in. That way, my job is done and I don't have to worry about Emma. Two wins, as far as I see it."

Dean tilted his head. "Couldn't you just tell them you don't want to do it? It's not like you're mission-ready yet or under their command. I'm sure they'd understand."

"But that could just end up with them sending someone else to go get her. Emma could still be part of my team again, which would be great to avoid."

"I guess. Look, you knew her and I didn't. And you've talked to the Crossmans more than I have too. If you think lying is the right—"

"I do," I said, too quickly and firmly.

Dean didn't say anything else. I searched him for any sign of emotion, approval or concern, but all I sensed was his usual blank chill.

EMOTIONALLY UNSTABLE

I'm not wrong. I couldn't make the same mistake in trusting her that I had before. Just how many chances did someone deserve, after all?

My tour of Limbus had been on Friday afternoon, and the comic convention was that weekend. On Saturday, I fidgeted around the house, trying to let the day go by until enough time had passed during which I could have had a reasonable conversation with Emma. Mom and Dad were both out working in the shop, so when it got to half past three, I sat down with Dean in the kitchen and dialed Dr. Crossman's number.

"Livvy, it's good to hear from you. How are you doing? Did you get a chance to go and talk to Emma?"

"I'm fine, but ..." I wasn't even nervous. I'd rehearsed the script in my head so many times already. "I went and found Emma, talked to her, but she's not interested at all in joining Limbus. She's refused to come in."

Dr. Crossman let out a long, deep sigh. "You really tried your best to convince her? You have to understand, it's vitally important she come in. We can't have an empath like her, with a criminal past, continuing to use her abilities in those ways. We don't have access to a blocker anymore so we can't even shut her down for everyone's safety. You're sure you tried everything?"

"Yeah." I gulped.

"Very well. Thank you for trying." Some muffled noises at the other end of the line could be heard. Something about dispatch, refusal, and *neutralize*.

"WHAT?" I choked.

"I said, thank you for trying." I could hear the shuffling of papers and more murmurs of discussion. "Head home, Olivia. We'll sort something else out."

My heart dropped into the pit of my stomach. "Did you say...?"

Neutralize? But Limbus didn't have a blocker, so it wasn't that kind of neutralize. Maybe they were going to capture her and imprison her in some high-tech empath prison. My gut told me it was more than that, or that it could easily escalate to more than that if Emma made capture difficult. Either way, I didn't want Emma to die. I just didn't want her on my team.

Panic spread through me. Dean gripped my hand, questions wrinkling his eyebrows. What had I done? I didn't want to tell Dr. Crossman that I had lied. I had no idea what the punishment would be for that. Not to mention the fact that I wanted Limbus to trust me. I needed them so that I could learn to better control my abilities.

EMOTIONALLY UNSTABLE

I had thoroughly screwed myself and Emma as well. There was no way I could admit my lie. But could I let Emma suffer because of it?

"Look, I can have another go. Maybe I can get her to come around."

"You aren't to approach Emma again." Dr. Crossman's voice was firm and chilling. "Things have changed. You should get back home as quickly as you can."

Cold sweat broke out on my forehead. "What's changed?"

There was a long pause of only quiet static on the line. "Olivia." Dr. Crossman spoke softly. "Ash is missing."

I gasped, and Dean held my hand, confusion all over his face. I shook my head and put the phone on speaker. "Ash is missing? Since yesterday?"

"After dropping you off, he had a date. Some girl I think you knew—Roxy? After the date, he never made it home. We've got agents out looking for him, but we are worried it was the leech."

"Emma's not the leech though. She couldn't be involved." My chest ached for Ash, and for Rayni. I couldn't understand how this had happened.

"No, but she's an empath flaunting her powers and could become an easy target for the leech if she isn't dealt with. We cannot, *cannot* allow the leech to grow stronger, which they do with every empath they drain."

Dealt with echoed in my ears. Dean's eyes were wide and his eyebrows low as he gathered what he could.

"We are working on things right now and when I have more news for you, I'll let you know. It is important that you follow the agency's wishes. Get home. Don't approach Emma again. Do you understand?"

"Yes."

"We'll be in touch." She hung up, but I sat there staring at the phone for several moments. I didn't know what to do or where to turn.

Ash was missing. Emma was going to be neutralized. I knew a secret empath agency would be serious stuff, but this was all too serious and all too soon.

One question wormed itself into my head, leaving my skin chilled. *What would Limbus have done if I didn't agree to join?*

13

"**A**re you certain she said neutralize?" Dean asked.

"One hundred percent," I said, throwing him a helmet and grabbing my own.

"And we're going ...?"

"Now. To Emma." I'd dragged Dean down to the garage but his understanding of the situation was lagging behind our bodies. Even my own body seemed to be acting before my head knew where it was at. After the phone call, I found myself throwing on my red trench coat and grabbing the convention address. It was only after we were at Dean's motorbike that I'd realized my decision.

351

I was responsible for leeching Jake, Jamie, and Donny. I wasn't going to be responsible for Emma being *neutralized* too.

My fingers smoothed across the shiny red helmet and I saw my reflection glaring back at me. "This is my fault. We have to warn her. There's no other option. They are going to treat her like a criminal and she's just a girl; she just made the wrong choices."

She did deserve another chance. I just didn't want to be the one giving it to her, but now I had to.

"Yeah. She can't be all bad. I don't know her, but I do know if she wanted us dead, she could have come into the hospital room that night and killed us right there. We wouldn't even have woken up long enough to fight back. But she didn't." Dean reached over and held my hand for a second, then put his helmet on and swung a leg over his bike.

I cringed as I put my helmet on. *What have I done?*

"Let's go. Fast. We've got to get to Emma first." I hopped on behind Dean and he revved the engine. "Just don't kill us, okay? Or I won't be able to beg my parents' forgiveness for this."

Everything in the neighborhood was quiet as the garage door opened. After a reassuring squeeze of my knee, Dean sped out. It felt like we were airborne for a second when we went from driveway to road. The back tire squealed as he turned, lined us up with the street, and we were off.

Dean gunned it, pushing the bike, and the road rules, to their limits. I wrapped my arms around his waist and we both bent forward, leaning into the ride.

The wind rushed all around us. Dean's focus on my empathic overload waned as he put all his attention to driving. On the bike, though, it wasn't that big of a deal. I caught wisps and whispers of emotion as we passed people on the street, but we moved too fast for anything to soak in. Which was a good thing, considering that a face full of asphalt awaited me if I were to fall and start convulsing. I closed my eyes and squeezed Dean tightly, feeling the hard muscles on his stomach tense each time we took a corner.

We made it to San Corale in only half an hour, a third of the time public transport would have taken. I pulled out my phone and loaded up the map to the convention center. Dean kept the speed up, bobbing and weaving through the traffic. I rolled with him, leaning when he leaned, becoming an extension of his body.

"There!" I yelled, pointing to a huge banner printed with *San Corale Comic Con*.

Dean pulled the bike up on the sidewalk as close as we could get, and we rushed inside. We pushed through the crowds of posing superheroes and families at the front entrance.

"Hey, Hey! You need a ticket," a woman in a high-vis pink shirt yelled at us.

"It's an emergency," I yelled back, and we ducked past the ticket check-point and into the main hall, scooting out of sight of security.

The number of visitors inside was immense. It was bursting with over-hyped children and irate parents and nervous fans. I reached back and grabbed Dean's hand. I couldn't risk being separated from him in here. Even with a direct connection to him my powers were *thumping*.

Dean held my hand tight as I practically dragged him along. I snatched a map out of the hands of someone dressed as a golden robot. "Sorry! Need this! Thank you!" I yelled over my shoulder, then scanned the map, trying to find the ballroom area.

I barged my way across half the main floor and off to the right where the entrance to the cosplay party room had another volunteer yelling at us for not showing a ticket.

"Where is she?" Dean asked, looking all around.

Everyone in the room was dressed up as someone or something from their favorite show or comic. Princesses and heroes, robots and soldiers, but now and then, between the colorful characters, I spotted people in bright blue shirts that had a logo printed on the front saying *Three Minute Miracles*.

I narrowed my eyes and scanned each one of them. They moved through the crowds, chatting in an overly friendly way to the other guests, or giving head and shoulder massages to them.

Up the back was a tall, busty blonde, her shirt incredibly tight, a diamanté covered fanny-pack slung over incredibly short shorts. She rubbed the back of a barely dressed barbarian and whispered in his ear. He looked entirely under her spell.

Emma.

It was the same wig she'd worn at the bank job.

We hurried in her direction. What was her reaction going to be? If I'd had more time, I could have eased into my reappearance in her life, but I had visions of a SWAT team appearing and whisking her away any second.

Emma laughed at something. Her eyes came up and met mine. Her smile dropped away.

Don't make a scene. We just want to talk, I prayed silently as we tried to get close enough to do so.

Emma backed up from her client, and her eyes darted around the room. "Stay back!" she yelled at the top of her lungs. "You monsters! I won't let you do to me what you did to my team!"

Every eye in the room turned to her, and then to Dean and me. So much for not making a scene. It became quiet as the entire party watched, trying to work out what was going on.

"We're not the bad guys. We're just here to talk." I lifted my hands in peace.

"Talk to my fist, bitch!" Emma lunged, leaping from her position superhumanly high to land right in front of me.

Someone in the crowd yelled, "Aw, naw, she didn't!" and that seemed to be enough to make everyone think this was some kind of floor show.

When Emma jabbed her fist at my face and I dodged it fast enough to seem choreographed, the crowd broke into applause.

"Emma!" I shifted left to avoid an uppercut. "Really!" I blocked a head-height kick with my forearm. "Listen to me!" I thrusted both hands against her chest, shoving her back across the space the crowd had cleared around us. "You're in danger."

She skidded to a stop. The spectators cheered. I guessed it was better than them assuming we were in a real superpowered fight, but we had to get clear of here before someone got hurt for real.

Dean pushed through the mob and moved closer. I felt a chill extend from him. Emma's fists lowered and her face contorted. "No!" she bellowed.

She slouched like all strength had been sapped from her. With a half sob, half growl, she plunged a hand into her shimmery bag and pulled out a small, silver gun.

My heart stopped.

No. No not again.

Emma pointed the same gun she'd wielded at the bank job, alternating its aim between Dean and me.

I stepped in front of Dean and wrapped my arms around him so he couldn't move. I couldn't lose him. I couldn't see him shot again. I'd do anything to stop that from happening.

Emma roared in frustration, and then threw the gun at us.

It plinked as it hit my shoulder then landed on the floor at my feet.

I exhaled and blinked. *What in all of insanity just happened?*

I slowly let go of Dean, somehow sure one of us was bleeding. We looked into each other's eyes, both uninjured and totally baffled. The crowd muttered amongst themselves, also confused about where our little performance was going with that development.

I stared at the gun for a long moment then picked it up.

It's a fake?

My head snapped up, seeking Emma. She'd pushed through the audience and was forcing open a locked exit at the rear.

I grabbed Dean's hand again and raced after her.

The door exited out into a loading dock, surrounded by

stacks of cardboard and wooden pallets. Emma jogged past a parked forklift, but the area was surrounded in high fences and all the gates were closed.

"Wait! Please!"

Emma skidded to a stop, boxed in by crates. She looked like a cornered animal, her eyes wild and her blonde wig askew. "Just leave me alone!"

I stopped where I was, giving her space. "I don't know if you know about Limbus?"

Emma showed no sign of recognition, only suspicion.

"It's a secret organization of empaths, and they are coming for you. We came to warn you."

"Why? I don't know what you're talking about." Without taking her eyes off me, Emma leaned back and grabbed one of the gates, giving it a tug and a shake. Chained shut.

The alley extended down around a corner and out of sight, and Emma eyed that potential exit.

I called out, "They know everything about you. Everything you've done."

Emma froze. Her voice was a child-like whisper. "Everything?"

"But if we go to them before they come after you, I think you've got a chance."

"Oh, I don't know," came the muffled voice of an older

woman. "I'd say you've missed your chance."

The voice had come from above us, and the three of us looked up the straight-walled convention building. Lined up along the roof stood a dozen figures covered head-to-toe in black.

Each had a large assault rifle, aimed at Emma.

14

bolted with all my enhanced speed to stand in front of Emma. "No! She wants to come in. She never refused."

The figure in the middle of the team lowered her gun and bent her head to talk through some device on her wrist that glowed. "Olivia Mirawi and Dean Lasslow are here. Yes. Interfering with the target."

Emma whimpered. I kept my arms outstretched as though I could create a shield with them. "Is that the Crossmans? Tell them I messed up, that I never came to see Emma until now. It was a lie."

There was some more conversation I couldn't hear, then

each of the agents lowered their weapons, and stepped off the edge of the building. I gasped, but they all landed with perfect precision and continued to stroll toward us as though that first step hadn't been such a big one. "You kids are in some trouble."

Dean stepped over beside me, and the agents' march slowed. Some visibly shivered, and others stopped in their tracks.

"Are you sure?" I hissed to Dean.

"It's okay. They should know," he whispered back.

Unlike the younger empaths who might have never been in the presence of a blocker before, these older agents seemed to know exactly what was happening, and all looked at Dean.

"Is he—" the lead woman asked.

"Yeah, a blocker," Dean replied. "Which means you don't have to worry about Emma. If you think it needs to be done, I can block her permanently, instead of whatever else you had planned. She wouldn't be a threat to anyone."

"No," Emma cried out, dropping to her knees. "Please don't take my powers away. They're all I have. I can't go back to what I was before. Please. I'll do anything, join whatever secret club, do whatever I have to do. Just don't take my powers."

"Jesus," the lead woman spat. "Chill out, kid. Plans have changed. Boss is on the way."

"Stay put and get comfortable." A man told us. It was hard

to see who was who, because the uniforms they wore included silky balaclavas that covered their faces. Up close, their outfits seemed much more slimline and high-tech than normal police gear. They didn't have bulky flak vests, but still had large belts with many things holstered in various compartments. Near their wrists were soap-bar sized screens, with a slight curve to fit their forearms. Some had maps and info loaded on theirs. On others, the screens were black, with just a few small heart-shaped lights showing. They all looked ready for anything.

The agents spread out, some taking positions at the entries to the alley to make sure our business stayed private, I figured. A few more remained standing guard around the three of us.

Emma had started crying at some point and hadn't stopped. I sat on the oil-spotted concrete beside her and put my hand awkwardly on her shoulder. We still didn't know exactly what her fate would be. Or what ours would be. But I tried to be positive.

Dean sat on my other side, still breathing heavily from me dragging him around at superspeed. I probably should have carried him. I giggled at the mental image of me running through the convention center, cradling Dean in my arms.

Dean bumped his shoulder softly into mine. "You did good."

"You too. Letting them know what you are was really brave. I didn't want to put you in this situation. I wanted you to be free from the expectations of all of *this*." I gestured to the ninja-like secret agents surrounding us. "Aside from being our plan B. I'm sorry. You're here because I didn't do the right thing."

Dean smiled, shaking his head. "I'm here because you saw your mistake and did everything you could to fix it. If you didn't, if you didn't care the way you do, I wouldn't be by your side." He paused, licked his lips, and looked at his feet. "I love that you care so deeply."

Love? My heart made a whirring, thudding noise loud enough to echo off the buildings around us.

Actually it was a helicopter landing on a building across the street.

Felt like my heart though.

I held Dean's hand and we waited.

An agent opened one of the gates to the street with some kind of lockpicking gun. A couple more agents, in suits rather than tactical gear, walked in, followed by Dr. and Mr. Crossman. They marched toward us, looking really, really *cross*.

15

Dr. Crossman pointed to Dean and I and snapped her fingers. "You two, with us, now."

Emma looked up, her face streaked with make-up blackened tears.

"What about Emma?" I asked.

"She'll be going with them," Mr. Crossman said, indicating the agents waiting around us.

Emma tensed, begging me with her eyes, and I tightened my hand on her shoulder. I shook my head.

Dr. Crossman pinched the bridge of her nose. "She will be fine, I promise. I don't know what kind of impression you have of our organization that has led to this mess, but the agents here were only ever intended to bring her into protective custody, and would have done a much cleaner job of it than the drama you presented the convention with earlier."

"But you said neutralize. I heard you."

Dr. Crossman squinted as though confused before seeming to remember. "Well, congratulations on your excellent hearing, but you took that completely out of context. Now let's get you home before your parents find out and blame all of this on us."

I let go of Emma and stood up. She sat up and hugged herself. I felt bad leaving her there, but I tried to trust the Crossmans, and hoped they no longer had a reason to take things any further.

"This way," Mr. Crossman said.

Dean got up too and pointed the other way. "My bike is out the front."

"The agents will make sure it's returned to you."

We didn't argue anymore; it wasn't worth it. We followed them out and across the street to another building. It was a hotel, and I watched as one of the suited agents used their powers of suggestion to have hotel staff allow us all up to the helipad on the roof without an eyelid batted.

As we rode the elevator, Dr. Crossman said, "We seem to

have had something of a miscommunication. Or a number of them. But I thought I'd been clear on telling you not to get involved again. Like we don't have enough to worry about right now with Ash missing."

I hung my head, ashamed of the mess I'd caused. "I'm really sorry I lied. And that I thought you were going to kill Emma. They were really only ever going to bring her in?"

"Of course." Dr. Crossman sighed.

"And not hurt her? Even though you thought she'd refused to co-operate?"

"They would have used whatever force was necessary," Mr. Crossman admitted.

I nodded. I knew it could have gone worse for Emma if I had left things as they were. "She's going to be okay though now, right? With those agents?"

The elevator dinged and the doors opened to a windy rooftop. The sun was low across the city, glaring off shiny skyscrapers. A slim, matt-black helicopter sat still before us.

Dr. Crossman patted my shoulder in a stilted attempt to be comforting. "Now we know she was never against the idea of joining Limbus, Emma stands a better position than when we thought otherwise. Lying to us was a mistake, but you've proved you're a good person with how you reacted to what you thought was going to happen. Don't worry about the rest. The agents will clean everything up."

I flushed red with embarrassment. "I can't believe I thought you were going to have her assassinated."

The two suited agents headed over into the helicopter, taking the front. Mr. Crossman paused and looked back at me. "Your father mentioned you're in therapy, and I hope you continue to keep that up. It seems that your past traumas are affecting your judgement of current situations. You seem to be looking for the danger in everything."

The four of us headed over and got into the back passenger section of the helicopter. It was relatively comfortable, and I tried not to be scared as the blades started spinning. Maybe I really was looking for the danger in everything.

Dr. Crossman pulled her seatbelt on and spoke to Dean. "And as for you ... I had a feeling you were more than just an overprotective boyfriend."

I glanced at Dean, mostly to see his reaction to being called my boyfriend. It didn't seem to faze him a bit. "Yeah. I only found out I was a blocker after Livvy found out she was an empath, so I really don't know much about this stuff either. Sorry we didn't tell you sooner."

"You didn't trust us yet. Understandable, I suppose." Dr.

Crossman's tone was soft and guarded. "Do you think you'd be interested in joining us at Limbus too?"

"Now you know about me ..." Dean looked at me and shrugged. "Where she goes, I go."

"That's great to hear. A blocker is someone we've needed at Limbus ever since we lost Mr. Kairu, two years ago. Your skills will be very useful, and I'm sure we can help you develop them too."

Dean nodded, and the spinning of the blades grew louder.

I asked loudly, "What now?"

Dr. Crossman pulled on a headset. "Emma will be brought into Limbus headquarters. We have secure rooms where empaths of questionable safety can be kept."

I remembered the windowless room I had talked to Ash in, and the heavy-duty locking sounds the door there had made. Would that be Emma's life now? Imprisoned in that small gray space?

My own stuff-ups were leaving me feeling soft towards her, as much as the idea of her being at Limbus made me pouty. "We all have lapses in judgement sometimes."

"That's why we believe in second chances. What happens after that will be up to Emma now." Mr. Crossman put his headset on as well, and smirked. "And as far as your parents are concerned, we're happy to keep all this quiet if you are."

Lying had gotten me into this mess, but since it had all been a big misunderstanding anyway, and things seemed to have turned out fine, I figured this was one time my parents could be left out of the loop.

Soon the helicopter was too loud for talking. There were headsets for us too, but Dean left his off, and Mr. and Dr. Crossman seem to have switched to their own channel to talk to each other, so I took mine off again. I tried to enjoy the flight, and by the time we were nearly home a beautiful sunset had filled the sky with apricot and pink tones that reminded me of how Dean had blushed.

We landed on a sports oval two blocks from home and Dean and I walked back alone from there. After all the excitement, we were still home before six, and before my parents. We went in through the garage, surprised to find the bike already returned; the empath agent must have driven it back way faster than Dean had ever dared to go.

We had just started making some spaghetti for dinner when Mom and Dad got home.

"Do anything fun today?" Mom asked.

"Nah. Pretty boring, really."

My phone buzzed and I put down the wooden spoon I'd

been stirring the from-a-jar sauce with that was only for when it was my turn to cook. I frowned, seeing it was Dr. Crossman's number, and answered quickly.

"Olivia, I thought I should let you know, Ash has been found."

"That's great," I said. I met Dean's enquiring gaze and put my hand over the phone, relaying the news in a whisper to him. He nodded and quickly caught up my parents on the situation.

Dr. Crossman kept talking though, and all the blood drained from my face. "Oh no …"

"What is it?" Mom asked.

"Ash, he's … they have him back at Limbus, but he's been drained by the leech."

16

Dean and my parents chattered behind me, and I tried to focus on Dr. Crossman's voice. I hushed them, then put the phone on speaker.

"With your parents' permission, I would like for you and Dean to come in first thing tomorrow. We can send a driver. We need to take some precautions, keep you safe."

Mom's eyebrows twitched, then she nodded.

"That's okay," I said. "Could we visit Ash?"

There was a pause. "You can see him, but you know what state he'll be in. He's non-responsive. Although it doesn't look like there was much of a fight, his body was just … discarded.

Left out in the elements for almost twelve hours, so it might be a bit confronting to see him in that state."

Mom covered her mouth with a hand. She looked furious.

"We'll see you tomorrow." After sorting out the final details, I hung up.

I waited with stiff shoulders for my mom to explode, but instead, she just wrapped her arms around me and kissed me on the top of the head. "I know I'll have to get used to you being in situations less safe than a perfect plastic bubble, but this is all just too close to home. I'm too young to be this gray."

I hugged her back tightly. I remembered the feeling of pure grief and darkness I'd experienced when I drained the powers from Jake, Jamie, and Donny. It was horrible. It made my skin crawl. *But someone is out there doing that on purpose.* And had done it to Ash. Cheerful, grinning Ash. Maybe I had been paranoid about danger everywhere, but how could I not be with that evil out there?

The next morning, my parents waved us goodbye as the driver arrived out front. They had offered to come with us, but I'd told them we would be all right on our own, mostly in an effort to make them feel like things were fine because I was so obviously okay with everything.

When an unfamiliar driver got out, with no Ash and Rayni greeting us with smiles, I knew I wasn't really okay.

The driver was a stout man with an obvious combover and rosy cheeks. When he ushered us into the car, his face got even redder and he blotted it with a handkerchief from his back pocket. He wasn't very talkative, which was fine with me.

The entire way to Bellston Main, my thoughts swirled over the last few days. I wanted answers. Who could have done that to Ash? Would he be all right? Would we all be all right? As if Dean could sense my unease, he laid his hand across mine, calming the tension in my chest. We didn't talk, but we didn't need to. We both knew how each other was feeling, even if my empath powers weren't working on him.

The driver's nervousness rubbed off on me, and I checked the GPS on my phone a couple of times to make sure we were going the right way, but we always were.

When we arrived at the Limbus building, Mr. Crossman was waiting outside for us. The driver dropped us at the door and almost seemed to be relieved to have us out of his care.

I glanced at the retreating vehicle. "Is he all right?"

Mr. Crossman glanced at the SUV pulling off into the back parking lot. "Mr. Graybiel? He's fine. Kind of a nervous man, not a full-powered empath but very in tune with emotions. Maybe a bit too much to fit in with regular types. We thought a job here might help him feel more included and understood."

I chewed my lip.

"Not seeing danger everywhere again, Olivia?" Mr. Crossman tutted.

"No," I grumbled. But considering what had just happened to Ash, I was sort of surprised that the company head wasn't *more* alert.

Mr. Crossman led us up to the first floor and past the ward where the drained empaths were kept. Where Ash probably was now too. We entered a room a few more doors down, with a nameplate labelled 'Dr. Felix Slate, Esq'. Inside was a small lab, with multi-screen computers occupying a few desks that were also cluttered in wiry electronics, empty coffee cups, and a few overgrown house plants.

Dr. Crossman was already there, sitting on a desk and talking to a pale, gangly, goateed man in a lab coat.

"Morning," she said, looking like she hadn't slept a wink. Her normally perfectly retro-styled hair was loose and tangled down the back of her neck. "Glad you got here early. I need to go through this with you. I have a couple of other meetings to attend to shortly."

EMOTIONALLY UNSTABLE

Dean and I stood shoulder to shoulder, both of us grasping our hands in front of us. Neither of us wanted to do anything wrong again so soon, and the gear in this room teetered like a tea shop a bull had already rampaged through.

The new guy collected some things off the desk and fiddled with them right up close to his face with one eye wide and the other squinted.

Dr. Crossman stood up and smoothed the wrinkles from her blouse—the same one she'd worn yesterday. "I'll get straight to the point. We want you both to agree to wear a special tracker and panic button device so we can better keep you safe."

That must have been the precautions she mentioned vaguely last night. Now I wished my parents had come in. Dad always had something to say about invasions of privacy in the digital age. It also felt something like a punishment. My nose wrinkled in disgust as I said, "You want to keep track of us all the time?"

"For your own safety," Dr. Crossman emphasized. "It's been three months since the leech's previous victim, but that was in Bellscroft. And now Ash was found in Bellscroft as well."

"My town?" I'd imagined the leech as a shadowy figure prowling the alleys of the city at night, not strolling around my sleepy suburb.

Dr. Crossman nodded, her lips thin. "It could just be a

coincidence. We still don't know anything about who this leech is. But it's better to take precautions. We're not going to be listening in or following your every move, although we will station some agents permanently in Bellscroft. This will all be for 'just in case.' Just in case you need help. Just in case you go missing. We'd be able to locate you and be there to assist as quickly as possible with one squeeze of the panic button."

It sounded reasonable enough, but … "I don't know."

Mr. Crossman sighed. "Trust us. We aren't the danger you keep seeing everywhere."

His wife rubbed her eyes. "Outside of your training sessions with us, we want the two of you to be able to continue your lives, keep going to high school, doing normal teenage things. The minors we have living in the building are only here because their parents are empaths as well, or they otherwise come from unstable family environments and are better off here. You two are better off at home, as long as we can keep you safe there."

I agreed with that at least.

"And we can only do that if you agree to wear the tracking devices." Dr. Crossman waved a hand at the lab guy, and what he was holding.

I checked in with Dean, and he shrugged. I had to make the call. Maybe it was time I made the decision to trust these people.

"Okay, I agree."

"Me too," Dean said straight after.

The lab-coat guy looked up at us then, but his eyes remained one wide, one squinted. "Hands please." His voice was way deeper than I'd expected based on his appearance.

"Sorry, I missed the introductions. This is Felix, one of our R&D guys," Dr. Crossman said.

Felix approached, holding a couple of rubbery wrist bands with a wide section at the front. They looked a lot like fitness trackers. He unclicked something to open them and dangled them before us. "Waterproof. Nearly indestructible interior fibers. Once I lock it on your wrist, it can't be removed by force by an attacker. I mean, unless someone takes your hand off. Let's hope that doesn't happen though! Press the front with your fingerprint until it turns orange to activate a caution beacon, or squeeze the two sides until it flashes red if you're in a real doozy of a dilemma. Also has a watch function. Pretty nifty really."

Dr. Crossman rubbed her eyes some more. "Felix will pair it to your fingerprints now. You can unlock and remove it with your fingerprint only, but we'd prefer you just leave them on all the time."

I took a deep breath and held my hands out. Felix took the

red-colored band, pressed my right index finger to the top until it flashed green, then clicked it onto my left wrist. Dean got a black one.

"One tap turns the watch on and off. Three taps to unlock. Ooh, and you can even pair it with your phone to manage the watch features and some other cool stuff once you get approved for a Limbus account on the system." Felix's eyebrows bobbed up and down.

"Um. Cool. Thanks," I said, turning the watch on and off.

Mr. Crossman held up his own wrist then, showing off a gray tracker. "In case it makes you feel better." Dr. Crossman also pushed up her sleeve revealing a purple one.

Strangely it did, but also worse at the same time. Between the trackers, Ash, and Dr. Crossman's worried, sleepless appearance, the leech situation seemed more worrying than ever.

"Thank you for trying to keep us safe," I said, and I meant it that time.

Dr. Crossman nodded, and glanced again at her revealed watch. "I have to get to my next meeting. Walk with me?"

She didn't wait for a response, just started walking, and Mr. Crossman, Dean and I fell into line behind her. I waved a quick goodbye to Felix as we left him alone.

"Nice to meet you Olivia," Felix said, waving back. He

looked intently at me with his one wide eye. "I'm really looking forward to doing some experiments on you."

"Umm, what?" I asked as we left the room.

Mr. Crossman half-smiled at my alarmed look. "He could have worded that better, but Felix enjoys taking on the air of a mad scientist. You will be working with him during your visits here to understand more about what's happening with your absorbed powers, and hopefully help find a way to give them back."

"Your case is very interesting to all of us, honestly. Yours and Dean's," Dr. Crossman added. "We have your brain scans from your hospital stay, but Felix has some more precise scanners, custom made for empaths. We're excited to find out what we can learn about helping you, the drained, and even stopping the leech. We are worried they have the potential to become very unstable now they've taken in more proesthian powers."

I looked guiltily toward Dean. "I'm amazed they can still function. I can barely stay conscious on my own."

Dr. Crossman left a small shimmer of blue in her wake, but didn't look back as she led the way. "We don't believe the leech has absorbed any more blockers since Mr. Kairu. Blockers ..." She glanced at Dean. "... are very hard to find, since their powers only manifest when in proximity to a proesthian. With Ash drained now, the leech must be pushing what their absorbed blocker abilities can handle. It could make him or her act more irrationally. Attack more often. But it could also be a weakness we could exploit."

A coldness stabbed at my heart. "But couldn't that mean that Dean's a major target to be drained? If the leech needs more blocking ability they could be hunting specifically for one."

Dr. Crossman stopped walking, and held up her wrist to display the tracker again. "Another reason we're taking precautions."

Dean didn't say anything, or seem worried, but I reached out and held his hand anyway.

"We're positive we'll find the leech soon though. Don't worry. Things have already made a lot more sense since your relationship to Dean's blocking abilities were revealed. It's helped our elucidists better read the situation."

"Elucidists? Is that another empath type I didn't know about?"

"You'll meet one at your first training session. I'm sure he can explain their powers to you then." Dr. Crossman glanced at her tracker watch again, but didn't start moving. An elevator dinged down the hall. She gave her husband a nervous glance, and then with a nod, addressed Dean. "There is one other thing that we hoped to talk to you about, Dean. We'd hoped we could address it later, but under the circumstances ..."

She trailed off. Dean raised his eyebrows. "Yes?"

"Knowing how you were able to block and then reverse the blocking on Olivia, we were hoping that you could possibly try to reverse the permanent block on us." Dr. Crossman frowned deeply, and her words came out forced, almost embarrassed. "I know it's a long shot but we could really use our powers now with the leech issue escalating."

Dean shrugged. "I'm not sure I could. So far, I really only understand my powers in relation to Livvy and ... my feelings for her."

Dr. Crossman, sighed and nodded.

"But ... I'll give it a try."

Dr. Crossman pressed her lips together and smiled. "Thank you," she whispered.

She checked her watch again, swore, apologized, then dashed off to her meeting while Mr. Crossman filled us in on what times our weekly training sessions would be.

We decided to catch the train home, not wanting to keep relying on Limbus's drivers—and maybe also to keep from being a bit weirded out by the last one. I was used to doing the pub' transport thing anyway. Mr. Crossman was fine with that, now we had our trackers set up, and even supplied us with company City-Trans cards for free tickets.

I trusted Limbus more now, but at the same time, fear continued to bubble in my gut. I could imagine those bubbles drifting together to spell out the words, 'Danger is Coming,' like some kind of prophecy

Or maybe it was just a sign I needed my next counseling session sooner rather than later.

17

The next week went by in slow motion. Dean and I went to school as normal. We weren't kidnapped, no roofs collapsed on us, and no new empaths were found drained. Once or twice, what I guessed was a Limbus van did a lap past school and my house, but it never hung around for long. Maybe they were keeping a protective eye on other empaths in the area too.

Nati was twitchy for a while after her brush with the kidnapping adventure, but soon returned to herself after I made up a story about mistaken identities and re-assured her that the person they'd thought I was had since been captured. *I wish they really had.*

There were no new developments about the leech. I found myself itching to get back to Limbus for our first proper training visit. I wanted to stop feeling useless.

My parents ended up being pretty cool about the tracker concept. Dad even joked about wanting access to our location feed, but Mom told us they wouldn't invade our privacy like that, although thought the extra precaution from Limbus was probably a good idea.

When it came time to head back to Limbus, I could barely contain my excitement on the train ride. I hassled Dean the whole way there like a talkative squirrel.

"What do you think we'll learn? How many other kids do you reckon there'll be? How long do you think it will take me to work out how to put these powers back? Should we have brought some afternoon snacks? Is what I'm wearing okay? What do you think an elucidist is? We really can trust the Crossmans, can't we? Do you remember where the vending machine or cafeteria was from our tour?"

He shrugged a response for everything except for the question about my outfit to which he nodded, then blushed ever so slightly. I had changed after school into tight yoga pants and a red tank-top, and then, when I realized it was pretty cold out, borrowed one of Dean's hoodies.

384

EMOTIONALLY UNSTABLE

Mr. Graybiel picked us up from the station, but the Crossman's didn't greet us on arrival at Limbus. A spectacled, frizzy-haired receptionist told us we were expected in the training room.

We walked through the doors of the gym, and straight away I noticed a guy just a bit older than us. He had light-brown hair and skin a very similar color, and his large ringlets formed a halo around his head. He was tall and heavyset, not so much muscular, but more as if he'd never managed to lose his baby fat.

Rayni was there too, wearing an oversized dressing gown. She sat on a mat at the end of the large room with two other boys and another girl, all at least as young as her. They all had downturned mouths, and blue auras surrounded them.

She looked up when we walked in. I waved, and she managed a small smile before it dropped again and she looked away. It physically hurt seeing her so sad.

The older boy walked up to us with his hand out. "Hey, I'm Sebastian. Olivia and Dean, yeah?"

"Livvy," I said, shaking his sweaty hand.

"We doing nicknames? Bastian, then," he replied. "Sweet to have some people my age around again after, you know, with Ash."

"Yeah," I said, noticing a blue aura around him too. "Is this it? All the students?"

SELINA A. FENECH

"Yep, this is the class. Empaths aren't that common, really. Although I heard there might be another new student today too."

The doors opened again behind us as he spoke, hinges squeaking. My jaw dropped.

Mr. Crossman walked in, Emma right behind him. Another adult, wearing gym clothes, and a uniformed agent followed, the guard taking a post near the door.

My teeth clenched. I couldn't believe she was here already. She wasn't just some kid like the rest of us. She was a criminal. And they were just going to let her come and train with us? This was exactly what I didn't want.

From the look on Emma's face, she wasn't too thrilled with it either.

I tried to sound more curious than catty when I asked, "What is she doing here?"

"Emma has been very co-operative—"

I'm sure she's made it seem that way. I scowled.

"—so we think she's ready to join in. Bastian? We'd like you to work closely with her. We think your skillset and temperament would assist her greatly."

Bastian's eyes went up and down all of Emma, and he shivered awkwardly. He took a step backwards. "I can't work with *her*."

Emma's mouth made an *O* shape then slammed shut.

386

Bastian took a few large steps over beside Mr. Crossman and they both walked away, arguing rapidly and quietly.

"You two know each other?" I asked Emma.

"No." She sounded confused and fiddled with an orange tracker bracelet on her wrist. So she'd got one as well. She was protected too.

My lip twitched. "I can't believe they're just letting you off."

"Letting me off? Who do you think the prison guard is for?" she growled back, tilting her head to the agent at the door. Then she tugged at her tracker with her long fingernails, like she wanted to tear it apart. "And they have me locked down on house arrest with this thing. I'm far from free, which I blame entirely on you."

She glared at me, but I couldn't look her in the eye. I muttered, "Probably for the best."

Bastian and Mr. Crossman rejoined us, their conversation finished, and Bastian looking put out.

"Things don't always turn out how you expect. It will be fine. Train with her," Mr. Crossman said to him. He gestured for Emma to join us, and she hissed at Bastian as she passed him.

"Not like I want to train with an ug-fest like you either."

I wanted to slap her, but Bastian broke out into a charming, hearty laugh and squinty grin. "Okay, maybe I was wrong. I don't think we've got anything to worry about."

Emma seemed just as confused by his reaction as I was. Dean shrugged as well.

Mr. Crossman said, "Bastian is the elucidist I mentioned the other day."

"Oh, okay," I said, like I knew exactly what he meant.

"What the flip is an elucidist?" Emma snarled. Maybe it was good having her around, so I didn't always seem like the clueless one.

Mr. Crossman smiled. "Bastian, maybe you could show Emma a bit of what you can do?"

"Sure, boss-man Crossman." He unzipped his jacket and threw it to the side of the mat. His stomach pressed against his black tank top and although large, his arms had no visible muscles when he held them up.

"Emma, if you would like, please attack Bastian. Feel free to really go for it."

"Don't have to ask me twice." She flexed, and I could see colorful streams of emotions flowing into her from sources around the building, including fear from me about what Bastian was about to suffer.

She moved at blinding speed, red hair flying behind her, not holding back a bit. Maybe she thought this was her chance to show off, like this was a prison yard and she had to punch the biggest guy in the room. I winced, but Bastian ducked and swayed effortlessly away from every blow, bending like one of those inflatable dancing men outside of car dealerships. While Ash had been always a step ahead of me in our match, Bastian was five steps ahead of Emma without even using any super-speed.

She soon slowed down, eyes wide, teeth bared, sweat glistening on her forehead. She grunted, landed on her bum and smacked the mat with her fist.

"That was incredible," I said, still in awe. "How did he do that?"

Mr. Crossman smirked. "Elucidists can read people's emotions, much as other empaths can, but to almost precognizant levels. Emotions affect every decision people make, and elucidists can get a sense of someone's actions and choices even into the future."

"Wow, that's some next-level stuff," said Dean, looking impressed.

I side-eyed Emma, frowning. Is that why Bastian reacted to Emma like that when he first saw her? Just what did he sense in her future that he thought was so bad, but Mr. Crossman thought wasn't an issue?

Emma flopped back onto the mat and face-palmed. "Future

vision? For real? No fair! I must have looked so dumb!"

"Who cares how you looked?" Bastian shrugged.

Emma pouted her surgically enhanced lips, and she flushed red as her hair.

Mr. Crossman explained, "Elucidist powers are effective for short-term decisions, like which way an opponent is going to swing. But anything more down the track is often wrong. People's emotions and decisions can be changed or influenced by even the smallest things. But it can give us some ideas about what paths they might take." His tone was pointed.

Bastian begrudgingly offered Emma a hand and helped her off the ground. "Good match," he said, sounding like he meant it.

"That was pretty cool. I suppose. I'd never heard of elucidists before," Emma muttered.

Mr. Crossman excused himself and the gym instructor took over. He gathered all the students together, had us take a place on the mat, and follow him through a range of physical and meditational exercises. Some seemed very tai-chi-like, with a focus on centering our minds, developing a greater connection to our own bodies, and extending the reach of our senses in that calmed state. I awkwardly twitched through the elegant movements and fidgeted when we were meant to still our thoughts. Dean was a natural.

I kept my eye on Emma the whole time, but she seemed to be diligently following the instructor's directions, although she glanced sideways at Bastian a couple of times and glared at me a few more.

When training wrapped up, I grabbed Rayni before she left and gave her a huge hug. "I'm off to see Felix now for some tests. I'm sure we'll work out a way to restore the drained empaths. Then Limbus will find that leech and make them put your brother back."

Rayni sighed like she'd heard it a million times, and managed to twitch up the corner of her mouth. "We'll all do our best."

Bastian remained in the gym with Emma, sitting cross-legged as they faced each other on a mat, talking. I was comforted to see the adult agent still keeping an eye on her too, before Dean and I headed up a floor to the labs.

I felt good after the training, more focused and calm. Until I walked past the intensive care ward. The double doors had been left open, and inside I could see all the drained empaths in their beds. Two nurses moved around the room, rolling the corpse-like patients onto a different side to prevent bed sores. In the closest bed was Ash, his face as white as his hair. The cat I saw before was curled up asleep near his tucked-in feet. I swallowed hard. Seeing someone who had been so cheerful, so full of life and energy lying so still, felt like looking into a shattered mirror to some twisted, alternate dimension. I couldn't fathom it, what void they were trapped in. Could they sense anything? Or were they simply shells now?

I turned away, and Dean moved closer, his shoulder pressed to mine and our fingers entwined as we continued down the corridor.

We headed to the examination room, right next to the one where we'd met Felix last time.

The door was open and Felix waved us in, distracted by the circuit board of what looked like a CT-scan machine. There were three other high-tech medical machines in the room I didn't know the names or uses for, and a small side room behind a pane of glass filled with monitors.

"Hi Felix," I said nervously. He wasn't particularly old, but I felt odd calling him by his first name knowing he was a doctor.

He turned around to eye me for a second. "Oh, we are going to have some fun today."

He returned to the machine and I gave Dean a worried look, then hid it when Felix spun toward us. "You, there," he said, pointing to Dean and then an office chair in the sectioned off area. "You, there." He pointed from me to the bed of the CT machine.

Dean squeezed my hand then we went to our positions. I wriggled up onto the beige vinyl-padded platform. "Do I need to take off any jewelry or anything?"

"In case it gets ripped off you by the awe-inspiring power of magnetism?" Felix bellowed, then waved a hand dismissively. "No, not today. Different kind of thing."

I laughed nervously. "You've got an interesting bedside manner."

He stroked his goatee and looked at me with his uneven eyes. "Really? No one's ever mentioned it before."

He pumped some hand sanitizer from a dispenser on the wall then stood over me, placing small, round, sticky papers across my forehead. He clipped several wires onto each. He adjusted the last one and mumbled, "Don't worry. This will hurt me more than it will hurt you."

"What?"

"What?" He shrugged like he had no idea what I was talking about and backed away. He joined Dean in the sectioned off room, watching from behind the thick protective glass.

The hum of the machines startled me. Felix's voice came through a speaker next to my ear. "This will only take a second. You won't feel a thing. Aaaaand okey-dokey off we go-key."

The donut-shaped section of the machine lit up bright blue and the platform I laid on adjusted and moved into it. I licked my lips and tried to stay still, but ended up talking nervously. "I imagined learning to control my powers would involve stuff like meditating under waterfalls. I didn't realize how high-tech it would be."

The speaker buzzed again, and this time it wasn't Felix, but a pre-recorded voice of a sweet-sounding woman, directing me when I should hold my breath and keep still and when I could move again. It ran a few cycles and then Felix opened the door and said, "Hey! Do you want to see your BRAIN? Come on. Just rip those things off."

I blinked and sat up, unclipping the wires and leaving them on the bed.

"How was it? Okay?" Dean asked, as I walked in and flopped down in the third chair. He reached over and helped me pick the sticky tabs off my forehead.

"Yeah, no problem."

Felix tapped at a keyboard, and the large screen in front of him had a pretty generic-looking medical image of what I guessed was part of my brain. I didn't know the terminology but I knew the gray squishy stuff was important.

Felix coughed into his fist and pointed at the screen. "Check this out. It's exactly what I was hoping to see." He hit a button, and the cross-section view of my brain lit up, sparkling like a nebulous galaxy. "Your limbic system is firing up with four unique bio-electric signatures."

I couldn't quite see what he was referring too. "You mean you can see me, Jake, Jamie, and Donny all in there?"

"Bingo! Which it proves my theory was correct and I'm a genius."

"What theory? That I now have three extra dormant personalities?"

Felix smiled cheerily. "Yes! But that's good. They are all still there, all intact, and all distinct. It's great news. A bit more work on focusing and developing your powers, and you should be able to separate all three boys from your mind and expel them back out again where they belong. Imagine it." He looked up at the ceiling for a moment as if doing exactly that, then smacked his knee and laughed. "Imagine you sent the wrong consciousness back into the wrong body! Classic!"

I gulped. Great, there was an all-new terrible outcome I hadn't worried about yet. If I even could shoot bio-signatures out of me. "My powers have been all more on the absorbing end than the, er, expelling end."

"Pretty typical for a proesthian."

"Is that what you are too? Or—"

"Just a regular old Joe here, if Joe were a *mad genius*. My mother was an elucidist but it didn't pass to me. Lots of folk in Limbus aren't empaths, but know about them for some reason or another. Nice to help out with the super side of things though. My mother always said, 'In times of trouble, look for the helpers; they are the ones most likely to have candy in their pockets.'"

He plunged a hand into a pocket of his lab coat and pulled out a handful of cat kibble, then put it into a small silver bowl in the corner.

A second later, the black and white cat I'd seen before ran in, wound around our ankles, and started eating.

I reached over and ran my hand through its soft fur. It purred but didn't stop eating. "What about the cat? Is it an empath?"

Felix glanced back. "Kimmy? She used to be Mr. Kairu's cat. Still is, I suppose. I just keep the fluffball fed. She spends most of her time sleeping on the beds with the ICU patients. I think cats are natural empaths of a sort. They even have their own superpowers."

"Really?" I asked.

"Oh yeah. Their purr is at a sound frequency known to heal bone and muscle injuries. Pure scientific magic. You should hear Kimmy purring away in ICU. I'm sure she's trying to help them."

Kimmy mewed then hopped up onto my lap, kneading my thighs and purring loudly. I leaned down and touched my nose to the top of Kimmy's head. "Good kitty. They can use all the help they can get."

18

broke down crying for almost all of my next therapy session. We'd just started, still in small-talk mode, when I suddenly wondered whether Jake, Jamie, and Donny could still experience anything inside me. If they were able to observe my actions, my time with Dean, or my parents, or what I said privately in counseling. Then I was thinking about what I did to them, and Ash, and the leech, and trackers, and Emma, and *danger, danger, danger.* Then I was sobbing.

Debbie let me cry, and I'd only just pulled myself back together when time was up. I switched with Dean for his session and hoped my face wasn't too puffy and red as I sat to wait outside.

There was a ton of foot traffic moving through the mental healthcare facility that day. I frowned as a couple of nurses ran past. *It's probably nothing. Stop looking for danger everywhere.*

Two doctors walked past the waiting area and stopped, oblivious to me sitting there.

"He's always been non-verbal," one of them said. "But I can't find any medical reason for his deteriorated condition since lunchtime. He is completely non-responsive. It's too early to say but it seems like a coma."

The other doctor grunted. "Has Holbrook's medication been changed recently?"

A memory flashed through my head of the old man who'd made me feel cold. On the front of his shirt he wore a tag that said Holbrook.

He was really old, I tried to reason with my gnawing paranoia, but my body was already alert, trying to hear more. I pretended to be entirely engrossed in the two-year-old health magazine I'd been flicking through and leaned closer.

"No change to medication," the second doctor replied. "Sad, really. Poor guy had such a hard life; his extreme chronic depression was understandable. And now this."

"Let's get some tests run. A person doesn't just slip into a coma for no reason."

"No, they don't," I whispered to myself.

I watched the doctors walk away, sat up straight in the plastic chair and put the magazine away. My mind was screaming. *Holbrook was a blocker. The leech got him.* I took a deep breath and tried to calm myself down. This wasn't necessarily empath stuff. There were a lot of other possible explanations. How could I tell this wasn't just my danger senses misfiring? But everything in my churning gut said something bad had happened, was happening here.

I clutched my hands together tightly on my lap and attempted to do nothing but calming meditative activities until the door beside me opened again and Dean stepped out.

Debbie said her goodbyes to Dean then smiled at me. "I hope you're feeling better, Livvy. Keep up your mindfulness exercises, and remember I have lots more resources available for you if you need them."

I cleared my throat and tried to use my calmest voice. "Actually, there was one thing I was thinking about that I'd like to try that I think could really help ground me."

She raised her brow. "Really? That's great."

Dean's forehead wrinkled as well but he didn't say anything.

I nodded enthusiastically. "We passed by the common area

on the way in, and it looked like a really nice environment, and I thought maybe Dean and I could spend a bit more time here. Maybe even chat with some of the other patients, get a bit of perspective."

I held my breath, hoping that the therapist didn't think it was strange, inappropriate, or weird. After a few moments, she grinned, then waved for us to follow her to a reception desk nearby. "Mary, can you get me two visitor passes for the general ward? Thanks."

She turned back to me. "You've shown great maturity in our sessions, Livvy, and I trust you will again in any interactions you have with our residents. But I agree, it could be a healthy exercise for you both."

I wasn't sure if she thought it really was a good idea or if she was just taking pity on me after my big sob-fest. Either way, I thanked her, and we took our visitor passes and made our quick escape.

When we were out of earshot, Dean said, "You want to spend more time here? Why? Did you see something?"

I explained what I'd overhead from the doctors.

Dean listened but didn't reply.

"Okay, I know, I know. Livvy and her crazy conspiracy theories. Just humor me? Again?"

Dean looked at me thoughtfully with his cold gray eyes for a long moment. "Sure. What could go—?"

"No! Shh! Don't say the famous last words." I made a mouth-zipping gesture.

Dean half smiled, and we reached the entry to the common area.

Large windows made up an entire wall of the long room, and filled the space with cheery sunlight. Brightly coloured bouquets of gerberas filled vases in the middle of large tables that had board games and craft supplies spread on them. I spotted several carers wearing brightly colored uniforms, some interacting directly with residents, joining in the activities, others roaming and keeping an eye on things. One checked our visitor tags as we walked in.

About ten patients sat in armchairs up one end of the room watching a romantic comedy on a big screen. The remaining few residents were spread out, mostly alone or in pairs. Some wore basic scrubs, but the majority wore comfortable-looking everyday clothing.

Dean stayed close behind me, shielding me from the barrage of emotions that the place brought. "What are we looking for?"

I tried my best to remember. *Someone petite and blonde, and from a distance, basically androgynous.* In the corner, I

402

saw a boy-faced girl with the sides and back of her blonde hair buzz-cut, leaving only a tangled swirl on top.

"Her." I nodded in that direction.

The tiny, curve-less girl was maybe fifteen, wore scrubs, and sat perched on the arm of a floral-patterned recliner occupied by a middle-aged woman. The elder of the pair had short gray hair, dark-olive skin and a slouchy, rounded shape, mostly hidden under a knitted blanket. Her eyes were shut, her mouth closed but smiling, and as we approached I heard her humming a cheerful tune. Tiny wisps of yellow happiness spread from the woman toward the blonde.

"Hi," I said timidly. "Mind if we join you?"

The girl's eyes met mine, then Dean's. She full-body shivered and her face scrunched up. She looked like she wanted to run away. Then she tilted her head and stilled.

"You made everything stop," she said to Dean.

Dean's jaw dropped open.

"Told you," I mouthed when he looked my way.

The girl squinted at us both. "Pull up a chair. Docs say I need to be more open, but they don't know what it's like. People are much *much* too much. Normally. You two are different."

We're like you, I wanted to say. But I had to be careful. It made sense that without understanding their powers, and

403

without support, empaths could easily become emotionally unstable, diagnosed as who knew what and locked away. It made me feel good to have Dean there with me. I knew if anything happened, he could shut their powers down.

We dragged over a couple of plastic chairs.

"My name's Livvy, and this is Dean."

She eyed our visitor tags. Her eyes were dark, matching the circles beneath them. "I'm Sway. This is Marigold, but she doesn't talk much."

Marigold opened her eyes then, woken by her name. She looked at Dean, and shivered violently, despite the warm sunlight streaming down on us all.

Dean and I shared another glance. She felt his blocking power too.

Marigold pulled the blanket up tighter around her as though it could ward off his effect and turned away from us to look out the window.

Sway put a hand on her shoulder. "She's not being rude. Goldilocks is all sunshine and lemon drops normally. If only you could *see* ... but I think they've fried her with all the drugs she's on." Sway's eyes roamed around the room. "All the colors have stopped too."

I leaned back in my chair. She saw colors from emotions

too? Did that mean she'd absorbed other empaths like I had? It couldn't be that she was the leech … Sure, she could have gotten Holbrook, but not the others. I wasn't sure she'd been out of this building any time recently. Dr. Crossman had said some rare, highly talented proesthians had the color vision naturally. I hoped that was the only reason she could see emotions in shades like I did.

"Colors?" I asked, innocently.

"Bless me. It's my kind of crazy. A cute, curly, swirly kind they haven't found a label for yet." She twitched and slapped her ear.

Empaths. That was the label they should have, one that could actually help them. And I was sure now the man in the coma was one of us as well. That also meant there was a good chance all of their lives were in danger.

Sway reached into her shirt, pulled out a plain cookie and started nibbling on it. When she saw me staring, she ducked her face away. "They don't allow food outside of mealtimes."

A carer walked over and Sway stuffed the cookie down between Marigold's blanket and the arm of the chair.

"Time for group, ladies," she said, clapping twice.

Marigold started moving immediately, getting to her pink-fluffy-slippered feet and shuffling away, taking the blanket with her.

Sway groaned and slumped into the spot Marigold had left.

"Don't care. Group's not fixing my crazy, crazy, crazy. Momma used to say I was too crazy for the Lord."

"Come on, Sar—"

"Sway!" she barked.

"*Sway*, we don't want another incident, do we?" The carer seemed to notice Dean and me then, glanced at our visitor tags, and gave us an apologetic look as though she was sorry we had to see this.

Sway held out an arm as though inviting the carer to drag her away, which she did, in a gentle way, sighing audibly.

"We have to do something for them," Dean said.

My pounding heart was relieved he was onboard. "We really do. Because what if the leech has discovered that this is a good place to pick off undiagnosed empaths?"

Holbrook's 'new condition' had begun only that morning. My heart reached out for Sway and Marigold and I wanted to race after them, tell them what they were, keep them safe.

I turned to Dean and murmured the fear that had swelled inside me. "And what if the leech is still here?"

19

Dean and I left the common area and went down a quiet corridor for some privacy. I leaned against the stairwell door. I tried calling Dr. Crossman but it went to voicemail. I tried again. Same result. I started pacing, biting my nails, then noticed my wristband. "I'm going to try this out."

"Are we in a panic button situation?" Dean asked, fidgeting with his own tracker.

"I'll use the caution beacon. Hopefully that's enough to get Limbus's attention. We need to get them down here fast." I pressed my fingertip to the top of the tracker and waited until it glowed orange.

Not two seconds later, my phone rang. Dr. Crossman's name was lit up on my screen. I put it on speaker. "Olivia, are you all right? Did you mean to set off your caution beacon?"

"We're okay, but we're worried there's an issue here."

Dr. Crossman hesitated, and I heard some typing sounds. "You're at the Bellscroft Mental Health facility? Your location came up as soon as your beacon activated. Did something go wrong at your therapy session? The tracker really is only to be used for dangerous situations."

I could hear the patronizing tone in her voice. "I know. I pressed it because I think there are empaths here, some of the residents. I mean, I know there are. This isn't me being paranoid. Please trust me."

"Okay, it's something we can look into. I have contacts I can check in with to see—"

"No, you've got to come right now. One of the patients that I thought was a blocker? He was found in a coma around lunchtime."

"Today?" Dr. Crossman asked urgently. I heard more typing. I stared at the phone I held face-up in my palm. It had only just ticked over to three.

She didn't wait for an answer or for me to explain my fears. She got it. "We'll send agents right away. Find a safe place to wait. A crowded waiting room or something. We've got agents ten minutes out and I don't want either of you on the street alone."

A strange, harsh smell made my nose wrinkle. *What is that?*

When I didn't answer, Dean agreed, bringing my attention back to the conversation.

"Who were the other patients you think could be empaths?" Dr. Crossman asked.

"A girl going by Sway, probably with the real name of Sarah, and a woman called Marigold." I ran over a quick physical description for both as well, and as I did, the smell grew. The smell of something burning. We began to head off to find a waiting room, however, as my feet shifted, movement caught my eye.

Tilting my head to the side, I walked forward, stopping a few steps away from the emergency stairwell doors. Rolling gray smoke floated across the floor.

Suddenly, the fire alarm began to blare. Lights flickered overhead.

Sickly green energy seemed to seep toward me from every direction. Fear, so much fear. Dean grabbed my hand.

Dr. Crossman's voice was urgent. "Livvy? What's going on?"

I opened my mouth to speak when the door to the stairwell blew out, slamming against the wall. Flames shot from the entrance. I was hit by a wall of hot air. I pulled Dean away from the licking flames and we ran down the hall.

"There's a fire!" I yelled into the phone. Sprinklers went off, pouring cold streams of water over us.

"Get out of there! Take no chance … to … the …"

I furrowed my brow and tapped my phone against my palm. The screen was soaked and went black. The smoke chased us down the hallway.

The sound of glass smashing and people yelling came from all around. We saw more flames up ahead. The fire burned so hot that the water from the sprinklers didn't even touch it.

We took the next turn in a different direction, skidding on the wet carpet. A thin gauze of smoke surrounded us. People ran past the intersection up ahead.

I stopped at an emergency sign stuck up on a wall, squinting at it through watering eyes. The markings were all blurry.

Dean tugged at my hand. "We have to get out of here, Liv. The whole place is going up."

I heard coughing, and looked into the room beside us. A man sat still in a wheelchair, with no real idea what was going on. I ran over and grabbed the chair, then sped back to Dean. Even with him there, there were enough emotions swirling within the smoke for me to absorb. For the first time, I could

410

almost section out the influx, reading its source, floor by floor. My chest bulged with the feelings of fear, anger, and, there it was … relief. Taking in a smoky breath, I focused, sorting the emotions like color charts in my mind until I could see where the relief was coming from.

"This way," I yelled, my throat burning.

He nodded and I led the way, pushing the wheelchair in front of me. Around the next corner, a young woman was huddled, screaming against the wall. Dean took over pushing the man, and I threw the woman over my shoulder. We kept running. At the stairs, I used one hand to help Dean drag the wheelchair down. We ran out of the stairwell to the right, and through the exit door.

Patients and staff spilled in all directions over the concrete-covered outdoor area, relief all around at being out of the building. Fear and sadness mingled at how the structure roared and crackled, the flames engulfing it.

I put the woman down, still screaming, next to a nurse who was checking on some other people, and Dean parked the man in the wheelchair beside her.

I searched for Sway and Marigold.

I couldn't find them.

I spotted the nurse who'd taken them away for group.

"Where are Sway and Marigold?"

Her head snapped over to a small crowd of patients behind her and then up to the second floor. My eyes followed.

She stumbled over her words. "They—they should be here. In the panic, maybe they got separated."

"Stay here," I told Dean. Gritting my teeth, I took off.

"Liv, stop! You can't!" Dean yelled from behind me, but I moved out of his physical and blocking reach too fast. I placed my bet on the building being empty enough by now that I wouldn't get overwhelmed, hoping I could just reach Sway and Marigold in time.

As I hit the main hallway, I grabbed onto the doorframe, feeling that brick wall of emotions slam straight into me. I blinked several times and shook my head. I couldn't let it stop me. I blasted through flaming corridors, trying to use every bit of the fear rushing into my body, like if I could just spend the energy fast enough it wouldn't overwhelm me.

In the distance I could hear Dean yelling my name, and I had my own fear that he'd followed me in. But I kept going.

The stairwell was thick with smoke and smoldering piles of debris spotted the steps. I leaped over them, going so fast it was close to flight.

Bursting through the door to the second floor, I covered my

mouth with my sleeve. The smoke was so thick I could barely see. Flames rippled all over the ceiling.

I dashed down the corridor, dodging sparks and crumbled walls. I could barely see anything. Panic rose in me. *How am I going to find them?*

From behind me, I heard a bloodcurdling scream.

I skidded to a stop and backtracked to an intersecting hallway.

Silhouetted by the surrounding blaze I could see a person. I heard the voice of a man. He was holding a soft, round figure high above his head, a surge of rainbow energy vibrating around them, holographic against the flames.

The leech.

He had Marigold.

20

My heart whumped like it could burst from my chest.

On the ground was a much smaller figure—Sway, crawling toward me, screaming for help. "Monster! Devil!"

The man lowered Marigold down to where her feet barely touched the ground. Her head flopped limply. With a triumphant roar, he discarded her into the nearby flames.

My eyes went wide in terror. "NO!" I cried. It barely carried over the sound of the sprinklers, the alarms, the fire, and Sway screaming.

The silhouette grabbed Sway's ankle, pulling her back toward him. She slid along the floor, her fingernails clutching at the singed carpet.

The flames grew closer. They were immense, radiating so much heat it felt like my skin was melting. My senses swam, burning inside and out.

Sway flipped over onto her back and kicked at the leech, trying to scramble away. "Momma's not right. I'm not going to Hell! I won't!"

I could hear the strength in her kick as it collided with the man, but he didn't react at all. She was confused and untrained, didn't even know she had powers much less how to use them against the multi-powered leech.

I pulled my soaked cardigan off and dropped it to the ground. Mustering my speed, I barreled down the smoky corridor. I slammed my forearm across the man's throat, trying for a blow to his windpipe, trying to incapacitate him more in the already hard-to-breathe environment.

If nothing else, my appearance seemed to stun him. He dropped Sway and took a few steps back, all blurry, shadowy shapes in the smoke.

I looked down at her. "Get out of here!"

Her brow was furrowed and she looked at me with barely open eyes that streamed with tears.

I reached to help her to her feet, ready to carry her if I had to.

A hand grabbed the back of my neck. It slammed me down to the ground.

I landed hard beside Sway. I flipped, jumped to my feet, swung and missed.

The leech was fast. Too fast. Too strong. Something hard cracked against my shoulders and sparks flew all around. I smelt singed hair. I could barely see a thing. My eyes and throat stung with each wheezing breath.

I took another blow to the back and landed next to Sway again, who was mumbling prayers and crawling away. I tried to look but couldn't see where the leech was. The smoke was so thick now I doubted he could see where we were either.

I scooped Sway up into my arms and, using every last bit of speed I had, I dashed back the way I had come, careening into walls, rolling down stairs, and stumbling over ash-covered floors. Only sheer momentum kept us going.

We reached the ground floor, and I almost crumpled. Everything was too much. It was a struggle to put one foot in front of the other, but I kept going. *We have to get out.* I spotted a pale white square of light up ahead and hoped it was the exit. I hobbled blindly toward it and soon, the cooling effect of Dean's presence washed over me. I headed toward that feeling, and almost cried in relief as though he could heal every burn I'd received.

I stumbled out the exit with Sway in my arms.

I wasn't sure where we were but there was fresh air, and I felt Dean beside me, taking Sway out of my arms. He wasn't a proesthian, but he was strong enough to carry her petite body.

My vision cleared slowly, but faster than a regular human's would have, I imagined. We were in a side strip between the main building and an outdoor covered area. Sway had wrapped both arms tight around Dean's neck, almost entirely supporting her own weight as she clung to him.

I drank deep gulps of air into my charred lungs, basked in a few seconds of relief, then turned back towards the building.

"What are you doing? The whole place is going to collapse on itself. You can't go back."

"Marigold is still in there. The leech got her. She's *in the fire*. I have to save her."

Dean grabbed my wrist. I could feel his blocking power kick in hard and my strength sapped away. He wasn't letting me go anywhere.

"If she's in the fire it's already too late." His voice was rough from the smoke. "Don't be the hero who dies."

I tried to pull away, but I couldn't gather the strength. Tears welled in my eyes and I dropped onto my knees.

He was right. But it *hurt*.

Behind me I heard a loud slam. A figure stumbled out of an entrance at the other corner of the building, a black mask covering his face and hair. As I spotted him, he spotted us. The leech. He stood in the rain of ash and stared at the three of us long and hard.

I stood, ready to fight.

"Olivia! Dean!" a woman yelled.

I spun around. It was the lead agent from the convention center. She had bright pink hair and a scar across her chin. Half a dozen plain-clothed agents from Limbus ran up behind her, identifiable only by the matching tracker bands they all wore.

"The leech," I yelled. "He's—"

I turned back to find the space he'd been standing empty. *Gone*.

The lead agent signaled with her hands and three of her team split off, flashing away with empath speed in search of the man.

"Are you hurt?" She checked me over, eyes lingering over my ash-grayed skin and red welts, then glanced over Dean, still cradling Sway.

"Is this one of them?" she asked.

"Yes. Sway," I gasped between coughs. "Marigold ... he just

... he threw her in the flames."

The agent nodded slowly, and wrapped an arm carefully around me, leading me away from the devastation. She spoke to her team. "Let's get the kids safe."

Dean handed Sway over to one of the agents and they took us around to a van, which I got into gratefully. It felt like some of my burns were already healing, but I was wrecked.

Dean took a seat beside me and held my hand. "I was so worried I was going to lose you."

I leaned back against the headrest. "I'm sorry. I know that was a bit crazy, but I couldn't leave them in there."

"Don't apologize. You did you. You're a hero, through and through, Livvy. Ever since I first met you. Worrying I'll lose you comes naturally with that." Dean looked down at our joined hands. "But weirdly, I think it's helping me. Each time things get dangerous, but you come through okay, I build a bit more hope. But beyond that it reminds me how fragile life is, and that *I* have to come to terms with it. I can't control everything, or hide from everything, and blocking it all out means I just miss out on the good things too. Does that make sense?"

My tears flowed again, cleaning my eyes. "Yeah. A lot of sense. I get scared of losing you too. When Emma pulled that gun the other day ..." I gulped back a sob and rested my wet cheek on

Dean's shoulder. "Maybe I'm really not cut out for this."

Dean let go of my hand and wrapped both arms around me. There was a rigidness to his embrace that told me he still struggled between releasing his emotions and holding back, probably for my sake. I still snuggled into his awkward hug. "No. You saved Sway today. You identified her, you realized the threat, and you saved her life entirely. You're amazing."

I couldn't save Marigold though. The leech was one hundred percent monster, taking what he wanted then throwing away the rest. And the way he had looked at us ...

He knew our faces now. It felt like only a matter of time before he was discarding our used-up shells like we were nothing.

21

We were rushed into Limbus and straight to medical. Limbus only had one ward area, so we ended up on beds at the end of the room where the drained were, sectioned off only by curtains.

Dr. Crossman, Felix and a group of nurses were there, ready for action. Sway and I were covered in ash and burns, but were already recovering well on our own, thanks to our proesthian-enhanced healing. The team still got us to change our ruined clothes. They cleaned us up, spread medicated gels over the raw patches of skin, and made us sit breathing pure oxygen from masks for a while. When they found out we'd had physical contact with the leech, they checked our hands and under our nails for signs of his DNA, and sent our clothes to Felix's lab for forensics.

Sway stayed quiet the whole time, listening to Mr. Crossman explain to her the gist of what was going on. About empaths, proesthians, leeches, emotions and powers, and soon her face clouded over. It wasn't the same enthusiastic reaction I'd had when I first found out about empaths. Of course, I hadn't been in the psych ward for years being told I was crazy beforehand.

Dean had minor burns on one hand from when he'd tried to open a hot door handle and, without proesthian healing powers to help his lungs, he was going to have to stay on oxygen a lot longer than we did.

Felix also took my phone from me, promising to use his genius powers to get it going again after its dousing, then returned soon with it sitting in a bowl of uncooked rice. He left, the rest of the medical staff not far behind him.

Dr. Crossman called my parents, had a quick chat to them, then handed her phone over to me. I pulled my oxygen mask to the side.

"Livvy, honey, I'm so glad you're okay. Terry called a while ago and told us the facility was on fire." Mom's voice was frantic. Dad spoke too. They must have been on speakerphone together.

"We've been trying to call you ever since."

I glanced at my phone sitting in the bowl of rice on the bedside table, hoping it wouldn't have to be replaced again. "Yeah, the fire started just after our sessions finished. But we got out okay. A bit smoky and dirty, but we're all fine. Limbus just want to keep us here for observation a bit longer."

I heard a loud sniffle. "We're on our way, okay? We'll be there soon. We love you, Lollipop."

"Love you too, Mom and Dad."

"Tell Dean he's growing on us, too," Dad added.

I smiled. "Will do."

When I hung up and handed the phone back to Dr. Crossman, a movement caught my eye. From the doorway, Emma peeked in. She had a hand pressed onto her chest and a frown on her face. She caught me watching and her mouth opened a little then closed again. She frowned even deeper and disappeared.

Dr. Crossman took her phone and left too. Now they had more information on the leech, and he was growing so bold in his attacks. They were doing everything they could to find him.

I lay still for a while, breathing through the mask and doing every calming exercise I knew to release the tension from my body.

The ward was silent—almost too silent.

I rolled my shoulders and looked around the room. I could see Jake, Jamie, and Donny a few beds down. They lay on their backs, faces blank, hands resting by their sides. Mr. Kairu and the others I didn't know were also there.

Next to them was Holbrook, the man who had fallen into the coma before the fire started. Apparently, a nurse had gotten his bed down the emergency elevator before the sprinklers went off. The agents managed to do whatever they'd needed to take possession of someone who was a patient at a mental institute. I imagined the details were for them to know, and for me to act like I'd never heard.

In the bed to my right, Dean had dozed off. I envied him. There was no way I was getting some rest with these *bodies* all around us. I stared at the lines of his face for a while, but he remained so still it brought me no comfort. He lay face up, hands by his sides, just like the bodies. Fear clogged my throat.

I turned the other way. The bed to my left was empty, the sheets folded back where Sway had been. When had she left? I pushed myself up into a sitting position, looking for her. She couldn't have gone far; the staff would have never let her leave the premises.

Still, she'd gone *somewhere*. Unable to find rest either, probably. Every time I closed my eyes, I could see Marigold's body being flung into the fire. I hated it. I wanted the image out of my head.

I pulled back my covers and stepped down into a pair of slippers a nurse had given me along with the pale blue scrubs I wore, slightly too big for me and rolled at the waist.

Quietly, I moved to the doorway, wary about going too far from Dean. There was no sign of Sway out the main door; the hallway was empty. There was another door leading to a fire escape. She might have taken that. I stood on tiptoes to look out the small, high window in the ward. Below, I could see the stormwater drain that ran across the back of the Limbus property, and a tiny figure sitting on the edge of it.

I calculated the distance with my eyes. I should be okay that far from Dean. It was one floor down, but only a pathway width distance between the building and where Sway sat.

I pushed through the heavy fire door and tiptoed down the plain concrete stairs.

Sway turned to me when the external door closed with a thud. She sat on the weed-cracked concrete, her knees tucked up to her chest.

With my hands shoved into the shallow front pockets of my pants, I walked toward her with care. I didn't want to spook her. I had no idea where her head was at after everything.

As I sat down beside her, she gave a partial smile. "Can't rest either?" she asked.

"Nope."

She nodded, her eyes dark. "Monsters make it hard to sleep. I've met monsters before."

Down the slope of the wide drain channel, a small shadow moved. A rat, poking its head out of a grate. Sway leaned forward, pulling her legs down into a cross-legged position. She reached into the front of her scrub shirt and into her bra, pulled a cookie out, and tore off a crumbly piece. She threw it near the rat. The rat spooked at first, then eased toward the morsel, took it in its little claws, and ran back for cover.

"Tastes too salty smoky now," Sway said, breaking more pieces and throwing them down into the channel. "Sorry I got so clingy with your man."

"Oh, that's okay?" She caught me off guard. I hadn't thought twice about it at the time, having just escaped a catastrophic fire and death.

"His, *blocking*, is it? I just really needed it. I needed to feel *less* then, after feeling *everything*." Sway looked so small.

"I get it. And I really didn't think anything of it. Guess I'm not the jealous type." I also trusted Dean. A rush of warmth filled me. *I love him so much. I have to tell him.*

EMOTIONALLY UNSTABLE

"You realize how good it is to know I'm not alone in feeling this way? That I'm not a nut nougat brain? At least, not completely." Sway tilted her head back, looking up at the dusk-tinted sky. "I used to take Marigold up onto the institute roof sometimes, just her and me. I liked being able to feel nothing but her golden light. And it was the only time I could get her to talk, when it felt like just me, her, and the sky. I don't know how she managed to stay so happy. I wish she could have known, too. That she wasn't crazy."

My eyes stung, too dry for more tears. I closed them and saw Marigold, the leech, the flames. "I'm sorry you lost your friend. I wish I could have saved her."

Sway swatted then scratched the side of her head. "There are worse ways to go. Mr. Crossman said that when this leech thing drained her, she fell into a coma. She wouldn't even have felt the fire."

I tried to see the comfort in that, but it was hard.

Sway tossed the last of the crumbs down into the drain then wiped her hands on her scrub-covered thighs. She looked back to the building, but didn't make any move to return to it. "Empaths, huh? All these slippery, shiny emotions ... I never used to know what was really real before. Nobody else seemed to *feel* the way I did." She turned her hands over and smacked one palm to the other. "There were times when I thought my emotions would make me burst like popcorn. Or I would get so sad ..." She trailed off for a moment and then picked up again. "So sad I felt like I could swallow the world with my grief."

I shivered, folding my arms tight around my chest. I knew that feeling. That was how I'd felt when I stole the life force from Jake and the others. Like I could have swallowed them whole.

Sway reached her hands up toward the evening star, the first pale sparkle in the still bright sunset. "When I was angry, I just knew if I reached up, I could tear down the sky."

She pulled her fists closed and down to her chest. "But then they would drug me up and I would relax. And all the rainbow light would just simmer out of my pores."

"I'm glad we were able to get you here safely. Now Limbus can help you, train you, teach you."

She let her hands fall into her lap and looked at me with a thin smile. "I wonder where my life would be if I'd known before now. If I could have done anything to control myself enough to stay on the sane side of the line. My own parents tucked me away so they wouldn't have to look at all my feelings every day."

I thought of my mom and dad, probably still on a train on their way to me. "My parents have been pretty cool with it. I'm really lucky to have them, especially with the incredible stuff-ups and ridiculous danger I've been in. I'm surprised we all haven't short-circuited our emotional systems. I've been hot mess after hot mess even with a great support network. Being an empath can be a bit extreme. So yeah, welcome to the team?" I chuckled wryly.

Sway cracked a small smile. She rested one fist on her hip and put her other straight out in the air. "With our powers combined, we are the Emotional Wrecks!"

We both broke out into relieved, hysterical giggles. It felt good to let it all out, as though the laughter healed me as much as the tears I'd run dry.

Non-funny thoughts returned quickly though. Because I did have powers combined. Powers I needed to return. Although …

I gasped.

Sway jumped. "What is it?"

I put my hand out, touching her arm like she was a savior. "What you just said, about combining empath powers. You gave me an idea." Chewing my lip, I ran the thought over and over again in my head. It was definitely something. Something we could try. Something that might actually work. I kept my mouth closed, not wanting to jinx it.

I hopped to my feet and Sway looked up at me, confused.

"Good idea? Bad idea?"

I stared off down the length of the storm drain, spaced out, worried, and hopeful.

Sway stood up in front of me and tapped her finger to my forehead.

My eyes met hers, and a smile reappeared at the corners of my lips. "An idea of how to put the drained empaths back into their bodies again."

22

On our way back to the ward, Sway detoured and flagged down an agent to send for the Crossmans and Rayni.

When we reached the ward, Rayni was already there, sitting cross-legged on the end of her brother's mattress, talking to him softly.

Sway returned to her bed as though she'd never left.

I rushed over to Rayni, full of enthusiasm. When I got closer, I could see the blue aura surrounding her in the dim light, and even more clearly, the tears on her cheeks. I didn't want to get her hopes up too much in case this didn't work. I reined myself back in. Leaning my hip on the side of the bed, I cautiously explained my plan. I had to get her to understand it because she was the key component. She and I had to work together to make it happen.

Her young round face watched me intently as I tried to explain the concept, still so new and nebulous, even in my own mind. I was worried she wouldn't get it at all, but a bright sparkle of comprehension flared in her eyes. When I finished, she looked up and away for a moment as though doing math in her head.

"Actually, it could work," she said, with a small, cautious smile. She reached down and squeezed her brother's foot through the blanket.

Dean had woken up while we'd talked. He took his oxygen mask off and came over beside us. He stood there with his arms crossed, his face straight, as always. He probably wasn't thrilled at the idea of waking up the guy who'd shot him. Neither was I, but that wasn't the point. If this could be done, there was a chance to save everyone. We just had to trust that Limbus could manage Jake, Jamie, and Donny appropriately once they were awake again.

The Crossmans arrived at the same time, and had brought Felix with them.

"No luck on a clean DNA sample yet," Dr. Crossman reported.

"Have you thought of some other detail about the leech that could help? Is that why you called us?"

I shook my head and pointed at the three boys. "I was talking to Sway, and she gave me an idea. An idea of how I could return their powers. I want to try it now."

Felix's face lit up with excitement, but Dr. Crossman was more hesitant. "Let's hear the idea first."

I walked to the foot of Jake's bed, not even wanting to look at him, but it was necessary. "We combine powers. I was watching Rayni the other day, and I could see how the emotions flowed from her and through other people when she pushed them out with her emogen abilities. I think those powers could help me push out all of this inside me."

Dean spoke softly. "Would you be able to do that without pushing out your own ... self?"

"I think so. In the fire, I was able to channel and sort the emotions I was feeling into unique streams to find our way out. We know from the tests there are four distinct patterns in my head, and now I'm focusing on those, I can really feel them. I can feel who they are, their energy, which one is which."

Dr. Crossman's normally unflappable expression looked close to tears, but her voice remained steady. "And you want to try this now?"

I nodded, keeping my eyes from making contact with Dean's. "I want to be just me again, so things can be at least more normal in some ways. I do have one concern, though."

All eyes were on me, waiting. I puffed out a breath. "The leech was strong. So strong, and so fast. Sway, or probably any normal empath, couldn't stand a chance. Even as I am, all charged up, I could barely hold him off. I was only just fast enough to get away. I'm worried we need this"—I held my fists up in front of me—"this extra power I have, or we won't have any way to fight the leech."

Dr. Crossman shook her head adamantly. "Olivia, I admire your bravery but it's not your job to fight him. It never should have been. Leave it to the grown-ups and let yourself just be you."

Dean took my hand and I looked up into his face, still smudged with ash. His gray-eyed gaze was intense, making me shiver. "You're more than enough on your own. For anything."

I wanted to kiss him. But the kissing would have to wait.

And if this worked, that wait wouldn't be long.

"Okay. Okay, should we start?" I gestured to Rayni who came to stand behind me. "I've already talked it all over with Rayni."

"One more thing first," Mr. Crossman said. He took his wife's hand and they nodded to each other. "Assuming this works, Dean, we want you to block the three boys permanently as soon as they are awake."

My mouth popped open. I had hoped Limbus would do what was needed to deal with the three of them, but hadn't expected they would choose that path. Maybe it was easier for them to decide, since they were blocked themselves. After they were disowned by their own sons, maybe they thought there really was no hope for them.

"What about second chances?" I asked, unsure.

"We don't have the resources for second chances right now—not with having to focus everything on the leech." I could hear pain in Dr. Crossman's voice. "Jake and Jamie, with everything we've taught them? They could be a huge risk in so many ways. Even once blocked, we can't trust them not to continue pulling cons, or take revenge. We'll be sending them to regular authorities for their crimes as soon as it's safe to do so."

Mr. Crossman nodded. They'd clearly been over this together already and were firmly on the same page. "We'll help them how we can with legal aid and observation. If we feel there's a chance for them to turn their lives around with Limbus when the rest of the danger has settled, we can extract them from the legal system at that time."

Dean said, "Sounds like the best option to me." There was no emotion in his voice. I could only imagine everything running through his mind, given he was the major victim of one of the crimes the Crossman boys committed.

The Crossmans called a few agents up into the room just in case, and had me run over the finer details of my plan with Felix to see if it seemed sound. Felix smiled a wide, glittery smile, nodding along. He gave me a double thumbs up approval. "Oh boy, I can't wait to see this."

"Okay, Rayni. Showtime." I took position in front of the three beds the boys were lined up in.

Rayni came and stood beside me, her hands on either side of my back. "We'll do our best."

"Dean?" I found him with my eyes, standing to the side of the beds. "Can you drop your blocking on me? Completely? We need to let Rayni take control."

He frowned, then nodded. "You've got this."

A rush of nerves was the first thing I felt. Then a rush of emotions. The building was fairly empty and quiet, but even the controlled feelings of the Crossmans seemed extreme.

I gritted my teeth, then sensed Rayni's presence pushing through me. It cleared the emotions from me almost as fast as I could absorb them. My chest seemed to explode in a rainbow of colors.

I looked at the boys and closed my eyes, focusing on their

energies in my own body. Each energy was different. One, charming and gilded. Another, jittery and mischievous. The third, stoic and solid.

I moved my body into one of the meditation stances we'd been taught in training, and calmed my mind. I imagined each energy inside me as a stream, and then let them flow outwards with the current Rayni had created.

Sway gasped. *It's working. She can see it happening.*

I kept my eyes closed and focused.

I doubted anyone else could see the energy moving, but I could feel it escaping me. It was heavy, and the pressure on my chest grew. I spread my legs apart, stabilizing my body, and opened my eyes.

Tendrils of light flowed out of me toward the three I'd drained, and I could see the same vibration in the air I had seen around the leech and Marigold. My eyes watered and my lips peeled back as the pressure intensified, burning through me. I tried to hold my focus.

Jake began to stir. With a convulsion of my chest, the flow of light toward him ceased. He was back.

Dean was beside him instantly, shutting away his powers.

I couldn't slow the stream rushing through me. Jamie's light ended next. I grunted, releasing the last of Donny's energy, and the tendrils disappeared. But only Sway and I could see that.

Rayni kept pushing, and the flow through me cracked and fractured something inside. I came loose. I floated out of myself. I watched as Jamie and Donny's bodies twitched and woke. I watched as Dean shut them down.

I watched my body wobble and fall.

"Stop!" Dean yelled. He brought up his blocking ability and it flew over my body to Rayni's. I snapped back into my crumpling self.

Dean was there to catch me.

"Hey, hey, Liv? You okay?" He placed a hand on my cheek.

"Whoa." My head was swimming, something still loose, but everything felt like it was there. "Yeah, I'm here. All good. You don't have to block me so strong."

Dean furrowed his brow. "I'm not."

Looking back at Rayni, it was obvious from how she was plopped down on the floor, exhausted, that she wasn't using her powers on me either.

But I felt so … little.

I sat straight up, searching for signs of my powers.

There. I could sense the Crossmans' happiness and worry at the return of their sons. I could sense Rayni's relief and pride. I could sense Felix's joy and excitement. I could even sense a flutter of something warm coming from Dean.

I could no longer see emotions as colors. My powers were there, just smaller, back to what they once were. I had grown so used to the overwhelming excess, it took a while to remember what being *just me* felt like. "I may be totally less superhuman cool now, but it's so nice to just be me again."

Dean helped me to my feet; my legs were still shaky. He wrapped an arm around my waist for support. He smiled, one of those sparkling smiles I rarely saw from him. "You're still my superhero."

My cheeks grew hot, and I leaned into him, wrapping my arms around his waist too, feeling the warm flutter inside him growing.

"It really worked," Mr. Crossman sounded like he couldn't believe it. Dr. Crossman and Felix had both begun checking vitals on the three waking patients.

Rayni had taken a seat back on Ash's bed, watching him with a tired smile, and Sway watched from her own bed with her eyes and mouth wide open.

"What is going on? Where am I?" Jake's voice was harsh and croaky. His crusty eyes narrowed as he spotted Dean and me. "What did you do?"

I flinched and cuddled closer to Dean. How could I explain

everything I'd done? Everything that had happened and was happening?

Jake caught sight of his parents, and his pale skin flushed red. His eyes were wild with confusion as he took in the space, his brother, and Donny waking up beside him, and the other still unconscious patients.

Dr. Crossman started talking quietly to him, and Mr. Crossman beckoned Dean, Rayni, and I over. "Leave it to them now. You've done your part."

Rayni looked up at Mr. Crossman with wide, hopeful eyes.

He frowned back at her, gently. "You know we can't return your brother or the others until we get the leech in custody. This is a great reason to have hope though. We know now that it can be done. Thank you, Livvy."

"No problem." I shrugged, and yawned wide. It was still early evening, but I was exhausted.

Mr. Crossman's phone pinged and he checked the screen. "You parents have just arrived downstairs."

A wide grin split my face. I couldn't wait to see them. To go home.

My happiness was only tempered by knowing the leech was still out there. How did Limbus plan to catch the leech? And how could they make him do what I'd just done?

EMOTIONALLY UNSTABLE

Although I wasn't as strong anymore, I felt proud of what I'd achieved, and somehow, that made me feel stronger. I was the heroine, walking into battle, ready to save the world. Somehow it felt like things were going to work out.

Beside me in the bowl of rice, my phone vibrated into life and dinged with missed calls and messages.

Felix barked a laugh. "Told you I was a genius!"

23

I smiled at my parents as I stepped out of the elevator and into reception.

Mom rushed toward me and grabbed me into her arms. She let out a cry of affection. "Oh, I was so worried. I can't believe there was a fire. Of all the things we have to worry about, some random fire happens." She brushed my still ashy hair from my face and kissed my forehead.

I realized Limbus hadn't said anything to them yet about the leech being there, and that maybe the fire wasn't so random after all. I would tell them later, after the other news. Maybe after a shower and some sleep.

Dad stepped forward. "Uh, Livvy? Where's Dean? Shouldn't he be closer to you than this?"

Mom let me go just to arm's length, looking around for Dean too. I grinned at them both. "I don't need him to be close by anymore. I worked out how to return the extra powers. I'm back to normal me."

Mom's mouth popped open and she hugged me again. "That's wonderful! I know it's been hard for you, managing that."

"What about the boys? Are they actually awake?" Dad had just an edge of worry coming from him.

"It's okay. Limbus is dealing with them. I don't know if we'll even ever see them again." I explained what had happened, how Rayni and I had worked together, and the plan for the boys. "Dean blocked them all permanently—well, at least maybe permanently."

"Where's Dean now?" Mom asked. I loved that she seemed concerned for him as well.

"Well, that's what I mean by *maybe* permanently. Mr. Crossman asked if Dean could stay and work with Rayni to see if Dean could unblock the Crossmans. Now we have new options with combining powers they thought it was worth a shot." I yawned again, my mouth stretching wide, then smiled sleepily at my parents. "They said they'd only try a few things, what with all the other drama, but thought it was worth attempting ASAP since it would be super helpful if they had their powers again. I was going to wait with Dean and call you up to us, but he reminded me I don't have to always be near him anymore. He could tell how tired I was and said I should go home with you."

My heart still felt fluttery at the possibilities for Dean and I in our relationship now. And from the kiss we'd shared when he walked me to the elevator. From the words we'd spoken to each other. I knew we could be apart from each other now but I wanted to be closer to him than ever before. Although I also really wanted a shower and my own clothes and my own bed in my own home.

I started shuffling to the exit where a driver waited to take us to the train station. Mom and Dad walked on either side of me, keeping my slow, sleepy pace. Dad patted me on the back. "This should be really good for both of you."

"Does it feel weird not having Dean here?" Mom asked.

I looked up, as though I could see through the floors of the Limbus building to Dean. "Yeah. I'm so used to having him near me all the time. But that couldn't have gone on forever."

My mother smirked. "I get the feeling he would have done it forever if he had to."

My heart fluttered faster, part love, part fear. "Still, I didn't

444

want him to feel obligated or forced to be with me. He needs his freedom, his own time. I want our closeness to be his choice."

Mom put an arm around my shoulder as we walked. "Damn, we raised you good."

I stuck my tongue out at her.

"What do you think he'll do now?" Dad asked. "You know, with all that free time."

"Take up knitting?" I shrugged. "I don't know. He said he'll come back home tonight, when they are done here. But long-term …"

A sharp sliver of doubt stuck like a splinter into my happiness. *What will Dean choose to do now?* I didn't want to doubt our relationship, but just moments after we were able to be apart, he'd sent me away. I shook the feeling off. I was just overwhelmed. I couldn't doubt him after what we'd just shared.

"He might want to go home," Mom said gently. "Regardless of his father's failings as a parent, family is family. Or maybe Limbus has room for him, like the other kids who board here. But if Dean wants to—and I don't know how your father feels about it, but as far as I'm concerned—he's more than welcome to stay with us as long as he wants."

"He's a good kid," Dad said in agreement.

I blinked tears from my weary eyes. "Yeah, he is."

We stepped out of the main doors. I stared down at the slippers on my feet, not even caring I'd be riding the train looking like this. The driver was Mr. Graybiel again, and he gave me a less nervous, warmer smile when he dropped us off at the train station.

I dozed on and off along the way home, leaning my head on Dad's shoulder, my mom's arm still supporting me.

I felt the separation from Dean like I'd been cleaved in two, and insecurity continued to build the longer we were apart. I was afraid that he wouldn't want to come back to our house. Maybe living at Limbus was the best choice; it would probably be really good for him. It would be selfish of me to not let him make that choice.

But I wanted to be selfish. I wanted to be the teenage girl all over her teenage boyfriend, and for the first time, I finally could be. I didn't want to be apart from him at all.

But being a teenage girl and having normal teenage worries seemed distant to me now. I wasn't the same Livvy I was when I'd been handing out blankets at the shelter. I wasn't even the same Livvy who was in the park that night with Jake's gang, fighting for my life and Dean's. And I couldn't expect Dean to be the same either. I just hoped that our new, different selves worked as well together as our old selves did.

EMOTIONALLY UNSTABLE

When we got off the train, we got a taxi from the station back home, and I went straight into the shower to wash away the smoke and ash from my hair and skin.

I wobbled into some soft, clean pajama pants and a T-shirt. When I crawled into bed, I pulled my knees to my chest and wrapped my shirt over them down to my ankles, cocooning myself.

Mom knocked on the door and came in, pulling the blankets up and tucking me in. She smiled a warm, motherly smile. "You've been through quite a bit, *again*. Get some sleep."

My eyes flashed to hers and I sucked in my lips.

She smirked. "When Dean gets back, I'll poke my head in and let you know."

She could read me perfectly. "Thanks, Mom."

It was only just past nine, and I tried to wait up for Dean anyway. Yawning, I closed my eyes and remembered the moment we'd shared saying goodbye at Limbus, feeling every tingling touch, reliving every joy-soaked word …

Dean held my hand and walked me from the ward to the elevator. My whole being felt light, wobbly, joyous at just being *me* again. At finally ridding myself of the powers I'd stolen. I grinned from ear to ear.

A smile spread slowly on Dean's lips as well, which made me even giddier. I kept throwing glances at those smiling lips of Dean's and warmth grew and grew inside me, and I could sense it from him too, being set free.

I pressed the elevator button, and turned to stand face-to-face with Dean. He took my other hand as well, holding both between us.

"Livvy. Everything … can be different now," he said softly, looking down at our hands.

I only had eyes for his lips.

He continued, "I'm going to make an effort not to push down my emotions anymore. It's going to be hard, but I'm ready. I'm ready to feel again. Feel everything. I think I have been for a while, but I've had to be careful."

For me. He has had to keep blocking everything away so he could keep me stable. I frowned, but he kept talking.

"But now, I want to allow myself to feel, to want, to fear. To *love*."

I looked up into his gray eyes as a single tear rolled out of one, making me gasp. Never, *never*, not in all the tragedy or danger we'd been through, had Dean ever cried. Ever.

"Sorry," he said, almost automatically, shame in his eyes.

He reached a hand to wipe it away. I grabbed his wrist and stopped him.

"No. Never apologize for feeling. You can cry or laugh or do anything you need to do." I put my palm onto his cheek, holding the tear between us. "It's beautiful. *You're* beautiful."

Suddenly I was flooded with warmth and love. Streams of kind-heartedness, pride, and excitement flew through me, filling me to the brim. I could feel everything he had been blocking from himself for so long. I could feel how he still grieved for his mother, how he was saddened by but still loved his father, and lastly, his contentment at being close to me, his fear for my safety, and his overwhelming desire to be with me, in every possible way.

I stood up on my tiptoes and placed three quick, feather-soft kisses onto Dean's lips. I felt the smile on them grow, and then Dean grabbed me around the waist, pulling me into him and our kiss grew deep and strong. Every danger we'd shared, every loss and every fear, was washed away in a tidal-wave of *love* swirling around us.

The elevator dinged beside us. Doors opened and closed again. Dean lifted me from my feet and we spun in slow circles, our lips pressed hotly together.

Down the hall, Felix yelled at us to get a room.

Everything felt golden and sundrenched and like I could kiss Dean forever.

I slipped away from the memory and into sleep, swimming through the waves of visions I had seen over the last few weeks. Coming back to school and to Nati. Rayni's pale rainbow hair. Sway sharing a cookie with a rat. Ash's face fluttered by, smiling big at the bus stop. Dean hooked his fingers into mine.

But then things started to get dark.

I stood in the center of a pitch-black space. Red light grew as flames flickered all over walls on every side, boxing me in. Smoke rolled over my bare feet. I heard a striking laughter that made me sick to my stomach. Then, as if someone had stabbed me through the back and into my heart, a piercing pain took over me. My mouth fell open and I wheezed, only small moans escaping. The leech stood on all sides of me. So many of him. Moving so fast, surrounding me. He was everywhere and everything all at once and he was stealing my soul.

I struggled and fell backward onto the ground, tried to swim away through the smoke and darkness, but the leech was too fast. He grabbed me by my heart and lifted me high above his head. I looked down into his face and he seemed … *familiar.*

450

EMOTIONALLY UNSTABLE

I gasped awake, slippery with sweat. My eyes shot wide open and I sat straight up in the bed, grabbing at my chest. Looking around my room, I blinked in relief. It was a nightmare. Just a nightmare.

The clock on my phone's lock screen told me it was one in the morning. No other notifications were on the screen.

I frowned. Had I slept through Mom telling me Dean was back? He had to be here by now.

I picked up my phone, making sure there weren't any missed messages. I climbed out of bed and when I stepped out of my room, I noticed the light was still on in the kitchen. I squinted as I walked downstairs and into the light, seeing my parents still sitting at the kitchen table. Each with a coffee mug in one hand and a phone in the other.

"Why are you both still up?" I mumbled groggily. "Why didn't you wake me when Dean got back?"

Mom and Dad frowned, looking at each other, then back to me. "Lollipop, honey—"

Acid sickness rose in my throat. "He did get back, right? Where's Dean? Is he here? What's going on?"

A rush of sad worry spread from my mom to me. "Dean's missing."

24

"Missing?" I swallowed bile, unable to accept the concept. "He could still be at Limbus. Maybe they're just still trying things. Maybe they went later than they'd thought they would."

Even as I said it, I knew it couldn't be true. Rayni was already tired, so she couldn't have lasted this long.

"We called Limbus twenty minutes ago when we started getting worried. Dean left there at ten thirty."

"Then he should be back by now." I stepped left, then right, panic driving my actions, but I didn't know where to turn. I glanced again at the phone in my hand—no messages from

Dean.

"Stay calm. Dean has his tracker. If something was wrong, he would have pressed the panic button. The trains might have just been held up. Limbus are checking."

My voice was louder than it needed to be. "Have you tried calling Dean?"

Mom bit her lip. "He's not answering."

"Lollipop ..." Dad put out a reassuring hand, but I was already moving.

Maybe it was nothing. Maybe he was just enjoying being free from me, on his own. Maybe his phone was flat. Maybe he was enjoying some complete solitude for a change. Maybe he'd fallen asleep on the train and missed his stop. Maybe, maybe, maybe swirled in my head but gave me no hope. I had to find him.

I ran for the front door, grabbing my red trench coat and throwing it on over my pajamas. I didn't take time for shoes. I dashed out onto the street, barefoot, while my parents yelled after me.

I built momentum, my feet slapping the tarmac on the empty roads. I sought and absorbed fear from every source I could to go faster. I drew in the fears from children's bedrooms where they had nightmares about monsters. I went faster, and faster, because I knew monsters were real. I prayed the monster hadn't gotten Dean.

The threat of the leech created an all-consuming fear within me. It was unlikely the leech would strike again so soon. It was unlikely the leech would know where Dean was. That was why Limbus had been fine with us taking trains home.

But the leech had seen our faces.

At the speed I was going, I would reach the train station in five minutes. I caught glimpses of myself in the shopfront windows as I passed, just a red streak flashing by. It didn't feel fast enough, and I wished I still had the three boys' powers as well.

My phone buzzed in the palm of my hand and I checked it quickly as I dashed down a side alley. It was Limbus.

I answered. "Do you know where he is?"

"Olivia." Dr. Crossman's voice was concerned. "Your parents told us you ran out to find Dean. We really need you to go back home where you'll be safe. We're activating your tracker until you get back."

"WHERE'S DEAN?" I yelled.

There was a shuffle and some mumbled voices. "We've activated tracking for him already, and I'm looking at Dean's location now. He's at the Bellscroft station—has been since we got your parents' call. We already have agents on the way to check, but he hasn't pressed his beacon or panic button. You really should go home."

I wasn't going home. I didn't hang up, but took the phone away from my ear, shoving it into my coat pocket.

I'm going to find Dean, sitting there just fine. He'll have fallen asleep waiting for a taxi at the station. He's just enjoying a moment alone. This is fine.

I ran faster.

The night air was icy and my breath burned cold through my chest and throat, but I didn't slow down. Greater than any fear I absorbed from my surroundings was my own terror, white-hot in my veins, pumping through me, pushing me even harder.

I rounded the corner to the train station.

The main entrance through the ticket turnstiles was all the way around the other side. A couple of drunks were arguing down the road. No one else seemed to be around as I looked through the chain-link fence at the platforms.

I clung to the fence with clawed fingers and leaned my head against the wire, staring through it for any sign of Dean.

Breath caught in my throat. Something flashed down in the gap on one of the tracks. The same way my tracker flashed now it had been activated.

I could hear a train in the distance.

Tightening my clawed grip on the chain-link fence, I tore it apart. I took off across the empty train station, leaping from platform to platform toward that flashing beacon.

The train was in sight now, heading for the track the flash had come from. I reached the platform and jumped down onto the tracks. I almost froze entirely when I saw … but I had no time to freeze.

My heart raced as I raced headfirst toward the train, toward the body between me and it.

The train's horn blared. It zipped past, clipping my elbow as it went by.

I stood on the platform again, shaking all over. Dean was lifeless in my arms.

I cried out as I slumped to my knees. *This can't be happening. Not now. It can't.*

I held my ear to Dean's chest, listening for his heartbeat. It was there, but slow, weak. Tears choked me as I stared at his pale and purple features.

"Dean? Dean, please wake up," I begged, but I knew there'd be no reply.

I pulled the phone from my pocket. All strength had left

me. I was numb, shivering, could barely breathe.

"Olivia? Olivia, are you there?" Dr. Crossman's voice was frantic.

I managed to get just one more sentence out before dropping the phone. "Dean's been drained."

EMOTIONALLY
POWERFUL

THE EMPATH **3** CHRONICLES

1

The elevator dinged beside us, but I didn't want to separate my lips from Dean's.

My body felt light and giddy after having just emptied myself of the other powers I had drained. Yet the world felt so full now, of new possibilities. Of romance. I could taste the salt of Dean's tears and the sweetness of his tongue and didn't care that half of Limbus stared at us from down the corridor. Dean and I embraced each other with needy arms, living only for this kiss that we had been denied for so long.

Dean slowed down first, drawing back softly. I didn't ever want the moment to end, but then he did something that filled my heart even more.

He pressed his temple against mine, and whispered into my ear, "I love you."

I didn't even have to think. The words shot up from my very heart itself. "I love you too."

Dean squeezed me around the waist and kissed my cheek slowly. "Everything will be different now. Everything will be amazing."

My eyes were on Dean, his shallow breaths, his purple lips, his closed eyelids.

His hand was cold and still in mine.

Machines helped him breathe, monitored all his vital functions, pumped nutrients and fluids into his body that couldn't support its own needs. They whirled and beeped, matched by others around the Limbus ward, the only sound in the room.

It had been more than a week since the leech had got to Dean. A week of sleepless nightmares and unstoppable tears.

I squeezed Dean's hand. I had dragged him into this life, the world of empaths. This was my fault. *All my fault.*

The moment I found Dean at the train station still felt like a dream, or a nightmare. I had slumped, curled up beside Dean's lifeless form on the platform concrete. The agents close by had arrived, then the Crossmans came, and my parents, and everyone tried to console me, tell me it was going to be okay, but I was lost.

My chest was tight with heartbreak; I wanted, *needed,* to be with him. His body was here, but I knew he wasn't. Not the real Dean.

"Hi Livvy. Back again, I see." One of the nurses pushed the curtain aside and smiled at me with pitying eyes.

"Every day," I replied, trying to force a grin.

Limbus had been good about letting me come in and see Dean whenever I wanted. They knew I needed to be here. I couldn't tear myself away from him. It was too soon. I felt guilty every time I went home, but I also knew there was no chance Dean would spontaneously wake up on his own. My parents had been understanding too, but I knew it wouldn't last forever. Eventually I would have to join the land of the living again.

Kimmy followed the nurse over and jumped up onto the end of the bed. She walked up to nuzzle a soft nose-kiss for Dean and me, then curled up into a black and white purring ball beside Dean's tucked in legs.

The nurse took readings and jotted down some notes on a tablet screen with a stylus. "Just normal checks."

"Any changes since yesterday?" I asked, already knowing the answer.

She patted her hand on my shoulder. "No, sweetie. But as soon as there are, you'll be the first person I tell. I promise."

I nodded and waited for her to leave the area again. There would be no changes, no life returned to Dean, until the leech was brought down and brought in. And Limbus seemed no closer to achieving that.

I tiptoed to gently pull the curtain that surrounded Dean's bed closed again. I didn't know why I moved so quietly. It wasn't like my noise was going to wake anyone. Moving back to my chair, it felt like a strong current blew through my head, bringing a weird sense of detachment with it. My vision blurred. I grasped the chair back with one hand, holding tightly to my forehead with the other.

The feeling dissipated just as quickly as it started and I blinked, looking around. *Weird.*

Sitting, I put my legs up, resting them on the edge of Dean's bed and holding his hand. I spoke, not because I thought he could hear, but because I needed to imagine him with me.

"Let's see. What do I have to tell you today? I slept in your bed again last night. Although it's starting to not smell like you already. Mom and Dad are missing you too. Dad keeps cooking more for dinner than we need, forgetting he doesn't have a teenage boy to feed anymore."

Tapping my fingers on Dean's hand, I stared at his pale face. He was still Dean, but the stillness of his body made him look like he was made out of wax. I kept imagining him opening his eyes, stretching his arms, and yawning, like he was just waking from a nap. And every time I imagined it, my eyes filled with tears.

"So anyway," I said, clearing my throat, "I've got training this afternoon. I figure it will be good for me, but it will be hard without you there. I hate the feeling I'm going back to my life, without you. It makes me feel like I'm giving up on you. But it's not helping anyone, sitting in here moping either. The longer I do this, the longer you'll be out. The only way to save you is to find and capture the leech. I need to help. I want to be the hero that saves you."

The word hero made me laugh at myself. I've been such a superhero, sitting in here, crying and holding my valiant hero's hand while he lay helpless in bed.

I couldn't keep waiting for Limbus to fix this. They didn't seem to have any leads. The leech was either way too lucky or way too clever for them.

But I had a shot. The leech knew my face. Knew what I

could do. He'd gone after Dean right after he saw us. He'd felt … familiar.

And the fact Dean hadn't used his panic button must have meant the leech didn't seem like a threat to Dean until too late. Maybe it was someone we knew.

That was something I could work with. I'd drained people before; I'd restored people before. I would find the leech, and take everything he'd stolen from the others, even if it made me explode, and I'd put all those powers back where they belonged.

After I'd restored him to his body, Jake had told his parents he hadn't been aware of anything at all, of any time passing or any feelings or thoughts during the time I had drained him and held his powers inside me. I wondered if Dean was the same. He was a blocker, which had to be a bit different. I had only given the power back to proesthians like me. I didn't even know if I could give back a blocker's powers. But I couldn't think about it at that moment. I couldn't dare imagine not succeeding. Last time I did, I cried so hard I vomited in the sink.

I pulled Dean's hand to my lips and kissed the back of it. "I promise, one way or another, I'll get you back." I looked around the room, at all the leech's victims. "I'll get every single one of you back."

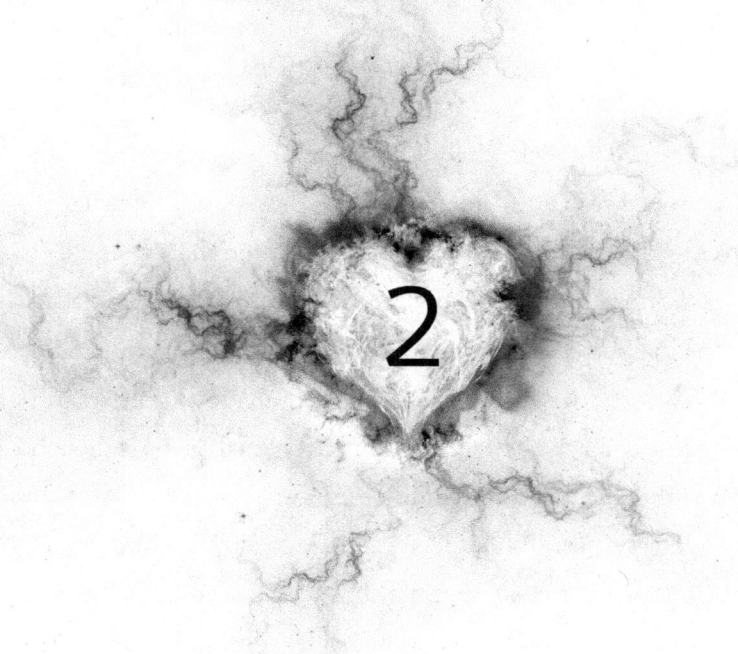

2

The Crossmans looked more nervous with every passing day. Dean hadn't managed to restore their powers that night, before he was drained. From what I'd heard, he was really close, but close wasn't what they needed. They were anxious about the leech, and being powerless left them relying entirely on the other Limbus agents.

I noticed one day they had both started to carry concealed firearms. It felt like everyone was waiting to hear the news the leech had struck again with every passing hour. But after Dean, everything had gone quiet.

Limbus had ramped up training for us younger empaths. Our teachers had begun introducing a lot more aggressive self-defense into what had been mostly meditation and focus classes before. They probably wanted us to have some chance of defending ourselves, or at least the illusion that we could.

I didn't fear the leech anymore. My fear had been replaced with pure hatred. An anger so deep that it changed me. I could tell from the way my parents looked at me that it wasn't necessarily for the better. I let that anger burn deep, as though it was the fuel that I needed to keep going.

Security overall had been increased both at Limbus and within our household, and the times Mom and Dad allowed me to catch the train I always had at least one agent with me. Mostly, Limbus drove me anywhere I needed to go.

Home was the only place I didn't have a full escort. I hadn't been to school. My parents let me take sick days. I missed Nati, but how could I explain any of this to her?

When I walked into the gym, the room was quiet, but there was a whisper of excitement from some of the younger kids. They watched Felix, who stood beside a metal trolley with plastic crates stacked on top, twiddling his goatee. Bastian, Emma, and Sway were in the middle of the room, sitting beside each other, cross-legged with their eyes closed. Rayni was with the few other younger kids, who I now knew were Ada, Cam, and Max. She seemed a bit brighter than she had for a while.

EMOTIONALLY POWERFUL

I couldn't see color auras anymore, but could still sense sadness in her underneath her smile.

My eyes still felt raw and my mouth was fixed downwards. How long would it take after Dean's draining for me to be able to put on a brave face like that?

For now, all my energy went into training. It was essential in order for me to grow physically and mentally stronger. I needed anything I could get if I was going to start hunting down the leech. Of course, I hadn't divulged that plan to the Crossmans, but I was sure they suspected. They knew where I was and how angry I had become, even without empath senses.

The Crossmans were deep in conversation together, checking things on their tablet screens, before Mr. Crossman spoke loudly, addressing the room. "All right, everyone, gather around. Felix has brought something for you all."

Everyone came closer, and Felix reached into one of the boxes. So that was where all of the excitement was stemming from. Some of the kids must have already known what was happening in training today.

"You get a superhero suit, and you get a superhero suit!" Felix cried, as he pulled black jumpsuits out of the box and chucked them into waiting hands.

One landed in my grasp, and I rubbed the thick, silky fabric between my fingers. I glanced over at one of the uniformed agents in black standing guard near a door. It looked almost the same as what they wore. My eyebrows went up.

A rush of chatter filled the room. The younger kids were so excited their emotions were flooding over. It was like a domino effect, catching to every empath in the group. Even I managed a wry half-smile.

Felix clapped his hands together. "Okay, I know you are all dying to play dress-up, but I need to explain the suit to you first so you don't rip holes in these things, because they aren't cheap." He dashed out of the room briefly then came back in, pushing a mannequin wearing one of the suits. Felix rolled the mannequin to the front of the group and stood beside it. "These are the same kinds of suits that the grown-up operatives wear, just scaled down for you guys. With a shrink ray!"

Everyone oohed and awed.

"Not actually with a shrink ray." Dr. Crossman clarified dryly. "These suits have a lot of features that can help an empath utilize their powers, or help with things an empath's powers can't. You kids are very talented, but sometimes that isn't all there is to it. Strength, speed, and toughness can't solve every problem you are going to face. From now on, you'll be wearing these during training sessions to learn their features and get used to them, just like our adult operatives."

Felix pointed to the different features of the suit as he went, starting with the soap-bar-sized flat section near the wrist. "Capacitive-touch smart-screen that—once fully activated—links up to the Limbus system, GPS, telecom systems, vitals monitoring, and more. Plus, it has pretty heart-shaped notification lights! That was my design choice. Utility belt contains various tools for covert operations and survival in many conditions, including tasty ration packs. You don't get those yet either. The fabric has bio-electric protection, and is blade- and bullet-proof."

I ran my hands over the soft fabric again. As the material moved, the light caught on small metal fibers running through. The suits sounded pretty impressive. I doubted they were leech-proof though.

Felix went on and on, explaining every single device, then let the excited group split up to go and try the suits on.

I made my way towards the bathrooms in the corner of the gym, then noticed Emma heading that way too. She locked eyes with me, and we stopped. She bit her lip, then opened her mouth as though she was about to say something.

I spun on my heel, heading out to the bathrooms down the hall. I wasn't in the mood to interact with her. I fumed, imagining she was happy, that in her mind Dean deserved what he got. Or even worse, imagining having her pity us.

I hated that Emma had been getting the full team experience the whole time I'd been mourning Dean. I'd been hearing glowing reports of how well she'd been doing. How clever and talented she was. Emma had even officially been let off 'house arrest' at Limbus. Not that it meant anything right then. She, Sway, Rayni, Bastian and the others who lived at the agency were pretty much on lockdown, unable to go out in town without extra permissions and security.

I closed myself into a toilet stall, despite having the whole bathroom block to myself. I undressed and then pulled the suit on, one foot at a time. It looked far too small at first, but slipped on snuggly and smoothly. The black material was like spandex or Lycra, but it was far lighter with a subtle scale-like texture, and a thicker vest area. I zipped up the front and stepped out. As I pulled my hair back in a ponytail I looked into the mirror.

The old me would have been giggling with excitement. I looked like a superhero. But the new me had red-rimmed eyes with dark purple smudges beneath them, and a hard grimace.

Part of me wished I could feel that innocent giddiness again. Maybe one day it would come back. I didn't want this serious girl in the mirror to be the permanent version of myself. But I needed her right now.

EMOTIONALLY POWERFUL

Back inside the training room, the kids were being paired up to practice some karate-based self-defense moves to experience the full range of movement the suit provided. Bastian and Emma paired together as normal and were already suited up and sparring.

Bastian had pulled his brown ringlets into a puffy top-knot. He shook his head at Emma and slapped his forearm. "No. I know you can do better than that. You know it too. Don't worry about the external. You've got what you need inside. Go again."

Emma nodded, moving through the stances a second time to strike a blow that made Bastian laugh and clap. She pushed her red hair back over her ear, exposing her clear eyes, the natural pink to her cheeks. *Huh.* She wasn't wearing any make-up.

Sway walked up next to me, wrinkling her nose and tugging at the fabric around her non-existent hips. "I guess this is better than scrubs."

I looked at her petite, boy-like figure, and the shaved-side blonde pixie hair swirled on top of her head. "You look like a cartoon character. In a good way."

Sway smiled and her eyes glittered. When I didn't smile in return, she followed my gaze to Emma and Bastian. "You two have some history, hey. She told me a bit about it."

I pursed my lips. I could only imagine what Emma had been

telling everyone. Because I doubted any of it was the truth. I started some warm-up stretches and muttered, "I can't believe everyone thinks she's so great. How does she deserve this …?" *When Dean* … I gulped away a sob and firmed my expression.

Sway moved her face close to mine, inspecting me wide-eyed. "You really don't like her?"

"She's so … superficial and selfish." *Like I used to be.*

"Really? Wow. I haven't noticed. She's more of a thinky-thoughtful, tries-to-be-bestest-friends girl." Sway bent over beside me, stretching as well. Sway and Emma had been in rooms just down the hall from each other since moving into Limbus.

I imagined them bonding, up late chatting on each other's beds, and scowled. "Sounds like how I first saw Emma. Before I learned the truth."

"If it's worth anything, I think she's sorry." Bastian's voice startled me from my stretch. He'd come over beside us without me noticing. I bristled and stood up straight, but Emma hadn't followed him. She was over with the Crossmans.

"Emma's not what I expected either." Bastian shrugged his round shoulders. "She's actually a total egg-head under all that razzle dazzle. She's just spent so long pretending to be what she thought she had to be in order to be accepted, to survive."

A vivid memory of Emma's pre-cosmetic surgery photo flashed

through my mind. She'd done so much to escape who she was. Maybe in the right, accepting environment, she could be the real her. And maybe the real her was nicer than I imagined.

I wasn't sure though. "Then why didn't you want to train with her? What did you see with your future vision that made you flip out when you met her?"

Bastian's brown cheeks glowed. "You know that elucidist powers don't always play out accurately."

Emma and Rayni came over before he could elaborate any further. They both held water bottles, and there was a vulnerability in Emma's smile I hadn't noticed before.

She tucked her hair behind an ear even though it hadn't fallen free, cleared her throat and said, "Hey, Livvy."

"Hey," I grunted. It was the first direct interaction we'd had since the comic convention and a tense silence built.

Bastian looked around at the four of us. "Wow, it's becoming a bit of a girls' club in here."

Sway scrunched up her lips in a pout. "I don't always feel like a girl, if that helps."

Emma tilted her head thoughtfully. "Are women more likely to be empaths than men? Women are naturally more in tune with their emotions."

Rayni's eyes lit up. "Actually, if you really look into it, that whole 'emotional women' and 'unemotional men' thing as a premise is nothing more than a sexist societal construct. Fairly damaging on the men's side too, making them bottle up their emotions—" Her eyes zipped over to me and her mouth clammed shut. I took a deep breath, my jaw twitching.

Sway beat her chest like a gorilla. "Crush the patriarchy, raaar!"

Bastian feigned terror. "I'm completely outnumbered!"

I snapped, "What? You're feeling put out because you're the only guy your age not lying in a coma?"

The smiles on everyone's faces dropped. Anger sizzled under my skin, and from the way Sway looked at me, I wondered if she could see my aura glowing red.

"Have you already forgotten about Dean? And Ash?"

The tremble of Rayni's bottom lip made me turn away. I bent to grab my water bottle from the mat then stalked off, filled with fury and shame.

Because for a moment, I had been enjoying myself too.

From behind my back I heard Emma tease Bastian. "Why didn't you see *that* coming?"

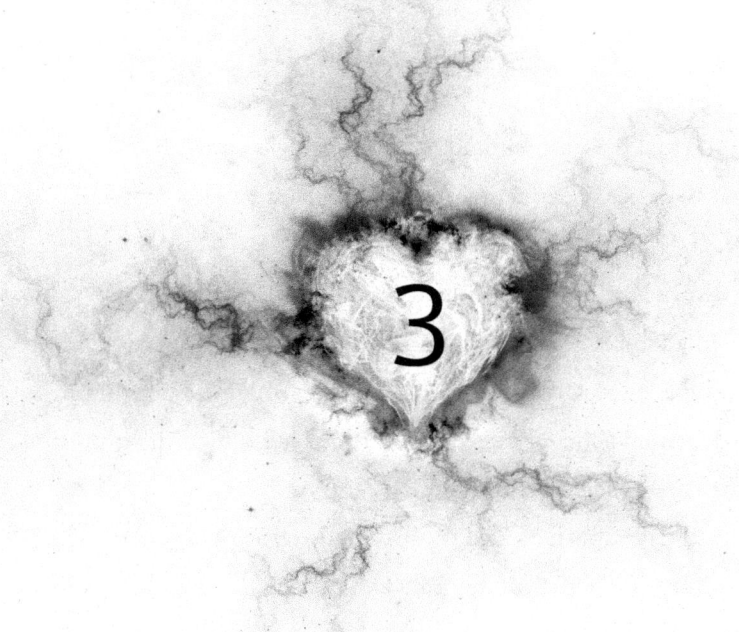

3

Dad had garlic and ginger sautéing in a pan, sizzling softly as he chopped vegetables. Mom sat next to me at the kitchen table, her fingers tapping away on her laptop keyboard, and she mumbled and muttered occasionally under her breath about insurance claim bureaucracy bull—her eyes would flash to me—*dirt*.

I had my head down on my folded arms, staring at the beads of condensation on my glass of water. Trying to do nothing, think of nothing. Another week had passed. I had started going to school again. I kept training. Nothing changed. Dean didn't wake up. The leech was still out there. I could have exploded from frustration. I wanted to rip the world apart, hunting for that monster. I wanted revenge and justice and to not feel all this hate all the time.

So I sat and did nothing and took slow, deep breaths.

I had kept up with my therapy sessions, out of a new office. Because the old office was at the institute, where all the buildings had been evacuated after the leech burned one to the ground. After he murdered Marigold.

My fists clenched, and my breathing was not slow and deep.

"This is almost ready. Can you set the table?" Dad called across the kitchen counter to us.

I started sliding my chair back, but Mom shut her laptop and smoothed her hand down my hair. "I'll do it." She stood up and kissed me on the top of the head, then went to the cupboard.

Plates clattered in her hand and she put them out around the table. I sat up so she could put one in front of me. "Thanks."

"No prob, bub," she said cheerily.

When she'd put three plates down, she still had one in her hand, hovering above the table. Her gaze flickered to me, then she took the plate back to the cupboard, probably hoping I hadn't noticed her slip-up. I wondered whether Dad was cooking too much food again. He'd started excusing it as 'making leftovers'. But it felt like he wanted to be sure, that just in case by some miracle Dean woke up perfectly fine and walked in the door, there'd be a meal for him here. I liked that idea too. But I knew it wouldn't happen.

Dad placed a huge serving bowl of stir-fry and one of rice into the middle of the table. Enough for us three and way more. *Bingo.*

"I'm glad you're here for dinner tonight. It feels like you've been at training or visiting Dean in all your spare hours," he said as he took his seat, "which is completely okay. But we've missed you."

"I've missed you both too." I smiled thinly, helping myself from the mountain of food. My stomach gurgled, hungry from the extra exercise and training. And below that I could feel my pull to Dean, that need to be close to him that lived deep in the pit of my being. "I want to be with Dean, too. I want to be there for him all the time like he was there for me. But it's not helpful. There was a point to him being by my side. It's actually kind of counterproductive for me to spend all of my time next to him. It won't wake him up."

Mom paused with the serving spoon in the rice. "Oh, Livvy-bear. We wish there was something we could do. We've racked our brains, and the Crossmans', on how we could help, but in this situation I'm afraid we're virtually useless."

I smiled, honestly and warmly. "You're far from useless. You help me so much just being here for me. I need you both to be my parents, and I'll handle the empath stuff."

Mom side-eyed Dad then, and I could tell they were edging around a conversation. She cleared her throat and put her cutlery down. "Livvy, you're not planning anything rash, right? We know you're determined to fix this, to save Dean, and we're worried you're going to try and do it alone."

After taking a deep breath, I sipped my water. It bugged me how they could always see straight through me. I appreciated that they cared, but I also knew I'd do anything I had to do to save Dean. *Anything.*

Unfortunately, so far, I had *nothing*. I didn't even have to lie. "I don't have any crazy plans."

Mom squinted at me like she really was trying to read my mind. "Because you're not alone, you know that, right? We all want to save Dean, and the others, and stop that criminal from hurting anyone else just as much as you want to. You have all of Limbus trying to help."

"And us," Dad added. "At least to keep doing the parent thing."

"Thanks, guys." I poked at my food, trying not to cry. "I love you."

"Right back at ya, Lollipop," Dad said with his mouth full.

Mom looked like she had something else to say when the doorbell rang.

Dad frowned. "I wonder who that could be. You expecting anyone?"

Mom shook her head. "Nope."

I scoffed at the tiny spark of foolish hope, imagining it really was Dean there, miraculously woken and come home for dinner.

Still, I sat frozen in place as Dad went to answer the door. *Limbus could have done it,* the hope reasoned. *Caught the leech, restored everyone. It could happen at any moment.*

Dad greeted someone happily, and I could hear his and another man's laughter.

"That's brilliant news. Come in! You have time for a beer?" Dad returned to the kitchen, followed by Terry. "You'll never guess who got promoted again!"

Mom hopped up and greeted him with a hug. "So soon? That's amazing! Congratulations."

Terry flashed his million-dollar smile. He wasn't in uniform, just wore jeans and a tucked-in polo shirt, but he still had that authoritarian police presence he always had.

I forced a smile. He wasn't my favorite person. "Hi Terry," I said, without getting out of my seat.

"Olivia, not getting into any new adventures?" He walked

past and patted me on the back, then took the empty chair across the table from me. He watched me with sparkling eyes. I worked hard not to roll mine.

Dad grabbed two beers from the fridge. "You're welcome to some dinner too; we've got plenty."

"If you insist." He grinned, taking a bottle from Dad and popping the top off.

Mom set a plate and silverware in front of him. She took her seat again and raised her water glass. "To your promotion."

"To Captain Pence." Dad chinked his bottle to her glass and Terry joined them.

"Just honored to serve my town." His tone gave me an uneasy feeling, but I tried to ignore it. Terry had always been a good friend to my parents, no matter how much he creeped me out. He held out his bottle to me and I clinked my cup against it politely.

"It's not as safe a place as people believe," he mused, taking a swig of his beer. "A strong police force is important to keep everything in check. There are bad guys around every corner."

Mom chuckled nervously. "I'm sure it's not really that bad. Most *bad guys* are just people society has failed in some way."

"Even those kids who trashed your shop, Jolene? Thugs with no respect for anything or anyone—that's what they are.

Menaces to society that will only get worse unless they are locked up or put down."

Dad tutted and gave Terry a stern but friendly look. "You know how we feel about the death penalty in this house."

Terry smiled an apology, but a shiver ran down my spine. I could sense a rising mix of emotions, a humming jitteriness in Terry that set my teeth on edge.

He ate a mouthful then pointed his fork at me while he spoke. "Your parents are big softies, but if they saw what I saw every day, their minds would change. For example, just last night I saved a woman's life, down in Bellston Main. A drug addict had her at knife point, trying to shake her up for cash—maybe more."

Mom sucked in a loud breath and gave Terry a warning look, but he kept going.

"I was able to intervene because I've done what I've needed to do to be in a position of power. In the war of good and evil, you've got to consider the greater good. I did what I had to, to save her life, before something really bad could happen."

He paused as if I was supposed to say something back, but I could only stare, aghast and confused. His tone, whatever message he was trying to get across, was creeping me out more than he had ever done before.

"How about you, Olivia?" he asked.

"Huh?"

"You must be starting to think about what to do after high school. Ever thought of joining the force?"

I stared around the table, all eyes on me and a heavy awkwardness setting in. "Not really. I don't think I'm the crime-fighting kind of girl."

Dad coughed and cleared his throat.

Terry helped himself to seconds of the food, piling it up and scraping the serving plates clean. "Oh? I would have thought, after your recent experiences, you might have gained a certain appreciation for that side of the world."

I stiffened. Just how much had my parents told him? They looked as confused as I felt though. "And what side of the world exactly is that?"

"You know ..." He laughed. "The helpers—those who are powerful enough to help the powerless. Police, EMTs, that sort of thing."

My shoulders dropped a little, relieved.

"Or people with abilities like ours. Empaths." He winked at me and I dropped my fork.

Cutlery clattered near Mom and Dad as well, but my eyes were fixed on Terry.

484

EMOTIONALLY POWERFUL

My jaw wobbled as I tried to find words to deny what I was, and shocked to find out what he was, but he talked over me.

"No point denying it anymore. You know, I was almost thrown off my suspicions about you when that bleach-haired punk in your class ended up being an empath too. I'd set up that little ceiling incident to force something out of you but ended up getting him instead."

"Getting … Ash?" My breathing became rapid and panic made my vision blurry.

Mom gasped. "Terry? What are you—"

"Eat your dinner and be quiet," he replied tersely.

Her mouth closed and she smiled softly, and she and Dad robotically ate their dinner.

I jumped to my feet, my chair falling to the ground behind me. My mind raced.

"Isn't it amazing? The things we can do." He grinned at me like we were best friends, and took another mouthful of his food. "Getting ahead in life, making a real difference. It's all about power. This power. As much of this power as you can get."

My whole body turned to ice and my legs nearly buckled.

It's him.

4

It's him. Terry's the leech. He's sitting at dinner with my family, telling me *he's the leech.*

I didn't know why. I didn't care what his motives were. I only knew I had to *stop him.*

I leaped straight over the tabletop and threw the hardest punch I could.

Everything spun around us, the wind from my movements sending napkins flying and plates crashing to the ground.

As my fist approached his cheek, he casually reached up and grabbed it.

It felt like I'd hit a block of steel. I cried out in agony as bones in my hand cracked.

He gave me a pitying look. "Olivia, please. I'm just here to tal—"

I swung my other fist, landing the uppercut under his chin. My punch glanced off him. He didn't even blink.

He snatched my second hand out of the air so fast I couldn't see it, and pushed against me.

My legs bent as he forced my back down onto the table with enormous strength.

Staring at me from above with menacing eyes, he grunted. "That was just rude, Olivia."

Plates crashed and clattered. My parents jolted into awareness. My mom cried out, and Dad heaved his chair back. "Let my daughter go right now."

Terry's mouth twitched and his eyes twinkled. He was drinking in their anger. They were only making him stronger. My chest flooded with sudden fear for my parents. I eyed the Limbus tracker bracelet, but Terry still held both my hands firmly.

He chuckled, like we'd just had a misunderstanding, but didn't let me go. "Now, now. Let's just put this all behind us, shall we?"

Mom bellowed, "Get out. Get out of my house!"

Terry sighed, and he flung me like a wet rag against the wall.

The plasterboard buckled beneath my impact and I crashed into a side table, falling down into a pile of smashed photo frames and broken ornaments. I saw stars. Punch-drunk, I flailed, tried to focus.

Terry stepped toward my terrified parents, waving his hands and chin in time as though conducting an orchestra. "My old friends. Come now, let's not fight."

I sobbed as my parents both smiled and nodded at him like puppets.

I squeezed both sides of the tracker with stinging fingers, preparing to set off the panic button. Terry shot me a smile and wrapped a hand around the back of my mom's neck, lifting her off the ground. I snatched my fingers away from the tracker before it flashed red.

"Stop!" I dragged myself up onto wobbly feet. I wanted to rush him, but I knew I wasn't as fast as he was. And Limbus's reaction to the panic button wouldn't be fast enough either. "Please, *please* don't hurt them. They aren't part of this."

"I really would hate to have to harm anyone. You won't make me, will you? No more sucker punches?"

I cradled my broken hands and nodded.

Terry put my mom back down on her feet, then brushed back his messed up blond hair with his hands, sighing. "I think

Jolene and Craig here are going to come for a ride with me."

A whimper escaped my mouth. "No, please don't."

Terry tilted his head to the side as though considering my plea. "You see, I am pretty sure your parents are *persons of interest* in a string of robberies downtown. I think it's best I take them into lockup. Just for a while. That should give you time to think about my offer."

"What offer?" I growled.

"To join forces, of course." He smiled, and it dripped with satisfaction. "I know what you did to those three boys. I know you're like me. You understand the scope of what people like us can *really* become. And with my help, you could be so much more."

My head shook and my lips twitched with overflowing hatred.

"Think about it," Terry snapped, *commanded*, and I felt the force of his command stronger than I'd ever felt Jake's power of suggestion. I forced it away only by the pure might of my anger.

Terry herded my parents toward the door. He stopped in front of me and picked a piece of broken glass from my shoulder. I whimpered as it slid free of my flesh. "But if you tell a soul about this, I can promise you right now, you'll never see your parents again."

With a million-dollar smile, he tapped the tip of my nose. "So, think on it long and hard, *Lollipop*. I know you'll make a good choice."

5

I didn't know how many hours I lay on the floor, curled in a ball. Aching all over, inside and out. Weeping. Choking on sobs.

It had been dark a long time before I could move again. My empath powers had worked to heal my physical injuries relatively quickly, at least enough to achieve basic functionality. I was sure parts of my hands were broken, and although I could move my fingers again, they still throbbed.

But it was nothing to the emotional pain that crippled me.

I should have pressed the panic button straight away. As soon as I suspected anything. Before he had any reason to threaten my parents. I could have played it cool, hidden it under the table, kept him talking.

I shouldn't have tried to take him on my own.

Coulda, shoulda, woulda etched repetitive patterns into my brain, scratching away my sanity.

My imagination tortured me, showing me Limbus arriving in time, the agents taking Terry down, bring him in, forcing him to restore those he'd drained. I had Dean back. Happy ending.

But instead, I had this.

Nothing.

Terry had taken everything from me.

I groaned and moved into a sitting position, my back against the wall. I angrily picked pieces of rice and glass off my clothes.

How did I miss this? I should have guessed it was him. The leech had felt so familiar, but I didn't connect that to Terry.

Not Terry, a pillar of our community. Not Terry, always there to help out. Not Terry, with his shining blond hair and winning smile. Terry, who deep down had always creeped me out, but I'd ignored that instinct because he was my parents' friend. Mr. Everyone Agrees He's A Great Man.

I stared at the tracker on my wrist. I could still press it. Still ask Limbus for help.

I needed help.

EMOTIONALLY POWERFUL

I was so wrong. I can't do this alone.

Tears started again, but I couldn't press the button. I'd seen firsthand what Terry was capable of. How he used people, used them up, discarded them. I didn't doubt for a second he could keep my parents locked up forever. Or worse.

The kind of control he had over them was unlike anything I had seen before. They moved like zombies, unable to control their own minds. His power was above and beyond anything I could even comprehend. And he was still after more.

And he wanted to make me *like him.*

I had to stop him. Somehow. I wasn't sure any amount of training could help me become strong enough to beat him head to head, and I couldn't drain him if he was beating the snot out of me. I rubbed my face on my forearms, trying to dry my tears, trying to soothe the tension headache that grew, trying to fight exhaustion, trying to think.

I just had to find the right time.

He had to have some weakness. And I would find out what it was.

The next day, I was woken by dawn's pink light streaming into where I lay on the tiled dining room floor. I blinked, looking around, hoping it was all just a dream, but the state of the room proved it had really happened. The place was trashed. Sticky bits of stir-fry congealed in blobs around the room, surrounded by spray patterns of rice. Family photos lay scattered, escaped from their smashed frames.

Terry was the leech. And he had my parents.

I picked up the closest photo, of Mom, Dad, and I, dressed up as baby owls for book week when I was seven. Looking at it almost tipped me into the abyss of hopeless despair.

But then, a cold resolve took control. And with it came a plan of action.

I didn't dare call Limbus. I sent them a text saying I had the flu and wouldn't be coming in for training. In case Terry was tracking my phone, I wanted proof I hadn't outed him. I figured that was the kind of power he'd have, in his position.

I tested my body, stiff and sore from sleeping on tiles and probably also from getting thrown almost clean through a wall. I shuffled to the closest window and looked out onto the street. A cop car was parked a few houses down, right on the corner.

It wasn't Terry, but if he was police captain now, he wouldn't even need to use his empath suggestion powers to have someone keeping an eye on me.

I checked a back window. There didn't seem to be anyone

watching the footpath that ran along the back of our yard. Only from where the cop was parked on the corner, he'd be able to see both ends of where the path came back out again.

But I was placing my bets on Terry not knowing about Dean's bike.

I changed out of my food and tear-stained clothes, and into a pair of Mom's cargo pants and one of Dean's biggest hoodies. Along with the full-head helmet, I hoped that would be enough of a disguise to make me unrecognizable. I stuffed some granola bars in my pockets, and left my phone on the table.

I went into the garage and carried Dean's dirt bike up into the house, through the laundry door and out the back gate. I was a sweaty mess by the time I got there, but as I edged out onto the pathway I couldn't see anyone around.

My hands shook as I swung my leg over the bike. I was glad Dean had shown me once how to ride, but now I had to do it on my own it all seemed very scary.

The engine roared to life. Adrenalin and fear raced through my veins. The bike throbbed beneath me. "Here goes nothing."

I wobbled back and forth for a moment, bunny hopping and having to put my foot down a few times before plowing into a neighbor's fence. But I managed to straighten up as I left the path and went out onto the road.

I kept a slow and steady pace, checking the rear-vision mirror a few times, but the cop hadn't followed me. I was free.

And I was going to find Terry.

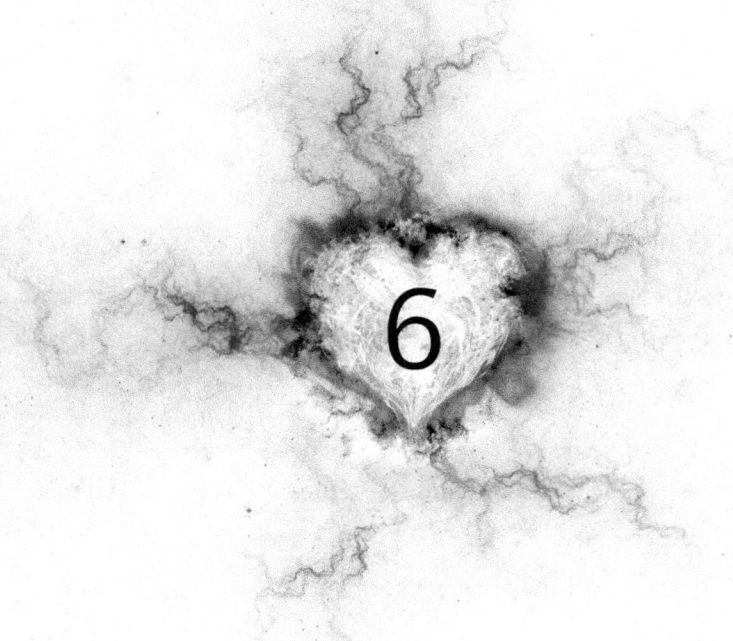

6

My first day of stalking Terry yielded nothing. He spent the entire time at the police station and stayed late. I tried to wait for him to head back to his house, or anywhere alone, but was too exhausted to keep my eyes open.

I went home, parking Dean's bike a block away and sneaking in through the neighbors' backyards. I crawled into bed, and even my tears and pains couldn't keep me awake.

The next day, I trailed Terry from function to function. First, a press announcement on Main Street. Then lunch at the golf club with the mayor. Then an inspiring speech for new cadets visiting the precinct. I kept my distance and kept my helmet on whenever I could, staying out of the way and out of sight.

Both nights, I went home exhausted and without having found any chance to take out Terry, or any clue as to how. Both days, I left my phone at home and went into full-on stalker mode. Obsession drove me. I barely ate, spoke to no one—there was only Terry.

Three days later, in the late evening, I was about to give up for the night when Terry came out of the station. He was talking to another officer. "I'm going to head home and have dinner with my family. They haven't seen me in a while. I bet you got this, right?"

I couldn't see the other officer's face, but he nodded and Terry smiled, patting him on the shoulder. I ducked back behind the alley wall as he walked over to his car and pulled out.

After giving him some distance, I followed on Dean's bike. I kept the lights off. The slight night-vision I got from my empath powers and abundant street lighting was enough to see by. I also kept my emotions as off as possible. I didn't want Terry to sense my raging hatred for him, so I locked it all away. I channeled Dean, trying to be cool, calm, and contained. I doubted I'd become a blocker overnight, but it was surprisingly easier than I thought to shut it all out when I didn't want to be feeling all that pain.

EMOTIONALLY POWERFUL

A few days had given me a lot of practice in reining in my emotions, and also at riding Dean's bike. I had been almost constantly on it during daylight hours.

We left the town and headed up a curvy mountain road, surrounded by pine forest. I leaned into the curves, the cold air whipping past me. I knew Terry lived on the outskirts of town, but I had never been there. I didn't think my parents had ever been there either. This was my chance to find out where he lived. Where he slept.

With fewer vehicles on the road, and less lighting, I slowed down and kept back, worried a few times I'd lost him. Then, up ahead I saw him slow down in front of a tall, ornate iron gate which opened automatically for him.

I stopped and waited as he drove down the long gravel drive and turned his lights off. I turned my own engine off and rolled the bike over behind a thick redwood.

I left the helmet behind too; there were enough bushes and shadows to keep hidden in, and I was worried the shiny surface would reflect light and be spotted. I crept up to the property on foot, and climbed over the high brick walls, checking for security cameras as I went.

As I came around through the side garden and saw the house itself, my mouth dropped. It was a mansion—massive and richly detailed, like something out of a movie.

Through the lit windows I could easily see inside, where chandeliers shimmered, dangling from the ceilings in most rooms, gilt-framed paintings were hung on the walls, and everything looked pristine, stunning, and unjustifiably expensive. There was no way Terry afforded all of this on his cop salary alone, no matter how many promotions he had arranged for himself.

Jake and his team's lifestyle seemed a much more fitting explanation. So much for all of Terry's greater good talk. He was using his powers to serve himself.

I ducked behind a formally sculpted hedge. From there, I could see into a kitchen and dining room where people moved about. There was a tall, beautiful blonde woman wearing a neat fifties-style dress and apron, moving plates from the kitchen to the dinner table. There, two infant children with strawberry-blond hair sat in high chairs. The woman looked really nervous, fussing over the layout of dishes and center ornaments on the table. The kids weren't fussing, but their heads drooped. They looked wiped out. Should they have been up so late?

Terry walked in behind the woman and kissed her on the cheek. She froze for a moment, then spun around and took Terry into her arms, kissing him and smiling broadly. He patted her on the butt, then rubbed each child on the head, waking them and making them look around, bleary-eyed, before taking his seat at the head of the table.

The little boy's chin wobbled, his mouth opened wide, and his face scrunched up.

The woman spotted his reaction to being disturbed and rushed over beside the child when the loud wail escaped his lips. She knocked a spoon out of a dish as she went, splattering soup across the table. She looked panicked, staring between the soup and the screaming child, the other kid now set off as well. And then to Terry who had risen from his seat and stalked towards her.

"Oh, enough!" Terry snapped, and the crying boy's face went blank, along with the girl beside him. "I come home from working all day and have to deal with this? Can't you keep the kids under control and serve a simple meal? Do I really ask so much from you?"

Terry's hand snapped out and he grabbed his wife by the throat. He picked her up in the air, holding her there for a long moment while she clawed at his hand, her eyes bulging.

I gasped loudly, putting my hand over my own mouth as fear and anger rushed through me.

Terry's body went rigid and he put his wife back onto her feet. His head whipped towards the window. I ducked down flat onto the ground.

Calm. Controlled. Cold. Feel nothing.

I counted to twenty. No doors opened, no footsteps came, and no one grabbed me from my hiding place.

"Clear this mess up," Terry commanded, and I dared to look up again.

His wife held her throat, her shoulders heaving with hard breaths, and tears streamed down her face. Terry patted her on the shoulder and just like that, she was smiling. She kissed him on the cheek, and fluttered around the room, cleaning and serving as he sat down again.

I backed away, keeping to the shadows until I got over the wall and then bolted for the bike.

That poor woman. Those kids ... how long have they been his prisoners?

I couldn't help them yet, but I might be able to help my parents. If Terry was just sitting down to a large meal, it could be enough time to get back to the station and possibly break out my parents. It was a long shot, but if I could do it, I could take them to Limbus and then let everyone know what was happening.

I grabbed the helmet and bike and rolled it farther away before starting it up. I didn't think he could hear it all the way out there, but I didn't want anything tipping him off. I sped back to town, ditching the bike in the alleyway I'd been staking out the station from. If I were able to get my parents out, we'd need some other transportation. I would come back for it later.

I left the helmet on and visor down. It restricted my vision a bit, but I was pretty sure there would be surveillance cameras here. Sneaking around the outside of the police building, I crouched down behind a side door I'd seen a couple of police using for smoke breaks.

I extended my senses, feeling for the presence of nearby emotions. It wasn't quite X-ray vision, but enough to give me a feeling of where people where around me.

Like when my parents had waited angrily outside of Dean's door when I had been in there with him without permission. I missed them all so much already. The idea of sneaking into the station terrified me, but I had to get my parents back, and then I could get Dean back.

I kept low and hid in the shadow of a dumpster until I sensed someone on the other side of the door. Just one person, by the feel of it. The handle turned. I was right. One female officer pushed out through the door and wandered over near a streetlight, cigarette in hand. I dashed to the door before it swung closed and slipped inside.

I had been in the station only once before. I must have been eight or nine, and Terry had taken my class on a tour. Always smiling. Always helping out. Had he leeched anyone then? *Had he even known he was an empath at that time?*

I roughly remembered where the holding cells were, and sprinted down the hallway on soft feet, as silent as I could.

I sensed two people headed my way and I backed up behind a filing cabinet. They went the other way at the corner of the corridor. They were eerily calm and content in their work, despite the late hour. It gave me little power to work with, and I wondered how much of that was their captain's doing.

Up around the corner, I snuck through an unoccupied bullpen office that backed onto the holding cells. I peeked out from behind a cluttered desk. *Mom, Dad.* They were there. I could have shouted for joy. But two guards stood in front of the cell, their expressions stiff and determined. Under orders, I was sure.

I knelt down and ground my teeth. I had to do something, but there wasn't enough emotion at the moment to build up my strength and speed. It was the happiest, calmest police station ever.

My eyes fell on the fire alarm on the wall beside me. This might be my only chance. I could only risk hiding under a desk for so long, and had no other way to get the guards out of there. I shrugged. It was worth a shot. I waited until the guards looked away, then lunged up, pulled the alarm, then dove back under the desk.

A high, jangling bell rang throughout the station. I stayed completely under cover.

"We have a drill scheduled?" one of the guards asked.

"Captain Pence said we should keep an eye out for anything that seemed off," the other replied. "Let's go and see what's going on."

They walked right past where I was crouched. I held my breath.

As soon as they were through the door, I grabbed a ring of keys from a rack on the wall and hurried to my parents' cell. Everything was labelled so it didn't take me long to get the door unlocked. I swung it wide open.

"Quick, let's go!" I hissed.

They both looked up at me, confused.

"It's me, Livvy." I popped the visor up, even though they should have known my voice. I frowned.

"Lollipop, so nice to see you." Dad beamed, but he didn't move from his seat.

Chills prickled up my spine. "We have to go, like, *now*."

"Why?" Mom laughed softly. "We're perfectly happy here. We're happy to stay here as long as we have to. We're not going anywhere."

No, no, no. I squatted down in front of them, grabbing their hands. "You have to snap out of this. Terry is controlling you. You don't want to be here."

They just smiled, shrugged, and didn't move.

I had never compelled anyone with my powers before, but I tried then. I focused all my willpower on making them listen to me, making them think that my suggestion was exactly what they wanted to do, *had* to do. "Come with me, please," I pleaded.

Neither of them even blinked. Terry's powers were just too strong, even without him being there. I knew Jake's powers had some hangover time before they wore off, and he had just one proesthian's worth of power.

I growled in frustration. There had to be another way. I considered trying to carry them but wasn't strong enough. Maybe if I still had four empaths' worth of power in me I could have, but not anymore.

The alarm blaring overhead cut out suddenly.

Silence.

The cops knew there was no fire. They'd be back any second. I gripped my parents' hands and pulled them up to kiss them. "I'll come back for you, I promise." Then I flicked my visor back down and turned away.

I quickly locked the cell again and put the keys back, hoping I could get out unnoticed except for the unexplained false alarm. But as I passed by the desk I'd hid under, something caught my eye. A kraft brown folder lay there, with a label on the front that read, "Limbus."

That is so very, very far from good.

I could sense people just down the hall, but paused to flip the folder open. I gasped. There were pictures of Dr. and Mr. Crossman inside. A picture of the pink-haired agent. One of Rayni, the day she and Ash picked me up from school.

And it was all there, on a detective's desk. My heart raced. Was Terry getting his station to investigate Limbus for him? To hunt empaths for him?

What could be worse that this?

"Hey, you! Don't move!"

Two cops stood in the doorway, their guns aimed at me.

Oh, yeah.

That could be worse.

7

I couldn't talk my way out of this one. Not that it was a particular talent I possessed, but I didn't want the cops to have more reason to work out who I was and pass that info on to Terry.

I threw the folder in my hands at the men. It broke apart in mid-air, paper exploding everywhere. A rush of fear and anger spilled from them to me. It was just what I needed.

I absorbed those emotions and focused my powers. Before the fluttering sheets had reached the floor, I raced toward the cops.

As I reached them, I dropped and slid along the floor on my knees. I grabbed one each of their ankles, and with a sharp tug, toppled them over onto their faces.

I launched back to my feet and dashed out the door without looking back. I hoped I hadn't hurt them much. I didn't want to hurt any of them. But I had to get out of there.

I took off at top speed down the hallway, no longer worried about being spotted, just trying to get out as fast as I could. Three more police rounded the hallway corner in front of me. The view of my blurringly fast figure drove fear through them and into me, sending me faster. I kicked off the wall beside me, ricocheted off the opposite wall, and flipped myself over through the gap between the cops and the ceiling, spinning my body with sheer speed and instinct. I hit the floor on the other side on my knees, rolled forward in a somersault, then sprang up onto my feet again. I reached the side exit before they'd even had a chance to turn around.

I burst out of the station and into the cold night air. A gust of visible breath fogged the inside of my helmet as I panted hard.

But I didn't dare stop.

I fled to the alley and took off on Dean's bike, adrenaline drilling through my whole body.

I'd made it out. I could have almost screamed with relief.

But I knew it was bound to be short-lived. A helmeted intruder was going to be something reported to the station captain. And security videos would be reviewed. And it would be clear to Terry just from context, even without seeing my face, who I was. I shuddered to think what he was going to do once he found out.

Because I hadn't been able to save my parents.

Terry had my whole life in his hands.

8

sat slumped on the couch, staring at the blank television screen.

After getting home from the police station, I had fallen asleep there, and when I'd woken in the morning, I couldn't find the energy to go out again. There seemed to be no reason to keep hunting Terry. It all felt so pointless. I was sure he was going to come to me any second now, to punish me for trying to free my parents.

So I just sat, and stared, and waited.

My stomach grumbled. There wasn't a lot left in the fridge or pantry that I knew how to make into a meal. Empty pizza boxes were already piled up on the coffee table alongside a handful of unopened letters.

The last cash I'd rustled up from around the house had been spent on fuel for the bike. I hadn't wanted to use my parents' credit cards for anything other than fast food deliveries, worried if I used them out of the house I'd be tracked. Until last night, I'd hoped I'd gotten away with the illusion I hadn't stepped foot outside.

There were some missed calls from Limbus, but I sent them another text from my mom's phone, explaining I was still sick. Last time they activated my tracker, it flashed, so I figured they bought my excuse and hadn't felt the need to check in on me yet.

If only I could go there. I wanted more than anything to zoom down to Limbus on Dean's bike, and then climb into the hospital bed beside him and curl up, holding him. I hadn't seen him since Terry took my parents and I felt his absence like a hole in the chest.

But going to Limbus was too big of a risk. Terry was already investigating them. He knew of their existence, but I hadn't seen any photos of the Bellston Main Limbus building in the folder. I could only hope he never found out where they were. And that meant keeping my distance, from them, and from Dean.

I whimpered and flopped over onto my side, crushing a

crinkly, empty chip packet.

A knock on the door reverberated through the empty house.

I was on shaky feet in a flash, desperate to bolt. *He's come for me.*

But ... why is he knocking?

I tiptoed hesitantly toward the front door. I extended my senses, trying to pull in any emotion from the other side. *Regret. Fear. Sadness.* No way it was Terry. Curious, I cracked the door open.

Standing on the other side was Dean's father. He looked worse off than he did the last time that I'd seen him. His gray eyes twitched over red cheeks, and his nose ran. There were holes in his shirt and sweatpants, and he only wore flip-flops. The sky above him was gray and heavy, and a cool breeze made me shiver.

"Mr. Lasslow?" I squeaked through the gap.

He wobbled, obviously drunk. But the anger he'd shown in the past wasn't there. "I want to talk to my son." He squinted at me. "Tell Dean I want to talk to him."

Oh. Oh, no. What was I supposed to tell him? The truth? His son was an empath and was drained of all his powers, and was lying in a coma in a secret agency headquarters? That was enough to confuse a sober person, much less a drunk one. I sighed and stepped out on the porch, shutting the door quickly behind me before he could decide to push past and go searching for his son.

"How did you find us?"

He held up a piece of paper with my mother's handwriting on it. "They sent me a letter. Gave me your address. In case of emergencies, it says."

Emergencies. My whole life was currently an emergency, and this man, who'd insulted me to my face more than once, showed up drunk? Wanting something?

I scowled. "Is this an emergency? Because Dean's not here and even if he was, I doubt he'd want to talk to you."

"He's my son. He'll talk to me if I say he has to talk to me." He spat the words, but shuffled uncomfortably back and forth.

"He doesn't belong to you. He's not a thing to be controlled, like you tried to control your wife." I stepped closer, uncontrollable anger burned through me, tightening my fists. "You wouldn't let her go, wouldn't deal with your own emotions from losing her, and wouldn't help Dean deal with his. He was a child who needed to mourn his mom's death, but you left him feeling like it wasn't even okay for him to cry. He had to crush all of his emotions so completely it broke him." *And he became a blocker. And he was drained because of it, just when he was starting to heal, just when*

514

he was starting to open up … I thrusted both palms into Mr. Lasslow's chest and knocked him off his feet, down onto the front path. "You broke *everything*."

He looked up at me from the ground, his eyes wide and watering. The look of complete heartache on his face made my stomach turn.

It wasn't him I was angry at. Not really. I hadn't wanted to hurt him, but I couldn't deal with him here, now, on top of everything else. I just wanted him gone.

I rubbed my eyes, finding them wet as well. "Just get out of here. Get sober. Deal with your emotions instead of drinking them away, and maybe you'll be in a place for once where you could help Dean deal with his. I know you lost your wife, but Dean lost her *and* you. He needs his father back. He needs you to be able to look him in the eye and tell him you're sorry for the way you left him all alone in the world."

He stumbled back up to his feet and looked around wildly, his teeth clenched. For a second, I thought he was going to rush me. But then he wiped his eyes with the back of his sleeve, spat into the herb garden, and hobbled away crookedly, swearing and muttering.

I felt about the same as I shuffled back into the lonely house. I was way harsher than I'd needed to be, venting all my anger out onto Mr. Lasslow, but I really did want him to be better. For Dean.

If Dean ever woke up again.

My eyes filled with hot tears.

I wish Dean was here. I wish anyone was here.

On the hall table in front of me, my phone flashed and hummed. I stared at it for a moment, fearful of what could be on the other end. Slowly, I reached for it, blinking my eyes clear so I could read the screen.

A call from Nati. I sobbed in relief, and need. I needed to hear her voice. I needed to not be alone anymore.

I answered, trying to hide my shaking breath. "Hey, Nati."

"Hey girl," she said, and I could hear the smile in her tone. "So, I was thinking, since you like to play hooky from school these days, you wanna come over and do a little sisterly bonding?"

I bit my lip. I wanted to see her so badly, but could I, without putting her in danger?

Nati took my silence as an answer. "I know you're probably stuck like glue to Dean, but I haven't seen you in forevs. I need you over here, no buts, buttface. As long as you aren't contagious."

I looked around my empty home. I had to get out of there before I snapped entirely. I'd just have to sneak there the best I could, but with all the secret coming and going I'd been doing,

I'd learned a few new routes that I hoped might still be unnoticed. "Screw it. Yeah. I'll be over as soon as it's dark."

"Holy herringbones, the sky is going to fall!" She giggled. "I'll meet you out back of my house so you can get in the gate."

"Wait." I was terrified I'd made the wrong decision, that this was going to be another mistake, another loss. For all I knew, Terry was bugging my calls. But he must already know Nati was my friend. If he'd wanted more hostages, he'd had plenty of chances. Still ... "Instead, can we meet"—I bit my tongue, careful not to say too much—"at that place with the crazy sundaes?"

I held my breath, hoping she wouldn't give it away.

"Brilliant idea! Ice-cream for dinner it is!"

"Perfect," I replied. "See you soon."

I hung up, smiling, my heart pounding. Even if Terry knew I was going out, as long as I didn't get followed, he wouldn't know where.

It was only early afternoon, so I waited, pacing anxiously around the house, talking myself out of cancelling. Soon, the sky through the windows darkened, and the heavy clouds released a sprinkle of rain across the suburb.

I grabbed a large black raincoat of Dad's, put it on over Dean's hoodie, and left my phone behind. Peeking out a front window, I saw the cop car still sitting at the corner up the street, right in view of the front of the house and the exits to the back pathway.

I crept out into the backyard, and listened, extending my senses to check for anyone outside. The rain had everyone indoors, and created a gray veil over the world, almost inviting me to disappear into it.

I jumped over the neighbor's fence and dashed across their yard. I went like that all the way to the end of the block, over and across every neighbors' property, over the pathway itself, and continued on until I reached the yard at the opposite corner of the block to the cop. Rain splattered my face, and my fingers were chilled as I watched through the palings for my opportunity.

A few cars passed by, driving slowly, lights and wipers on. Then, a few minutes later, there was a removals truck. I pulled the hood drawstrings tight, zipped out through the gate, and grabbed the back of the truck, jumping onto the bumper.

I travelled like that for two blocks until I hoped I was clear, and before anyone saw me riding that way, then hopped back off and went to collect Dean's bike.

I reached the games arcade dripping wet, my fingers numb and my cheeks burning.

Leaving my hood up, I carried my helmet, my raincoat rolled

up under one arm, and walked through the dinging games and hyped-up children to the secluded booths up the back. Screens flashed around me of colorful characters racing cute cars, kawaii photo booths, and gritty shoot-'em-ups. One kid was being way too zealous with the Whac-A-Mole. I hoped Terry wouldn't find us there, since I'd only mentioned food, and this wasn't strictly a café or diner.

I spotted Nati in one of the booths, happily scrolling through her phone, ringlets hanging down over a sequin-streaked shirt.

"Why do you look like you just escaped a super-max through the sewage drain?" she asked as I ducked down onto the seat across from her.

I wiped matted wet hair off my face, readjusted my hood, and faked a laugh. "Thought I'd walk over."

"You are so weird." She frowned, and I could *feel* her worry. She eyed me up and down, then held my gaze until I had to look away or risk bursting into tears.

She tsked. "All right. What's going on? And don't BS me. I know something is up. The look on your face is breaking my heart."

I gaped. Gulped. Crumpled. I wanted to brush it off, make up some excuse, but I had nothing left in me. I hadn't told her before because I didn't want her to think I was crazy, because it was all so much. But now, it had all become so much I would go crazy if I *didn't* tell her. I stared at her with tears in my eyes and just exploded.

I spilled everything. From the first time I met Jake, to Dean's powers, to where he was now and how the leech stole my parents. The only detail I left out was who the leech was.

Her mouth hung open and she just watched and listened until I finally stopped rambling.

She sat back in her chair and crossed her arms. "I ... wow, that's some crazy stuff. Hold on, let me process." She waved a waiter over and ordered two of the most extreme ice-cream-piled-on-sugar-piled-on-candy sundaes they offered. "That's to help us process," she told me, and then leaned forward on the table toward me. "Okay. Superpowers. Crazy adventures. I mean, it makes sense. It makes total sense, actually."

"Uh, really?" I wiped my eyes with the sides of the hood.

"Uh, really." She echoed me sarcastically. "Weeks away from school all the time? Surviving roof cave-ins? Getting abducted by shifty clandestine agents? I kind of already figured things weren't in the realm of normality for you anymore."

I pouted bashfully. "Sorry I didn't tell you sooner."

"Nah, I get that this is an area requiring total secrecy." She hushed up quickly as the waiter brought our sundaes over, pausing until he was gone. "You're in some seriously dangerous doo-doo right now. And I have no ideas for anything I can do to help."

I picked some cotton candy off the ice-cream and let it melt on my tongue. "This is helping already. I just needed to get it out. Dealing with all this, all alone—it was eating me away, rotting me from the inside."

Nati wrinkled her nose and reached out, taking my hand. "You need a place to stay? Can you come to my house?"

I shook my head. "Not safe for you or your family."

Nati sighed and stabbed her spoon at her ice-cream. We devoured our sundaes in silence for a while. "Babe, this sucks. I really wish I could do something. Can't you blast me with energy and give me powers, too?"

I snickered, and then sniffled. "I wish. I wish you could be in this with me, but I'm also happy that you're not. It's hard, being like this, having these powers when they still aren't enough to save the people you love."

Nati slid off her seat, came over to my side of the booth, and wrapped her arms around me. "You're enough. I know you've got this, Livvy. You know why?"

"Why?"

"Because even before this whole superpower deal, you were

a hero. I would always see you, how no matter what came your way, you would tackle it head-on, with heart and guts. You're the best person I know."

"I don't feel like I've been very heroic lately," I muttered. *Dean's dad probably doesn't think I am, either.*

She just shrugged. "You're in a bad place, and I mean, come on, kind of understandable. But you're going to pick yourself up. You'll look inside yourself and see you have what you need to win this. You have enough love inside you to change people, change the world. If you have emotion-based superpowers, you have a heart that is unstoppable."

My nose wrinkled and I hugged Nati back. Her words were exactly what I needed to hear. I had spent too long dwelling in places of fear and anger. I wanted to find my answer, my hope, my courage, in *love*. Because it was the one thing I was sure I had that Terry didn't.

"Thank you," I whispered. "I love you."

"I love you too." Nati placed a sugar-sticky kiss on my cheek. "Now, let's get seconds, 'kay?"

9

Bringing Dean's bike to a stop behind a parked SUV, I put one foot down against the curb so I could lean out far enough to see. Terry had pulled his cruiser over up ahead.

After the talk with Nati, my spirits had improved, and my determination grew with them. I'd started following Terry again, since he hadn't decided to come after me yet. Maybe he hadn't found out about what happened at the station, or hadn't worked out it was me, or perhaps he was just too arrogant to care. Regardless, I decided to continue my surveillance of him, to find a time to make my plan happen.

I would wait until he was alone.

I would take the first chance I could to drain him, before he suspects, before he can fight back

I would absorb everyone he held inside him.

And I would hope my heart was big enough to contain it all.

Nati believed I could do it. I just hoped she was right.

I'd followed Terry all the way down to Bellston Main, growing more worried all the way that he'd discovered Limbus's HQ. But we ended up on a small nightlife street with a club on the corner, an open-all-hours kebab store, a diner, and a Japanese restaurant.

Terry strolled into the diner, and through the window I watched him order at the counter, watched him flirt with the lady who served him his takeaway coffee. Watched how he didn't even pay.

When he came back out, he set his cup on the roof of the car while he checked his phone. Everything inside me wanted to take him down right then and there. But despite Nati's pep talk, I knew I had to be patient and at least wait until I wasn't in the middle of a busy street where everyone could watch me straight up assault a uniformed police captain.

He opened his car door and I started the bike again to continue the trail.

Then something in my chest thumped.

EMOTIONALLY POWERFUL

I put my hand to my heart and swallowed hard. Someone's emotions were raging nearby, and it was sinking right into me. Feelings of happiness, excitement, nervousness, and ... *love*. And the emotions felt so familiar.

It was how I felt for Dean, the excitement and surprise of finding a love beyond anything I could have imagined.

As the sensation grew stronger, I realized that the familiarity wasn't just because I knew those feelings—it was because I recognized *the people* they came from.

My eyes darted, trying to find the source. A couple came out of the door to the Japanese restaurant, giggling and holding each other tightly. Both were tall, and both had hoods pulled up over their heads. The girl reached forward, her sleeve inching up. On her wrist was an orange Limbus tracking bracelet, and I glimpsed red hair.

Emma? What was she doing out here? And who was she with?

They turned, both looking up, and the light hit their faces.

Bastian? My jaw dropped. Emma and Bastian ... *together?*

"What bizarro world is this?" I growled to myself.

Then it hit me. If I could feel them, so could the leech. And Terry knew about my adventures with Jake and Emma. He could have files. He could know what she looked like.

My eyes snapped back to the cop car. The coffee still sat on top, but Terry wasn't there.

Where did you go? Panic brewed in my belly. "Get out of here," I begged in a whisper, watching Bastian and Emma strolling together into the tree-filled park down the street. They had no idea of the danger they were in, but I felt every part of it.

My eyes landed on Terry again, prowling out from behind a building, going toward the park entrance. His smile was dark and ominous. He'd sensed them. *He was hunting Emma.*

Once in the shadow of the trees, Terry picked up his pace. I had to do something, and I had to do it fast. My grip tightened on the handles of the bike.

I hit the gas and took off, speeding out onto the street. I skidded around the corner, and gunned it, jumping up the curb. People tumbled out of my way, yelling in my wake. I kept going. Racing across the grass of the park, I dodged trees and newly planted flower beds.

Bastian and Emma were right up ahead. Terry stalked behind them.

The happy emotions I'd been feeling from the couple shifted suddenly to fear, and Emma buckled, folding in the middle. Bastian caught her, oblivious to the cause standing just down the path from them, already draining Emma's life away.

EMOTIONALLY POWERFUL

Busy sapping Emma's powers, Terry also seemed oblivious to the roar of the bike racing toward him. I put my head down, aiming directly for him. I went faster, as fast as I could go.

At the last second, Terry looked up with wide eyes. I leaped from the bike, and it plowed into him. They tangled together, bouncing and dragging across the grass twenty feet in a roar of scraping metal.

I rolled across the ground and slid to a stop between Terry and Emma.

Pulling off my helmet, I looked back at her and Bastian.

Bastian shifted his focus between all of us, eyes squinting then going wide, his whole body shivering. He grabbed Emma's hand and started pulling her away. *He got it.* Elucidist powers were really something.

Emma held her ground though, staring at me like I was mad. "Livvy? What have you done to that cop?"

The bike lay on top of Terry and both were still, surrounded by a cloud of settling dust. I held my breath. I only wanted to stop him, not kill him. If he was dead, then Dean …

A low, angry groan came from beneath the bent metal.

I yelled, "He's the leech! You've got to go!"

Both of Emma's hands went to her mouth, her head shaking. "We can help—"

"We can't." Bastian's tone was crushed, yet determined. "I'm sorry Livvy. I'm so sorry."

I inhaled sharply, fear twisting its tendrils into my heart with his words. Bastian tugged harder at Emma's hand, and she looked at me one more time. "But—"

"Emma, we can't survive this. Livvy …" Bastian looked at me with sad eyes. "Livvy *can*."

Emma's face crumpled, then she turned away and they ran. I watched as they took off, Emma using her proesthian speed to help Bastian move faster, and they disappeared into the shadows of the park. I nodded to myself. It was better they wouldn't be here for this, for what I had to do.

My body ached from hitting the ground. I pulled myself to my feet, holding tightly to my knees to keep upright. I dropped the helmet and took in a long, deep breath, pulling my powers into focus. Strength filled me and I stalked toward Terry, letting loose my pain and despair. *Losing Ash. Losing Marigold. Losing Dean. Losing my parents.* I let my grief swallow me so I could use it to swallow him.

I stood above Terry, who grumbled and twitched under the broken bike.

Darkness overwhelmed me, ravenous, angry, and cold, and I let it feed on Terry. I sensed the first touch of our consciousnesses.

528

EMOTIONALLY POWERFUL

Terry roared in anger, throwing the bike up and off of him. It flew through the air and crashed into a tree trunk behind me.

I gritted my teeth, tried to hold my focus. The drain on him wavered, failed. I couldn't get a grip on him; all the energy was too jumbled, too tightly packed, too massive. My own mind felt like it slipped and slid around in my body, and sometimes out of it.

Terry got to his feet, cricked his neck, and dusted off the front of his uniform. "What on earth do you think you're doing? You stupid girl."

"Stopping you!" I cried, pushing deeper into my despair, pushing the energy out toward him.

It seemed to have no effect at all.

He strolled toward me. I kicked him as hard as I could in the stomach. He braced, then kept coming. I swung wide, meeting his jaw with my fist. Blood splattered from his lips, but he kept coming. He grinned wide, blood covering his teeth, then backhanded me across the face so hard I flew through the air into the same tree the bike had hit.

My back cracked as it hit the trunk, and I tumbled down in an avalanche of broken bark, landing badly on the hot, pointed metal of the bike. I cried out, whimpered, and hurried to get back up.

Terry appeared in a flash by my side. His hand wrapped around my throat. My eyes went wide and I wheezed for air. I clawed onto his wrist as he lifted me up off my feet. Tears poured down my face. I swung my arms, my legs, but I couldn't reach him.

He's going to drain me. This is it.

I winced, waited. His grip tightened, crushing my throat, then he slammed me to the ground with bone-cracking force.

Air rushed from my lungs and I didn't have enough left to cry out.

Through pain-blurred eyes, I watched as Terry stood over me, shaking his head.

"I've known you since you were a little girl," he barked. "I've given you every opportunity, but you keep trying to fight me. Why? Trying to save your parents? Trying to drain me? Can't you see it's pointless? *I am a god.*"

He lifted one knee and brought his foot crashing down onto my ribs. I screamed, a dry, cracked scream, and curled into a ball.

"You could be too. That's what I'm trying to offer you. Be my apprentice, my disciple. I know you have it in you."

His foot landed again, deep in my lower back. Pain blinded me. Bile rose in my throat, hot and stinging. I tried to pull my body together, pull my powers into focus, but everything swirled.

"I'm offering you power. We could rule this world. If you'd stop being so stubborn."

Again and again he struck out, hard leather boots crushing me to a pulp.

"You've been brainwashed to think there are heroes and villains, good and evil, but real life isn't a fairy tale. One day, you'll understand that. Only power matters. And imagine how powerful we could be together."

He bent down over me, grabbing me by the top of the head, wrenching my face up close to his by my hair.

I lost all control of my emotions. I wept hard, useless tears for my own pain, for my imprisoned parents, for the love I shared with Dean that felt so impossibly lost. I roared in anger and fear, my throat as raw as my bloodied, bruised body, as raw as my heart. I tried to lift an arm to fight back, but it wobbled weirdly. I whimpered.

I have to survive this. I have to win this.

Bastian said I could survive this.

"Next time, I won't stop," Terry hissed into my face. "This is your last chance to consider my offer. Join me, or you will become just another vessel to drain the power from. Either way, you will only make me stronger."

He slammed the back of my head into the ground. My eyes

went wide and then fought to close. The entire world spun around me, falling, falling into darkness. *Bastian said I could survive. Bastian ... said ...*

10

Reality flashed around me in painful, disjointed moments. In between was only fog and darkness.

Two blurry figures, argued. My hands moved, held and controlled by someone else. I thought I was crying.

I was alone. I could feel every sharp twig and pebble pressing up from the cold ground into my mangled body. Everything was pain. Light flashed. Barely enough strength remained to remember to breathe.

Then darkness. Then more voices. Surrounding, urgent. I screamed when I was lifted and moved. Agony smashed my consciousness out of existence.

I came back to a strange sensation of softness rattling beneath me. I was moving, rolling. There was so much light, glaring down in bursts overhead right through my aching, puffy eyelids. I tried to reach my hands up to block it but someone grabbed them and put them back down by my side.

"Livvy?" It sounded like Dr. Crossman. I couldn't see, my face swollen up around my eyes. "Don't try and talk. Just stay still. We've got you."

"Get her over on the table," Felix yelled out somewhere above my head.

I was lifted, slid effortlessly to the side by unseen hands. Something sharp entered the back of my hand. The pain began to fade, and I faded with it.

I slipped into a deep sleep, floating through a darkened dream world. I could feel the coolness of Dean nearby, shifting to warmth, like he was wrapping his arms over my shoulders and holding me close. I could smell the ylang-ylang fragrance of my mom's candle collection, and hear the laughter of my father in the distance. I could taste the sugar-sweet friendship of Nati. I couldn't move, and everything remained dark. But I wasn't afraid. I wanted to stay there, safe from pain, safe from suffering. Safe in the darkness.

But the world around me began to shudder and shake. All

of my emotions surged forward, slamming hard into my chest. I could hear Terry's loud maniacal laughter all around me and panic crept through my veins.

I screamed out. "No! I won't be like you! You can't have me!"

There was a gentle pressure on my shoulder. My heart rate slowed, and a calm warmth spread through me. I could hear Rayni's voice near my ear. "Livvy, it's just a dream. You're safe. Just open your eyes and you'll see. You're safe."

I nodded in understanding, my brain quickly switching from dream mode to awake, helped by Rayni's control over my emotions. I took a deep breath, slowly opening my crusted-shut eyes.

I was in the ward at Limbus. Rayni stood beside me, and behind her, sitting in a row on the side of an empty bed, were Sway, Emma, and Bastian. *They're okay. They got away.* I swallowed relief down my dry throat.

Dr. Crossman placed a straw to my lips. I sipped the iced water slowly, gratefully. Felix checked my IV lines and blood pressure.

"How are you feeling?" Dr. Crossman asked. "We've got you on some pretty strong pain relief but let us know if it's not enough."

I looked down at my body in the bed. My left forearm was in a cast. My mouth tasted bloody. I could feel a low-level ache in my back and head, but didn't want it all gone. I didn't want to be numb completely. I had survived. I was alive, and the pain reminded me of that. "I'm okay. I'm fine."

"Kids these days have a strange definition of fine," Felix muttered. Then he patted me on the knee and I tried not to wince. "Your proesthian powers give you slightly faster healing though so you should really be fine soon, but I suggest staying in bed for now in case of complications."

Mr. Crossman folded his arms over his chest. "We are really glad you're okay, Olivia. But what in the world were you doing out there? We thought you were home with your parents, sick, then we found you like this in the park after you pressed your emergency button."

"I don't remember doing that," I mumbled, my head still foggy.

"Unsurprising. You've been out for fifteen hours." Dr. Crossman checked the watch on her tracker. "It looked like you'd driven a motorbike into a tree. But this clearly wasn't just a bike accident. What happened?"

I licked my lips and frowned. I wondered if I could pretend I didn't remember anything. I slowly turned my head. It crushed me to see all the others Terry had drained there beside me. I had done everything I could and failed. I didn't know what else to do.

Mr. Crossman put his hands on his hips. "We've been trying

to reach your parents, but no one's answering the phone or the front door. Olivia, you have to tell us what's going on."

My lips wrinkled with sadness, making my words shaky. "The leech did this."

Dr. Crossman's eyebrows went up. "Are you sure it was him? This isn't his normal behavior. I mean, he's certain to be in an unhinged and violent state of mind, but you weren't drained."

"I'm sure. I know who he is. I've been following him for a while."

Rayni gasped beside me, and I shied away from her confusion and disappointment.

"Who is it?" Mr. Crossman demanded.

I shook my head. "I can't tell you."

"What? Why not?" Dr. Crossman's professionalism cracked and she cried, "Why do you feel like you have to do everything alone? Why don't you trust us?"

"I do trust you. I wish I could have come to you. But he has my parents!"

Dr. Crossman put a hand over her mouth. "Oh, Olivia." She came over and sat on the side of my bed. "How long? Since you first called in sick? You should have told us. We could have helped."

"You don't understand what he's like, how strong he is. If

I say any more, if anyone goes after him, my parents stand no chance."

Mr. Crossman seemed confused still. "Why? Why has he taken your parents? What does he want from you?"

He's a friend of the family. I've known him since I was eight. "He knows what I did, draining Jake and the others. He thinks I'm like him. He's power crazy, wants me to join him." I lifted my bandaged arm. "This was my last invitation."

Dr. Crossman stood back up and paced. "This is madness. You have to tell us who he is. We have to stop him."

"He's *unstoppable.* I started following him after he took my parents, hoping for some chance. Last night, when I saw ..."

Bastian and Emma both had scared looks on their faces, and Bastian gave a tiny shake of his head. At first, I thought they just didn't want their forbidden date to be discovered, but then I realized they were actually helping me out. Because they knew who the leech was too. They'd seen him. They were keeping the secret too, for me.

"I thought I saw him go to attack someone, so I ran my bike into him. I tried. I tried to drain him and get everyone back, but he's too strong." My words devolved into sobs.

Rayni took my hand, all her calming ability lost in our shared grief.

EMOTIONALLY POWERFUL

Mr. Crossman, Dr. Crossman, and Felix all stared at each other for a long moment. "We need to contact the agency heads." Dr. Crossman's voice had grown cold. "If he's really that powerful, has become this bold and violent, it may not be worth trying to capture him anymore. We may just need to take him out. Otherwise, who knows how many people he could hurt?"

"What? No," I said, pulling myself up in bed. "What about Dean? And the others? If the leech dies, they're gone for good."

"Then you have to tell us who he is so we have a chance of catching him before he gets any stronger, or hurts more people," Mr. Crossman replied.

"But then the people he'll hurt are my parents." My teeth ground together in frustration. "It's like I have to choose between my parents and Dean. This isn't fair. I can't tell you who he is and I won't let you kill him."

The machines I was hooked up to whirred and beeped wildly. Felix's one larger eye grew even bigger. "Whoa. Time out. Shh, shh, happy thoughts time," he sang to me, then gave the Crossmans a firm look.

Dr. Crossman sighed deeply and crossed her arms. "All right, enough for now. But Olivia, I want you to really think about the consequences here. We cannot afford to have civilian casualties in this."

"But we can afford to have empath ones?" I snapped back.

Her expression softened. "In this situation, we may not have a choice. These things aren't easy decisions. This room is filled with our friends and loved ones too."

I turned my head away. A few beds down, there was Dean. And Ash. Mr. Kairu with his faithful cat, Kimmy, on the end of his bed. Old Mr. Holbrook from the institute, and three more grown-ups I never knew, but the Crossmans had.

"Time for the patient to rest," Felix ordered.

Dr. Crossman patted the bed beside me, and she and her husband walked away, whispering together. Rayni, Sway, and Felix followed. Emma hopped up, and for a moment, she grabbed my fingers and squeezed them. Her lips were pressed thin, then she and Bastian left too.

Alone in the room with the drained, and too exhausted to move, I just stared at Dean. At the line of his profile, his eyelashes resting on his cheeks, as though he were sleeping. He was still so beautiful it made my heart ache, and I longed to see him move, to smile, even to see him cry again.

If the leech died, I never would.

But they still didn't know who the leech was. Working out it was Terry would be pretty hard unless you knew him. And I was the only one in the whole group who did. Police Captain

Terry Pence, working long hours, serving his community. Who would ever have suspected?

I had hope that I still had some time. Time to heal, grow strong again.

Kimmy pounced at the end of my bed, and chirped a high meow. I wriggled my fingers, and she came up to me, curled at my side, and purred loudly as I scratched her chin. She probably wasn't used to her bed companions returning affection. She snuggled up beside me, lulling my senses with her healing purrs.

I was terrified there was no answer, no way to stop Terry. That his powers would grow and grow, leaving bodies behind in his wake. But I was equally terrified of him being discovered, hunted, and assassinated from afar, and losing everyone in this room. For me, for Rayni, and for the Crossmans.

We couldn't give up on them.

I wouldn't.

11

E veryone stared at me when I walked into the gym for the afternoon training session. The whole place went silent.

I knew why. I'd seen myself in the mirror while I was putting my training suit on. I'd healed remarkably well in the thirty-odd hours since Terry had beaten me, but I was covered in mottled sickly yellow and purple bruises, with one side of my face still swollen and the cast still on my arm.

Felix had reduced my pain meds and everything felt clearer again, but with the clarity came anxiety. Lying in bed doing nothing made it worse. I could only stare at Dean and weep for so long.

EMOTIONALLY POWERFUL

I pretended to ignore the shocked expressions as I moved out onto the mats where everyone had already begun warm-up stretches. The adult empath who ran the class raised an eyebrow at me. He probably knew I wasn't meant to be out of bed yet. But then his phone started ringing and he ducked out into the hallway to answer it.

I took a spot on the floor next to Sway, who winked at me. Rayni was just behind us, and Emma and Bastian were on the other side of the few younger kids. Everyone was in their Limbus suits, and I was glad that training in these was still a thing since two weeks ago, and I hadn't been the only person to show up in a skin-tight bodysuit.

I slowly moved into a leg stretch. Everything ached as I lined my torso up and bent low over my thigh. When I raised back up, Emma and Bastian sat in front of me, and everyone else in the room had stopped stretching.

"Hey," Emma said. She swirled her long, red hair around a finger, and cleared her throat. "I umm ... I guess I wanted to say thanks. For saving my life. This time ... and last time, too."

She seemed so different to how I'd once known her. Thoughtful, vulnerable—anything but shallow. I smiled with one half of my mouth. "Thanks, for saving mine too, I guess. Figured it was you and Bastian who pressed my panic button for me."

Bastian nodded, his brown ringlets dangling around his sad eyes. "I'm so sorry we couldn't stay. I was certain if we did, he would have drained us. It was intense, knowing what could happen, but knowing it would only be worse if we stayed. Just, whoa, man."

"That man's insane," Emma said. "Seeing what he did to you. I can't believe anyone is that cruel."

"Shoulda seen what he did to my Marigold," Sway said, leaning into the conversation. "But I object to the term insane. I know plenty of sugar-pop insane sweethearts. That man is a *monster*."

Rayni shuffled up closer on my side. "Actually, calling him a monster feels like an understatement."

I frowned. "Wait, wait. You stayed and saw what happened?"

Emma looked at Bastian and shrugged. "Not really. We left a phone to get video before getting to a safe distance. We came back for the phone and to press your panic button before getting clear again."

"You *filmed* it?" I narrowed my eyes. "For, like, a keepsake, or what are we talking about here?"

Bastian tapped his forehead. "I'm not sure exactly, but everything in my senses was telling me I needed to record it. That it was something Emma needed, that would help stop the leech somehow. I can't explain it, and I don't even know if it will amount to anything. My powers—they aren't exactly always accurate."

I snorted. "Like when you freaked out about Emma when you first met?"

Bastian's cheeks went red and he pushed his hair back. "Actually ... that one kind of played out pretty much as I saw."

I sat up straight, imbuing my tone with a heavy dose of sarcasm. "Really? You didn't want to be anywhere near her, and now you're both sneaking out for couples' night?"

Sway gasped dramatically beside me then whispered, "Just joshing. I knew these lovebirds have been at it for ages. Can't keep secrets from the queen of institution sneak-abouts."

Bastian gestured between him and Emma. "This *was* why I didn't want to train her. I saw us together. And I saw *her*"—he waved a hand at her fabulousness—"and I felt like that whole concept was not a place that was going to work out well for anyone. But then she insulted me to my face and I figured it was a misreading."

Emma ducked her head, embarrassed. "I was so used to judging people's worth based on appearance. But the environment here ..."

"A bit different to high school or a team run by criminal con artists?" I snarked.

Bastian shrugged. "Hey, I mean, I judged her based on appearance, too. But then she opened up a bit and I saw who she really was. We've got a lot in common under the surface."

Emma crossed her legs and put her hands in her lap in a pose we used for meditation. "Under the surface is somewhere I hadn't looked in a very long time. Because I was worried I was just as ugly on the inside as I'd once felt on the outside. Now, I feel like an idiot for ever letting myself feel ugly, and for the ugly things I did. Because I know it was always my choice."

Sway twitched and scratched her ear. "Self-love propaganda. Don't bully-beat yourself. It's hard to feel good inside when everyone creeps cruelly around you, telling you the opposite."

Emma's bottom lip wobbled. Bastian reached across and held her hand, and she put her other hand on his, and then he joined in with his second hand too, and they both were smiling at each other.

"Uh, okay, enough with the googly eyes," I groaned, but couldn't help the small smile that grew on my face. "And thanks, for not telling the Crossmans who the leech is."

Emma shuffled closer into our circle. "I want you to know I'll do anything I can to help. I want to stop the leech, and get Dean back."

I nodded a thank you, and blinked away tears before they could fall.

Bastian put his arm over Emma's shoulders. "I'm in too. Liv, you saved our lives. We'll keep your secret and anything else you need to save Dean and the others."

"Me too," Rayni said, her voice small. "I want my brother back. We can't let Limbus kill the leech before we get everyone back."

Sway's face was dark. "I want payback for Marigold. But Livvy saved my life too. So I'm in for saving anyone she wants saved."

I sniffled. "That's really sweet, guys, but I have no idea what to do now. I don't have any plan. The leech? He's just too much. What he's capable of—I don't even know how to describe him."

"He's a straight-up psychopath, for starters," Bastian said seriously. "It took me all of one look into him to know."

"Psychopath? He's so good in the community though." *Why in this wild world am I defending him?*

"Actually," Rayni said, "psychopaths often make big efforts to help other people out, to cover their darker urges, or as another way to manipulate people and situations."

"He clearly likes to be in power, and pretending to be the good guy is a great way to have power," Bastian added.

"Which explains him being"—I glanced from our small group to the few younger kids doing a bad job at eavesdropping—"in his career choice. I can't even imagine the ways he's exploited that. How is he an empath and a psychopath? How can he hurt people so easily?"

Bastian raised his hands palm up. "I can only guess that while his empath powers can absorb emotions, he doesn't actually have them himself. He might be able to label the feelings he absorbs but he doesn't experience emotions like we do, especially compassion. He's an empath without empathy. He can use other people's emotions brutally against them and never feel bad about it."

I shivered. He'd known exactly how to take my love for my parents and turn it against me without so much as blinking. And his arrogance—he didn't want me because he felt anything for me. He probably just wanted to be seen as the great teacher to a student, the master to a thankful slave. He just wanted someone to appreciate his power and make him feel more powerful.

Emma's head hung down, her face curtained by her red hair. "I hate that I used to do that too. Use my proesthian powers to get whatever I wanted."

I shook my head. "The difference is you're here, doing the work to be better. You're changing. He will never understand what he's doing is wrong. He's a predator, and there isn't a single person he doesn't consider prey."

Rayni bit her lip and looked up at me. "Livvy? I think it would help us to understand all of this more if you told us how draining works. How you did it. We know you didn't know what you were doing at the time, but if you told us maybe it could help us understand what the leech can do, and how we can stop him."

I took a deep breath. "It was horrible. Like being so desolate and devastated that I wanted to let go of all control and consume everything around me. I thought Dean was dead and I just turned into a black hole."

Emma put her hands over her mouth and leaned into Bastian. "I'm so sorry."

I shrugged. "That was … that specific situation though. The more I've thought about it, the more I've realized it's like opening up the inlet taps of your powers fully. To soak in every single emotion, every bit of energy that the other person has. As empaths, we absorb emotional energy on a regular basis, but just small amounts. When you drain someone, you take everything."

Bastian straightened up with a concerned look under his furrowed brow. "You don't think, in theory then, that it could be done to normal people too? Not just empaths?"

I shrugged. "I guess. Only they would just be losing emotions and not powers."

Bastian's eyes went wide and he started tapping on the suit's screen on his wrist. He held it up, showing us a news article. "Maybe something like this? Tuesday evening, authorities were called to the scene of a major gas leak in the Bellscroft area. Twenty people were found unconscious and have yet to be revived," he read aloud. "But they don't know where the gas came from."

"You think it's the leech going after normal people? Like, maybe a bunch of normal people might equal the power boost of one empath?" My chest grew cold and I wrapped my arms around my shoulders, wishing they were Dean's arms and starting to lose hope they ever would be. "Maybe the Crossmans are right. Maybe the best thing at this point is to end this. He's just too dangerous."

Rayni grabbed me with both her hands. "No! We can't. We have to get Ash back. We can't abandon him."

I squeezed my arms tighter. "I don't want to abandon any of them. But I don't have a plan. I don't know what else we can do. I tried draining the leech and it didn't work. Nothing I've tried has worked."

Sway put a hand on my shoulder. "But you didn't have all

of us with you then. We can think of something together. Team Emotional Wrecks, remember?"

I laughed softly. "Go team."

"What about you, Bastian?" Rayni asked. "You were there with him; you know what he looks like, what he thinks like. Can your powers see any further into what we could do to beat him?"

Bastian shook his head and sighed. "I wish they worked that way. I really do. I would have to be around him more to read anything else, something I don't think he's going to just let me do."

"Not without draining you and getting your powers for himself." I shuddered at the thought of Terry with elucidist powers. "You really didn't get anything else from that encounter? Anything from his personality to guess what he's going to do next?"

Bastian scrunched his face up in thought. "I mean, if I had to guess, I'd say Terry would come after Limbus next."

Just as he finished his last word, alarms blared through the building.

12

We all stared at each other, not daring to speak or move, as alarms sounded around us. Ada, Cam, and Max shuffled over closer to our group.

"Maybe it's just a drill?" Emma offered.

Gunshots rang out from somewhere in the building.

Ada shrieked and covered her mouth.

We were on our feet instantly.

Shadows moved past the frosted windows in the entry doors to the gym. One of them stopped directly in front of it.

A deep voice bellowed. "Drop the weapon. Get your hands up!"

The sound of the gun hitting the floor echoed from the hallway into the training room. "My name is Vincent Crossman. I'm responsible for this workplace and those in it. You have no reason for this use of force. I want to speak to the officer in charge, and I want to see a warrant."

"You need to come with us," the other voice said. "And we'll use any force necessary."

"Show me your warrant or I'm not going anywhere. I will not move."

There was a rustling sound and the doors shook. Then more sounds of arguing, yelling, and struggling. A gunshot boomed, making us all duck to the ground.

Following the shot was a thud, the sound of a body hitting the floor. Blood seeped under the door and Bastian moved back, fear on his face.

Rayni grabbed my arm and slapped her hand over her mouth, whimpering quietly. More shouting came from outside. Another loud bang echoed out from the other side door. Seconds passed in stillness, only the suppressed crying from Ada breaking the silence. Then the door burst open.

We all jumped, Emma, Bastian and I moving to the front of the smaller kids.

Dr. Crossman stood there, panting heavily, holding a handgun in both hands, her finger on the trigger. Behind her on the floor, blood pooled and spread. Lying to the side, surrounded by that red ooze were two pairs of feet—Mr. Crossman's, and a uniformed cop's. I swallowed with a dry mouth. *Were they ... dead?* Dr. Crossman's face was ice pale and a spatter of blood flecked her white suit-dress. She did a quick headcount of the room. "You're all here, all okay. Thank God."

Rayni squeaked, "What's happening? Is Mr. Crossman—?"

Dr. Crossman gave a single sharp shake of her head. "No time. We have to move. Police are attacking the building; it's madness."

"It's the leech." I swallowed hard. I couldn't keep the secret any longer, not while Limbus agents, while Mr. Crossman, died around me. "He's the police captain in Bellscroft. I'm sure this is him, controlling these cops."

She inhaled audibly. "If he knows about Limbus ... we have to get you all out of here. There's a team of agents trying to hold off the police. I have to go and tell them what's happening. We may have a chance to catch the leech, but you kids have to be safe. Bastian, I'm trusting you to get them out of the building. Now."

"But we can fight," Cam said, stepping forward.

Emma nodded. "We want to help stop the leech."

Dr. Crossman looked from her to Bastian and me. "You're helping by getting the kids to safety. Even that is a more massive responsibility than I want to put on you, but I don't have any other option right now." Her eyes drifted down to the ground, to her husband's still body. Her expression glazed over, then she snapped out of it, looking back up at us. "I'm trusting you to do it. The kids need you. They can't face the leech. Just look at Livvy."

Everyone turned, and stared. My skin prickled, the ebbing pain of my bruises clear proof of the leech's powers.

"If you don't succeed, that's the *best* outcome you can hope for. And I'm sure you all know the worst." She checked her gun, then stepped back to look down the hallway. "I have to go. Stick together. Play it smart. Be careful. Quickly now, while it's clear."

Bastian nodded. Emma too.

"Let's go," I said. I took Rayni's hand in one of mine, and Cam's in the other. Bastian took Max and Emma paired with Ada. Dr. Crossman nodded to us and ran off to the left. We stepped out of the gym and ran right.

I made every effort to turn my head, and those of the children, away from the bodies behind us. We dashed toward the elevators. Sway ran behind me, crying "Insides should not be out!" over and over again. Emma, Sway, and I had the ability to move the fastest, and the three younger kids were all proesthians too, and did a good job at keeping up. The slick fabric of the suits reduced our friction and we sped faster.

I hit the emergency door shoulder-first, barreling through it. Concrete stairs led up and down, the path splitting before us. Rayni stopped, digging her feet in like a mule and staring upwards.

"We're not leaving without them," she said, and I knew exactly who she meant because my heart was dragging me up the stairs too. "We have to take them with us."

Bastian breathed heavily. "We can try and get them down the stairs, but you'd have to carry them." He pointed to Emma, Sway, and me.

"We can help; we're strong enough," Ada declared.

"Safest to stick together, too," Sway added.

Bastian looked over us all, focusing his powers. "Go and get whoever you can carry out. You get *one trip*, that's it. I'll get transport lined up out back."

"On your own?" Emma squeaked. "I should go with you."

I counted in my head. "Emma, we need you. Even with all of us, someone will still have to carry two people to get everyone out in one trip."

Rayni looked crushed, and I knew she was wishing she had proesthian powers too. "I'm going for my brother. I have to."

Bastian nodded. "I know you do. Don't worry. I'll be okay."

I squeezed Rayni's hand, then lifted and swung her around onto my back. Looking at the three younger kids, I said, "Keep up, okay?"

"No problem." Cam shivered, but his face was determined.

I bolted up the stairs. I held onto Rayni's legs and she hugged tightly to the back of my neck. The three other kids were right behind us, with Sway bringing up the rear. Emma dashed ahead of me, opening the door as we reached the next floor up where the ward was. The stairwell was the one Sway and I had once snuck out of, that opened up right outside the ward.

I came to a skidding stop at the double doors. Felix stood to the side, his uneven eyes panicked. He put his finger to his lips and pointed inside.

I peeked in through the windows and Rayni did too, over my shoulder. She gasped and pushed off my back, landing on her feet.

There was an officer standing next to the first bed in the ward. Ash's bed. Lifting Ash out from under the covers.

Before I realized what she was doing, Rayni had slammed her fist to the button, swinging the doors open. "Get your hands off my brother!"

The man's face was dazed and slightly confused. He dropped Ash, who fell back in a rag-doll slump on the mattress. The cop reached for his gun.

Rayni put her hands up in the air, but not in surrender. Her teeth clenched together and her nose wrinkled, and the sheer waves of negative emotion streaming from her brought tears to my eyes.

The officer's face crumpled and his legs buckled. He wailed in grief, clawing at his hair and face.

"Rayni, stop," I breathed, barely believing the power she had over him, this sweet girl who had pushed happy, calming emotions into me before. I'd never seen what she could do with negativity.

The man smashed his forehead with both fists. His arms stilled for a moment, then, shaking, he reached again toward his holster. He took the pistol in his hand, struggling as he tilted it up toward his temple, desperate to stop the anguish.

Rayni's eyes flashed and the air radiated around her. I reached for her arm. "Rayni, stop. This won't make any of it better."

Tears streamed down her face, and she let out a deep breath, releasing her emotional hold over him. "I'm sorry."

The cop dropped the gun and fell down weeping.

EMOTIONALLY POWERFUL

"See something new every day in this place," Felix muttered.

"More coming!" Sway hissed, herding the three kids into the ward. Footsteps came from down the end of the hall, and we all ducked inside out of sight.

"They're going to find us, for sure," Cam whined.

My head snapped back toward the cop. The way he looked around wildly, confused, gave me hope. "Hey, hey, get up."

He looked up at me, and around at the other kids. "What's going on? Captain told us this place was a terrorist network, had to bring everyone in by any means. But you're kids. This feels wrong. It's all wrong."

Jackpot. Rayni had knocked Terry's control off him. But I'd never successfully controlled anyone before. "Emma, need you, quick."

She stepped up beside me.

"Tell our friend here that the people he wants are upstairs, right up on level ten. And he needs to get all the police up there right now if he wants to help keep us kids safe, which I'm sure he does."

Emma nodded knowingly, and knelt down low beside the man, using every ounce of charm and suggestion power she had. "You understand?" she finished.

The sounds outside grew closer.

The cop stood, brave and determined. "Got it."

Sway opened the doors for him, slamming them shut right behind as he left.

We all held our breaths as muffled voices came from directly outside. And then footsteps again, going fast, away from us.

I exhaled loudly and looked around the room at the other kids, and the people in beds, and Dean. "Come on. We need to get these people out of here. Felix, help us unhook everyone and then grab whatever you need."

He gave me the thumbs up and got to work. As he took each patient off their monitoring machines, someone was there to scoop them up. Ada, Max, and Cam each managed one of the grown-ups each, and Sway took Holbrook, leading them away.

In the distance, floors up, gunshots sounded again, making us freeze, and then move faster.

"I can take two," Emma said. She had Mr. Kairu, over one shoulder, and reached out her other empty arm.

"You sure?" I had Dean in my arms. Rayni stared desperately between me and Ash, the last remaining. Emma nodded firmly, and I swallowed my heart as I put Dean into her arm and she ran off. Rayni climbed up onto my back again and I lifted her brother in my arms.

I checked around the room, over all the empty beds.

Felix had thrown a bunch of tubing, IV bags, and medication in a cardboard box and was looking around under a cupboard making kissy noises.

"We have to go," I snapped.

"But—"

"Now!" I couldn't carry him too. But when I yelled, he moved surprisingly quickly. I chased along the hall after him, down the stairs, and out the back exit. We arrived just as Emma lay Dean down beside Mr. Kairu in the back of a van. There were two there, each packed with moving and unmoving bodies. Bastian sat in the driver's seat of one, with Sway, the three kids, and their patients. Emma climbed into the driver's seat of the second van.

I lay Ash down next to Dean, and Rayni climbed off my back, stepping carefully around them.

Everyone was piled up horribly. I didn't know how long they'd last without proper medical support. But at least we were out.

Felix dropped his box into the passenger seat next to Bastian. "We following protocol? Know where we're going?"

Bastian nodded.

"See you there." Felix took the passenger seat beside Emma. He reached out the open window and slapped the side of the van. "Go, go, go!"

I stepped up into the van as the engine revved. As I reached to grab the back doors to close them, I looked up at the Limbus building, hopefully not for the last time.

I hoped Dr. Crossman and the agents would do just what we all wanted them to do.

I hoped we'd be returning here soon, triumphant, safe, ready to have our loved ones restored into their bodies where they belonged.

Through a window a few floors up, a shadowed figure stared back down at us. I could feel in my heart that it was Terry, and a deep, uncontrollable anger took over me. I wanted to beat him the way he'd beaten me. I wanted him bruised and bloodied and defeated. I wanted to strangle the life from him, and the only thing stopping me doing so was the lives of my loved ones he held in his grasp.

I slammed the doors on him and those dark, hateful emotions, and we sped away.

13

Rayni sat on the van floor, squeezed up against the wall, cradling Ash's head. I mirrored her on the other side, holding Dean in my lap. Mr. Kairu, gray-haired and gaunt, lay held between us. We did what we could to protect them from the swerves and bumps of our wild escape.

"I'm sorry about back there, with the policeman," Rayni said in a tiny voice. "I just got so angry."

"It's okay. I understand. I'm angry too. And scared. And just upset in every way. Everything about what Terry has done to me, to us—we can't pretend it doesn't hurt." My eyes remained on Dean, and I pressed a hand to his cool cheek, willing his body to hold on.

563

"I can't believe Mr. Crossman is dead." Rayni wiped her nose on the sleeve of her black Limbus suit. Her rainbow hair had been in a tight braid at training, but had been pulled loose and tangled somewhere along the way. I wanted to see her back in a bright cardigan, smiling like a prim fairy princess, like she did when I first met her. Before she had seen such horror.

"Me either," I replied.

"I hope Dr. Crossman is okay. I hope she and the other agents made it out. Or that they've already captured the leech."

I closed my eyes, trying to hope the same, but it seemed so impossible. "At least we got everyone from the ward—" I cut off, mouth turning down. *Oh, Kimmy.*

We left Kimmy behind. Somehow it hurt even more, imagining that sweet cat, confused and abandoned in the building. Wandering the empty beds, looking for her sleeping owner. Finding Mr. Crossman where he lay lifeless and bloody. If Terry had taken over the place, I was terrified to think of what casual cruelty could befall a cat which happened to cross his path.

The brakes went on. We all lurched forward like we'd been washed up on shore.

Felix tapped on the cargo barrier. "Everyone stay there. I'll get the keys. Gosh, I hope I remember the code to the lockbox."

He hopped out, and through the front window I saw the

other van pulled up beside us in front of a large but unassuming suburban home in a quiet leafy street. It was well kept and a bit old-fashioned, with a wide porch and attic windows.

Felix dashed around the front yard a few times, flitting like a white moth in his lab coat, then the double garage doors opened and Emma drove us in. I could hear the rumble of the other van as it parked beside us and turned off.

A few seconds later, Felix and Emma opened the back for us as the garage doors whined closed.

I placed Dean carefully down and stepped out over him and the others.

"Where are we?" I asked, looking around the tidy garage, neatly stacked with storage tubs and buckets.

"Limbus safe house. About halfway between Bellston Main and Bellscroft. Everyone out," Bastian replied, hopping down from the other van. He opened the back doors of his vehicle and Sway, Ada, Cam, and Max climbed out, looking wide-eyed and bleary. "Our home away from home. Should have everything we need for a while. Food, gear, cash, beds."

"Bathrooms? Man, I need to pee so bad," Sway declared, running through the adjoining door to the house. The other kids followed, muttering about hunting for snacks.

I turned to pick up Dean and bring him in.

"Leave the patients for now," Felix said. He paced behind the closed garage door, pulling cat kibble from his pocket and snacking on it absently.

"Umm, you seem worried," I said.

He crunched a piece and looked up at me, eyes darting while his brain made calculations. "I'm not worried. I'm fully brown-pantsing right now. I don't think we can stay here."

"The safe house isn't safe?" Emma asked.

"Maybe, for a little while. But if the leech gets Dr. Crossman or any of the senior agents, if he thinks to interrogate them before whatever else he does to them, he'll have access to the Limbus system. Then, *whoosh!* Goodbye safe houses." Felix made his hands like a rocket, zooming them away.

Rayni's face looked drained, hollows deep around her red eyes. "Actually, not just safe houses. If he gets access to those files, he will have the details and location of every empath known to Limbus ... on Earth. No one will be safe. Nowhere will be safe."

Bastian leaned face-first into the side of a van and groaned.

"Then what do we do? Where do we go?" Emma hugged her arms around herself.

"We stay here for now. We have to hope the leech doesn't get that far, that the agents can stop him," Felix said. But from the look on his and everyone else's faces, they had just as much hope of that as I did. "But we prepare for the worst. We load up everything we can into the vans, everything we might need. And we keep watch. First sign of trouble and we're out of here."

Emma nodded. "Good plan."

Rayni glanced back at her brother, then at me. "I'll take first watch."

We split up, Emma trailing Bastian to load up the supplies he selected, and me trailing Felix to do the same. Even though I knew Rayni had headed upstairs and was watching the street from one of the attic windows, I still checked between the closed curtains every time I passed a window too. So far, the coast looked clear, but we weren't sure how long it would stay like that.

We dragged some bedding into one van and moved all of the patients into it, looking somewhat more comfortable than they had during our first trip, then used the other van for supplies. We took a quick trip up to a bedroom and Felix unlocked a floor safe filled with cash, which we loaded into the vans. A lot of what we needed was right there in the garage. We went through the storage crates and buckets and found weapons, long-shelf-life food supplies, and even throwaway cell phones. We weren't sure whether Terry had the info or ability to track everyone else's phones yet, so we all took a burner, and connected up our numbers. My own phone was still back at home, a place I wasn't hopeful I could ever go back to. The place my parents were taken from. *Are they still okay? What will Terry do to them now?*

There were some medical supplies there, but Felix grumbled about it not being enough. It was mostly first-aid gear. Quality first-aid gear, but not the machines and medicines needed to maintain more than half a dozen coma patients. Still, we took everything we could.

Emma rounded up the kids, grabbing duffel bags out of the hall closets and loading them with blankets, toiletries, snacks, and anything else they decided they wanted on their way through the house.

Sway returned to the vans with a loaded backpack and what looked like a dozen energy bars stuffed in her shirt. "This place was finger-licking loaded! Want one?"

She offered an apple-flavored ration bar to me and I took it gratefully. I sat down on the back bumper of the van and bit into the crumbly pastry.

Felix hopped from one foot to another, looking more nervous than ever. "We really should get moving soon. I keep expecting leechified marines will burst in when we least expect it, but then I am expecting it, but still, I think I won't have expected it *enough* to stop them bursting in."

Bastian carried a plastic crate over and balanced it on top of the others. "All we need to do now is figure out where we're going to go."

Sway pursed her lips. "Anybody got any ideas? Long-lost cousins who own huge secluded mansions far away?"

Emma handed Bastian a duffel bag and he squeezed it between the crates and the van ceiling. "Well, there are some places Jake used to take us that were pretty secluded and safe, but the nearest one I know is hours away."

"We need to get the patients back onto proper medical support asap." Felix shook his head.

I narrowed my eyes, looking at Sway.

She wriggled her eyebrows back at me. "What?"

"I was just thinking," I said, "we need a big place with medical facilities, and it needs to be somewhere the leech won't suspect. And I think I know where that is. But Sway's not going to like it."

Sway's eyes widened with understanding. "For freaky real? You're going to make me go back there?"

"Sorry." I winced, then explained to the others. "I think we should go to the institution."

"Didn't it burn down?" Emma asked.

"One building, yeah. And so they cleared out the rest of the place, but there's another whole building there, sitting abandoned. There could still be supplies and things too. If we're halfway to Bellscroft already, it's close."

Felix rubbed his goatee. "That could be ideal."

Sway dragged both palms down her face, whining.

I stood up and gave her a hug. "You'll be fine. You know what you are now. You're with us, one of us, and we're a team, remember?"

"Uh, guys," Rayni said, poking her head in. "Whatever plan you have, I think maybe now would be a good time to implement it. A cop car just did a drive-by."

"Butt biscuits," Felix hissed. "I stopped expecting it!"

Bastian looked faint. "That means … it means the leech got control of Limbus."

My arms were still around Sway, and she squeezed me back tightly. For a moment, she was all that held me up. Terry had won. He had everything. I didn't want to think about what might have happened to Dr. Crossman and the agents who'd tried to face him.

"And it means someone's seen the lights on here, and there will be more police on the way," Emma said, heading up into the house. "I'll get the kids."

I took a few steps after her, leaning to look out the window onto the street. It was empty again, for now. My tracker watch said it was almost six p.m. but dark clouds made it seem much later at night, and in the distance thunder rolled.

My tracker …

"We have to leave our trackers here!" I dashed back down to the garage, and moments later was joined by Emma and the remaining kids. "If Terry—the leech—is in the system, he could activate them and find us anywhere."

Everyone triple-tapped the fingerprints on their trackers, unlocking them and dropping them to the floor.

Emma started crying. "I can't. I can't take mine off."

Bastian growled. "They still hadn't given you clearance over it? Felix, can you fix this?"

Felix's shoulders slumped. "Not without my computer. It got left behind. I could hack it. Estimate of twenty, thirty minutes though."

Emma's lips tightened. "We don't have that time." She took her left hand and squeezed it in her right hand. She cried out, buckling at the waist as her thumb bones snapped, and the tracker fell loose to the floor. I cried out in sympathy.

"Done," she said, cradling her hand as everyone stared at

her with gaping mouths. "But someone else has to drive the second van now."

"What about these?" I asked Felix, holding up my arm with the digital display pad built into the Limbus suits we all wore.

Felix's eyes trailed back from Emma to mine, watering. "No problem. Not activated yet. I mean, they have Wi-Fi, but no GPS or other things the full-function models have. They were supposed to be just for training, never meant for use in the field."

"Okay. Let's move then."

Bastian put his arms around Emma, supporting her over into the passenger seat of the supplies van. Felix took the other driver's seat and I climbed in beside him with Sway, Rayni and the other kids in back with the patients.

The garage door opened out onto the street as a gust of wind made a cloud of dust and leaves dance along the footpath in front of us. Thunder grumbled and grew closer as we floored it out of there.

14

We made short work of the chain-link barriers that had been set up around the burned out Bellscroft Mental Healthcare facility and drove the vans right up to the front door of the only remaining building on the lot still standing.

Everyone pitched in, carefully carrying out the patients and unloading everything inside before Bastian left to get the vans parked in the underground carpark, out of sight. We hadn't seen any police cars following us, and could only hope we'd made it there untraced.

As I carried the last duffel bag inside, I looked back across the leafy courtyard to the blackened and crumbling remains of what was once the main part of the institute. A shiver drove through me as I remembered the crackling flames, my scorching skin, and Marigold, thrown into the fire. I turned away and headed in after the others.

The smaller side building had been filled with admin offices to support the main institute. It had survived mostly untouched, but there was a small layer of fine ash covering every surface, blown across from the blaze.

A quick investigation revealed the building owners had only cleared out the patient files and medicines, then just locked up and left the rest.

We quickly found a larger storeroom filled with machines and things that made Felix groan loud sighs of relief, and his eyes lit up again when we found a room where salvaged hospital beds had been lined up against a wall.

Everyone worked together to clear out the furniture from a large meeting room and set the beds up in there, get the patients into them, and help Felix hook up everything he needed to. He was going to have to rotate some of the machines he didn't have enough of for everyone, but for now, the patients were safe and stabilized.

I held Dean's hand for a few long moments while Felix fussed around by torchlight, muttering about only having enough medical supplies for a few days. I wasn't sure if we'd even last that long before the next attack came, the next tragedy struck. I rubbed my eyes and headed across the hall where everyone else was making camp.

Although we had power back on, we kept the lights off, knowing it wouldn't do for anyone to see lights on in a supposedly abandoned building. One small LED lantern set to low sat on the floor near the door. Ada, Cam, Max, and Rayni had rolled out foam mattresses and sleeping bags in the middle of the break room. Cam and Max sat on one bedroll, hugging each other and crying, and Ada just lay wide-eyed and still, curled into a ball on her side. Bastian and Emma sat together on a two-seater sofa, and Sway paced.

"This place smells like a mixture of burnt cheese and hospital disinfectant," she snarled.

"But it's safe." *I hope. For now.*

"Safer than anywhere out there," Bastian muttered. "I'm pretty sure we're all considered wanted criminals by now. That Terry bastard could have the entire regional police force out looking for us."

I took in a deep breath and rolled my shoulders. I wanted to lay down and sleep, straight on the floor if I had to, even though it was probably only seven at night. "Felix has got the security monitors up and running and is keeping watch, so we will see anyone coming. We've got enough food to last us a few days or so. We just need to hunker down in here."

Rayni sat up on her sleeping bag, arms wrapped around her knees. "Then what? We live here in hiding forever? We can't. We have to do something. We have to stop him."

She was right. We had to do something. Every part of me burned to act, to save Dean and my parents and everyone. I wanted to rip Terry limb from limb, but I was just so defeated. I didn't know where to start.

And everyone in the room was looking to me.

I shook off the morbid hopelessness that had been creeping into my bones, and clenched my teeth, took one big breath, and nodded. "Okay. We need to deal with Terry right flipping now. Otherwise, he's going to drain every empath he can find in the Limbus database. He's already stupidly powerful, and we don't want him getting any more so, or there'll be no where we can hide."

I let them know everything I did about Terry, his life, his character, his strengths.

"What about his weaknesses?" Emma asked. "Things seemed pretty rough for you when you had drained empaths in you. He might be ten times as strong, but wouldn't he be ten times as weak in a way, too?"

"Yeah, okay. So, what weaknesses do proesthians normally have? Nothing is too small or ridiculous. We just need ideas."

"Actually, there are a lot of things that proesthians powers can't tackle," Rayni piped up. "They improve your input senses like vision and hearing a little, but there are many ways to cripple them, like extreme darkness, or smoke."

"Fire was pretty tough to deal with," Sway grumbled.

Bastian added, "Negative emotions like sadness can be debilitating in some situations. Or just the presence of no emotions at all to use."

I tapped my lips, thinking. "Can we do that?"

"What?"

"Get rid of all emotional energy from around the leech?" I directed my question to Rayni. "Like you did for me, back when you guys first kidnapped me?"

Her mouth wobbled. "Maybe. I could try and pull it off, but depending on how many people there were nearby, it would take a lot out of me. The angrier they are to start with, the more it takes to bring them down to a baseline. I could only do it for a short amount of time."

Bastian focused in on both of us, understanding. "You want to get back there, ambush Terry like he did us?"

I nodded. "I doubt he'd be expecting us to hit back so soon. He thinks he's won."

Bastian nodded. "Yeah, I think Rayni can do it. When I was getting the vans, I spotted maybe a dozen cops at Limbus. Rayni's strong; I could see her managing to calm them. But doing that will mean none of you proesthians will have emotions to draw from either. You won't have any powers."

"I know. But we'll have each other. And we have an emogen," I pointed to Rayni, then to Bastian, "and an elucidist. I don't think Terry knows about you guys. Or at least, he won't until he gets done studying the Limbus info banks. I don't think he's ever come across your types before. That's another advantage we have."

"Plus we have these sexy, sweet super-suits!" Sway said, posing with a fist up in the air.

I cracked a smile, but had to admit that the suit made me feel safer and stronger too. Being bulletproof counted for something. "If Rayni can keep any cops in the building calm and out of our way, we'll be taking the leech on as normal people. One middle-aged man versus all of us—it's better odds than trying to take him with his powers. That is, if you still are all in." I looked around the room, and everyone nodded, even Ada, who'd sat up to listen, and Max and Cam, who'd stopped crying.

"Then we do this. Now. We do whatever we can to incapacitate the leech while he's powerless. After that, I'll drain him and restore everyone back to where they belong. Done and dusted," I said.

Everyone got to their feet, ready for action. I didn't want the kids to come, but I could see from the looks on their faces they were determined, and they had proven themselves capable today.

"It's a good plan, but ..." Rayni stuttered. "C-could we do this without you?"

"Without me?" I repeated, confused.

She grimaced. "If something happens to you, we have no way of getting everyone back from the leech. No one else knows how to drain and return people."

"I—" I looked down at my arm, still covered in a cast, and remembered the warning Terry had delivered along with the beating. Next time he saw me, either I joined him, or I was his next victim. But I had to go. I had to face that monster and beat him down. My blood boiled for revenge. "I'm going. And if it looks like we can't take him down, if it looks like he's got me, I will kill him before he can hurt anyone else."

"Are we really at that point?" Emma asked in a small, high voice.

Bastian frowned at me for a long while. "Livvy needs to go.

579

And we will protect her at all costs."

The circle of suited-up empaths in front of me nodded as one.

We were doing this.

I wished I could promise the ache in my heart that we'd succeed.

15

A *moment.*

That was what I needed with Dean. Just a moment to explain to him where I was going, and what we were doing. I doubted he could hear me, or even knew that I was close, but if I didn't say it then, there was a chance I would never say it at all.

I sat on the edge of the padded gurney and rubbed my hand over his. I spoke softly, so those outside couldn't hear. "You're gonna be so mad." It felt like just yesterday that he wrapped his pinky around mine as we stood side by side in the schoolyard. Back when he was being my stalwart hero, keeping the emotions at bay and helping me to find my stability. I smiled, imagining him already frowning at me. "But this has to be done. I think we've got a chance to take Terry down together."

I had to believe we had a chance. But saying it out loud didn't help the sinking feeling inside. I was terrified to go back into that building, to see what had become of those who were left behind trying to fight Terry and his hypnotized police force. Terrified of seeing bodies, like Mr. Crossman's, and the cop Dr. Crossman had killed in return. The sound of those gunshots echoed again in my head.

I sighed, and poked at the cast on my arm. My ulna, which was apparently one of the two bones in the forearm, had been fractured the last time I went head to head with Terry. But I no longer felt any pain. I wriggled my fingers, wanting more freedom of movement, as though every bit would count. I dug my fingers into the plaster, cracking it away.

Emma appeared at the doorway to the makeshift ward. "We're all set."

"Just a minute," I said, then turned back to Dean. "Before I go, I have to tell you two things. The first is, I'm sorry if you wake up one day and I'm not here. And I'm even more sorry if you never wake up."

Tears pooled around my lashes. The thought of never seeing

Dean open his beautiful gray eyes again was too much. "Second thing is, don't worry about the first thing, because I will come back, and when I get back, you'll be back too. We'll be together again, like we should be."

There was a shuffle in the hallway outside. Emma was still there, waiting for me. I grimaced. *Couldn't she just give me a moment?*

"I've got to go," I whispered, leaning over to Dean's cheek. "Get your sleep because I will be back soon to wake you right up. I love you."

I pressed my lips to his cold skin and breathed him in. Letting go of his hand, I hopped down from the bed and headed out the door.

"Everyone's in the van," Emma said, falling in step beside me. She shot me a few sideways glances. "I know you find it hard to talk to me. And I don't blame you for that; I've done some pretty awful things. But I want you to listen."

I said nothing, just kept walking beside her, the rubber soles of our suits nearly silent down the linoleum hall, adding to the eerie quiet of the abandoned building.

"When I was younger, before Jake and everything, I used to get bullied pretty bad. All those hateful emotions used to burrow into me, cut through me. I didn't know I was an empath, which made me feel everything so much more. There was this one guy ..." She rubbed her hand around the thumb she'd broken earlier, bending it slowly back and forth as though testing it. "I took one of my dad's fake guns to pull a revenge prank on him. He didn't find it very funny. He attacked me and my powers kicked in for the first time and there was a big accident and ... he died."

I frowned, but still didn't reply. I could tell she wasn't finished and I wanted to speed along through whatever point she was trying to make. We reached the front door, and she stopped in front of it, blocking my path.

"That was when I first started feeling bad on the inside as well as the outside. And no amount of cosmetic surgery fixed that. Everything felt horrible inside me, and I used that to justify doing bad things, like I had no choice." Emma tucked her red hair behind one ear, looking through the door windows at the van out the front. Her eyes sparkled, wet with unspent tears. "You and the others, though? You've made me feel like I could be good again. And it's the hardest feeling ever. Because making that choice means it was *always* my choice to be bad."

I fought off a grimace. Was she trying to apologize? Make up somehow? I didn't have the emotional space for her as well as everything else, but I tried to say something helpful in return to keep us moving. "That gun—the one you had at the convention, and at the bank—it was always a fake, wasn't it?" I asked, and she nodded, looking embarrassed. "That was a choice you made. While Jake and the others were literally shooting innocent bystanders, you always chose not to. I think you've always been better than you think you are. I know you've been crushed down, made to feel small. I'm glad you're finding people to help you find yourself and your worth again."

I nodded to her and tried to push past and out the door, lips twitching. I'd dealt enough with her feelings when so many more important things were happening. Emma reached out and took my wrist, turning me toward her. "That's why I wanted to talk to you, to get you to listen. Because I feel like I'm seeing you getting crushed down in every way. I can feel the anger just dripping off you, and that's with you trying to block it. It's like you're going to explode and I'm worried about you."

"You're worried about me?" I choked up, frozen mid-step. *This was about me?*

"I've felt those same vicious emotions, that pain and anger. I know how easy it is to let that darkness in. I don't want to see that happen to you." She pulled me in toward her, and caught unaware, I tumbled into her arms, squeezed by them as unexpected tears spilled from my eyes. "Darkness isn't going to get you what you want."

I wished I could have said she was being ridiculous, but I couldn't. Darkness had been trailing behind me every day since I found Dean. It called for me, beckoned me, and pulled me down into its grasp. It was the feeling that I could be justified in doing anything I had to do to stop Terry. I could even kill him, or anyone who stood between me and getting my revenge. I had been relying on that darkness to keep me going, to have the will to commit to the violence I knew lay ahead, to be able to lead others into the same, and to risk their lives.

I shook my head. Emma was wrong. I needed those feelings to beat Terry.

"Thank you," I told her anyway, as I backed out of her embrace.

Emma wiped her cheek and laughed. "Come on. Let's go defeat the bad guy, then maybe after that, you and I can start over fresh."

There was so much vulnerable hope in her tone then I almost called the whole attack plan off. How could I be leading my friends and some innocent kids into this mad plan?

The darkness whispered back. *Because you have to. You have to be a monster to defeat a monster.*

I steeled myself and smiled. "Ready or not, here we come."

16

A soft rain had blown in. Thunder rumbled in the distance, as though calling us to action. We were all huddled together on the slope of the stormwater drain around the back of Limbus, having used it to sneak up to the building. Rivulets of water ran down the concrete under us and a small creek had formed in the channel below, dragging leaves and old drink cans along.

The suits we all wore seemed to be somewhat waterproof, but my face and hair were slick and cold from the rain. I blinked it out of my eyes as I narrowed them at the building before us. I wanted to get in there and get this over with. I was eager to claw out a victory and return to Dean and wake him up.

"Right, we all know the deal," Bastian whispered, sounding jittery. We had gone over and over our strategy on the drive in. Before that, when we had explained our plan to Felix, he'd told us it was the kind of plan only teenagers with no sense of their own mortality could make, then wished us luck with such solemnity it made me tear up.

"Powers stay up until we find Terry. We're aiming for as few encounters with cops as we can on the way. Once we have Terry in sight, Rayni does her thing and powers get nulled. We rely on training and numbers, and we do whatever we can to take Terry down while Livvy tries to drain him."

Easy peasy. My mouth tasted of acid and I gulped it away. Everyone looked so confident in the plan that it scared me. They all seemed so confident in *me*, and I couldn't shake the feeling I was using them just to get to Terry.

"Terry will still be a fight," I said, almost hoping to scare the others off. "Even without his powers, assume he's still dangerous. He's been a police officer for years, and we can expect him to be armed."

Bastian looked at me long and hard, and I shied away from what he might be reading in my future. But he nodded and said, "We've got some protection from our suits. But we should maybe grab weapons along the way, too."

Weapons sounded good. I wanted to beat the ever-living snot out of Terry. Then, when he couldn't even crawl, I would take his powers and everyone else's that he'd stolen. There were probably far more than I even knew about, than I even knew whether I could contain or not. It was worth the risk to me though. I would do anything to beat him.

Sway put her hand on my shoulder. "How you holding up? You're glowing hot as a jolly red poker."

I nodded. "I'm fine. I'm ready."

Bastian patted me on the back. "Then let's go. We can do this. Let's take Limbus back."

"Hear, hear," Rayni said. She looked a few years younger than normal, with her hair plastered down over her small face.

Everyone nodded and looked to me. Bastian, Emma, Sway, Rayni, Ada, Cam, and Max.

Call it off. Someone's going to get hurt.

I clenched my teeth. *Everyone's going to be hurt if we don't stop Terry.*

I led the way, dashing over to the emergency exit door, and ducking behind a dumpster. Everyone followed close behind. The team was pumped. I could sense their hope, excitement, and fear.

I quietly tried the door. *Unlocked.* I doubted we were just

589

lucky. Terry thought he was a god. What god needed to lock his own doors?

We snuck up through the concrete stairwell, staying quiet, and calm, and unnoticed. I extended my senses out, trying to track any presence around us, trying to find Terry's location.

Sway found him first. "Uh, gross," she said. "That's him, total gangrenous guts."

She took the lead, and we went up a few floors and out into a quiet corridor.

"*Back, back!*" she mouthed, gesturing wildly. I sensed it a moment after her—a couple of people headed our way. We ducked around a corner. Two officers, in ragged uniforms and looking out of sorts, patrolled past us. When they went the other way, we let out our held breaths so simultaneously, it was almost comical.

Sway crept forward down the hall, around a bend, and turned left at an intersection. We all followed.

There was blood on the floor here, a dropped gun there, but thankfully, no other horrors. *Not yet.*

I eyed the gun, but Bastian snatched it up first.

"*In there,*" Sway mouthed when we reached a hardwood door with a shiny brass nameplate. Dr. Crossman's office. I could feel Terry now too. But I could also sense the presence of a half a dozen confounded and conflicted bodies between us and him, and more above and below us, throughout the building. If we could clear some out, it would mean less for Rayni to deal with.

"Ada, Cam, Max," I whispered. "I want you guys to draw the cops away. Let them see you, then just run for it. Lead them in circles, buy us some time, then just get out of here and get back to the van once you're sure you've lost them."

They seemed unsure at first, as though catching onto the fact I wanted them gone too, but agreed silently. The rest of us hid in a supply closet across the hall while the three kids opened the office door. It only took a second for someone to notice them, and the chase was on. The three kids no doubt fed off my fear for their safety, using it to go faster, pursued by stomping, squeaking boots down the corridor.

I was worried Terry would chase them too, and was ready to burst out and get in the way if that happened. But I didn't sense Terry move at all, and now, he was alone. We crept across the hall, quietly opening the door.

Terry sat with his back to us, typing away at the computer.

Rage flared through me, and I almost leaped across the room to smash his face in.

But then Rayni's turn was up, and suddenly everything was calm. No fear, no anger—nothing came from within me or around me. My muscles practically drooped, and had I been capable, I would have been scared at the loss of my powers.

But even without my rage, my powers, I knew what I had to do.

"Go!" I hissed. Emma and Sway ran in first, and I tried to join them but Bastian had my arm grasped tight in his hand.

"No," he said, with disturbing, calm clarity. "Something's wrong."

I ripped out of his hold and snatched a heavy award plaque off a shelf and went after the others ... just in time for Terry to rise to his feet and brush off the attacks Emma and Sway tried to land. I was inches from striking his face with the heavy plaque when his hand snapped up and he grabbed me mid-flight.

Sway and Emma tumbled into opposite corners of the office with striking cracks.

Terry held my wrist, squeezing it high in the air, wrenching my body with it. I gasped and cried out, dropping the award. It thudded beneath me. *What's happening?* He still moved so fast. Was still so strong. While none of us had any powers available at all. How?

The drained civilians. Could they be acting like an emotion store inside of him? I didn't know. I couldn't be sure of anything except that he was infinitely stronger than us, and our plan was sure to fail.

Terry swept back his blond hair with one hand, keeping me held in the other. He was wearing a bulletproof vest over his captain's uniform, and blood stained the cuffs of his shirt. He almost sounded disappointed. "I could sense you children approaching from a mile away. And now it's come to this. I told you what would happen."

His body pulsed with energy and it struck out, opening up and feeding, crawling inside me. I felt sick to my stomach, waves of power lashing and dragging at me. Terry was draining me, right there in the middle of the room.

Emma was back on her feet, wobbling as she picked up the office chair and swung it across Terry's back. It bounced right off him. Rayni stood in the doorway, sweat dripping from her furrowed brow, trying futilely to push the emotions from Terry. Sway pummeled him with fists, completely ignored, less of a threat than a mere mosquito.

Bastian stared. Calm. Studying.

There was a pull in my chest that took my breath away and my consciousness was set adrift, floating out. I tried to hold onto it, hold onto myself, but the suctioning whirlpool of darkness before me was too strong. *Terry* was too strong.

Emma screamed something, but I couldn't hear her. For a

moment, I stared over at her through Terry's eyes, then back into my own face, seeing it slacken and pale. Helpless. Sinking out of the world.

A clapping boom rang out, shocking me back into my own body. I blinked as Terry stumbled back a step, still crushing my wrist in his hand, but dropping me onto my feet.

Bastian yelled behind me, "Rayni, stop. They need their powers back, now!"

I turned and saw him aiming the handgun he'd taken at Terry. He squeezed the trigger again and the sound crashed through the small room, pounding in my ears.

Terry stumbled a second time and released his grip on me, clutching at where the bullet had struck. The bulletproof vest blocked each bullet; each shot barely winded him.

Sway ran forward, speeding fast, grabbing me and dragging me out of the office. My powers were coming back too, but my body was still processing what was happening, still swimming back to myself.

"Get out of here, all of you, now!" Bastian yelled, firing off another shot. It hit Terry in the hand where he had been brushing off the previous one and he howled, more in anger than in pain.

"Take Rayni!" Bastian barked at Emma when she hesitated beside him.

EMOTIONALLY POWERFUL

"But what about you?"

Terry gathered himself and began a slow march forward.

Bastian pulled the trigger again. "You have to go without me. Trust me and just go. Now. I'm almost out."

Emma looked between him and Rayni, anguish twisting her features. She snatched Rayni up into her arms, rushing out of the office. Sway supported me into motion and we followed.

Behind us, shot after shot went off.

As we hit the fire-escape door, Bastian pulled the trigger one last time, the gun making nothing more than a clicking sound.

"Go!" he bellowed.

Terry roared. Bastian cried out.

Emma wept and sobbed as she ran down the stairs with Rayni. My head spun, thoughts spinning loose, fading in and out. I tripped, tumbling down one flight, then Sway lifted me entirely.

We were out in the rain again, back down the street to the van where the three kids waited.

Emma's chest convulsed with sobs and the muscles that strained to keep them in check as she got into the driver's seat and sped us away.

Empty-handed. No victory. No one saved.

Nothing but another dreadful loss.

595

17

My head was tilted limply back against the cinder-block
wall of the break room, staring at the LED lamp by the
door. I avoided the vacant stares of the others. The worn linoleum
floor was hard and cold, numbing my body whenever it touched
it for too long. I cuddled my knees, and let the numbing effect
spread up through my body.

I didn't want to move, to think. I didn't want to feel. I let
my emotions grow numb as well, especially the deep yearning
to be with Dean. All I desired was to curl up beside him, draw
strength from him, as though even in his coma, he had more
life in his body than I did right now.

596

But I couldn't do that. I couldn't face him. Not when I'd promised I'd return and wake him up, and instead had come back with nothing but the burden of another shattering defeat.

As much as I desperately wanted to go to Dean, denying that need was the least punishment I deserved. I was almost surprised I still felt those urges, that I still had love in me after so much darkness had taken root inside.

I wasn't sure how long it had been since we got back. Felix had seen our faces when we came in, seen that Bastian wasn't with us. "I'll keep monitoring the patients and the security," was all he'd said. He'd looked drawn, helpless, as I was sure we all did.

Ada, Max, and Cam had cried themselves to sleep some time ago.

Emma's wrenching sobs from the kitchenette corner had quieted into regular sniffles. Sway and Rayni had slumped onto each other's shoulders along the wall beside me. No one spoke. No one moved. We were paralyzed in grief and surrender. I had no idea if Terry would track us back here, and who he would take from us next, and I wasn't sure anymore if any of us still cared. We were broken, every one of us.

Emma flopped forward from where she leaned in the corner, landing on all fours and slamming the ground with her fists. "I can't believe it happened like that. I can't believe we lost Bastian."

Everyone stared at her with wide, red eyes, as though she'd broken the spell of paralysis on the room.

"I don't know how we went so wrong. We didn't stand a chance." Rayni's voice crackled with emotion.

Sway patted both her hands in a rhythm against the sides of her head. "Perilously pumped-up parasite. Terry, Terry, terrifying. Monster from hell, can't take me. Won't. WON'T!"

Rayni made soft hushing sounds and put her arms around her.

"He was unstoppable, and now? Now he has an elucidist's powers too." Emma whined and pulled at her hair. "What do you think he did with Bastian? With ... his body?"

My voice came out hoarse, flat, and unconvincing. "Maybe Bastian's okay. Maybe Terry won't recognize him as an empath, or is keeping him hostage for some reason."

Emma sniffled again, wiping her nose on one of a million used tissues piled around her like clouds. "Let's be real here. I mean, look how Ash was left. Look how Dean was left. That callous bastard has his meal and just leaves the wrapper on the ground."

She got up and paced, and I could feel anger replacing her sadness, shedding off her in waves. "I can't stop thinking about that stupid video."

I squinted at her, confused. "What video?"

"The one Bastian insisted I take of Terry beating the hell out of you in the park that night," Emma replied. "I still don't know why he felt we had to do that. I keep thinking if only I'd worked it out, worked out the reason, it would have been the key to doing whatever needed to be done and everything would be different."

I rolled my head back and forth on the wall behind me. "It's just a video. What do you think it could do? Earn us some getaway cash selling it off to some sadistic sicko?"

"I don't know! But Bastian thought it would be important."

"Then maybe Bastian was wrong," I snapped. Whatever hope she was trying to rouse, I wasn't having it. I'd had enough of hope. Of trying and planning and losing, losing, losing. There was a poisonous glob of depression sludging through my veins, heading straight to my heart.

Everyone went quiet again, and still, and even though I couldn't see it anymore, I imagined the whole room filled with blue like we were deep underwater in an ocean of sadness.

I leaned my head back and scrunched my eyes closed. I felt light and dizzy since almost being drained by Terry, disconnected in the way I had on and off since giving Jake and the others their

599

powers back, but this time I couldn't shake it. It was like I'd been undone from inside of me. *Get a grip,* I ordered myself.

I floated back and forth, seasick with the sensation, rocking in an ocean of grief. I tried to breathe through it as I teetered away from myself, out of control. A rush of sadness and anger pushed me, splashing over the edges of my mind.

I panicked as I fell, spinning wildly around the room. My body remained motionless behind me.

I landed in warmth, another body. I wanted to cry out, but had no body, no mouth of my own. *What is happening?* I looked out through Rayni's eyes at Sway, and then over at my motionless body.

I gasped back into myself. *What was that?*

I snapped my own eyes open, staring at Rayni. She didn't seem to notice what had just happened, and had returned to calming Sway.

I stared at my hands, trying to ground myself. There had been a moment when Terry was draining me when I'd felt as though I looked back at myself through his eyes. Had that been real, too? In those moments, there had been so much panic and chaos I barely knew what was happening. But I had felt something like that—that feeling of being outside myself, but still aware.

600

EMOTIONALLY POWERFUL

After I'd woken them, Jake and the others had said they weren't conscious of anything while they were drained, but maybe something else was happening with me, after everything my powers and body and mind had been through. Maybe I could put myself inside someone else's mind, and still be aware of myself.

And if I could do that, could I control the other person?

I had to try, to send myself out on purpose, to see how much control I had.

I closed my eyes again, sat up a little higher and crossed my legs, untightening my fists. I embraced the sensation of disconnection, letting myself flow away, like I was a trickling waterfall. I set my sights on Rayni a second time, building a sense of her essence in my mind. Her kindness, her cleverness, her bravery. With a rush like a surging wave, I lifted from myself, floated, and landed again within her.

My first instinct was to rush back to my own body again, but I fought it.

I saw what she saw, heard what she heard.

Rayni spoke to Sway, her voice sounding different through her own ears. "I can ease the sadness away for you if you want me to help you calm down."

Sway's face was wet and snotty, and she shook her head

601

continuously in a hard rhythm. "My feelings are me. Ferociously, ferally, forlorn. Hearts are hard to have, but I want to stay me."

Rayni didn't seem aware of my presence at all. I tried to will her to look over at me, but she didn't. I tried to focus on one of her arms, attempt to make it move. My focus was strong and deliberate, but she didn't shift even an inch. I was nothing but a tourist in her body. I was there, aware of all of myself, my heart, and my feelings that made me *me*, like Sway said, but I couldn't control anything.

My spirit sank, thinking of Dean, of how I hadn't been able to wake him, of how much I loved him and missed him and how nothing seemed to lead to a way to save him.

I felt movement. Rayni pushed herself off the ground without any explanation and walked out of the room, taking me with her. We went across the corridor and into the makeshift ward, and I expected her to sit with Ash, as she often did. But instead, she went right over beside Dean, and placed a hand on his cheek.

The oddness of the sensation, of feeling Dean's skin beneath another person's touch, of Rayni being drawn to him, shocked me back into myself. I inhaled sharply as though breathing myself back in.

My eyes watered, and my whole body tingled.

Rayni shuffled back into the room, a small frown creasing

602

her forehead.

"Weird," she said.

I tried to show no sign of my racing heartbeat. "You okay, Rayni?"

Her doe eyes flashed over to mine. "Um ... yeah. I think. Just not sure why I went in there."

I opened my mouth to tell her what happened, excited by my discovery, by its potential, but I stopped. As puzzle pieces locked together in my head, I started to realize what it could mean, what I might have to do, and that I couldn't tell anyone. "You're probably just overtired," I told Rayni. "Try and get some rest."

She nodded, then went back to sit beside Sway.

Suddenly, everything was clear. Everything that I'd been through, all the emotions, all the clarity and all the fog, had culminated into one huge realization.

These new powers I had meant I could stop Terry, but only with sacrifice.

I couldn't drain Terry from the outside. I couldn't take him with violence, with darkness. Not in an ambush, not with numbers.

But I had a chance to push his stolen powers out *from the inside*, because he wouldn't even know it could happen. I could make him think he'd won. I would be defeated, and drained, and exactly where I needed to be.

I needed to be in Terry. Then I could get him and his powers where they needed to go. *To Dean.*

Terry was strong. Could my love for Dean be stronger?

Would he go to Dean, as Rayni did?

He will. He has to.

I had new hope, a hope that I could use the power of my love to overcome Terry, but I still couldn't let go of the darkness inside me. I still needed it.

Because for my plan to work, I was going to have to do something unthinkable.

18

bent over the small table next to Dean's bed, scribbling quickly with the pen and paper I'd scrounged up from an abandoned office. I wrote out my message, hoping he would understand, folded it, and tucked it into the front of his blue scrubs shirt, out of sight.

"I'll be back soon. Just remember I am always with you, no matter what happens." I tried not to feel like I was saying goodbye. Leaning over, I kissed him gently on the forehead and smiled as I pulled back. "I love you."

Knowing this could be the last time I looked at Dean with my own eyes almost paralyzed me. But at least even if I didn't, even if we never saw each other again, I would have brought him back, and the rest of the team, and stopped Terry hurting anyone else. And in a way, I would always be with Dean, even if my body wasn't.

Knowing what I had to do next was even harder.

I wasn't sure yet how I was going to get Rayni alone. But I knew it had to be done. Maybe everyone else would be asleep by now. All of this would be a lot easier if Rayni were asleep. I could already imagine her little face staring at me in fear, wondering why I was hurting her.

Walking slowly away from Dean's bed, I let my eyes linger on his face for just one more moment before reaching the door. When I turned away to the hall, Rayni was there in front of me.

My eyes stung. My throat closed up.

"Hey," she said, almost cheerfully compared to before. "I was just coming to find you. You okay?"

I tried to smile, chuckle, brush it off. "As good as could be expected. What did you want?"

"Actually, it's Emma. She's just worked something out; she wanted me to tell you."

I glanced across the room where soft shadows moved against the low light. People were still awake. I tilted my head back. "Sit with me and tell me all about it in here? I want to stay near

Dean a bit longer."

Rayni shrugged, and headed into the ward. I closed the door behind her. When I'd gone to get a pen, I saw Felix had fallen asleep in front of the security monitors, so I hoped we'd have the ward to ourselves for a while. For long enough to do what needed to be done.

We sat on a couple of office chairs that had been wheeled in. Rayni had one of the phones from the safe house in her hand, and she looked at me with wide, bright eyes.

"What has Emma worked out?" A small fear twitched in me, worried Emma had somehow discovered my plan.

"The video. She realized what she could do with it. She knew trying to blackmail Terry probably wasn't going to work. But then she had this other idea." Rayni turned the screen of her phone on and held it up for me to see.

It was loaded to a So-Snap account, where the top post was the video, titled 'Bad Cop Beats Up Girl'. It was public, live, and the hits on it were ticking up faster than I could count.

I wasn't sure how I felt about hundreds of thousands of people seeing me get beaten to a pulp. "And this is a good thing?"

"Actually, it could be a great thing," Rayni said, checking the numbers again herself. "The section of video she loaded doesn't really show anything that gives away empath powers.

It just looks like Terry in his uniform, kicking a girl on the ground. It's gone viral crazy fast. She's uploaded it to other accounts too. We figured the more the better."

I wrinkled my forehead. "But why?"

"Well, it's another weakness Terry has—a lack of social media savviness." Rayni's nose scrunched up at her own joke. "So, proesthians have the power to influence and control people, but it's based on attraction and likability, right? So what happens to a proesthian's suggestion powers if everybody in the world hates them?"

My jaw dropped. "No more cops on his side. No more anyone on his side. No matter how much empath power he's stolen, he couldn't possibly overcome that kind of hatred."

Rayni nodded like a pleased teacher. "He'll still be powerful, but he'll be alone."

My eyes shifted, searching. That was good. But I still had to follow through with my plan. This would make it work even better.

I forced myself to grow cold, hard, determined. I took both of Rayni's hands in mine. "I'm glad Emma worked the video out. It will help. But I've also got my own plan. One I have to do alone."

Rayni blinked and looked back up at me. "You know you

don't have to do anything on your own. We're supposed to be a team."

I smiled at her, my lips fading to a frown. "I have to do this. I'm sorry."

It was time. I had to drain Rayni. I had to steal her powers.

Because I couldn't complete my plan alone. I could only push everyone's powers back out of Terry from inside him if I had Rayni's powers too. My plan meant sacrificing myself *and* Rayni, which made it infinitely harder. I knew I was risking her life without her consent, without her knowledge.

But it has to be done. I took in a shivery breath and closed my eyes, envisioning my powers, the dark pit of despair inside me. I opened myself to darkness, and opened my eyes again, focusing in on Rayni.

She looked back at me with confused, innocent eyes, her pastel rainbow hair pale and grey in the dim room. My nose and throat burned.

Come on. Take her powers. You need her emogen powers to do this. It's the only way. Do it.

I held my breath, clenched my teeth, and squeezed her hands in mine.

My plan was nothing without Rayni's powers, but I just couldn't bring myself to do it. I couldn't hurt her like that, violate her like that. I hated the idea of causing her any fear or pain at all.

Emma's words stirred within my memory. *Darkness isn't going to get you what you want.*

Tears flooded my eyes, and I covered my face with my hands as great sobs burst from my mouth.

Rayni's small arms wrapped around me. "Hey, it's okay."

"It's not. You don't understand. I was going to drain you," I gasped out between sobs and sniffles.

She stiffened for a moment, then pulled me in tighter. I could hear tears in the waver of her voice. "Is that what you need? To save everyone?"

My plan felt so risky, so impossible, I wasn't sure I'd save anyone anymore. "I don't know."

Rayni's voice was soft in my ear. "You do know. You wouldn't have even considered draining me if you didn't think it was worth it."

I pulled away from her, looking deep into her dark eyes that knew too much for someone so young. "It was wrong. I was wrong. Nothing is worth doing that to you."

"Tell me the plan, and I'll decide."

I choked back my tears and told her everything. "I can't do it without you, but I can't ask so much from you. I can't promise it will work."

Rayni sat for a moment, processing, chewing her lip. "Actually, the only thing we know for certain is that if we don't try, it won't work. I want to try. To save my brother and everyone else. So, it's okay. You can drain me. I trust you will do everything you can to get me back to my body."

The tears I had choked back broke through my seal and streamed down my face. I pulled her close to me and kissed the top of her head. Maybe we really could do this. Together. With love, and trust, and hope, instead of darkness.

"Thank you, Rayni. You really are an amazing person. If this works, I'll make sure you're the first to get woken up."

She looked around the ward, at all the empty bodies, and my chest ached imagining her that way. But she smiled and said, "It will be really nice to see my brother's smiling face again. Because I'm sure we can do this together." She turned back to me. Her smile faltered, and although she brought it back quickly, it wobbled on her lips. "What do I need to do?"

I reached out and brushed a strand of pastel hair back from her face. "Just close your eyes. You'll be back before you know it."

19

Draining Rayni was still difficult, no matter whether I had her permission, her blessing, or not.

It also felt different. I hadn't done it with darkness, or ravenous grief. I had done it with *love*. I had opened myself to her completely, taking her into me as though bringing her into a protective embrace. That was where I would hold her, keep her safe, until I could put her back where she belonged.

With her body safely tucked in beside her brother's, I made a quick adjustment to my letter to Dean, and set a few final pieces of my plan in place.

I felt strong, more in touch with my powers than ever before.

EMOTIONALLY POWERFUL

Rayni's powers alone weren't enough to tip me into unstable territory, and the combination of her emogen abilities with my proesthian ones meshed together, humming inside me.

But I had to test them, to know I could harness those unfamiliar skills to complete the most important mission of my life.

I headed back to the office with the security monitors and gently woke Felix. Where my powers in the past all required absorption, I focused instead on pushing outwards, sending waves of calm to Felix as he yawned from his sleep.

I told him clearly that I had drained Rayni, and I was going alone to the police station to free my parents.

He blinked and nodded to me like I'd told him the weather report predicted a cloudy day. "Righteo then. I should probably tell the others."

He yawned again, shuffling slowly down the hall, floating in a serenity I knew would crash away when I left. Hopefully right in time to rouse the others to action.

I made a run for it. I needed to get as far as I could as quickly as I could. I used my burner phone to call for a ride-share and headed out to meet it a couple of blocks away.

The driver gave me and my outfit some weird looks. I told him I was going home from a superhero-themed fancy-dress party, and he laughed in understanding. It was late now, and the streets were quiet and empty. Headlights created a shimmering glitter in the rain as we made good time getting back to Limbus.

The rain grew heavier, coming down in thick swathes by the time we pulled up in front of the building. Thunder boomed overhead like a warning. I ignored it. I had done everything I could think of to make this work, now I just had to *finish it*. My plan wasn't foolproof, but I had to try, for Dean, for Ash, for Bastian, and for Rayni.

All I had to do now was get in front of Terry and hope he didn't see right through me and my plan. That any powers he had from Bastian wouldn't pick up the subtle distinction between what I wanted, and why I wanted it. Because the truth was that I *wanted* him to drain me, and that was exactly what I wanted him to think.

I paid the driver with cash from the safe house stash, and stepped out into the rain. The plain front of the Limbus building loomed before me, the concrete turned a dark gray from being soaking wet, sickly yellow light shimmering out of the few windows.

I ran up the steps, blinking the hard drops of rain from my eyes. The front door hung crookedly from broken hinges. I took a tentative step inside. There wasn't a single cop in sight, and none I could sense with my powers nearby. No rush of emotion, no yelling, no gunfire. It was absolutely silent except for the patter of driving rain.

I ran my fingers gently over bullet holes in the walls, and found them still warm. It was obvious that something had gone down there between the time we'd escaped our last failed attempt on Terry, and now. Something I was sure had been caused by Emma sharing that video.

Carefully, I walked forward. My boots crackled on broken glass. I stepped over a puddle of blood on the floor. I shuddered. There must be bodies. Where were they? There were adult empath agents from Limbus I still hadn't seen anywhere. Not drained, not dead. Maybe they had realized it was futile trying to fight and gone on the run. But then how did Terry get into the Limbus system? He must have captured at least some of them, and if he had them I was sure he'd have drained them. *What has he done with the bodies?*

What will he do with my body?

At the front desk I paused, whirling around. From the corner of my eye, I caught the shimmer of something reflecting off the flickering lights. Breathing heavily, I stepped forward and looked behind the desk. It was a cop, shot in the neck, dead. His body laid crumpled there as if he had been thrown over the desk during a fight, illuminated with the blue glow of a screen. Acid swirled in my stomach.

The monitor that lit up the grisly scene was paused on a moment in the video where Terry had struck me hard in the face.

I turned away from the body, but the vision had burned into my mind. Was his death on me? Or on Emma for having shared the video? It was clear it had caused Terry to lose control of the police force. Just the sheer hatred for Terry that half the online world was no doubt feeling for him at this point would have affected his abilities, and the few cops who were still under his control must have been shown this video by those who shook off his influence sooner.

It had cleared my path. It had set them free, but there had been a cost. Maybe some, before they got the heck out of this hellhole, had tried to face Terry themselves, and failed.

No. I wouldn't blame myself for every life Terry took. That was all on him, one hundred percent. And soon, I would stop him for good.

I extended my powers again, trying to sense anyone nearby, pushing as hard as I could. *Oh no.* What if Terry had been killed when he lost control of the police? Or if he had disappeared, been forced on the run?

The unmistakable force of Terry's unstable powers drifted

down to me from above. He was still here. Him, and just a few others.

I headed for the stairs and took them three at a time, running toward the center of power like a moth to a flame.

Fear came from nearby, fueling me and sending me faster. *There, just up ahead.* I sped around a corner, and down the hall, then jolted to a stop. A woman in police uniform stumbled out of a doorway in front of me. She wove back and forth, rubbing her head and pulling strands of gray hair loose from what had once been a tight bun.

She held a gun in one hand. The other hand was bloody, matching a huge stain on the front of her shirt. She saw me and froze.

"What's happening here?" Her voice was a plea.

I put my hands up, focusing both mine and Rayni's powers, hoping between the two of them, it would be enough. "You have to leave here. You want to go home and wash the blood off."

She nodded slowly, as though drunk, and started shuffling away.

"You're not going anywhere," Terry snarled. He stepped out of another room up ahead. His blond hair stuck up at all angles and his face was splattered with blood and twisted with fury.

The police officer hesitated, looking from me to him with

fear in her eyes.

"Raise your gun, and shoot the intruder in the leg," Terry commanded.

Her arm raised. The safety clicked off. Tears sparkled on her cheeks.

I kicked back with my powers, struggling against Terry's control. I pushed with everything Rayni had, with the images of Terry beating me, of the body of the officer's fallen companion downstairs. I could see faint glimmers of the force of Terry's power and mine, meeting and swirling around the woman as we pulled back and forth, vying for control. The cop herself stepped back and forth, her eyes falling from me to Terry, again and again, her body shaking, jerking, confused.

"Go, run. Get out of here!" I yelled, putting everything I had into the words.

She took off. She ran and was out of sight before Terry could reestablish dominance of her again.

He squinted at me, more with intrigue than anger.

"That was surprising," he said, rubbing blood off his chin. "I thought for sure you would have forced Officer Jansen there to shoot me. But I forgot you weren't to know Jansen is quite a good shot. That you couldn't have seen like I can see that she could have gotten a shot through." He gestured to his damaged bullet-proof vest and torn up shirt. "In every decision, every emotion, so many details, so many possibilities. It's hard to see the truth. I'm still getting used to these *elucidist* powers."

He rolled the word elucidist off his tongue as though trying it out for the first time, as though it was merely a novelty to have learned of this new type of empath and that he hadn't drained a friend of mine to do so.

"Limbus told me eludicists often get readings wrong, that there are too many variables." I planted the idea in his mind, hoping to throw him off whatever he might be reading on me now as he looked me up and down, eyelids twitching.

He seemed more unstable than ever. How many more empaths had he drained since Dean?

"What I pick up from you now? That is surprising as well. After all you've done, I didn't take you for the type to give up." He moved closer, but slowly, as though suspicious.

"I'm not giving up. I'm making a deal," I replied.

Terry stuttered out a chuckle that edged on evil laughter. "You think you're in a position to bargain? All right, Lollipop. What's this deal you want to make?"

I held my arms out to my sides. "I stop fighting you, just like you read. I give in. You can drain me, but you have to let my parents go, free and unharmed."

A sly grin remained fixed under his wild eyes. "What about all your little empath friends? You're not going to beg for them too?"

"I'm not an idiot. I know you'll go after any empath you can find. I know what power means to you. But you only have my parents because you wanted me, and here I am. They aren't empaths; they have no more value to you."

His nose twitched, and he crossed his arms over his chest. "Smarter than I thought. So the deal is you give up your life for your parents'."

I scoffed. "What life? Spending the rest of my days on the run? Always looking around corners, terrified of you? It's hardly a choice. I would rather my parents be free."

He walked closer and circled around me like a vulture. I let him feel my fear, my worry, my anxiety, and even my anger. There was truth in those emotions, and I needed him to know my sincerity.

He stopped and held his hand out to me, business-like. "It's a deal then."

I shook his hand, not knowing whether he was telling the truth or not. It didn't really matter either. I just needed him to drain me and to do so without suspicion. If he planned to go back on our deal, then it was even better; we'd be going into this with him feeling like he'd won over me in every way.

"Now, keep still," he whispered in a hoarse, deep voice. "This might sting a little."

Okay, Rayni, here we go. Together.

His grip on my handshake tightened until my palm cracked. I winced and cried out, my knees buckling, but his other arm shot out, holding me in place by my shoulder.

A feeling surged through me, like he was ripping the literal soul from the deepest parts of my body. I groaned loudly, my teeth chattering as his powers drew me from my body, tearing shreds loose, stripping me down to nothing. My eyes went wide and my breath caught, allowing no sound to escape my lips.

At the last drop of my powers, my very being rose upward and out of me. He released his grip.

I watched through his eyes as my body hit the ground. *Empty.*

20

The noise was incredible. Without a body, without my own physical self grounding me, everything was feeling, emotion—everything was *sense*. I felt like I was in a bone-dry field before a thunderstorm, except I was the storm. I could feel, smell, and taste it all at once, a thrumming power, the bloody tang of energy, the swirling hurricane of dozens of spirits trapped within one. It was deafening. Drowning.

I reached out tentatively, exploring those spirits. Within the spinning pandemonium I noticed individual essences, like strands of silk tangled into a cocoon. I knew the names of some of those strands, could feel their beings slumbering within that nightmare. One drew me in, cool, calm, and stable. Without my body, my heart could not react, but my love did. I was made of love now, and that love wanted Dean. I wanted to dive deep into the tangle of essences, to be with him, to cling to him like a life-raft. But I had to keep every bit of my focus on my goal, or we would all be lost. I had to hold tight to myself, and to my love, because that was what would save Dean. That was what would make him whole again.

I strayed too far and was thrashed about in the storm, careening up and down with the current, pulled into the dark clouds. I kept my embrace around Rayni strong, keeping her safe. She was still there, her pattern entwined within mine. I hoped she didn't feel any of this.

I could no longer see through Terry's eyes, no longer hear or witness what happened. I fought my way back to the surface, back to consciousness. *I am me. I must stay me. I must stay aware. For Dean. For everyone.*

I rose into awareness. From inside, through dreamlike vision, I saw my body, still and pale, lying at my feet. No, *Terry's* feet. *I am me.*

He knelt beside me, shook me once, then, satisfied, started patting me down. If I still had breath to hold, I would have, but it was the body I'd left that's chest rose and fell automatically without me.

He lifted my limp arm to see the built-in screen in my suit, and checked through it, as I'd hoped he would. I'd also planted clues on the burner phone zipped into my pocket, just to be sure.

I gave him the location where the remaining empaths were hiding. I let him know they were at the institution, because that was where I had to make him go.

We had to get to Dean. All that mattered now was getting to Dean, and remaining *me* until then.

I could feel Terry's gloating triumph. It was sickening but, at the same time, satisfying. He might have thought he was winning, but he was falling right into my hands. I just had to *stay me.*

But the vortex of power dragged at me, pulling me down. I could only hear the chaos of noise, thunderous static like grating screams. My vision grew dim. I glimpsed Terry throwing my body over his shoulder, and then sank away.

What is he going to do with me? The thought drifted through me, calmly, like the final thought I had before falling asleep. I merged with darkness and sound.

That's just my body. I am me. I must stay me!

I tried to build a sense of urgency inside myself, to slap myself into control. I struggled against the sucking void and

624

for a moment I saw again. We were on the road, driving. Not far from the institute. Already? It was only seconds ago we were at Limbus. I'd lost time, completely unaware. I fainted away again as utter terror took hold.

Nothing.

I wasn't me anymore. I wasn't sight, sound, touch, thought. I was only love. Love for my parents. Love for Rayni, Sway, Emma, Bastian, all the Limbus team. Love for Nati. Love for …

Dean.

I reached for him, called for him, focused all of my love on him, and held onto it fiercely.

And then I felt him.

It was like having butterflies in my stomach, only at that point, I barely remembered the concept of having a body. I could have been gone for seconds, or decades. There was no sense of time. Then existence, the world, started coming back. Footsteps, padded down a long hallway, taking me closer. Closer to Dean. Closer to the surface. Closer to *love.*

I broke through again, exploding into consciousness, awareness of my surroundings crashing into me.

I was inside Terry. Terry was inside the institution.

Annoyance spilled like acid through Terry. He was pissed. He prowled up and down the corridors, finding the place quiet and empty. Relief flooded me. My plan to get the others out had worked, but I still knew they could come back at any time. I had to get Terry to Dean, now.

"Where are they all?" Terry looked into the break room, with empty sleeping bags scattered on the floor, then at his watch. It was almost two a.m. I felt the bitter tang of suspicion grow in him.

I overwhelmed it with love. I let loose everything I was made of. My heart filled with hope, the desire to see Dean whole again, the need that drew me to Dean. I made Terry feel it all.

For a long moment, he didn't move. I was terrified I'd failed, that his lack of empathy would mean he wouldn't be drawn to Dean as Rayni had been.

Then he looked over his shoulder, across the hall to the ward where the drained lay. He turned. He walked.

Terry went past each and every empath laying silent and still in their beds. All his victims. He stared down at them with no emotion. There was no guilt for the taking of their lives, no realization that he had done all of it. Instead, there was a void, as if he were looking at inanimate objects and not real, living and breathing human beings.

"What a waste of resources, keeping these useless shells alive," Terry muttered.

EMOTIONALLY POWERFUL

I wish I could punch you from the inside right now.

He moved on, a small sense of confusion within but otherwise oblivious to his destination or the cause of it. I sent out another wave of emotion, pulling him closer and closer to Dean's bed. He flicked the IV bags as he passed by them.

The nearer we got to Dean, the more aware I became. I soared above the chaos, made of love and power. I was me. I was ready.

Terry stopped and looked down.

I looked through his eyes at Dean's calm and sleeping face. So beautiful. *Love. Hope. Need.*

And then, *fear.* It swarmed my being, almost overwhelming me. This was it. I might only have a moment before the others returned, before Terry took control again and left, before he decided to destroy these shells for good.

Okay Rayni, let's do this.

I drew on Rayni's powers and my own. Summoning all my strength, all my love, I directed the hurricane of energy up, up, and out. Straight through me, pushed along by Rayni, down into Dean. I slammed all those powers, all those spirits out of Terry.

They flowed torrentially down into Dean's chest. His body jolted and shook wildly. The energy kept pouring, filling him to bursting. *You've got this, Dean. You can do this. Please.*

"What? What is happening?" Terry roared. He leaned over and clutched his chest, groaning. Pain laced through him like fire turning to ice as energy rushed out of his body. A small dribble of spit was strung from his mouth and he dropped to his knees, gripping tightly to the railing on the side of the gurney. "No!"

As the last of the stolen powers flowed out, I released my hold, slipping through as well and falling into Dean. The final impression I got from Terry was complete and utter panic, anger, and confusion. Then, for a moment, there was complete freedom, leaving one body and landing in another.

I sank down into Dean. Back into the swarming cacophony of all those energies. But being inside Dean was different to being in Terry. There was love here, and loss. And even the loss had found a place with peace. It held us and soothed us. We drifted, weightless and formless.

The pull to fade away was hard to fight, but I had to stay, had to hold on just a bit longer.

Because now I had to help Dean, and hope he was as strong as I believed he was.

21

slept. Deep, and unaware. Painless. Dreamless. Then a rumbling reverberated through me, bringing consciousness with it. I was moving, surrounded by energy. I fell without warning and as I landed, I unfolded. Connections reset as I awoke, my senses kicking in. I could feel my fingers, my toes, my face, and my heart, ready to explode.

Where am I? The last thing I remember, I was at the train station …

My eyes shot open and my lungs gasped in air as if I had never breathed before. My body jolted up from the bed and then landed back, uncurling from the sudden exposure to life.

Everything burned. Power buzzed like a swarm of angry wasps trying to sting their way out of me. My vision swam, all blurry light and streaming rainbows.

What is this? I was filled with so much feeling. I struggled to place myself in the present, the room around me completely unfamiliar. I sat up, squinting through the glare at myself. I was in scrubs, on a hospital bed, but this was not hospital. I tried to track my memories to this point, to find sense in the situation. *I was going home to Livvy. The cop she knew met me at the station. He ...*

He was the leech! He drained me.

The rattling of the rail on the side of my bed drew my attention downward.

And he's here.

Rising from the ground, the leech staggered, his skin drenched in sweat and a look of fear on his face. Green and orange shimmered around him. There was a pause, a moment of pure silence when the two of us stared at each other. We spoke through our eyes only, his full and wild, mine confused and quiet. Had he given me my powers back? Why?

His hand jerked out and grabbed my throat, squeezing. "Give them back to me!"

I cried out, but not because of his assault. I barely felt it.

Power surged inside me, godlike, unstoppable, unbearable. I felt *everything*.

My body moved stiffly, an un-oiled machine with a super-charged battery, jolting and lurching. I reached up and clutched the leech's hand in mine. His eyes widened as I squeezed, prying it from my neck.

It took almost no effort to push him away, sending him crashing across the room, like brushing off an ant. I had awoken bursting with strength and unanswered questions. I searched the hazy space with my gaze for Livvy, feeling as though she was there, that she must have done this, brought me back somehow, but I couldn't see her. Just the leech, me, and others who were drained lying still in beds around me. Yet I felt anything but alone.

The leech stumbled, regaining his footing. He glared at me, teeth bared. A darkness grew around him, a vibrating energy, dragging against me. I swung off the bed, pulled the IVs from my arms and placed bare feet down onto the cold floor. I stalked toward him, loomed over him, his attempt to drain me forced back by the sheer power pushing against my seams.

I picked the man up into the air by his shirt collar. "What have you done? Where am I?"

He whimpered a laugh. "She tricked me. She did this."

631

"Livvy? Where is she?" My heart echoed my words.

"Dead, if she's gotten what she deserved!"

What does that mean? The word *dead* sent my head spinning. *She can't be …*

The leech's face was mad, his eyes flickering wildly around the room. My nose wrinkled in disgust. I held so much hatred for this man, this monster, inside me. More hatred than I thought could come from one person, as though it came from many. It blazed out of my every pore. I marched with him in my grasp to the wall and slammed him against it, relishing in the feel of his collarbone cracking under my hand.

He moaned his words out. "That power is mine. And I won't let you keep it."

Terry's hands thrusted upward, slamming into my chest. Again, I felt the burn and tension pulling at everything that I had, the way it felt when he'd first drained me.

Without a thought, I snapped his wrists. His screams echoed through the ward. I let him go and he slid down the wall.

Anger pumped through my veins. Every bit of emotion I had ever repressed and more pummeled through me, directed at the leech.

He had no chance. I could feel it now, how he was so weak and I was so strong. Every bit of power he had stolen—it was all in me somehow. Including my own, which was all I needed.

I stood tall with my hands out and took in a deep breath. I used my blocking ability as Livvy had helped me learn to do, as my love for her had helped me understand. I extended the chill out, cutting off the leech's powers, and shutting him down for good. With the additional energy inside me, it took only seconds.

Lying on the ground, his eyes opened wide and he grabbed at his chest with crippled hands. "No. No. Put it back. Give my powers back to me. I need them!"

"Like you needed all the powers you drained? Needed to take lives?" I growled, my voice hoarse from being unused for so long. "Where is Livvy? What have you done with her?"

He tilted his head back, laughing through tears. "I threw her body away like the trash she was." His face quickly changed to anger and he roared in pain as he grasped for the gun holstered at his belt. But every moment drew out for me in slow motion. I saw everything, moved faster than he could. He felt as strong as a cornered animal, fighting for his way out. I felt more powerful than I ever had before. So powerful that it scared me. I'd had the skills of a blocker, but never the super-abilities of a proesthian, this speed, this strength. I snatched the gun from his hands, flung it behind me, and pushed my hand down on his throat.

He snarled, feral and wild. "I should have ripped what was left of her to pieces!"

"WHERE IS SHE?"

"I'll never tell you!" Terry breathed heavily, his eyes shifting back and forth, spit dripping from his lip.

The normal restraint I had known my whole life snapped like a twig as he licked his lips and laughed. I lifted him up, crushing his windpipe in one hand as I punched him hard in the jaw. His head flew back and then bounced forward, blood dripping from his mouth. He continued to laugh, as if it meant nothing to him, as if pain was something he welcomed. His reaction only made me angrier. I couldn't control the churning emotions within me. So many of them, unfamiliar, overpowering.

I punched him again, and again. Blood splattered and his eyes rolled around in his head. Devastated rage bellowed out of me. My muscles tightened, fury clouding every other sense in my body.

He grumbled and groaned, his eyes already swollen and bruises forming on his cheeks.

As I tightened my grasp around his throat, blocking every chance at breath, bringing the leech to the edge of death, a warm sensation blew through me.

634

It pushed the anger in my chest down and away. I could feel … I could feel *her*. I could feel that same warmth that Livvy always made me feel when she was close. I let go of the leech, and stumbled back, horrified at my own anger, at my violence.

I hit a bed and leaned against it, grabbing at the front of my shirt. My eyes watered and a lump formed in my throat. *I know where Livvy is. She's here, in me. I can feel her. I can feel her love.*

My head began to spin and I grabbed it. She had somehow done all of this. Driven the powers from the leech into me. All of them, including hers. And now she held me back from committing the unthinkable.

He must have gotten her. I turned and stared at the leech, bleeding and barely conscious, finding that the all-consuming anger I had before was no longer there. In its place was an embracing wrap of love, protecting me, keeping me stable. She was with me, helping stop the emotions rampaging inside me from tearing me limb from limb.

I snatched the tubing from the IV stand beside the bed I'd woken up in and bound the leech's hands together with it, then tied him to the radiator that he was slumped beside. He groaned and snarled at me, but had no fight left in him.

Once I was sure he wasn't going anywhere, I took a moment

to breathe, to sort through what could have happened, how and why. Sweat rolled down my forehead as I stared up at the colorful lights of emotion swirling around me. How long had I been gone?

I wondered where everyone else was, how Terry ended up here with me. Where *here* was. Was everyone else drained? Dead? Was I the last one remaining?

But most of all, if Livvy's spirit was within me, with all the other drained powers, then where was her body, and what was I meant to do next?

22

I felt seasick from the roiling emotions within me. I had spent so much of my life trying to feel nothing, the sheer immensity of feeling made me want to claw my heart out. I tried to block it off, shut it away, deny it, but there was just too much. My hands clutched at my chest, trying to hold myself together.

Something crumpled beneath the thin cotton of my scrubs top. It felt like paper. I reached in and pulled out a folded letter.

Dean, read me! was scrawled on one side in Livvy's handwriting. My heart pounded.

I glanced back at the leech to be sure he wasn't going anywhere, then unfolded the letter, more confused than ever, and desperately hoping it held answers. Shimmering halos of color swam across my vision, and I blinked and squinted, trying to see the words. My head throbbed.

Dean,

If you are seeing this then the first part of my plan worked! That's the good news. I'll get to the bad news soon.

I know you'll be confused. You've been gone for a while and you've missed so much. But I need your help for the next steps now.

If everything went to plan, you should have every person the leech drained inside you. I can't imagine how it will feel. I'm sorry if it hurts.

But I've seen your heart, how strong you are, how much you have carried in your life. I know you can do this. And I will be helping in every way I can.

Because here's the bad news. For my plan to work, I'm going to be one of the people the leech drained, so I'm in there too …

I clenched my teeth as pain and fear forced a groan up through them. I knew I could feel Livvy with me, and it was true, but the reason why almost shattered me.

I'm sorry. I had to let him drain me. It was my last hope, because beating him from the outside seemed impossible, but I had a chance to do it from the inside.

If you're awake, then I did it, and now we have to do it again. We need to get all those people, all that power, out of you and back where it belongs.

Just in case I'm not able to stay aware of myself, I've written instructions on what to do as best as I can explain below. I'm sorry you're probably waking up alone. I had to send the others away so the leech didn't get them. I hope they will be back soon to help you. I don't know what will happen to the leech if this works. I hope he's not a problem for you.

I looked back over at him again through the curtains of emotional color. He was more awake now, groaning and crying like a child throwing a tantrum, a ball of blue and red energy. He tugged at the tubing binding him to the radiator but it held strong. Disgust both at him and the damage I'd done to him made me shudder and turn away. I looked to the final words on the letter.

Now, let's save everyone, you and me together.

Remember, I am inside of you, guiding you. I'll be with you until you get me back to my body too. And if you can't, if something has happened to me for whatever reason, know that I chose this, and it's not your fault. Everything will be okay.

I love you,

Livvy

PS Wake Rayni up first. I promised.

Rayni first? I could have burst into flames. Livvy should be first. I needed to find her, put her back together, but I had no idea where she would be. She hadn't given me any clues in her letter on how to save *her*. I hated the way the letter sounded, as though Livvy didn't expect to come back from this.

I grunted in frustration and glared around the room, furious at the bodies lying there, that they would get to wake up when Livvy was out there, somewhere, alone. When my eyes fell on Rayni, her small face calm and empty, tucked in next to her brother, a sob of emotion escaped my throat. Livvy was right. I had to put all these people back as quickly as I could. I could barely see, barely think, like this. There was a mess inside of me, a mess that made me lightheaded, heavy, and unwell. I had to rid myself of some of this energy before I couldn't take it anymore. And these people deserved to be made whole again.

"Livvy? I don't know if you can hear me …" I gulped. I hadn't experienced anything the entire time I was drained. It was like lights off, lights on, and nothing in between. But she must still be aware. If she let herself get drained, had some plan, *this* plan that had worked up until now, she must be in there, awake, in some sort of control.

My body still felt my own, to some extent. It didn't move against my wishes. It just felt full to overflowing. But she had been drained by Terry, then from the inside pushed everything out into me. That was some amazing power, but if anyone could do it, it was Livvy. I believed Olivia could do anything. "Livvy, you did it. I'm here to put everyone back in their bodies with you, and then we'll get you back too." I carefully folded the letter back up and put it in my pocket. "I love you."

I held my breath. A clock ticked. Rain splattered on windows. I didn't know if I was expecting a reply of some kind, but I didn't get one.

I moved over close to Rayni and Ash's bed. My chest extended as I filled my lungs with air in deep, cleansing breaths. I had read over Livvy's instructions and was ready to try my hardest to follow them, but as I stood at the bedside, looking down at Rayni, I felt something else taking over.

"Woah," I gasped.

Pressure filled my chest. Light drifted out from my body in a long, bright stream of spinning color. Wisps of energy flowed down over Rayni, lighting up her face as though she glowed from the inside. I waited, staring openmouthed as her pupils moved beneath her eyelids, her lips twitched.

She shot straight up, taking in gasping breaths. First breath, she stared at her hands. Second breath, she turned her head, taking in the whole room. Third breath, she looked up at me, her jaw dropping and tears shimmering in her eyes.

"Livvy did it? She really did it?" Her voice was a high-pitched whisper.

"She did something all right," I said, irrationally jealous that Rayni already seemed to know more about what Livvy was doing than I did.

Then Rayni threw herself into my arms, hugging me tightly. I looked down at her rainbow-topped head and patted her back awkwardly. She shivered against me. "I'm so happy it worked. I tried to be brave about it, but it was pretty scary being drained, even by Livvy."

"Wait, what?"

"It's okay. She needed my powers to push everything out of the leech. Isn't she here?" Rayni leaned back away from me, looking around the room again. "Did you revive me first?"

642

I nodded. "Livvy's letter told me to. I don't know where she is."

Rayni mouthed a slow *"oh"* as her eyes flickered back and forth, trying to work things out. "Terry, the leech—he took over Limbus. Livvy said she'd look for him there first, then draw him back here to you, so she's probably still there."

"And where is here?" I asked.

"Bellscroft, at the burned down institute. Part of it, at least."

I breathed in and recognized the ashy smell on the air. We were in Bellscroft, and Livvy was all the way down in Bellston Main. I hated knowing she could be so far away, if she even was where Rayni thought she would be. "We need to get to her," I whispered.

Rayni nodded, a sharp, single nod. "Right. I'm here to help. But I think we need to sort you out first. I can feel all of that energy inside of you. How are you even standing?"

I grunted. "I don't know either. But I have no choice. I have to keep going, get everyone put back in their bodies, and find Livvy. But I still barely understand what's happening."

Rayni grinned wryly. "I'll try and fill you in as best as I can, and I'll do what I can to ease things for you until we get all that power out of you."

She put her hand on my wrist with a smile. Instantly, my

643

muscles relaxed and I felt calm and clear again. "Thank you. Okay, let's wake some people up."

Rayni climbed down off the bed. She wore what looked like a black superhero suit. *I really must have missed a lot.* She wobbled for a moment on her feet, then took up position behind me like she had when Livvy revived Jake and the others. "Okay, are you going to do them all at once like Livvy did, or just one at a time?"

My eyes grew big and I looked around. "I'm not really sure I'm the one making that decision."

"Okay, well, can we try and start with Ash?"

I looked down at her brother's motionless body. He was gaunt compared to how he'd appeared the last time I'd seen him. "Of course."

As though she knew we were ready, Livvy seemed to kick off the process again from within me, and I signaled for Rayni to do her part. I watched the energy flow back into Ash and we both stood there holding our breaths, waiting for him to wake.

Ash's eyes were slower to open than Rayni's, his lungs struggling harder to draw breath ... but he woke. He choked on his words, looking around frantically. "The leech, he's, he's ..."

"It's okay. It's all okay. You're back." Rayni's cheeks were wet as she flopped onto her brother's chest.

644

We gave Ash the ten-second recap before leaving him to rest and recover as we continued around the room, reviving empath after empath. I didn't know most of them, but I felt each of their energies, unique and sparkling as it left me, returning to where it belonged.

One by one, they awoke—some confused and terrified, others relieved and thankful. All weak, bodies struggling with their return to life. We needed a doctor, but I couldn't wait any longer to get these powers out of me. Time ticked by, and my impatience grew. It was all taking too long. Way too long. Livvy was out there somewhere and I needed to find her. I needed her.

We reached the final bed where Mr. Kairu lay.

And nothing happened.

"Livvy?" I questioned, but again, there was no form of response, and this time also no help from within. *Liv, are you okay? Don't lose yourself in there.*

There was no way to know what was happening with her, only that every second taken felt like she was slipping away.

After reviving all the others, I had experienced enough, sensed enough, to understand the process. At least I hoped so, as I stepped up to do it without Livvy's help. I knew Mr. Kairu was a blocker, and the last one other than myself left to be returned, so it was easier to separate his energy out than the others.

I signaled Rayni again and we worked together, pushing his essence into his body.

It was done. Every drained empath in the room stirred, coming back to life. I felt a huge relief. That was a lot of energy lifted off my shoulders. I still felt powerful—countless more energies dwelled within me. Rayni told me maybe Bastian had been drained too, and other adult empaths from Limbus, and even civilians. But I already felt more stable.

"How long has it been?" croaked Mr. Kairu, just as other voices filled the hallway behind us, along with a storm of footsteps.

Sway appeared in a flash beside me, also wearing one of those black suits. She was saturated, her face in grim shock. "Oh my good gurgling God. They're awake!"

The whole team piled in right after, crowding the space.

"What on earth?" Emma was there in the super uniform as well, with three younger kids dressed the same, all soaking wet, looking ready for a fight. Their expressions shifted quickly, and the explosion of mixed emotions coming from them almost knocked me off my feet.

Felix pushed through next, took a look at all the moving

patients, and started dashing around between them. "Vitals! Vitals! No, don't move! My kingdom for a nurse!"

I recognized Dr. Crossman next. She looked in a bad way, like she'd just crawled out of a minefield. But she stepped over to the patients as well, rolled up her sleeves, and got to work helping Felix check everyone over. "How did this happen?"

I opened my mouth to answer.

"Ray-ray!" Sway yelled over everything else, glomping Rayni and knocking them both back into a bed.

"Dean?"

It took a moment for me to spot the person who'd spoken. My eyes shifted over to the doorway where Livvy's parents stood. They looked scared and wildly angry. Livvy's mom reached a hand toward me. "Oh, Dean. You're back. It's so good to see—"

Her eyes landed on the leech.

Her scream halted all the reunions and questions shooting around the room as everyone took in the man who had been hidden, huddled and still against the radiator he was tied to.

"It's okay. He's blocked; he can't do anything to anyone," I said, wincing away from the tidal wave of fear and anger smashing through my muscles.

"How? What happened here? Where's Livvy?" Emma asked.

"She wasn't at Limbus?" I shot back.

Emma frowned. "I don't know, we weren't there. Last thing we knew, she went nuts and drained Rayni, then took off, saying she was going to the police station to save her parents. We went after her but she wasn't there at all. The whole place was in riot, with Terry losing his control over the cops. We got her parents back, and Dr. Crossman too."

Rayni pushed forward. "Actually, Livvy said she was sending you guys off a different way so you wouldn't be here when the leech was. She had it all planned out, told me everything before I let her drain me."

"What?" half the room seemed to ask at once.

I itched to move. I needed to get going, to find Livvy, but we all needed answers. We took a few minutes to exchange as much information as we all had, and the picture of what had gone down became much clearer.

"So she's still in here somewhere," I finished up my part of the story, tapping my chest. Livvy's parents held each other, hands over their mouths. "But we don't have her body."

Emma put her hands on her hips. "Then we need to go find her! And we need to go fast. The weather is getting crazy out there, and who knows where she's been left by that monster."

She shot a glare at Terry, and he smiled over broken, bloody lips. "I'll never ... tell."

"We'll find her. Maybe the others too." Rayni exchanged a knowing look with Emma, who pouted. "There's still time."

The adults in the room looked at each other. Dr. Crossman grabbed a duffel bag and started throwing medical supplies into it. "Okay. Dean and all proesthians with me; Rayni too. We'll go to find the survivors. Felix, stay here and look after this lot. Mr. and Mrs. Mirawi, please stay here too. Help Felix and the others."

Livvy's parents seemed unsure. I could feel they desperately wanted to go and find their daughter, but were still shaking off the fog of having been trapped mentally and physically by Terry for so long. Livvy's mom glared at him with such hatred she glowed a red so bright I could barely look at her. I knew he deserved it and more. And Livvy's parents deserved to have their daughter back.

I stepped forward and wrapped my arms around them both, hoping Livvy felt that embrace as well.

"It's okay," I said. "I'll do everything I can to bring her back."

Mrs. Mirawi squeezed me tight. "I know you will."

23

Rain smashed against the windscreen of the van. Emma drove, speeding along empty late-night roads running with streams of water. Thunder rumbled in the background, and flashes of lightning ricocheted across smothering clouds.

I leaned forward, looking out ahead of us as though it could get us there sooner. The wipers were going as fast as they could, racing my heartbeat. All of us were scared of what we would find back at Limbus. Emma caught me up on as much as she could on the way. I couldn't believe what they had all been through, what Livvy had suffered while I lay drained and useless. I could still hardly believe what she'd done, giving herself up for her crazy plan. We had to find her.

As we drove down the last stretch of road, I saw the Limbus building up ahead. There were no cars parked out front, and no signs of life or movement anywhere.

Emma swung the van to a screeching halt right at the front steps, sending up a wave of water.

We knew our plan. Everyone loaded out straight away, sprinting off as fast as their powers could take them. The three younger kids were to stay with Dr. Crossman, keep her safe and helping prepare the ward for treating incoming survivors. Emma would search the top floors, Sway the middle section, and Ash, who'd insisted on coming, was looking after the first floor. His powers had him healing up fast, but I worried even searching a single floor would be taxing for his body, which had been out of action even longer than mine.

Rayni would stick with me, searching the ground floor and basement. As much as I was probably the strongest right now, I also had so little experience using these powers, which burbled, unstable as a live volcano, inside me. I alternated between blinding speed and fumbling, head-splitting pain. As a whole, I moved as slowly as Rayni, and I needed her powers to manage the swell of emotions. We were the last into the building.

On the way through the lobby, Emma was moving something

behind a desk, out of sight. "Don't come over here," she told Rayni, looking pale and green. "It's a cop. He's dead."

First body found, and found dead, when we had hoped to find survivors to rescue. Emma, Rayni, and I shared the same grim face, and probably the same hope it wasn't the start of a pattern. Emma nodded to me, then sped off to her area. I could hear movement upstairs, pounding feet racing from room to room as the others searched.

Rayni and I continued down the hall toward the offices, then the gym. Holding my breath, I poked my head in each room, but there was no one, dead or alive. Papers and furniture were strewn around, bullet holes and blood splatters marred some walls and floors, and lights flickered, but there were no survivors. No Livvy.

We picked up the pace, racing down the stairs to the basement. Rayni tried to find out how to get all the lights on, but I went ahead, able to see just enough in the dim glow of the computer servers. Nothing.

By the time we got back to the lobby, Ash and Sway were back already, and Emma appeared a second after us. Frowns wrinkled every face and a green glow of fear filled the room.

"Nothing?" I asked, confirming the unspoken.

They all shook their heads, their lips tight.

EMOTIONALLY POWERFUL

I paced, frantic. "They have to be somewhere. There have to be bodies. Could he have sent them off somewhere else? He sent Dr. Crossman down to the station for interrogation. Maybe he—"

"Shh!" Sway hissed. "You hear that?"

It was hard to hear anything over the storm lashing the building.

Emma's eyes popped wide as well. "Is that—?"

"Mew! Mew!" Sway shouted, running toward the rear emergency exit.

I threw a look at Emma as she started to move too, hoping for more explanation.

She shrugged. "It sounds like the cat, Kimmy. Sway really liked the cat."

She followed after Sway, and then the rest of us did as well. As we filed out the doorway into the downpour, I had a horrible thought—that the cat would be the only survivor we found.

Rain whipped around us, into my eyes. Water in the storm drain rumbled and gurgled as it ran past behind us.

Sway was down on all fours near a dumpster, sharing mews back and forth with the black and white cat that hid beneath it.

"She won't come out. Keeps hissing at me when I try and pick her up."

The bedraggled cat circled the dumpster wheel, mewing and rubbing against it.

"Omigod," Emma gasped. Her eyes were wide as she pointed to the opposite side of it. "A body!"

We went around, and there were two, piled beside each other behind the bin. Adult Limbus agents in uniform. Emma ducked over quickly, holding their wrists. "Alive!" she yelled over the thunder.

"He wouldn't ..." I whispered, realizing what had happened. I felt Ash's eyes on me, but when I looked at him his gaze had followed mine to the hulk of the dumpster. He flipped the lid open.

"He would," Ash replied, the blood draining from his face. "Those two were just the overflow. It's full of bodies!"

Everyone moved quickly, pulling out person after person, checking for life, and rushing the victims back into shelter, to medical care in the ward. Rayni couldn't carry anyone, but managed to lure out Kimmy, and had her held tight in her arms. I climbed right into the dumpster, lifting the victims out and handing them over, checking each face. My heart tightened each time a face wasn't Livvy's.

"No Bastian? Livvy?" Emma came back after her last trip in.

"That's it. It's empty." I climbed out, my whole body felt on fire from tension. "Where is she? Where did he …"

He'd run out of room. Livvy would have been the last person he drained.

I squinted against the rain, checking up and down the pavement behind the building, running over to the side of the stormwater channel.

A body lay at the bottom in the muddy, rushing water. It was face up, identity obscured by tangled brown hair.

I put one hand back and slid down the concrete slope on my heels. I landed in the knee-deep water. The current ran fast, white rapids building around caught up trash and debris, tripping me and tugging at my every step as I splashed toward the black-clad body.

A roar came from upstream. A huge wave of floodwater approached, racing me. It rushed past, pushing and tumbling around me. I lunged, trying to catch the body. The water caught them first and they bobbed up and down on the murky surface. I tried to move with the tide but it was too fast and the body washed into a tunnel downstream.

"No!" I screamed. I was almost pulled under into the current as well.

Emma splashed down into the edge of the channel beside me, grabbing my arm and steadying me in the stream. The others moved around the edge up top, watching.

"That could have been anyone," she said, but it wasn't of any comfort.

The concrete drain tunnel was waist-high, and the water reached three-quarters of the way to the top of it now, and rising. The force of the flooding water was incredible, and everything from tufts of grass to old bike wheels swirled in it. I stepped through, gauging my strength against the water's. The thin material of my scrubs clung and twisted around me, soaking wet.

"I'm going in," I said. "We need to get that person out. Maybe they are okay, stuck in part of the tunnel. I can go in and look for them."

Emma pulled back on my arm. "That's crazy. Do you know how dangerous it would be in there? What if the current gets you?"

I shook her off. "I've got this. I'm conscious, but whoever is in there isn't. There's still some breathing space but there won't be much longer. I have to get in there."

"At least take this so you can see." Emma pressed some controls on the screen built into the wrist of her suit and it lit up bright like a flashlight. Then, using a combination of her teeth and brute strength, she ripped through the tough material of her suit and pulled the screen off and handed it to me.

"Thanks." I took the light, ducking down neck-deep into the water, bracing myself at the entrance of the tunnel as the current tried to pull me in, and down. Emma was right, the water was moving really fast, but that wasn't going to stop me. I needed to get to Livvy. I needed to find her. And if she was the one in that tunnel, she only had a little time to be rescued, if any at all. Unconscious, she would surely drown.

"What's he doing?" Ash yelled. He circled around in front of us, above where the water disappeared underground.

"He's going in!" Emma yelled back.

I gripped the top of the tunnel and took a deep breath.

"Wait! Dean, wait. Over here!" Sway shouted from somewhere.

Ash disappeared from view above us, then he called back, "It's washed the body over here. We can see it through a grate."

I climbed on all fours, up the slope in a flash of speed. Emma and I reached the top at the same time, and saw the others surrounding a large steel grill.

Sway had a thin arm squeezed through, reaching down and holding something up, keeping it from being dragged down and away again. Pressed against the grate was a body. I could see flesh but couldn't make out who it was. A whirlpool of floodwater flowed through the chamber beneath the grate. The level was rising higher and higher.

"It's bolted into the concrete." Ash frowned at me.

I strained against the metal with both hands. I pulled with every bit of strength I could drag in from the powers within me, from the anger we all held inside us at how these victims had been left, discarded like rubbish.

Concrete shifted, small cracks formed.

"Come on, open!" I yelled at the grate.

Everyone reached in, joining me, hooking their fingers through the metal squares. We braced our feet firmly into the mud that burbled out of the grate beneath us.

"On three, everyone give it all you've got," I yelled above the sound of the racing water. "One ... two ... three!"

With a collective grunt, we pulled. Steel whined and groaned as it bent, and with a loud crunch the grate ripped right out of the concrete setting, throwing chunks into the air. Ash and I held it up as Emma took hold of the body so Sway could get her arm free. Then we threw the grate over to the side.

The body was dragged out onto the concrete, Emma leaning over it. I knelt down beside her.

She looked up, her eyes red with tears lost in the rain. "Bastian. It's Bastian."

I looked down into his face, his normally brown skin so

pale and cold. My lips twisted and I smashed my fists down onto the concrete.

I wanted it to be Livvy.

Ash leaned over Bastian, checking for a pulse. "He's breathing! He's alive. Get him into the ward, quick."

Emma lifted Bastian's large body with effortless strength.

I watched as she disappeared with him inside and felt all my hope disappearing too.

I got back to my feet, pacing and tugging at my drenched hair.

Sway had both hands over her mouth and was hopping from foot to foot, sobbing and laughing and wailing. I felt the same. We'd found a friend. Saved him. But we were still missing someone we all loved.

I shook my head, looking around us. "She's got to be here somewhere."

Ash wiped his white hair off his face. His teeth chattered. "She might not be in there. She was his final victim. She could be anywhere."

I nodded and looked down at the broken drain. There was a ton of debris collecting at the lip, spilling over it. Twigs, leaves, and small branches pushed through the paper and plastic trash, creating a cover over the muddy water. I shook my head, turning away.

Something caught my eye and I stopped. Disbelief froze me for mere micro-seconds. Then I landed on my knees in the mud, raking through the flotsam with clawed hands.

"Fingertips," I shouted at Ash. "Someone else is in there."

I couldn't reach far enough, the water swirling and dragging away whoever was there. I jumped down into the filled chamber, chin deep, holding onto the top edge with one hand and reaching down as far as I could with the other, finding human flesh. I grabbed onto it, pulling hard. "Get us out!"

Ash and Sway reached in, grabbed me under the armpits and pulled against the sucking water, sending me and the body flying up and out of the drain.

I fell back into the mud and muck.

Livvy landed right on top of me.

"Livvy?" I gasped. I grabbed her face and tilted it up toward mine, wiping pieces of stuck leaves and the tangle of hair off of her. "Hold on. Hold on. I've got you."

She was ice cold. I pressed my fingers to her neck. My hands clattered and I couldn't feel anything outside of the rampage of my own heart and emotions.

There seemed to be no signs of life from her at all.

The next moments skipped in time with my thundering heart.

Thu-thump. I cradled Livvy tight in my arms. I ran.

Thu-thump. We were in the building, in the ward.

Thu-thump. Dr. Crossman injected something straight into Livvy's chest.

Thu-thump. Rayni watched from the side, clinging to the cat, crying into its fur.

Thu-thump. Defibrillation pads attached to Livvy's bare skin. *Clear.*

Thu-thump. Machines beeped, beeped, buzzed.

Thu-thump. The rainbow of emotions grew so bright, I couldn't see. I was burning out from the inside.

Thu-thump.

"Dean, DEAN!" Dr. Crossman shook me, yelling. "She needs to be back in her body. Her proesthian healing powers, it's her only chance. *Now! Put her back now!*"

24

I've never felt so cold. Too cold to even shiver, I felt like if I opened my frozen eyelids, they would snap.

Warmth teased at my slow, lurching heartbeat, spreading through my veins, connecting me back to my arms and legs, to my face, to my powers. Breath gurgled in my chest. I wheezed, and felt hands on mine, holding tight, squeezing more warmth into me.

"Livvy?" It was Dean's voice, choked with worry.

I'm here, I tried to answer, but I wasn't sure I was, where I was, what I was, other than tired. *So tired.*

"She's stabilizing. You did it."

More voices, muttering, celebrating, crying.

Sound faded in and out. "She'll probably need some time to ... Can restore the others ... Here when she wakes up."

Everything faded out again.

I felt wrapped in a cocoon of love, joy, and relief. It warmed me as I listened to the sound of my heart growing stronger. Then I heard more familiar voices again, pushing their way into my dreams.

I opened my eyes just a crack, squinting at the real world. Dean leaned over me from one side, and Dr. Crossman from the other. More blurry figures stood behind them. They all looked so pale and drawn that I wondered for a moment if we were all dead, just ghosts now.

Remember. Remember where you are, what happened.

I had been out of my body for so long, through so many other bodies, that everything felt surreal. The last thing I remembered was helping Dean restore people in the institution. No ... I remembered a cat, meowing. Maybe rain. Mostly nothingness, big gaps in time and awareness. I had struggled to stay, to remember myself, but even now everything blurred.

"Am I me?" I croaked.

Dean brushed his hand down my cheek. "Welcome back, sleeping beauty."

Still half dreaming, I imagined being trapped in slumber for a hundred years. My eyes popped open wide. "How long, how long was I gone?"

He chuckled, a sound of pure relief. "It's okay. Not long. You've only been back in your body a few hours. But it was in bad shape. You've been resting and healing."

My body—damp and wrapped in blankets and heat pillows. *My* body.

"What happened? After—"

"Is she awake?" It sounded like Emma.

Dean stepped to the side, and I blinked my vision clear to see the ward at Limbus, full of people. The bed I was in was raised into a semi-sitting position, and I could see every other bed in there occupied. Bastian was beside me, and adult agents in the rest, only a couple I recognized. Some were already up, gingerly moving around the room. Sway, Rayni, and Ash sat together, in clean scrubs and warm blankets. Kimmy was cleaning herself at the foot of my bed. Emma was just coming in through the doorway, followed by my mom and dad. Everyone stared back at me.

"We did it? We really did it?" I whispered.

"*You* did it," Dean replied.

Someone started clapping, and soon the entire room erupted in applause. Emotions overwhelmed me and I giggled, and cried, and clung to Dean's arm, and then to my parents when they rushed over to me.

"Mom, Dad! Oh, man, it's so good to see you being yourselves again."

"I went to get them as quick as I could." Emma smiled, shyly.

"Thank you." I smiled back sincerely.

"Oh, honey," Mom cried, wrapping me up in her arms as Dad patted my back and my hair. Mom squeezed me tightly, and I squeaked, and had to push her away, gently. Pain radiated through me, and the bruises, the aches from my encounters with Terry resurfaced. She shifted away, but kept her hands on mine. "Sorry. I was just so worried we'd lost you. I still don't understand half of what's happened. But I'm so happy you're here with us."

Dad shook his head. "I can't believe it was Terry all along. I'm so sorry we didn't know, that we couldn't help."

"Where is he?" I asked, panicked at the sound of his name.

"He's done. I've blocked him permanently. It's over," Dean told me.

"It was a risky plan, what you did, but it worked. You got almost everyone back." Dr. Crossman smiled thinly, and I heard the pain in the word *almost*. I knew she was thinking about her husband, shot during the attack. I even saw a faint shimmer of blue around her. I felt around within myself, checking for any sign of other empaths attached to me, an excess like the last time I was able to see the color of emotions, but it was just me. Maybe my powers were stronger now, after everything.

I stared at her, her skin unmarred and healthy, a glow of strength coming from her. I had the vaguest memory of her, through Dean's eyes, arriving at the institute after being rescued by the others. She'd looked like death warmed over then. I couldn't place my jumbled memories properly in a timeline, but she couldn't have healed this fast since then, not without—I gasped.

"Did Dean unblock you?" I asked her.

She half smiled. "He did. He's done some amazing things while you've been gone."

Dean shrugged. "I figured I should try, since she was pretty beaten up and needing to work so hard for everyone else, I thought it would help if she had her powers back. It ended up being pretty easy. I still have a bit of a power boost. Plus having had the consciousness of the blocker who shut her down in the first place inside me—that probably helped."

"Stop it," I scolded. "You are amazing."

"It has helped," Dr. Crossman said. "I've already been on the phone to the police to start sorting all this mess out. We have a lot of cleaning up to do, and I'm going to need my powers to make sure the leech takes the blame for all of this as he deserves, in a way that makes enough sense to the police and doesn't blow Limbus's cover."

"Sheesh. Have fun with that." I winced.

Her eyes glinted. "You are talking to a reformed con-artist. This will be child's play."

She checked my blood pressure, and seemed happy enough to detach me from the IV lines running down to the back of my hand.

"Hey, can you also get someone to check in on Terry's family?" I asked, as I pressed a cotton ball to the hole left by the needle. "He's got a wife, and two young kids. I saw them, the way he treated them. They've been suffering under control for who knows how long."

Dr. Crossman's forehead wrinkled, and she nodded, patting my hand and leaving me with Dean and my parents.

More people were moving around the room now. Other proesthians—who hadn't been sucked through a stormwater drain and almost drowned—were healed up and heading out, keen to rebuild their lives and home here at Limbus.

"Is it just me, or does your mouth taste like mud and dead leaves?" Bastian called over to me, smacking his lips together. Emma was still picking twigs out of his hair, a look of fondness softening her eyes.

"Our bodies went on an adventure and we missed it all," I replied.

"Pretty glad about that, honestly," he said.

I stretched my arms over my head. I was sore but other than that, I felt great. Seeing Bastian and Emma reunited, Ash and Rayni—it felt amazing to have helped do that. My heart hurt for Sway, knowing her friend Marigold would never come back. But she seemed happy, sitting surrounded by new friends.

I smiled at my parents, then up at Dean. His hair was still damp, and his gray eyes sparkled. "How are you going?" I asked. He had held so much power inside him—I couldn't imagine how that felt. I put a hand to his chest. "What's going on in there now?"

"I've still got more in me than there should be. It's confusing, and sometimes feels overwhelming, but I'm coping." His nose wrinkled, and the rims of his eyes turned red. It was strange, seeing him express emotion so visibly, but I liked it. It made me love him even more.

I pushed myself more upright and wrapped my arms around his waist, pressing my ear to his chest. "I knew you could do it. I knew your heart was big enough to save us all."

25

I paced up and down the hallway at home. *He's late. Why is he late? The last time he was late, things were not good.*

The wall beside me smelled of fresh plaster. It had only just been patched up again from the damage when Terry had thrown me across the dining room and almost right through it. The look on Dad's face when he'd seen it and the state of our house when we'd returned was one of bemused despair. They'd just gotten it back together after the earthquake, and there were all new holes in the walls. I'd apologized profusely for the piles of pizza boxes, and motorbike wheel marks on the floor from when I'd dragged it through the house. My parents had just hugged

SELINA A. FENECH

me, and we'd all worked together to make the house our home again, removing the marks of what we'd suffered through.

Dean had stayed with us for the first few days, but then Limbus had offered him his own place. A small apartment, close to my home and school, on the Limbus budget. We'd talked about it, and decided it would be good for him, and us. I'd miss him being around all the time, but it would feel more normal, which we needed. We could go on normal dates now, be a normal boyfriend and girlfriend, and be told normally by my parents to remember sex safety when I stayed over at his place.

Limbus was helping Dean get back to normal in other ways too, which was what he was doing now. Dr. Crossman had been using her authority and powers to get access to the civilians Terry had leeched, and taken Dean and Rayni to them that afternoon to get the last of the excess energy out of Dean and back to where it belonged, hopefully saving more people at the same time.

He said he'd come over for dinner tonight, and I'd been waiting for him to arrive since an hour before he said he'd be here.

I knew I shouldn't be worried. Terry was gone, powerless and locked away. Dean was safe with powerful friends. But I knew I would always worry about Dean, because I loved him.

EMOTIONALLY POWERFUL

And when he got here, he would finally be just him again. Well, just him, and Marigold. Those powers would always be his now, since there was no way to return them to her. He was now both blocker and proesthian. I loved watching him learn to control the new abilities. Now he could match me, speed for speed, strength for strength, heart for heart. He was powerful in every way, and we felt powerful together.

He told me the more he's been opening up, the harder he's been finding it to control his blocker powers. I wasn't particularly sad to see them fade if it meant having Dean be true to himself and his feelings.

My new astral-projection-type powers seemed to be sticking around, but I didn't try and use them. It felt too strange, too risky. I still felt detached sometimes, and more than anything, I just wanted to be me.

Mom popped her head around the top of the stairs. "Dean here yet?"

I checked the time. He was technically only five minutes late. I was about to reply when there was a knock on the door.

I raced to it and threw it open, bouncing on my tiptoes when I saw Dean there, a smile creasing the corners of his eyes, making them sparkle between dark eyelashes.

"Come on in," I said, formally.

"Thanks." He seemed bashful, re-entering the house that had been his home up until a week ago. He closed the door behind him and took a deep breath. "Smells good."

"Dad's making your favorite." I grinned, loving that my parents doted on Dean as much as I did. I started leading him down to the dining room.

Dean smirked and grabbed my waist, pulling me back to him. "I meant you."

I giggled as our lips met. We were broken apart too quickly by another knock at the door.

"Is someone else coming to dinner?" I called out.

Dad replied from the kitchen. "Nope. Can you answer that?"

Mom appeared at the top of the stairs, keeping watch. I could tell she was wary, but trying to appear casual.

I could sense one person behind the door. I rubbed my chest, a serious nervousness flowing through me from them. Looking up, I saw that Dean felt it too, with his new powers.

I opened the door, sure we could face whatever challenge the world threw at us, together.

Standing on the front step was Dean's dad.

I could almost feel the air rush out of Dean. Then I felt his anger build, and then, confusion, compassion, and a wary sense of hope.

I grasped quickly for his hand, and looked between him and his dad.

His dad had opened his mouth to speak, but stopped, frozen, seeing his son there, both of us together.

He looked different. His hair was brushed, his clothes clean, his eyes clear, the redness faded from his cheeks. For the first time, I could see some of Dean in him. Then I realized—he was *sober*.

"What are you doing here?" Dean asked. His tone was more puzzled than aggressive.

His dad cleared his throat. "I came to talk to you, to see you. I wanted to try again, after last time." He looked over at me, eyes creased and apologetic, then down at his feet.

In all the other chaos, I'd forgotten to tell Dean about his dad's previous visit. He'd come by when I was at my lowest point, and I was still ashamed at how I'd treated him. "I'm sorry. I didn't tell you he'd come by a couple of weeks back, when I was home alone."

Dean nodded, knowingly. Mom had approached, standing behind us. She put her hand on my shoulder. "It's okay. You have been pretty busy since then."

Mr. Lasslow nodded. "I have, too. I wanted to let you know, let Dean know, I've been sober since then, since that day."

Dean looked skeptical. "That's longer than I can ever remember you being sober. At least since Mom died."

Mr. Lasslow flinched like he'd been slapped. "I know. And I'm sorry. I'm so sorry you had to go through that, through her dying, without me being present and there for you."

Dean just listened patiently, his gaze intense. The war of warmth and cold I felt within him made me want to cry and hold him or forcibly make him and his dad hug each other, but I stayed still, letting them get through what they needed to in their own time and way.

His dad's eyes flittered between all of us, too uneasy to hold anyone's attention for too long. "I've had to confront a lot of demons. It's been hard, and I don't even know yet if I can promise I'll stay on track, but I want to. I'm getting help, and I'm trying hard, and … I want to be a family again. Our family was already so broken; I'm sorry I broke it even more." He took a deep breath. "I was hoping, umm, maybe you'd come back home for a while. Keep me company, let me take care of things, ugh, for a while."

Dean stared at him intensely, deep creases between his eyebrows. "I don't think that place is the best for me. Too many memories, mostly bad. I need a fresh start right now."

His father lowered his head and smiled uncomfortably. "Oh.

I understand."

Dean's face was blank, but his voice was kind and a new glow of warm love radiated from him. "I think a clean start would be good for both of us. I'm not going back to live with you, but I'd like you to come and move in with me."

Dean's father looked up at him with big eyes. Before he could say anything, Dean continued. "But I have to be clear—if you're moving in with me, you'll be living by my rules. That means you will try as hard as you can to stay sober, and I will try to be understanding of your addiction, and we'll both work hard, together, and with whatever outside help we need too. I want the dad I remember you being so long ago, but I also want more than that. Our home will be one with love, and respect, and we will be open with our emotions, both good and bad. We both need to learn to do that." Dean glanced back at me and nodded. I stared at him with awed, loving eyes. He turned back to his dad. "Can we work together to be a better family than before?"

Dean's father sniffled, shuffling his feet. "I'd like that more than anything."

Tears streamed down my face. "Omigod, hug already, you two!"

They did, in a big, crushing embrace. Over Dean's shoulder,

his dad looked at me and said, "Thank you."

I couldn't hold back anymore and wrapped my arms around them as well. Deep gasps of emotion came from both of them, shaking the shared embrace. After a few long minutes we separated, all of us wiping our faces and laughing.

My dad appeared, drying his hands on a dish cloth. "Mr. Lasslow, would you like to stay for dinner? We have plenty. As long as it's okay with everyone?" he said, directing the last question to Dean.

He nodded. "Sounds like a great idea. We've got a lot to catch up on."

26

As my family and Dean's family became closer than ever, I found myself missing my other family—the close friends I'd bonded with at Limbus. I'd seen everyone at Mr. Crossman's funeral, but it was a quiet and somber day. I missed the comradery of training, of fighting side by side, even when the circumstances that made us fight were so terrible. We had become an amazing team, and I missed all of them. Even Emma.

Limbus had put a pause on training for a while as the building was fixed up. Positions in the organization were filled and re-arranged, and people took time to mourn. I was so busy getting my own life back in order, I hadn't even found a spare moment to duck in for a casual visit.

After a few weeks, I received a golden envelope in the mail. A formal invitation to the re-opening of the Bellston Main Limbus building. Dr. Crossman called me personally after that and explained Felix thought a party would be a good idea to bring everyone together again, and to recommence from a place of celebration.

The event was semi-formal, and my parents spoiled me by paying for a sleek red cocktail dress I'd had my eye on from the boutique across the road from Mom's. Strangely, it made me feel as much like a superhero to wear as the Limbus suit did.

I got permission for Nati to come to the party too, and she, Dean, and his dad met us at our place before Mr. Graybiel, the Limbus driver, came to chauffeur us all. I thought it was the first time I'd seen Dean dressed up in more than basic T-shirts or hoodies, and he seemed nervous. But I didn't care what he wore; it was his heart I loved.

We hadn't told Dean's dad all about our powers and what we'd been through right away, but by the time the party rolled around, Dean had trusted him enough to explain. He'd seemed completely awed and humbled, and doubled down his efforts at self-improvement.

At Limbus, they had literally rolled out the red carpet, along with glittering golden streamers and huge bouquets of yellow roses, filling the foyer through to the huge gym room, which had been transformed into a formal gala. Everything seemed back to normal, and I tried to deny my memory showing me reminders of where blood and bodies had once been.

Nati clung to my arm, shimmying her hips. "This is amazing! I feel like a celebrity. I mean, I know it's you who everyone is looking at, but, you know, by extension."

The atmosphere in the gym was hopeful. Tentatively excited, even. Everyone chatted with joyous expressions. Tables were laid out at one end, and the other end was a dance floor. Currently only two people were dancing—Felix, and Mr. Kairu, who held Kimmy in his arms, waltzing with her to the upbeat music.

Ash and Rayni's parents were there, having been overseas during most of the drama. I was surprised to see their mother had white hair too, when I'd assumed the siblings had bleached theirs out. Maybe it was some kind of genetic thing. It was wonderful to see them all back together as a family. Although I couldn't help but wonder what top-secret spy mission they had been on that kept them away from their children during all the drama. And whether that sort of life was the direction mine was going.

I used to dream about romance, and action, and adventure.

679

And heroes. After all I'd been through, I wasn't sure if it was something I still wanted, now that it felt more possible, more real than ever. Everyone in this place treated me like a hero. In some way or another, I knew empaths and Limbus would always be part of my life, but would I be an agent? A teacher of empaths? A doctor or scientist? Dean and I had both been told we had the option of employment there. But we needed to at least finish high school first, which was all we really wanted to focus on now after all the excitement. We'd been scrambling and studying like mad to catch up. But it felt good, and normal. And I was starting to appreciate normal more than I ever had before.

Mom, Dad, and Mr. Lasslow split off from Nati, Dean, and I to go and mingle with the other adults. We went to find our friends.

On the way, I saw Terry's family.

His wife stood over in one corner, talking shyly to a couple of Limbus agents. She carried her youngest child on her hip, and the other hid behind the skirts of her dress. When Dr. Crossman had checked in on them, it turned out the children were already showing signs of being empaths. Terry's wife had a lot of abuse and trauma to heal from, so I was glad she was getting help from Limbus.

EMOTIONALLY POWERFUL

I wriggled my fingers in a wave to her, and she waved back even though she didn't recognize me. One of the agents beside her seemed to explain, and she put a hand to her heart, and I read a 'thank you' on her lips.

We found Sway, wearing a full tuxedo and sitting cross-legged on a grazing table as though she were a centerpiece, chain-snacking and laughing with Rayni, who stood primly in an A-line dress and lemon-yellow cardigan. Emma and Bastian held hands, smiling as they argued about the philosophical ramifications of the final episode of a cartoon from their childhood. Ash sat beside them, and beamed a mega-watt grin when he saw us approach.

I introduced them all to Nati, who greeted them with hugs like she'd known them for years, and then teased Ash about Roxy still pining for him.

"Isn't this fab-u-lous?" Emma exclaimed.

"I know, right?" Nati boomed back.

"And here's the guest of honor." Rayni bowed to me.

I gasped, suddenly terrified. "They aren't going to ask me to make a speech or something, are they?"

Sway picked up a fruit skewer and held it high in the air. "To Livvy! And Kimmy! And Dean! And all the save-the-day heroes!"

"That means to all of us," I said, picking up a skewer too, and tapping it to hers. Then I turned to Nati. "Including honorary empaths." Everyone joined in, tapping fruit skewers, until they somehow went from being stand-in champagne glasses to fencing swords and a couple of mock-fights broke out.

"You know what you guys need?" Nati said. "Superhero code names!"

I laughed. "Rayni, Ash, Sway, Bastian—these guys have supercool hero names already."

"What about you?" Nati pouted.

"Actually, Nati's got a point," Rayni said. "You're a real fair-dinkum hero now, you deserve a superhero name after all your ordeals."

Dean cleared his throat, side-eyeing me. "She's already got a nickname. Her dad always calls her—"

"Don't you dare!" I snapped.

Emma's mouth made an O shape. "Omigod, you have to tell us."

Dean grinned slyly. "Lollipop."

Sway squealed, her eyes glittery, then, with all reverence, she whispered, "It's powerfully perfect."

"Super Agent Lollipop!" Rayni crowed.

"You're stuck with it now." Dean laughed.

I punched him in the arm, but I couldn't begrudge him because the sound of his laughter was so beautiful. "What about you, huh?"

"I don't do nicknames," Dean stated, shrugging and leaning against the wall, and no one seemed to want to debate him on it, no matter how much I pleaded for back-up.

"Then Emma needs a name," I huffed.

"I had enough fake names while I was doing that whole criminal thing," Emma said, tucking red hair behind her ear. "I just want to be me for a while."

Bastian kissed her on the cheek, and I stuck my tongue out and made a gross noise. "Just kidding," I said. Grinning, I offered Emma a high five. She slapped my hand back then bounced on the spot, yellow joy radiating from her.

"Team Empaths forever!" Rayni cried. "With our fearless leader, Lollipop!"

I chased her once around the table before giving up.

The music grew louder, and more people moved onto the dance floor. Nati dragged Ash out, and Emma, Bastian, Sway, and Rayni followed. Ada, Cam, and Max were dancing too, and I waved to them. They were such brave kids, and seeing them happy made my heart full.

"You want to dance?" Dean asked.

"Maybe later," I said. "I've got another idea."

I took him by the hand, backing us towards the nearest exit.

SELINA A. FENECH

My heart pounded and we tried to suppress our giggles as we ran off down the hallway together, checking we weren't seen escaping, relishing in the danger-less excitement. I pressed the elevator button, and as we waited for the door to open, I looked up into Dean's gray eyes, once so emotionless and now filled with joy and hope, fear and desire, mourning and acceptance.

"I love you." I breathed out the words on a kiss.

The doors opened and I pushed Dean into the elevator and against the back wall. He wrapped his arms around me and kissed my neck with his own words. "I love you, too. My hero."

I swooned to his touch and didn't wait until the doors closed behind us before I started unbuttoning his shirt.

Our love swelled and swirled around us, burning like a new star being born.

We were love. We were power. We were each other's, entirely.

Heroes, together.

All my dreams had come true.

ABOUT THE AUTHOR

Whether it's painting artworks or writing novels, creating fantasy works is Selina's biggest passion. She lives in Australia with her husband and daughter and loves food, gardening, geekery, and all things fantasy.

Find out more about Selina
Official website www.selinafenech.com
Facebook www.facebook.com/selinafenechart